RE
for
Revenge

THE NORTHERN SINS SAGA

Book 1

NIK TERRY

Copyright Statement

Published on 1st March 2022 by Nik Terry.

The author can be reached by email on
nikterryauthor@gmail.com

Or Facebook https://www.facebook.com/NikTerryAuthor

Or Instagram https://www.instagram.com/nik_terry_author_/

If you enjoyed this book, please encourage your friends and family to download their own copy from Amazon and I would also love it if you could leave a review.

Contents

Chatpter One

❧ Ava ❧

The words in front of me jumbled. I was tired. The sofa I had been sleeping on for the last few weeks offered little comfort and sleep was at a premium in the one-bedroom flat between the parties and the arguments.

I pushed my head into my hands and read over the text again.

"Avery. Avery, Avery!"

The voice was distant at first, muffled, or so it sounded to me.

"Avery!"

"Sorry," I said, looking up into those light brown eyes, a familiar stabbing pain going through my chest.

"That report was wrong, Avery. All your figures. They were wrong."

I swallowed, a burn starting in the back of my throat. The paper I'd written was pushed back onto my desk, the edges tatty, as dishevelled as my mind.

"Look, Avery. We can't go on like this," the velvety tone of his voice rumbled quietly, "the Partners have noticed your mistakes this time. I think you should find something else. It would be better for the both of us."

I stared at him blankly, unthinking, tears pricking at the back of my eyes, surprised there were any left.

"I can help you find another job, another apartment?" Tom asked, keeping his voice low, "I have an old uni friend in the Newcastle branch. I can see if I can get you a job there."

Newcastle? That was miles away. And it was cold and wet and far away from my friends and my family. But then I didn't really have any friends. Not anymore. Not after this. I shook my head, anger pushing through the pain and numbness.

"I don't want anything from you. You've done enough."

His eyes narrowed, the furrowing of his brow making his face hard in the late afternoon light.

"Just get this shit sorted for the morning," he hissed, "and find another job. I want you out of my life, Avery."

Tom turned and walked away, my eyes trailing after him, watching the man in the expensive suit and the confident swagger as he walked away. No remorse, no regret for what we had or for what he had done. I was pathetic, gullible. I had been pulled in by those light brown

2

eyes and blond hair, the smooth charm and expensive gifts. How could I have been so stupid?

I stayed late to re-write the entire report. Tom was right, of course. I'd messed up the figures. The whole thing was a disaster. It was shit. I was shit.

When I wandered out of the office the City was in darkness. I only just made the supermarket before it closed, quickly picking up the essentials and then running for the last tube train out of the centre.

The clicker-clack of the train threatened to lull me to sleep. The coaches were almost deserted and I felt alone, vulnerable in the late hour. When the tube stopped at my station I bounded out, taking a quick look around at the station side, checking no one was likely to follow me through the dimly lit streets.

I walked home in record time, my arms and fingers burning under the weight of the plastic carrier bags that bit into my flesh and threatened to cut off my circulation. I checked every shadow, every doorway, watching for the gangs of kids and drug dealers that roamed the estate, the night their territory.

The flat was on the third floor and I'd had to take a breath half way up the concrete staircase, enjoying the cold breeze whizzing through the wind-tunnel, whipping my loose hair about me, strands of red blowing across my face. A door banged loudly below, deep voices shouting and swearing, others joining in. I picked my bags back up and raced up the last of the steps rounding the corner, the dirty red door a welcome sight.

The key missed the lock twice as I tried to juggle the groceries in my haste to get safely behind a closed door.

The flat was small. A kitchenette stood in one corner, offering a handful of cupboards and a dirty oven covered in food debris and dust. I quickly unloaded my shopping, my supplies standing starkly in the empty cupboard. There was a stale smell of cigarette smoke, alcohol and general filth, coming as much from outside as it was from within.

I stared round at the dirty couch, sagging and stained and the fake wood floor, rising up in places where drinks had been spilled. I'd been living out of the suitcase that was pushed against the corner of the room, a sleeping bag and pillow stacked on top waiting for me to crawl into tonight when the house eventually went quiet.

There were voices in the other room. Laughter mingling with grunts and moans and I cringed inwardly despite that this was what I came home to most days now. I raked around my bag for my ear phones, stuffing them in snuggly to drown out the noise.

The tap on my shoulder made me jump, my heart stuttering.

"You're twitchy, Avery," my mother commented, yanking the sticking door of a cupboard open overhead and pulling out a bottle of cheap vodka and two glasses.

I glanced at her bedroom, the only bedroom, at the far side of the flat. A body lay on the bed, naked. I chewed on the inside of my cheek.

"You have a good day at work, love?" she said softly, the steady glug of liquid as she poured two generous portions of drinks.

"Yeah."

"Any plans for the weekend?"

"No."

She grinned at me happily, grabbed the multipack of crisps I'd just bought and wandered back to her room.

My mum looked so much healthier since I'd moved in with her. She'd put on weight, the flat was better stocked with food and she took a shower every day which was probably because I was paying the electricity and gas bill. And I slept on the old sofa, ear phones wedged in my ears to drown out the sounds of her parties and the multiple partners she brought home.

And it was there I woke up to the feel of a hand tugging on my clothes, fingers running up under my top, the sickly smell of alcohol in the air around me. When I opened my eyes, his face was right in front of mine, dark eyes, the over dilation of pupils from multiple substances and the smell of years of cigarettes on the fingers that stroked across my face.

I squeaked, wriggling free from the last half of the sleeping bag that was still safely zipped up and pushed him backwards, my heart beating furiously.

"Get the hell off me!" I shouted, scrabbling backwards and away from the stale breath in my face.

"Ah, don't be like that. I only wanted a bit of company. Your mum's passed out and I'm feeling lonely."

His voice was scratchy, brittle.

"I'll make it worth your while," he continued, still much too close, pulling out a packet of white powder from the pocket of his jeans.

I jumped off the sofa, looking around for something to cover me from the eyes that raked across the shorts and vest top I wore as pyjamas.

"No. I don't do any of that."

"Suit yourself," he shrugged, pushing it back into his pocket, "but if you change your mind, I'll show you a really good time. Just ask your mum."

He winked at me and walked to the kitchen, rummaging in the cupboards for a couple of seconds, picking up a packet of rice cakes and then throwing them back in before grabbing a handful of chocolate bars, *my* chocolate bars and wandering back to the bedroom, winking at me as he passed.

Once the bedroom door clicked safely back in place, I let out a breath and padded to the kitchen. The glass of water shook in my hand as I brought it to my lips, my eyes fixed warily on the other side of the room. How had I got back here? I'd fought so hard to get away from this life, from these people, how had I slipped back into their grasp. I thought I'd moved away, bettered myself, but instead it was just some cruel twist of fate, tempting me with what I couldn't really have.

I picked my mobile from the floor beside the tatty couch and flicked through the contacts, my thumb poised over his name. Then, squeezing my eyes shut I pressed the green button.

The phone rang out for a few seconds, my heart beating faster with each that passed. Then the phone clicked.

"What?"

I could hear the ring of a female voice in the background. My stomach dropping at the sound yet I knew she'd be there.

"Get me that job in Newcastle, Tom."

"Will do."

The line went dead. I glanced about the dirty flat with its sparse furniture, a pang of guilt stabbing me in the chest.

Chapter Two

ജ Eli ര

Six months later

I sat back in the shadows, enveloped in the darkness as lights bounced around all corners of the club, catching the faces of the punters and dancing away again. The music beat in a low throng, deep and moody; a stage in the middle lit in a red backlight, and a soft spotlight picking up the naked dancer.

Tanned tits bobbed slightly with each movement, nipples pert. Her body was slim, the spotlight glinting off the jewelled piercing in her stomach and my eyes wandered down to the shaved pussy, and then the gap between thin, long legs.

I ignored the other girls that approached me where I sat, only half listened to their conversations as they stopped to talk to me, ignoring the purr of foreign accents. Eventually her dance finished and I waited for her to come back onto the floor. She'd covered up in red bra and knickers and red stilettos; heels so high she was in danger of breaking her ankle if she caught her foot the wrong way.

I smiled at her, encouraging her to approach me and she did exactly that, sliding in the booth beside me, her dark hair falling just past her shoulders. She smiled back at me, a mouthful of white but crooked teeth, dark eyes watching me behind long black, fake lashes and thick eye liner.

"How much for a private dance?" I asked.

"I'm the most expensive in here, babe."

"I know that, I'm wondering whether I'm gonna need a loan for someone like you?"

She smiled broadly then her eyes dropped to my hands and the wallet stuffed with notes that peaked open at her.

"I'm sure I can do you a good price."

I was sure she could.

The brunette stood and pulled tatty velvet curtains around us, shielding us off from the rest of the club. Music pulsed in the background and she began to move, swaying her hips to the beat, pulling her fingers over her skin and then straddling me so she was sat in my lap, her big tits just in front of my face.

By the time the dance finished she was totally naked. Not an unusual occurrence but my intentions tonight were strictly business.

"Does Ritchie pay you well?" I asked, searching her heavily made-up face for any subtle reaction.

"It's OK," she shrugged, "I make most of my money from stuff like this."

I didn't need to know what other stuff might be making up the shortfall.

"I'll pay you double what Ritchie pays if you come work for me."

"Where?" she asked.

"Opulence."

Her eyes widened.

"You're that rich guy that's been buying up Newcastle, aren't you?"

I tried not to roll my eyes in annoyance.

"I've been investing in the City lately, yes."

The naked girl continued to sit in my lap, looking uncertain.

"Look, here's my number. Give it some thought. I'd pay you double what you get here and all your tips are yours."

"All of them?"

"Yes. All of them. I pay the security, not you," I continued, knowing that Ritchie's doormen demanded a cut of the girls' tips for keeping them safe all night, even though the security guys were often half the causes of the bruises some of the girls wore.

She nodded tucking the business card between the small wad of notes I handed her and jumping from my lap to put her underwear back on.

*****

10

I sat in my car, far enough away that I was concealed by the shadows of the almost entirely unlit back lane. My coffee was now stone cold yet I sipped at it anyway and watched a few people enter and leave through back of the building I was staking out. The front of the building was a pub of sorts boasting a clientele of alcoholics, druggies and dealers. Those that didn't want to be seen entered and left by the back door which was why I had set up camp outside.

I'd been here a few hours watching, waiting but everyone I'd seen creeping into and out of the building were small fry; low level dealers sneaking away with product stuffed into bags and pockets or dropping off takings. That was until the big dark car drew my attention, light flooding over me and I slumped down into my seat instinctively.

Peeking over the steering wheel I watched the car pull into the yard at the back of the property, all four doors opening and four hulking figures climbing out. I focussed the camera, getting a closer look at the faces that moved in the night, a sudden flood of white illuminating them from the security lights they triggered. I managed to snap a few pictures until they disappeared inside.

A low green glow lit up the car from the screen of my mobile as I scrolled the list of names, finding the one I needed. The phone seemed to ring for ages before finally there was a split-second silence and then a gruff Irish voice answered.

"Eli? Why aren't you in bed?"

I ignored him.

"What business do the Volkov's have in Newcastle?" I asked.

"Didn't think the Russians operated in the North, Eli, so I've no idea."

"Come on, Cian, you mafia lot all know what each of you are up to. You can't tell me that you don't know why they're sniffing around Ritchie?"

"You're still obsessed with him, huh?" Cian asked, a hint of American twang creeping into his Irish accent.

I treated the remark with the silence it deserved.

"You sure it's the Volkovs?" he asked when I didn't respond.

"Certain. There's no mistaking Lukyan's ugly mug."

"OK, OK. I'll see what I can find out."

I hung up, resuming my watch over Ritchie's bar. The phone rang and I grabbed for it; the display showing an unknown number.

"Yes?" I answered much too sternly.

"Eli?" came the light feminine voice on the other end

"Uh huh?"

"It's Chloe. I'll take you up on that offer."

I grinned. Ritchie will be seriously pissed off.

Chapter Three

ᴇᴏ Ava ᴄᴈ

I massaged my temples where the pressure headache was building, the document on the screen overly bright as the office grew darker, afternoon fading as I sat deliberating over my work.

The strong smell of Jean-Paul Gautier got to me before Harry himself and I wrinkled my nose involuntarily.

"Great. Not the response I was hoping for from all the gorgeous single women tonight," he said, amusement ringing in his voice.

Light blue eyes sparkled at me as he propped himself on the corner of my desk.

"For God's sake, Harry, that's the report for Mr Fairbrother you've just sat on."

I reached forwards trying to save the document before the corners became tatty but he moved and instead I ended up groping his arse.

"Ooh err, matron; not in the office."

He flashed me a wide smile, his teeth brilliant white and perfectly aligned. Three thousand pounds worth of brilliant alignment, I reminded myself before Harry did.

"What are you doing working late, anyway?"

I sighed, my eyes flicking back to the screen where the presentation sat taunting me.

"I just can't get this lined up right. And you need it for Monday."

Harry removed his arse from my report and relocated it behind the desk, leaning over the top of me as he peered at the screen.

"Go on then, show me."

I tapped the document into presentation mode and flicked through each slide until the end.

"Avery, it's perfect."

"Ava," I corrected.

"Sorry. I forgot you're doing this whole 'new you' shit. Ava that's fantastic. Look, as your manager, I'm instructing you to go home. Or at least come and paint the town red, or black and white, or something … with me."

I rolled my eyes.

"I'm not going on a date with my boss. Been there and done it, remember? It didn't end well"

"I wasn't asking you out on a *date*. Just two friends…"

I shook my head,

"Okay, colleagues. Just two work colleagues…"

"No Harry. Just no. Now off you trot. All those single ladies are waiting for you."

He smiled again at me, reached for the computer and switched it off.

"Harry!" I squealed.

"Time to go home, Ava."

"I don't know whether I saved the last change."

"I'm sure you did. You always do. Now out."

My phone vibrated on the desk and I reached for it, my fingers brushing Harry's hand just as he whipped it off the desk before I could get to it.

"Meeting tonight at Cartier's, 8pm. From Kerry," he read it to me.

"I'm not going."

"Why not?"

"I, I, I'm too tired."

Harry sighed, placing my phone into my outstretched hand.

"Ava. You've been here months. It's time to embrace the City. And get over Tom."

I shot him a warning look.

"I'm over him."

"Yes, sure you are. When was the last time you had sex?"

"Harry!"

"What? I'm a friend advising a friend."

"You're a boss asking his staff personal information."

"Semantics," he shrugged, grinning at me, "but if you ever want help in that department…"

"Enough, Harry. Go. Find all those single ladies. Put a ring on it, or something."

He laughed, those light blue eyes lighting up his handsome face. With blonde hair, his lean frame and expensive suits reminded me of Tom. In fact, he smelt just like him. He was too familiar and every time I saw him my stomach would sink and I'd remember how broken I really was.

Finally giving in, I packed up my desk. Securing my laptop into its black bag and stuffing a folder full of documents on top of it, I slung my gym bag over my shoulder and left the office with Harry, parting company as we reached the street below.

The gym was on the way home which made it easier to motivate myself after a long day; offering me a guilt-trip if I walked past without paying a visit. But today I was feeling motivated, or maybe just looking for an excuse to hide from socialising. And excuses had been running out lately.

I ran, I rowed and did every piece of cardio equipment that was in there, my phone vibrating furiously every fifteen minutes. Despite this it seemed my house mate, Kerry, was not taking no for an answer tonight.

For a while I had come to the gym quite late. It was open 24 hours and whilst I'd tried to avoid people as much as possible it provided me with a means of escaping the relentless thoughts of Tom, of my old life that plagued me, even in the middle of the night. I'd been amazed at how busy it was in the small hours as I joined the club of those that couldn't sleep. And thanks to the muddle of thoughts and pained memories that tortured my mind I'd really started to shape-up. There was a hint of muscle on my stomach and my arms and legs were now lightly defined. I pulled on a thin-hooded top, slinging my bag onto one shoulder and waved a goodbye to Cameron as I passed his office on the way out.

Eventually, having caved in to the barrage of texts and threats of a week's worth of cooking duties, I put the finishing touches to my make-up. Red hair cascaded down onto my shoulders and draped mid-way down my back. It was always longer when I straightened it, taming the natural curls to straight locks. My green-eyes were framed with thick eyelashes made more dominant with the lashings of mascara I had applied and I had given my prominent cheekbones a pink glow.

I caught a taxi the short drive to the City's 'diamond strip', full of swanky wine bars, with modern decoration, light displays and extensive Gin menus. Kerry and her friends had secured a booth in the bar, an array of pretty cocktails dotted about round table. She pushed one towards me that looked more like a latte than an actual alcoholic drink, but I sipped on it gratefully, awkwardly sober as music bounced off walls and a jumble of bodies ricocheted off each as they moved around the busy bar.

By the time we got to the nightclub my brain was drowning in colourful cocktails with exotic names and all their effects. The club was packed tight and only getting busier. Modern dance tunes blasted out and I'd given up on holding any sort of conversation for fear of bursting eardrums. I hit the dancefloor with the group of girls, clutching a glass of prosecco, the alcohol swilling around my system giving me a false sense of confidence.

We danced and sang and danced some more till my prosecco had vanished. I checked my watch, squinting at the numbers as they moved and blurred, mocking me, taunting me. 1am. Tiredness threatened me suddenly. I beckoned towards the bar and stepped off the dance floor, leaving the girls behind.

I squeezed into a gap at the bar, catching the barman's eye and ordering another glass of prosecco. The club was getting busier and there was little space to wriggle out from the crowd that jostled and pushed for space and attention. I stepped back, turned and wobbled. Clutching tightly to my glass as I struggled to regain my balance I teetered, catching my foot against something. Stumbling forwards I watched the liquid fly from the glass, glistening in the pulsing lights as it sloshed against the man in front of me.

"I'm so sorry," I said.

I rubbed the wet patch on the man's white shirt, moving my hand over his chest. Muscles bulged under my fingertips, hard and solid, and his stomach felt like the ripples left on sand from the tide. I snatched my hand away; sure I could feel heat licking at my own cheeks. What was I doing? Had he noticed? Of course, he had noticed. The man towered over me watching me, his eyes the most vivid blue I had ever seen. I offered a weak smile, another apology slipping off my lips.

"It's OK," his voice seemed to boom above the music, "let me get you another."

I opened my mouth to tell him that it was fine and it was all my fault but he had already beckoned for the bartender. He leaned across the bar talking to the barman. He was so tall, and broad, huge shoulders stuffed into a dark suit and white shirt but without a tie. Thick dark hair was swept back across his head and a dark, well-trimmed beard covered the lower part of his face. And his scent, the mix of cedar wood and spice with the hint of masculinity; it made my head spin. I was sure I could actually feel my eyes dilating as I stood squeezed up against him, heat from his body radiating against mine, a tingle starting in the pit of my stomach. God damn it, I'd drunk way too much.

The barman poured a glass of Verve Clicquot; even the light gold liquid itself looking luridly expensive. I opened my mouth to tell the man it was just the house prosecco I was drinking, a hell of a lot cheaper than the champagne he'd ordered, but by then he'd turned back towards me, the delicate glass dwarfed in his hand.

"I, err, thank you. You really didn't have to. It was my fault."

"Don't worry about it," he answered, the same low rumble cutting through the air like the kind you hear from a motorbike, low, sultry and formidable, and it vibrated all the way through me.

With a sharp nod he stepped away from the bar and stalked off. I watched after him for a few seconds as he walked away; two other suited men following behind. Then they were gone, sucked into a sea of people and swallowed into the darkness of the club.

Chapter Four

ℬ Eli ℛ

I tilted my head back, trying to enjoy myself but only getting distracted. I clutched the whisky tumbler in my hand, swigging back the rest of the bronze liquid. I should be happy, should be grateful. I should be enjoying the blonde in front of me on her knees with my cock in her mouth. But instead, despite the use of whisky to still my thoughts, they whirled rampant round my head. Eventually I gave up, pushing her away from me and getting up off the settee and over to my drinks cupboard and pouring another.

"What's up, baby?" she cooed, following me into the kitchen and rubbing her fake tits against my chest.

"I've got things to do. I'll call you a taxi," I said gruffly, watching as she pouted her lips at me.

They were probably fake too and most of the time they felt good round my dick. Not today though. I left her waiting for her taxi whilst I jumped in the shower, taking my time in the hope

I was alone when I had finished. When she was eventually gone, I stared at my phone again.

'We've no idea about the Russians, mate. Could be drugs, could be anything. Kee,' the text message read.

Frustration simmered inside of me, needing only a little more gas and it would boil over into rage. I slammed the phone down cursing silently before yanking out clothes from my wardrobe.

*****

I sat in the office sulking. I'd been there hours, scrutinising the CCTV cameras from various bars and various angles, watching for something, anything that didn't look quite right. I knew he'd made a point of sending his boys into my bars. I just had to whittle them out in the crowds of a busy Friday night. But so far that had been proving tedious and I was bored. Really fucking bored.

I'd watched the revellers come and go, my eyes fixated on the screens looking for evidence of drug dealing transactions but the crowds, although good for business, were providing good cover for any planned espionage. I decided to walk among them instead.

Pushing through the back doors I forced my way carefully through the hordes of partygoers. The bar was heaving, bodies bumping against each other, a clash of perfume and aftershave. Still, I moved easily through the crowds. At 6ft 3 I was taller than many in there and my well-built frame and broad shoulders meant that most people stepped out of my way quickly. Instead of hiding behind my cameras I stood at the door, eyeing up the queue of revellers waiting to get their turn in my bar.

The air was cool as September started to ebb away but the women still wore little on their arms and the men only in t-shirts, no defence against the nip in the night air. Yet I did get a good look at the countless pairs of tits that passed in front of me. A brunette stopped and touched my arm seductively, flashing a wide smile and pushing out her chest further, which was unnecessary as her large round tits were barely contained in the thin scrap of material that was supposed to be a top.

I had a reputation. Fuck, I'd earned it. Women flocked to me, eager to be the one I took home for the night and I frequently obliged, sometimes it was just a quickie in one of the store rooms and sometimes they kept my bed warm till morning. Then they'd return to the same bar the next night, wiggling their chest at me in the hope they'd get round two. The odd one or two might be lucky but I rarely went there twice. I had no desire for a relationship and no need for one. I was fine by myself.

And tonight I just wasn't interested. My eyes fixed firmly on those entering looking for anyone who didn't fit or that didn't look to be there to get rat-arsed. The queue moved down and I stopped a few younger lads in their early twenties that I didn't like the look of, sending them on their way with one or two short words. I must have looked as grumpy as I felt for the next group of girls didn't even look at me as they walked in. It was hard not to notice the pretty blonde in their group, yet her eyes darted from mine. I was giving off some serious asshole vibes tonight that was sure.

There was no trouble. It seemed that nearly every punter was on their best behaviour. I'm not sure exactly what I was hoping for. That my suspicions be founded or that I had reason to smash my fist in someone's face?

A crackle came over my ear piece.

"Boss, we have some trouble at Opulence."

"On my way," I answered and then stormed off across the courtyard at the back to where my most lucrative club was situated.

The signage on the outside dripped excess; a black canopy over the door, emblazoned with black and gold writing and heavy gold-gilded rope marked out the walkway. The gold sign to the side of the door was lit up and two anxious looking doormen waited for me. The club shouldn't even be open yet so I wasn't sure exactly what was going on. Inside the lights had not yet been dimmed and the bar staff were setting up, wiping glasses and tables, straightening spirits on shelves. The stage was clear apart from the shiny pole in the middle.

"In the back," Micky muttered and I followed him behind the stage to the changing rooms.

Micky knocked on the door of one of the rooms.

"Come in," a female voice called from inside.

The girls inside were still dressed and hadn't yet changed into what they wore on stage but hair and make-up were in various stages of preparation. They all milled around at the far end of the changing room.

"What's happened?" I asked as I got closer.

The girls at the front parted unveiling one of the dancers sat in a dressing gown on a chair. Thick blood clumped at the bottom of her nose and there was an angry red cut across her eyebrow. Red stained her face where she wiped at her own blood I noticed as I got closer and tears still pooled in her eyes. Fuck.

I dropped to my haunches in front of her so I could see her better.

"What happened?" I asked gently.

"It was her fella," one of the girls said.

"I'm sorry, Eli. I didn't mean for him to be in here. He just promised to behave so I let him come up," the beaten girl muttered, keeping her eyes trained on her feet.

"It doesn't matter. Tell me what happened?"

"I told Toni to let him in through the back. He wanted money, but I didn't have any. I told him I'd give him my tips later. He just flipped and starting hitting me. I'm sorry. I didn't mean to bring any trouble here."

I clenched my jaw.

"Please don't fire me," Chloe begged.

"Ashley, call her a taxi and send her home."

The tall blonde standing behind her nodded at me. The beaten girl whimpered.

"Please. I just need some make-up. No one will know."

I tilted her chin up so she looked me in the eyes. The side of her face with the nasty cut was already starting to take on the blueish tinge of the bruise developing. Her eyes had filled with tears again.

"It's all right. Go home. Take a few days off. You'll still get paid."

She nodded at me, relief evident in the slump of her shoulders.

"Thank you," she whispered.

This smelt like revenge. I knew I'd pissed Ritchie off by poaching his best dancer but I hadn't thought he'd come after her.

"Where is he?" I asked Ashley, trying to suppress the growl in my throat.

"Mark and Donnie have him in the store room," she answered tilting her head in that direction.

I got to my feet and stalked out, balling my fists as I left the girls to finish getting their shit on. The man was sat on a bar stool, two big blokes stood either side of him, their arms folded over broad chests. He was wiry, not all that tall and dressed in grey jogging bottoms and an Adidas jacket that looked like it had been made from a bin bag. He fiddled with a lighter turning it over and over in his hands, refusing to meet my glare.

I knew he'd heard me come in; I'd made no surprise about it.

Eventually, he looked up at me, blood dribbling from the side of his mouth.

"Hey, boss," the older of the two doormen greeted me, "this one thinks he can knock around our girls. Seems he ran into a door too," he continued when he saw me study the man's face.

The great thing about the storeroom was there were no security cameras and no evidence to support any claims about those ill-placed doors. I continued forwards grabbing him round the throat and lifting him to his feet whilst the doormen took a few steps backwards giving me space. My fingertips dug into the soft flesh of his throat and his feet scrabbled against the floor as he struggled against my hold.

"What the fuck you come in my club for?" I growled at him.

He gurgled for a while until I released my grip slightly, realising he couldn't tell me what I needed to know with my hand wrapped too tightly round his throat.

"I, I, I just came in to see my lass."

I gave him a little shake.

"I just needed to borrow some cash, bud, that's all."

"So, you thought you'd knock her about a bit when she had nothing to give you?"

I had to keep a lid on this anger.

"I'm sorry. I didn't mean to."

"No? So what? You accidentally punched her in the face?"

The simmering anger inside me was threatening to blow the clean lid off. His hands scrabbled against mine.

"Did Ritchie send you?"

He looked at me blankly. I squeezed harder.

"I don't know who that is!" he spluttered, his voice making a hoarse sound as I pressed my hand tighter, feeling the delicate bones of his throat.

It would be so easy to squeeze just a little harder, feel the pop of those bones under my hand and watch as he choked on his own blood as it flooded his lungs. He strained his head back trying to get away from me as I stared into his woman-beating eyes.

"You touch one of my girls again, either in here or outside, I'll fucking snap your scrawny neck. Understand?"

He didn't answer. I squeezed harder.

"Y, yes," he rasped.

I let go reluctantly and he slumped to the floor gasping.

"Get this piece of shit out of my club."

I left him with my doormen. I was pretty certain he might fall into another door or two on his way out.

Now I was pissed. I needed a drink. Leaving the Opulence girls to get ready for their performance with instructions for both the girls and the security team that no one's girlfriend, boyfriend, spouse, significant other or fuck-buddy comes to pay anyone a visit tonight or any other night from now on, I escaped to the crisp, fresh night air.

By the time I walked round to the night club it was heaving. Revellers were dancing and writhing against each other as the drinks were flowing and the tunes banging. Really the number of people should be making me very happy but tonight I was in a foul mood, one not made any better after a run in with Fisty McFuckface. I waved a couple of the nightclub's security team to my side. They needed a debrief and I needed a drink.

Pushing gently through the growing crowd I was just about to wave at the barman when coldness spread suddenly over my chest.

"Oh god, I'm so sorry," I heard the sound of the girl's voice as she started trying to rub her drink from my shirt.

She glanced up at me nervously yet her hand slid down to my stomach, as if she was feeling muscles for the very first time. I met her gaze, hiding my smile, noticing the bright green of her eyes, even in the darkness of the club. They dazzled like jewels, captivating, hypnotizing, haunting. Fuck, I was staring at her.

"Here, let me get you another."

I guided her by the elbow back to the bar and waved at Danny ordering a glass of our best champagne. I don't know why. We had some pretty good house stuff. But those jewels in her eyes really needed something decent to complement them. I glanced at her again as I waited for our drinks to come. She was watching me, studying me, but dropped her eyes from mine as soon as she realised that I had noticed. She was petite with a shock of long red hair and sharp features. My hand brushed hers as I handed her the glass and she hesitated slightly.

"Thank you," she said and brought the pale golden liquid up to plump pink, natural lips.

Plump pink lips that would look really good around my cock. I knocked my whisky back, placed the glass on the bar and walked away before I became anymore distracted.

Chapter Five

❧ Ava ☙

Monday morning had come round very quickly. I groaned as the most annoying sound blurted out from my alarm clock and hit the snooze button for that ever-valuable, extra five minutes. But five minutes felt more like two when the clock yelled at me again, sounding like a duck with a sore throat. Eventually, I plucked up the courage to launch myself out of bed to be assaulted by the cool air.

It took twenty minutes to walk from the apartment I shared with Kerry to the opposite side of the river and I was soon in the foyer of our offices which occupied two thirds of the four-storey building. Taking the lift up to the third floor I quickly swapped pumps for a pair of black, patent leather heels. The lift doors slid back to expose a flutter of activity and the smell of freshly brewed coffee and I quickly settled at my desk, plugging my laptop into its docking station and pulling documents across two separate screens. Once I was set up, I grabbed a coffee from the kitchen and sat scrutinising the presentation I'd left partly finished on Friday. When I was absolutely happy with it, I attached it to an email and pinged it to Harry.

It was 9.15am when I was suddenly aware of someone standing over me. Startled, I looked up.

"Sorry, Avery," the middle-aged man in a smart navy suit apologised and I stifled my annoyance at the use of my full name, which always reminded me my mother was most likely on a bender when she chose it.

Martin Fairbrother, one of the partners, was stood beside my desk and I had been so wrapped up in finishing the presentation I had no idea how long I'd kept him staring at the top of my head.

"Avery, Harry's not in today. He's sick. We have a meeting with a potential new client at 2pm and I need you to prepare the groundwork."

"Oh, I, err. Well, I've not really led on this before," I answered apologetically.

"Avery, I'm sure you'll be fine. You know the drill. Can you have a scope to me by 11.30?"

"Yes, sure," I gulped running my work-load through my head and mentally pushing pieces of work around, "who's the client?"

"Antwill Industries Limited", Mr Fairbrother answered, "I'll have Julie set a meeting up at 11.30."

I nodded as he walked off before having a mini-panic. I had two big deadlines this week and hadn't anticipated this extra work on top. Damn, Harry. Most likely he was recovering from yet another heavy weekend and once more I was bailing him out.

I started immediately. I located the company website and read through their basic details before logging on and pulling their reports from Companies House, their latest filed accounts and the Company's Articles of Association and Memorandum. It seemed they had been around a long time. Family-run for many years, they had built the company from the ground and had a number of different businesses. Their most recent business acquisitions had been in the entertainment industry and I noticed the names of some of the bars in the area, despite my lack of experience with the Newcastle night life.

Itself, the company was hugely profitable or at least most arms of the company were. With a Head Office in Scotland, there was a huge manufacturing element with warehouses all over the country and an impressive turnover. Yet the entertainment side of the business looked chaotic. Filing deadlines were frequently missed, accounts not submitted on time. It stuck out like a sore thumb.

By 11.30 I was armed with background information and a number of suggestions about where the company could improve its processes and profit margins. I had put together, a pretty dramatic presentation and now I was sat in Martin's plush office on the top floor taking him through every detail.

"This is great stuff," he said when I had finished. "See you at 2pm in the Board Room, Avery, I want you to present today."

"I, err, OK", I stumbled over my words. "Do we know who is attending the meeting, sir? I just think I need to do more background work on the individuals."

I wasn't sure if I could pull this off and nausea was starting in my stomach.

"Don't worry, it's just one of the directors, not all of them," Martin answered.

Keeping tight control of the need to roll my eyes, I nodded dutifully.

Back at my desk I worked through lunch, running out to grab a sandwich and coffee from one of the small eateries down the road and scarpering back to my desk frantically trying to learn all I could about the company's officers.

64-year-old Alan Antwill had three sons who all were involved to varying degrees. There were pictures of Alan and the older two sons, Thomas and Timothy Antwill all over the internet, but the third, Elijah, was missing from my searches. There was a definite family resemblance in the older Antwill boys. Strong jaws, mid-brown eyes, light brown hair, tall and lean.

By 1.45pm I had been to the toilets, checked I hadn't smeared mayonnaise across my forehead, and collected my papers and laptop. My heart was already bounding in my chest and my palms were starting to leak a fine amount of sweat. I rubbed them on my trousers. I met Martin Fairbrother outside the Board Room and he ushered me inside. I took the seat beside him with our backs to the huge glass window which overlooked the River Tyne.

The room smelt of freshly upholstered leather and coffee, the slight smell of floral air fresheners just breaking the masculinity of the scents. I wasted no time setting up my laptop and connecting it to the projector, my presentation sitting boldly on the big screen to the side of us.

At exactly 2pm I watched the doors from the lift slide open and the figures of two people move towards us, shapes moving in front of the frosted glass of the Board Room windows. Noticing Martin had taken to his feet I copied, moving round the table behind him. Martin's Personal Assistant, Julie, opened the doors and beckoned for the man to walk in. But it wasn't the grey-haired man in his sixties that I was expecting to walk into the room, nor one of the older sons I'd seen pictures of, but a towering man with dark hair swept back over his head and a well-groomed black beard. His expensive navy suit strained over his arms and the white shirt pulled across a broad chest. But it was those bright blue eyes I recognised. A shiver ran down my spine.

Chapter Six

ഔ Eli ൽ

I sat in my car watching. I'd followed Ritchie from his home, staying well enough back so as not to arouse too much suspicion by driving the big black Landrover Discovery up his arse. That wouldn't have been very covert of me. Luckily these big SUVs were popular and there were plenty people in this area with money to buy one. I'd even resisted the urge to put a private plate on it. That would draw too much attention and I didn't need my ego massaging.

I rubbed my temples. I was pretty fucking bored so far and was finding out next to nothing. He'd gone in to a few of his bars, come back out again and currently he was sat in a pretty upmarket hotel restaurant having breakfast. Parked on the other side of the street I'd watched a tall brunette go in with him. She was slim, well dressed but a bit too made up for this time in the morning.

Ritchie liked a gorgeous woman on his arm but often they didn't last long. He was a collector, at least for a little while and seemed he appreciated a selection, just like I did. Only his women often ended up sporting bruises. I didn't need much extra help to hate him more than I already fucking did, but seeing his women having to hide facial injuries on a frequent basis added to the loathing. I suspected the brunette was covering up her face. Her hair fell over one side so I could only fully see the other side and the lashings of make-up she seemed to wear was most likely to disguise the blue and purple tone her skin had taken on.

I'd snapped a few pictures of the pair of them walking in and sent these on to my email. I waited, watching them at the table next to the window, Ritchie tucking in to breakfast whilst the brunette seemed to push hers around her plate; probably too sore to eat much. Eventually, two men, dressed more casually in jeans and black jackets trotted up the front steps before taking up the two spare chairs across the table.

I positioned my phone and zoomed in on the table. The men who joined Ritchie were well built and had a certain demeanour; the type of vibe given off by ex-military. They sat on the edge of their chairs, alert, scanning their surroundings, ready to jump into action. They wore thick soled boots on their feet, the type issued in the armed forces and that you then never get over wearing. The sort that you become so used to that you would wear them with any outfit, to any venue, given half the chance. I took a few quick snaps but both men were sat in a way that made it difficult to get a decent focus on their faces. Another military calling card.

'Recognise these?' I typed the email.

'Do you ever give up?' the reply came back almost immediately followed by another, *'not much I can do with these images. And if I did know I wouldn't tell you.'*

'Dick!' I responded.

A few moments later my phone beeped again and I smiled. He had relented after all. I grabbed up the handset eagerly, opened the email app and was immediately disappointed. The email was from my father. I sighed.

'I've set up a meeting for you at Fairbrother Williams Business Consultancy Services at 2pm. I want you to consider what they can do for the entertainment businesses. I've scheduled some more of the same with others. I'll send you the details. Dad.'

Fuck's sake, I scowled at the phone, grinding my teeth together. My businesses were running just fine. And I didn't need anyone digging around in them. It was typical of my father to interfere. I balled my fists. I really could do without this distraction but I also knew which battles to pick and this, with my father, was not one of them.

In truth he probably was right to have little faith in me. I'd never wanted to be a part of the family business and I'd gone out of my way at seventeen to avoid being coaxed or even forced into it. I'd joined the army. Not the Royal Air Force, not the Navy but the good old Green Army. My father was furious.

When I'd eventually left all of it behind me and returned home, he'd offered me company money to buy some businesses to manage myself. It had been very forgiving of him. Of course, he had expected me to invest in a manufacturing industry, as was the family way - instead I'd bought a pub, then a few others. After seeing how angry it made him to think the Antwill name was now associated with the lowly entertainment industry I bought a nightclub. And then I bought a strip club. That really was the icing on the cake.

I glanced at my watch and then back at the window. Ritchie and the brunette were sat finishing off their breakfast and the chairs at the table were now empty. I looked around hurriedly. Fuck! There was no one on the street, no one looked to be about to come out of the hotel entrance. I'd missed them and had missed the opportunity to get a clearer image. Fuck you, Dad, this was your fault, I cursed, thumping the steering wheel of the Landrover.

*****

It was just before 2pm that I reluctantly arrived at the offices of Fairbrother Williams on Newcastle quayside. The firm must have been doing well for themselves. Nearly completely covered in huge, panoramic panes of glass, the offices occupied two thirds of the building. Plush sofas dotted about the foyer made it feel more like the entrance of a hotel than an office block. My feet squeaked on shiny tile as I approached the concierge desk, gentle music filling my ears.

I was met out of the elevator by a well-dressed secretary. She looked me up and down intentionally slowly, her eyes lingering as she played with her earring. The ruffles on her pink blouse bulged over large tits yet her waist tapered off neatly into a tight black skirt. Her hair was immaculately styled and the same effort had been put into her make up. I glanced at her left hand. No rings. She smiled and then walked slightly in front of me, the wiggle of her hips slightly exaggerated. Nice.

A dark-haired man with an expensive suit met me inside the meeting room, offering a chubby well-fed hand in my direction. He was shorter, but what he didn't have in height he certainly made up for in width.

"This is Avery Edwards, Business Relationship Assistant," he said, gesturing to the woman beside him.

That shock of red hair was the first thing I noticed, only this time instead of falling down her back it was scooped up onto her head, loose curly tendrils spilling around her face.

"Ava," she introduced herself self-consciously and held out a slim hand.

I took it carefully in mine, looking at her creamy skin engulfed in my calloused bear-like paws. Her eyes held mine for a moment and there they were again those bright green orbs, entrancing me, pulling me under like a mermaid's siren. Fuck. Those eyes killed me, again.

Once we were seated Fairbrother opened the dialogue with the history of the firm, telling me the story of where they had come from and where they had got to. I'm sure he name-dropped some large clients, although I suspected Antwill Industries surpassed many, if not all of them.

Really, I barely listened to any of it. Instead, I watched the petite red-head across the table from me. She was exquisite and different, natural yet unnatural, with her sharp features and incredible eyes. My mind flittered a number of times to what she might look like under the tightly tailored trouser suit she wore. Her blouse was unbuttoned just a little; not enough to see the top of her tits but enough to expose the delicate dip at the bottom of her neck. She'd caught me looking at her a number of times but I refused to look away and instead enjoyed watching the flush rise in her cheeks, stark against her pale skin.

Eventually she took over the talking. Her voice wavered a little at the start but then she seemed to find her rhythm and I was captivated, although I wasn't sure whether that was with her presentation and the passion I could hear in her voice or just with the way her presence ruled the room. She'd carefully scrutinised my last accounts, highlighted some areas where she expected my profits to be better and outlined what the firm could do to ensure my businesses became more profitable, more competitive.

I didn't really care though. All I could think about was what she would look like bent over my desk, how she would feel around my cock, what that intelligent little tongue could do.

All too soon the meeting was over. I thanked the fat-controller-shaped Fairbrother for his time, shaking hands as I moved around the table from my seat. Then I took hold of the small hand of the red-head. I couldn't help but stare at her, taking a little pleasure in how I made her shift from one foot to the other uneasily, holding onto

41

her hand longer than I really should have. Even with those stiletto heels on she was over a foot shorter than me. I towered above her and she had to tilt her head back to maintain eye contact with me, exposing her slim neck. I liked that.

Chapter Seven

❧ Ava ☙

"Hey, Ava," Harry greeted me the next morning, pushing a takeaway coffee towards me as he approached my desk.

I looked at him quizzically.

"Coffee? What have you out in it? Arsenic?"

He laughed, propping an arse cheek on the corner of his desk and sipping at his own.

"Only Rohypnol, you'll be fine," he winked.

I took a tentative sip, recoiling at the sudden heat against my tongue.

"Harry, why have you bought me coffee? I mean I Iove coffee but...?"

"You saved my backside yesterday. I appreciate it. And yes, it was a serious hangover," he continued much more quietly, "Martin says you did a great job. Antwill couldn't keep his eyes off you."

Harry flashed me a knowing smile that said far more than I cared to focus on. It was true I had found the whole meeting uncomfortable. Elijah Antwill's eyes never seemed to leave me, it was as if my every move was being scrutinised, the stare of those bright blue eyes dissecting me as if they could unravel my every secret. He was intimidating.

"Well, you won him over anyway. He's been on the phone to Martin this morning and he wants us, well wants you".

I scanned Harry's face, sure I was missing something but not quite certain what. Reading my confused expression, he rolled his eyes.

"Ava, he has specifically asked for you. He doesn't want me or anyone else working on this, just you."

Harry smiled, but it didn't quite light up his face as usual. The contract for Antwill Industries would be huge, the fee astronomical.

"You should do it, Harry. I, I don't have the experience. I'm not a project manager. I just follow orders, directions, I don't lead on this stuff. That's you not me."

"You'll be fine, Ava. And I'll be right here when you need me. Antwill is coming in after lunch to sign the paperwork and then you're all his."

I watched Harry walk away, his words ringing in my ears. *You're all his.* Elijah Antwill had distracted me easily yesterday, had left me flustered and even now the thought of him made my cheeks burn.

By midday I was starving and regretting the extra time in bed this morning rather than in the kitchen making something from my lunch. Now I had to brave the cold October air. The thin dress I wore did nothing to ward off the chill that rolled off the River Tyne along with a damp mist which clung to every part of me making me feel more far more soaked than if I'd actually stood out in a shower. My heels clacked noisily on the quiet street as I marched back towards the office clutching a sandwich in one hand and a coffee in the other.

I rounded the corner, the ground floor foyer now in view and reachable in only a few strides as the rain grew heavier. With my head lowered against the thick drizzle I picked up my pace to a half-walk half-run. I didn't see him coming towards me; didn't see the man mountain that moved through the fog. And suddenly it felt like I'd collided with a stone wall, hands grasped my arms as I fell backwards, my ankle twisting painfully underneath me.

"Careful," the deep Scottish rumble came from above my head.

I glanced up, caught in the stare of familiar blue eyes.

"I, I'm sorry," I stammered, my eyes catching the brown stain across his shirt.

Pulling a tissue from my bag I patted at his chest, heat rushing to my cheeks as the coffee stain spread further still, clinging to hard muscle, his nipple poking through the fabric as wet and cold assaulted it.

"It's OK."

I barely heard the words as I rubbed the tissue back and forth, leaving spots of white against the stain, the tissue disintegrating under the effort.

"I'm so sorry," I murmured.

"Ava," his voice was sharper, more commanding, making me draw in a breath as my heart faltered ever so slightly, "it's fine. I'm fine. The only thing not fine is your coffee."

I snatched a peek at him and immediately wished I hadn't. His jaw was tight, tense, his eyes dark and stormy. I bet that shirt was worth more than my flat and I'd just ruined it with a latte. Shit!

Meeting his stare properly, I chewed on my bottom lip, my face flushed hot with embarrassment. He studied me for a second and then stepped back slightly.

"Please, after you," he said gesturing for me to go in.

"I, er, believe you are going to the fourth floor," I beckoned towards the lift, leading him to the doors just as they slid open.

How had I ever managed to give a presentation to him yesterday when today I was struggling to string a sentence together? Idiot.

"Thanks," he replied, his voice deeper than ever in the confines of the lift.

The space felt so confined, so small, like I was stood in the tiniest box with the biggest man. The biggest man who smelt so intoxicating; I could almost taste the sharp citrus in the air that fought against a woody, spicy scent and mingling with the coffee smell from the drink I had spilled all over his shirt. My head whirled, fuzziness filling my brain.

The ride to the third floor seemed to take for ever in the uncomfortable silence. I wanted to turn and look at him, take in all his features, search those eyes for what held me so tightly in his gaze. Instead, I stole glances at him in the reflection of the metal box, diverting my eyes at the slightest indication he had noticed me looking.

The sudden ding of the lift made me jump and his head turned towards me. I offered a shallow smile, chewing the inside of my cheek as I tried to stop the colour rising in my face. As the doors started to slide open, he turned towards me, his massive hand outstretched towards me. Instinctively, I slid my hand against his, warmth sending a wash of sensations over my skin and as his grip tightened around me, hard, powerful fingers gripping my skin, my stomach fluttered.

"Looking forward to working with you, Ava," he said, his voice a low rumble that seemed to echo round the lift.

"Me too," I squeaked, chancing a look at his face and immediately dropping my gaze when his eyes seemed to capture mine.

Heat leapt to my cheeks.

Chapter Eight

❧ Eli ❧

The blaring sound from my watch dragged me from a restless sleep. Pinching the bridge of my nose I fought the thudding ache of my head, silencing the alarm at the same time. I had all my bars and clubs alarmed and alerts came straight through to my phone. It was a great piece of technology until I forgot to remove my smart watch and was rudely awoken. Sleep was for the weak anyway.

I turned over, groping around for my phone and caught the empty whisky tumbler sending it crashing to the floor. The blonde beside me moaned and pulled a pillow over her head. The clock on my phone read 5.20am. I'd barely slept, having spent most of the night taking out my frustrations on the body of the woman who now lay naked and exhausted in the bed beside me.

"Hey, babe. What's going on?" the female voiced asked from beside me, sprawled across the bed on her front, bleached blonde hair cascading down her back as a fake tit peeped out from under her.

"Got to go. Issue at the nightclub," I grunted, "I've called you a taxi."

"I can just wait here for you getting back," she said, sitting up.

I shook my head, "got shit to do today. I'm not coming back."

She pouted her lips at me and pushed her tits together.

Ignoring her, I walked away into my bathroom locking the door behind me and standing under the spray of the shower, thoughts whirring through my head. When I'd walked out the office of Fairbrother Williams yesterday I couldn't keep the throb of my dick from my mind. The red head had fascinated me. She had an air of innocence about her; a vulnerability. Her tiny frame and slim figure and her eyes, slightly bigger than they should be in a small heart-shaped face, made her look so fragile.

I'd tried to bury my thoughts in Ashley, literally, but it hadn't been her face I had seen last night as I ploughed my cock into her. Every time I closed my eyes, I could only see the red of her hair and the emerald of her eyes.

It was nearly 6.00 am by the time I'd arrived at the nightclub to find the front doors had been rammed wide open and the foyer had been pretty much smashed to pieces. Micky had got there first, as was his job as head of my security team, but I'd followed behind sharpish.

"You're not gonna like this, boss," he said as I stepped into the scene of mayhem.

49

One of the front doors was hanging by one hinge, its frame twisted and tangled whilst the other seemed to have taken a nap in the middle of the club's dancefloor. It looked like a bomb had gone off, and I'd seen the aftermath of plenty of bombs to know that this is not what had caused this chaos; the rest of the club was incredibly intact.

I inspected the hanging door. There was paint smeared on the side, dark grey in colour and metallic; a car, a big one. As there was no abandoned and bashed up vehicle nearby my guess was it was something robust enough to drive off afterwards. And my next guess that this was someone sending me a message. And that pissed me off.

I looked around at my club. It was going to need some work to get it back up and running ready for tomorrow night. Wednesdays was a big thing with the City's student population and with two large Universities serving the City there was a shit load of students to be had. It was not what my mood needed right now, but I also needed to send a message right back.

We still had no front doors when Ava arrived for our scheduled 10am appointment to go over the initial paperwork.

"Yo, babe. Can I help?" I heard Danny call out from wiping debris from the bar top.

I peeked my head out of a booth in the far corner where I'd been squirrelled away, trying to call in some favours for some swift repairs to get us back open and watched as the small woman stepped gingerly into the scene of destruction.

I couldn't blame her for the way she was looking around nervously. There was now a gaping hole where the front doors used to be and even though I'd moved bits of broken wood out of the middle of the lobby it still looked like a hell hole. I strode over to the front of the club in a bid to get Danny to at least stick his tongue back in his head.

"Thanks for coming over, Miss Edwards," I said politely, holding out my hand to help her over some of the rubble that I hadn't yet tidied up.

"I'll manage," she said, and teetered precariously over the debris in a pair of black stiletto heels.

Stubborn little thing. I watched her pick her way through, my eyes trailing up her legs, pausing to take in the slim, well-defined calf muscles. Her coat was open showing the cut of her suit jacket which nipped in at her waist. Her flame-red hair was pulled tightly into a braid, showing off cat-like eyes that were watching me, intently. Busted. Had I made it that obvious that I was checking her out?

"What happened here?" she asked.

"Looks like someone drove into my club. Probably drunk," I lied.

I knew who was behind this mess.

I beckoned her to follow me back to the booth and watched as she slid carefully into the space across from me before rummaging around in her bag and pulling out a folder.

"Here are the initial proposals, Mr Antwill," her voice was soft and velvety and I liked the way she addressed me. Really liked it. And so did my cock as it twitched in my pants. Fuck's sake.

As I read the paperwork she'd brought with her I stole quick glances. Her eyes swept over the mess of paper on the table with my hand writing and doodles scrawled across each piece. Then she looked around the club, her gaze occasionally fixing in certain places then moving on in a systematic sort of way.

"This looks fine," I stated eventually and her eyes returned to me.

"Great, if you could just sign to state you accept the proposals."

"Where?" I asked.

"Just on the bottom of the last page, please," she instructed, leaning further over the table to point towards the section on the last page. Her blouse opened just slightly at the chest but barely enough for me to see anything. Fucking shame.

"I'd like to get started as soon as possible," she said, "I'll need you to send me a copy of the last three year's accounts and profit and loss sheets, as well as any performance information you have."

"Ah. About that. I don't have any of that digitally," I confessed, "but it's all here. Upstairs in my office. Just in filing cabinets."

I watched her frown slightly, her brow furrowing and narrowing her usually wide eyes to annoyed slits, like a pissed off cat. My cock twitched again.

"Ok, I'll need to work from your office for a couple of days. Would that be OK?"

"Sure."

It sounded like a good idea to me until she mentioned the time she wanted to start. I wasn't a morning person, not now anyway, and today was a one-off. I kept late hours and barely slept when I did eventually get to sleep so I resembled a zombie with a hang-over most mornings. Sleep was as elusive to me as my romantic relationships with women, only the latter was my choice. I'd had much of neither for years. Sure, I'd fucked plenty of women, but relationships I just didn't do.

"Thanks for your time, Mr Antwill," her tone was professional.

I watched her leave, picking her way back through the debris. Her coat covered her arse so I didn't get a good look at that. Next time. I would really like to see more, so much more. The shrill sound of my mobile ringing snapped my attention from the woman walking out my club doors, or the hole where my club doors once stood.

"You got me some info?" I answered.

"Yes and no," the voice on the other ended stated.

"Well, which is it?" I was impatient.

Another excellent trait of mine.

"You're right, it was a grey SUV that drove in to your club. Caused himself a fair bit of damage to the front end too. Pity, was a nice car; Audi. But looks like it was stolen. The vehicle reg brought up a totally different car so the plates were probably switched. Sorry, no joy in confirming who it is."

"Doesn't really matter. I know who it is."

"Yep, you're probably right. But you also know he doesn't make mistakes, Eli, so you ain't going to get any evidence. He hasn't made any mistakes in the last eight years so doubt he's about to start now."

"He will. He'll slip up one day. Then I'll have him," I replied before hanging up angrily.

It wasn't Joey's fault he couldn't get me what I needed but I was pissed off anyway.

Chapter Nine

ಬಿ Ava ಲ

It was well after 9pm before I got home that night and the apartment seemed quiet. At first, I thought there was nobody at home but then I noticed a pair of man's shoes just inside the door and a smell of aftershave lingering in the lounge. Two half-drunk wine glasses were left on the coffee table. I didn't need any more clues.

Too tired to eat and too mentally drained to even think about switching the TV on, I quickly scoffed a couple of slices of toast and crept into my room. Fortunately, the bathroom separated our two bedrooms but despite this I could still hear groans and moans coming from Kerry's room. I rummaged around in a drawer and found a pair of wireless earphones, stuffed them securely in my ears and then relaxed back onto my bed, thinking.

He was dark and foreboding, sinister almost. He made me shiver with fear, trepidation and....something else. The man approached me from behind and slid his hands down my sides, his fingers linking under the edge of my top, pulling it off roughly over my head. He spun me around to face him, grabbing a handful of hair and pulling my head back so I stared into his bright blue eyes.

I jolted awake, my heart beating a harsh rhythm in my chest that was echoed by the throb between my legs. For God's sake. That was all I needed, it was hard enough to keep my eyes and attention off him as it was.

*****

It seemed I was the first one in the entire offices that morning, having got up with some sort of renewed enthusiasm for my job and my new project, and my new client. I was so early the security guard had to come and unlock the door for me. But sat at my desk my mind drifted back to my dream, the heat and pressure rising in my core. I squeezed my thighs together saturated in embarrassment, feeling colour rising to my cheeks and thankful there was no one to see my weird blushing.

I re-wrote a report and analysed some data all before 9.10am then packed up and trotted across town to the nightclub. I wasn't sure what to expect when I arrived but it certainly wasn't the building looking so intact. It actually had doors this morning, and complete brickwork. In fact, there wasn't a shred of anything out of place. I buzzed on the intercom and waited.

A deep voice answered the intercom and excitement ignited immediately in my stomach, and somewhere else. Good God woman! It had been a while since…. The door was pulled open, and for a split second I was distracted by the heat that gathered between my legs until I looked up into the face of the ever-so-tall Elijah Antwill. He had to be over 6ft. In reality everyone was bigger than my 5ft small stature, but even so, he absolutely towered over me. And it wasn't just the height but the width of his chest and his shoulders. He was huge. I wondered where else he might be huge. Oh God! Stop me now!

"Good morning, Miss Edwards," he greeted me formally, ushering me in as I pathetically squeaked a greeting at him.

I'd bet he was used to stupid women going all to mush in front of him. Today it seemed like someone had deleted my entire vocabulary.

I followed him across the hard floor of the nightclub struggling to keep up with his long stride and feeling like I was about to burst into a run any minute. Coming to a stop in front of a door, Elijah Antwill swiped a key card and then pulled it open, beckoning me through in front of him before charging off again up a set of stairs.

We passed a number of stark looking doors that lined the corridor, not one had a window, or marking of any sort. We walked right to the far end of the corridor before he slowed and pushed open a door, allowing me to walk through first. I was instantly hit by chaos. It was an office I guessed but there was a jumble of papers strewn across a desk that I could only tell was such because it had four legs. That was all I could see of it. I couldn't tell what colour it was or what material it was made from as it was totally covered. A computer stood in the corner; an older boxy sort of thing sitting on top of a heavy hard drive. I wondered whether it actually had the ability to be switched on, let alone whether it even had any sort of Office package installed and internet connectivity. This was going to be fun.

The floor was equally littered with boxes of documents piled on top of each other, paper shoved in at all sorts of angles. I could feel a nervous twitch starting in the corner of my eye. The place was totally barren. No soft furnishings, no personal items, no photos of a wife, a child, a girlfriend. My stomach fluttered. Was there a girlfriend? Why the hell did I need to know? There was no pencil holder, no printer or photocopier, nothing but a scene of chaos in filing form. It was absolutely devoid of any comfort, any personality, just blank, vague.

Yet he was anything but. His presence was frightening yet intoxicating, his intense gaze, his huge frame, all of it should make me want to run away. Yet, I wanted to be closer, wanted to feel the ripple of those muscles under his shirt again, feel the heat from his body because I was stood so close, feel the brush of his lips on mine before he devoured me.

"It's a little disorganised" a low grumble came from close behind me, making me jump.

I turned towards him hoping I didn't look as flustered on the outside as did on the inside. He was much too close behind me, making my heart leap in my chest and sending a shivery sensation over my skin.

"Just make yourself at home," he continued, pushing a handful of dark hair back over his head.

My eyes focussed on his hands, like huge plates of meat with thick fingers. I wondered how they would feel inside of me. Shit! I forced myself to concentrate on something else but his fingers and instead noticed the scars on his knuckles, and across the back of his hand. A fighter maybe? A wrestler. I bet he could throw me down on a bed with some force. Oh fuck.

"Well, this is everything," Elijah Antwill said suddenly, breaking the silence and snapping me from another daydream. "All the documents you need are in here…. somewhere."

He offered what looked like an apologetic smile, although I wasn't absolutely sure. I looked around the boxes of paperwork, desperately trying to focus on something else.

"Most of the stuff you need is in the filing cabinet. I'll be downstairs if you need me."

And with that he left me in the middle of mayhem mountain. For a few minutes I just stood there, like a rabbit in headlights with no idea where to start, forcing pictures from my mind that had no business being there. Eventually I sighed, the feeling I'd bitten off more than I could chew settling down upon me, dampening the flames in my stomach. I took out my laptop and opened a document and I made a few lists. I always felt better, more focussed, with a list, any list; organisation amongst chaos, control in the madness.

I took my suit jacket off and rolled the sleeves of my white blouse up to my elbows, kicking off my heels so I was just in bare feet and sat crossed legged on the floor next to stacks and stacks of papers.

I spent over two hours surrounded by piles of invoices, account statements, staff rotas, personnel material, switching between kneeling on the hard floor to sitting with my legs crossed, to kneeling and back again. I was working on the last stack of papers from the cabinet when I suddenly got the awkward feeling of being watched. I looked up to see Mr Antwill just inside the door, his eyes boring into me. I tugged on the neck of my blouse pulling it up to ensure my cleavage was well covered.

"What are you doing?" he asked in a low, almost disapproving voice.

"I, err, your cabinet...."

"You've rearranged my whole cabinet?" he asked brusquely.

"It was far too disorganised so I've had to spend my time sorting it all out before I even begin to get any of this to give me any sort of information about you, I mean about your businesses."

I bit my bottom lip, my words coming out sharper than intended. When I looked up at him his usually unreadable face seemed lighter, as if he'd just smiled and I'd just missed it.

"I'm going to sort it all out into a better order for you," I continued, this time in a quieter, less pissed off tone.

"Can I help?" he asked softly and bent down in front of me to grab a pile of papers.

Without thinking I grabbed his hand before he could ruin the little piles I had placed all over his office floor. I let go of him almost immediately but my stomach flipping like a thousand butterflies had just been awakened.

"I'm sorry. I, err, I've got an order going here."

"Ok then, you tell me what you want me to do."

I looked up at him, into those captivating eyes and for a split second I had an urge to tell him something I shouldn't, something wholly unprofessional. I bit down on my bottom lip again, fighting the urge to blurt out and ruin my career and as I dropped my eyes from his gaze they settled to his crotch and lingered there a little longer than they should have. Shit. I could feel the heat of a blush rising to my cheeks and with my pale skin there was no hiding it.

Wincing I moved a leg. I had spent so long sitting on the floor my knees were aching and stiff. As I struggled to get to my feet, Mr Antwill held out a hand and I grabbed it helping me to stagger up onto numb legs.

"Thank you," I said trying not to make eye contact with him but noticing how huge he was now I was stood in front of him in my bare feet, tiny in his presence. Heat rose somewhere else.

"Really. I'm sorry my filing is not up to your standards," there was a hint of warmth in his voice, his lips tugged at the side a little, "Can I do something to help?"

"Actually, I need some dividers for the cabinet."

He nodded.

"There's a Smiths just a few streets up, they'll have them," I continued.

"I'll send Danny. Shouldn't take him long to go and bring some back."

"And I could really do with a coffee."

"No problem, I know just the place. Grab your jacket, oh and you may want to put some shoes on."

I glanced at my bare feet with my light pink, girly nail varnish and this time didn't try and conceal my embarrassment.

Elijah Antwill led me out of the nightclub and round the corner till we were a few streets away. Keeping up with him on damp streets in stiletto heels was not an easy job. I was sure I was taking two steps to every one of his massive long strides. At this rate I wouldn't need to go to the gym after work. Did this guy not do slow, or even anything other than speed stomp? The balls of my feet had already started to ache.

Then in a little side street he ushered me into a small café of no more than five tables, cute and intimate. We sat at a table in the window and a lady with dark brown hair, in her thirties I guessed, came across to take our order.

"Morning, Eli," she greeted him.

"Morning, Kell. How are you today?"

"All good, Eli. Just sloggin on."

"A regular Americano for me please," Mr Antwill ordered and then gestured towards me.

He shrugged out of the hooded jacket he wore over a black t-shirt and I couldn't help notice the way the top clung to bulge of thick biceps. A detailed tattoo ran down his right arm, a jumble of roses, crosses and all sorts of different shapes like a tapestry over his skin. The t-shirt dipped into a 'v' shape at the neck, the tiniest amount of dark hair peeking out and the hint of a necklace that he wore underneath. Pulled tight over his chest the material clung to the muscles of his pecs and a slim stomach, the small ridges of his six-pack just poking through the black top. I bit my bottom lip.

When I looked up at him again he was watching me intently and warmth flooded to my face instantly.

"I'm sorry about earlier," I deflected, "I didn't mean to be so abrupt. I have an issue with mess and er, organisation."

His lips tugged at the corners; the threat of a smile that he seemed incapable of letting develop.

"Paperwork is not one of my strengths."

"How long have you had the bars and clubs?" I asked, "I noticed it's a new business area for the company?"

"A few years. I bought the first one mainly to annoy my father."

I raised an eyebrow and he continued.

"He'd always wanted me a part of the family business but I found it boring. I'm not one for sitting behind a desk or shuffling papers," he looked at me pointedly, "so when I eventually retired from my other work he offered me money to invest. I bought a couple of bars. And I've since been building up an empire based on how much I can piss my dad off. The strip club has had the best impact."

I studied him. There was a tiny flicker of amusement, a tiny sparkle in his eyes that faded so quickly I wondered whether I had imagined it. And the accent? The gentle velvety rumble of a light Scottish accent and I could listen to that all day.

"And your other work?" I asked, sipping the last of my coffee.

"Army," he said gruffly.

"Sounds interesting. Guess they still have paperwork in the army though?"

"Ah but we don't have pretty little red-heads to organise it though."

I dropped my eyes into my coffee cup, searching for some speck of something to focus on whilst I tried to control the convulsion of my throat and the unexpected choking.

"What made you leave?" I asked when I managed to prevent my lungs from sucking in any more liquid.

"It was just time," he answered but his tone had changed and the expressionless mask that had lifted a bit at the edges returned.

"I'm sure your dividers will have come by now," he stated standing up.

I nodded, hastily put on my jacket and followed him from the café back to the nightclub.

Once back in his office I reorganised what I had pulled out of the filing cabinet, ordering them precisely and neatly and writing up an inventory of each drawer. That was better; a tiny flicker of order amongst the carnage. It had taken me near enough all day and there were still boxes and piles of papers and invoices that needed to be sorted out before I could even start. Really what this man needed was a secretary.

I locked the cabinet back up and took the key with me to find Mr Antwill before heading back to the office. I walked down the hallway of doors listening for voices but heard nothing. Doors were locked not just shut and there was no sign of Elijah Antwill up here. Still clutching the cabinet key, I went down the stairs and let myself into the nightclub itself.

It was weird seeing the place in the daytime. It was a lot smaller without a mass of human bodies crammed in, writhing away against each other. Hearing the creak of a door behind me I turned watching the hulking figure coming towards me with three boxes of beer piled on top of each other. Could he see me?

"Mr Antwill?" I asked tentatively as he staggered closer.

"Fuck!" I heard him exhale, "sorry, I just nearly ploughed into you with these. Wasn't expecting to see you."

"Sorry. I'm just heading back to the office now. I have your filing cabinet key."

"Great. Just put it in my left pocket, will you?" and he beckoned with his head to the side of his trousers.

I hesitated.

"I don't want to put these down and I can't take my hands off them."

I nodded and came round to the side of him. His jeans were tight against his waist and upper legs. I pushed my hand against him just enough that I could wiggle the key securely into his pocket and despite my efforts to complete the key-drop as quickly as possible, the tight fabric held my hand in place just to the side of his groin. I was sure my face was now glowing a bright shade of red. I chanced a glance up at him and sure enough there was a glimmer of something in his eye, a curl of his lips too, maybe?

Chapter Ten

ᬰ Eli ᬊ

The light floral scent of Ava's perfume lingered in my office and I could smell her every time I walked in. I could also actually get to my desk and although it still sported stacks of paperwork it was all neatly organised into piles. I didn't dare touch them. I thought she was about to bite my hand off when I went near them the last time and I expect she's the type to notice that they were a fraction out of place. Nope, I was definitely safer not even breathing near them.

I turned on my nearing ancient computer and eased my chair closer, careful not to disturb anything. I'd had a sergeant in the army that was obsessive like that; couldn't stand anything out of place or disorganised. Needless to say, I'd spent many an evening doing push-ups in the yard for not keeping my shit tidy. I'm pretty sure that was the start of my shape changing from a gangly teenager to the chest and arms of a killer; that and an impressive aim on the shooting range.

What I wasn't as good at was all the techno shit. I could pummel a man to death and shoot a hostile square between the eyes from 100m away with a pistol, I could plan huge missions to rescue kidnapped dignitaries but could I hell do all the fancy computer crap. Lucky for me we had others in the team with those skills and those people I still kept in touch with.

Once the computer, well overdue replacing, coughed and spluttered itself to life I logged in to my emails. I waded through junk email after junk email before Joey's name finally popped up. I really should buy a new machine, maybe something a bit more streamlined, but I couldn't be bothered with the hassle, and although slow, this one was reliable and I could work my way around it.

I opened the attachment Joey had sent and a young face smirking in a mugshot looked back at me.

'He's your driver. Low level runner. Got a bit of a record. I'm pretty sure you'll find him at this address....'

I looked at the address Joey had sent. The Byker Wall, a notorious rat-run for scrotes like this. It was a huge pedestrianised estate, hated by the local Police as its residents and criminals knew it like the back of their hand and could disappear easily. For me it was little different to the streets of Basra or Kabul and far less deadly. It was ideal for me too, I could also disappear and reappear so reconnaissance would be a breeze. I printed off the picture.

I spent the next two nights scoping out the estate, hiding in the shadows watching and waiting. The address Joey gave me attracted a lot of attention with visitors coming at all hours of the day and night. It took little watching to know he was running drugs from the address, but his operation was small fry and all I wanted was information; a clue as to what Ritchie was up to. I didn't expect this one to know much but I just needed a snippet of information and I could then join up the rest of the dots.

Ritchie was pretty thorough and so it hadn't been easy trying to follow the golden thread of command far enough up to get close enough to bury this fucker forever. I'd followed leads for weeks and then they'd turn up dead.

By Friday I'd gathered enough intel. When darkness fell I stood in one of the many alleyways that joined the parts of the estate to each other and waited. A group of youngsters came out of the flat, full of alcohol and high as kites. I'd watched them night after night, leaving at a similar time to head on to the local bars. Thankfully they were not the clientele that would get through my doormen. But it now meant there were very few people left in the flat.

I waited till the group moved around the corner then crossed the square and knocked three times on the door, just like the code I'd seen them using over the last few days. The door creaked ajar, the chain across the top stopping it opening more than a few inches. The kid was cautious but naïve. I pushed my shoulder against the flimsy wooden door; the door and the skinny one behind it bounced backwards, the chain giving a startled pop. I stepped in closing the door behind me.

The thin teen sat up on his backside, clutching his forehead where the door had hit him. I stepped over him. He was no threat and he wasn't likely to call the Police and incriminate himself and his friends in the process. The flat smelt dirty; cannabis and cigarette smoke, decaying food and unwashed bodies mingling into one overpowering stale stink. The small hallway was completely uncarpeted and human hair, dust and other muck drifted along in the draught created by the open door like tumbleweed. With a small push, the door to the lounge opened easily, it's effectiveness questionable. The thin wood was pitted with dints and holes some so large I could have almost walked through without opening it.

Three men looked up at me, confusion turning to anger.

"Who the fuck are you?" a dark haired one demanded but he wasn't who I was looking for so I ignored him.

The young dealer, Billy, had sprung from where he had been lying with his legs flung over a stained arm of a saggy armchair. I crossed the room and grabbed him by the collar of his hooded jumper, dragging him towards me. He struggled, arms and legs flailing, connecting with me but with no real power. The dark haired one lunged at me, as I'd expected he might, slashing forward with his excuse for a knife, the blade barely longer than a butter knife. My fist landed right in the middle of his eyes and he was out like a light as he collapsed round my feet.

Billy looked panicked now and struggled against me like an animal caught in a trap. The third man, who seemed barely over eighteen, got to his feet, clearly feeling obliged to do something to help his mates.

"Do yourself a favour and sit down," I instructed.

He listened, flopping back onto to the sagging sofa, his eyes fixed on me.

"Now, Billy, you and I need a little chat," I gave him a little shake to make sure he understood, "who told you to drive into my club?"

The kid went pale.

"I, I, I don't know what you're talking about."

"Yeah, you do. Maybe you need help remembering?"

"I told you. I haven't a clue what you're going on about."

I moved my hand around the back of his head before spinning him round and driving his face against the wall. Blood streaked down the tobacco-stained, cream walls as he crumpled in a heap at my feet. The third man looked like he was about to jump into the action again and I shot him a warning glare. Grabbing Billy again I yanked him to his feet, blood running through his fingers as he cradled his shattered nose.

"Wanna try again?"

"D, Dazza."

I gave him another shake to help his memory.

"Gray. Dazza Gray"

71

"Good boy," I sneered before letting him go and watching as he staggered backwards and sank into the manky armchair I'd found him in moments earlier.

"Sit," I instructed the other youth as I turned my back on them and left.

Chapter Eleven

❧ Ava ☙

"So, you had a coffee date with your Mr Antwill?" Kerry asked as she stood over the hob cooking a stir fry for tea listening to me regaling my day.

"It wasn't a date. And he's not my anything. He's a client."

"Uh huh," Kerry nodded at no one in particular, "and he's not the reason that you've found your sparkle?"

"What sparkle?" I nervously took a mouthful of red wine.

"These last couple of days your eyes have been brighter, you're less quiet, more energetic and you had more make-up on this morning. I don't think it was me you were trying to impress."

"Maybe I'm just having a few good days," I deflected.

"I mean, it's about time. You've been a right barrel of laughs these last six months and I get why, I really do, but the last couple of days you've been different."

Kerry spooned the stir fry into two bowls and pushed mine across the island in the kitchen to where I was perched on a stool.

"Army guys are normally a good fuck," she said suddenly and I nearly choked on a noodle, "it wouldn't do you any harm to have fun with someone. I can't recommend casual sex enough. It's about time you gave it a go."

I blushed uncontrollably and took another gulp of my wine.

We spent the rest of the evening gossiping, mostly about Kerry's sex life and last night's 'friend'. He was just a work colleague she'd told me. They'd been working together on a big job and having spent a lot of time together over the last week had become a little close.

"I had an itch," Kerry shrugged her shoulders "he scratched it".

*****

I buried myself in work for the rest of the week, trying to only think of Elijah Antwill on a strictly business level but every flitting thought incited a pulsing between my legs and sent my mind off to the land of dirty daydreams. I'd scheduled in some more visits to go through the contents of the filing cabinet for the next week, my heart beating that bit faster at the thought and the foreign feeling of excitement bubbled in my stomach, something I'd not felt for a long time.

By the time I'd finished work that night I felt mentally drained. I'd spent every few minutes fighting off wayward thoughts of the dark-haired man, refusing to succumb to the needs and wants

74

of my body but failing miserably. I stopped off at the gym hoping to out run the thoughts that plagued my brain.

"You OK, Ava?" Cameron asked as I passed his office on the way out, tired and red from the effort I'd put in just to still my mind for a few short moments.

"I'm fine, just tired," I gulped on the way out, my face burning red from the exertion.

"Training hard tonight, bad day huh?"

"Yeah, something like that," I mumbled, stupidly embarrassed at the thoughts the question invoked, the ache in my core returning.

Damn it, Cam. He rested muscled arms on the desk top as they flexed out of the short sleeves of his t-shirt, his eyes feeling like they were boring into me and for a moment I wondered whether he could see what I was battling with.

"Well, gotta go," I muttered.

"Have a nice night," he replied, dropping his eyes to the papers in front of him, a strained look returning to his face.

*****

"I'm in Gulliver's. Booth beside the door. Come get me when you've finished wherever you are," I typed a text to Kerry once I had eventually got myself motivated to get dressed and make it back in to the City centre.

Sitting back against the soft velvety cushions of the seats, I let my eyes wander around the bar. Lights bounced off the lavish purple and silver theme, momentarily lighting up groups of people as if purposefully picking out faces in the crowd. The throng of people round the bar was becoming deeper, the space filling up, a chorus of voices and laughter growing louder, more and more bodies pouring in from outside and surrounding each other, pushing to get served at the bar.

Even amongst the bustle of bodies all crammed together I could see him moving through the crowd. My chest jolted, my eyes fixated on the mass of the man wading slowly through the people three and four deep at the bar. He stopped at the group of glamorous women who I'd watched earlier myself. From afar I watched as a blonde girl turned to him and his hand came to rest on the bare flesh of her lower back. He leaned in and kissed her on the cheek and for a moment I wondered what his lips would feel like on my own skin. I blinked the thought away quickly taking a long swig of the sharp minty liquid in my glass.

There was a definite familiarity between them; the way she tipped her head to the side, her red lips glistening as the lights flashed across her face, her fingers fiddling with the buttons of the black shirt he wore. He clasped a hand over hers, studying her face and my eyes strained to read the lips moving as he spoke to her.

He looked up, his eyes seeming to scan the crowd and stopping on me. Could he see me in the dark recess of the booth? But his stare pinned me in place and I couldn't look away. I didn't want to look away. I swallowed my mouth dry but I couldn't even reach for my glass, my brain, my focus, my everything fixed on him.

The seat dipped beside me, pulling my attention away from him and the spell was broken.

"What are you doing here by yourself?" Harry's voice broke through my thoughts.

I turned my head to where he had slid in the booth beside me, almost unnoticed.

"Just waiting for my friends."

Harry shuffled in closer and slung his arm over my shoulders.

"Guess I'll have to keep you company until then," he slurred, alcohol sweet and strong on his breath.

He was far too close. I could feel the heat radiating from him, the strong smell of his aftershave almost suffocating, catching the back of my throat and sending me into a fit of shallow coughs.

"You know I've always liked you, Avery."

"Ava," I corrected.

"Ava," he repeated, "I always thought you were too good for Tom."

I frowned, recoiling at just the mere mention of his name.

"You know I always told him that too," he continued, each word dragged out longer with the alcohol muddling his brain, "I always told him he was a big shit for cheating on you all the time."

"All the time?" I asked, trying to mask the squeak of surprise in my voice.

"Uh-huh. The fucker really didn't know what he had. I kept telling him with a girl like you he should be going straight home, don't pass the strip club, don't collect two hundred pounds. I tried to make him go straight home to you. Fuck, if you were mine there was no way I would stick my dick in anyone else."

The pain hit me hard in the chest; pain I'd thought I'd exorcised. But even just the mention of his name, the reminder of him; that alone felt like someone had stuck a knife in my chest. And Harry's drunken words turned that knife in my chest viciously.

Harry reached forward, pushing a strand of my hair back over my ear, dipping his head towards me, his breath hot on my face. I moved away.

"Harry," I warned.

"I told him I would look after you," he mumbled towards my ear, moving closer still

"Harry, stop it!"

His hand grabbed the back of my head and pulled my face to his as he pushed his lips onto mine. I pushed against his chest, trying to get away from him. His other hand snaked up my thigh, his fingers groping, squeezing my leg. I shadow crossed the booth, the darkness growing blacker still.

"She said no," came the growl from somewhere above me.

Harry pulled away, confusion crossing his face and I followed his gaze.

Elijah Antwill towered above us, above Harry, his hand gripping the material of his shirt across the top of his shoulder. His face was dark, a wildness in his eyes as his brows knitted together. His lips were pulled into a sneer, angry and frightening and I backed away from him, from Harry.

With a rough movement he pulled Harry up onto shaky legs and bundled him out of the booth towards the doormen waiting behind him.

"What was that?" he asked Harry, although Harry had not uttered a word since Antwill's big hand clamped down on his shoulder, "you were just leaving?"

Chapter Twelve

ಖಿ Eli ಞ

The bars and clubs were busy tonight and I'd spent some time manning the security cameras, carefully looking for anyone out of place or suspicious. I doubted Ritchie's message would end with trashing my night club entrance. He'd retaliated, which meant I was finally getting to him, but it also meant that whatever he was up to was pretty serious.

A slim familiar form walked through my bar. She was alone as she ordered a drink and then went out of view of camera two. Zooming in on the screen for another camera I found her sitting by herself at a booth in the window. Was she waiting for someone or just drinking alone? I watched for a while, my eyes following every male who walked in watching to see if they approached her. Every second that passed, every second that she sat there alone gave me an odd sense of relief.

I left my office and wandered towards Gulliver's, cutting across the courtyard at the back which joined many of my bars and clubs together.

The front of the bar was covered with people jostling and pushing, trying to get the attention of the staff and order drinks. I weaved my way through them, gently moving them out of my way until I recognised a face in the crowd. Ashley smiled her best seductive smile. I hadn't seen her since the car-in-the-club incident and hadn't really had the appetite for her. Something else had piqued my attention lately.

She looked stunning of course, in an exaggerated way. The exposed skin under her jump-suit pulling the eye all the way down her chest, the bulge of her cleavage exposing very round, fake tits as the material of the black suit cut away all the way to her naval. The piercing in her belly button caught in the roaming lights of the bar, twinkling brightly, drawing my eye to where she wanted it. I smiled, shallow and indifferent, dropping a peck on her cheek.

My face lingered against her cheek as she said something in my ear but I wasn't listening. I was watching a figure join Ava in the booth, a heat igniting suddenly in my chest. He was slim and blonde, the pretty, boy-next-door type. He leant in close towards her, the over familiarity in the movement making me tense. Yet Ava seemed to pull away from him. Lovers' tiff? Some sort of domestic? I couldn't tell. Her body was angled backwards as if to create more space between them, her head moving as far away as she could get it.

I peeled myself away from Ashley, who was whispering something explicit in my ear which I hadn't listened to and stepped around her. With my eyes trained on the couple in the booth I watched intensely as I edged closer. The man suddenly grabbed Ava, pulling her head towards him as she strained trying to get away.

Anger now erupted within me and I advanced, the crowd in front of me moving quickly out of my way as I advanced towards them, sensing the darkness swelling in my chest. My hand clamped down on the man's shoulder, fingers sinking into the lean muscle underneath. He looked at me confused and annoyed. There was nothing more I would have liked right then than to punch him square in his pretty face. Instead, I pulled him to his feet, feeling his shirt tear under my grip and dragged him out of the booth.

"Get the fuck out my bar," I growled, pulling him away from my red head and into the awaiting arms of my doormen, "if I see you in any of my places again, I'll rearrange that pretty face for you."

I didn't even watch as the idiot was led outside and tossed into the street. I'd waded through the crowd at the bar and ordered a bottle of champagne giving myself a few moments to shake off the blackness of my thoughts, quelling the violence part of me would like to have inflicted. I didn't want Ava to see the monster that dwelled within me, the one that hid just under the surface.

Ava jumped slightly as I sat down beside her, fragile and twitchy and she eyed me suspiciously. I poured a glass of champagne and handed it to her and she stared into it for a second. Hastily I poured another, taking a large gulp from the glass, reassuring her I hadn't drugged it, that she wasn't escaping one arsehole only to be taken by another. Not yet anyway. I pressed the thoughts from my groin, instead losing myself for a moment in the green of her eyes, a raw innocence emanating from them. She pressed the thin glass to her lips, eyes focused on me as she took a tentative sip.

"What are you doing here alone?" I asked, an anxious fluttering in my chest that she still might be waiting for her date to arrive.

"I, I'm waiting for my friends," she answered, looking at me timidly.

I probably stared at her too long then. She was wearing the same perfume she'd left all over my office. Her brilliant red hair fell heavily around her shoulders, flames framing that delicate heart-shaped face. My eyes were drawn to her rose-pink lips as she sipped at the champagne and the slight bob of her slender neck as she swallowed. How I'd like to put my lips there, to taste her creamy skin. The top she was wearing covered the rest of her completely but I could still see the small swell of her tits underneath. I couldn't blame the dickhead for wanting to touch her. I wanted that too. And I realised then I had every intention of making it happen.

"Who was the dick head?" I asked suddenly abruptly.

"He's my boss."

I stared at her, gritting my teeth, keeping tight hold of the monster that stirred.

"And does your boss always touch you like that?" my voice laced with a darkness that surprised even me.

"No! He's just drunk. He's a good guy, really."

"Didn't look like a good guy to me. If I ever see him do that again…."

I know what I would do if he ever touched her again. Not that she was mine to protect, not yet anyway. A surge of possessiveness went through me.

"Thank you. But I can look after myself," she said sharply, a cool confidence returning.

I liked that even more. Maybe I'd underestimated the vulnerability of her tiny frame?

"I see you've been busy while you waited for us," a light feminine voice interrupted.

A group of girls moved around the other side of the booth and Ava looked up, giving them a warm smile.

"Who's your friend, Ava?"

The blonde was elegant and pretty but compared to Ava's unusual beauty she paled away into insignificance. Ava introduced me and the blonde girl smirked.

"Ah, so this is the hot new client you've been gushing about."

I looked at Ava and smiled at her. Yeah I'd make her gush.

"You've been talking about me then?"

Colour rushed to her cheeks, as she shot her friend a warning glare that I didn't miss. I leaned into her and whispered in her ear.

"Maybe I should I give you more to talk about."

She bit her lip, the colour in her cheeks now spreading down her neck, illuminating her pale skin. I smiled and got to my feet.

"I'll leave you to your friends. See you in my office Monday morning," I said, my voice low, brushing her ear with my lips, my face lingering just a little too close for just a little longer than it should.

Did I see her clench her legs together?

Chapter Thirteen

ಹ Ava ೞ

I was distracted all weekend with thoughts I shouldn't have. The feel of Elijah Antwill's beard scratching against the side of my face, the shivers going through me at the low growl of his voice and the brush of his lips across my ear. Every thought of him created a heat deep in my stomach and an ache between my legs.

I spent the whole weekend hiding from the whir of unprofessional thoughts about my client and escaping Kerry's interrogation techniques. I trained for hours in the gym trying to distract my mind and my body, pushing myself harder and harder, punishing myself for my wayward thoughts; thoughts that were making me weak. But nothing worked. I felt like I was caught in a spell. It was ludicrous.

I had nowhere left to hide Monday morning, and woke with a familiar ache eating at my core, reminding me that nothing I had tried over the weekend could control my feelings or tame my desires. Nothing. And yet my stomach bubbled with wary excitement, anxiety contradicting the anticipation. And then I had

Harry to face this morning, but despite the small knot of dread tightening in my stomach it didn't dull the wetness pooling between my legs.

"So, your Mr Antwill," Kerry ambushed me as I stuffed a slice of toast hastily into my mouth at the kitchen island, "are you gonna do that or is he free for me? I would so climb all over that gorgeous bastard."

I cringed, taking a gulp of my coffee and stifling the need to spit it straight back out as it scalded my mouth and throat.

"He's a client," I hissed.

"So? You don't have to *marry* him," Kerry shrugged when I rolled my eyes at her.

"I don't need to do anything with him."

Kerry shot me a look.

"No, you really do. It's about time you had a really decent shag."

I scrunched my nose up, trying not to meet her gaze. I hadn't been with anyone at all since I moved North, but she didn't need to know that. No one did. It was a can that did not need opening.

The office was reasonably quiet when I arrived, docking my laptop and grabbing a coffee waiting for the computer to whirr to life. I glanced around, my eyes settling on Harry's empty desk and for a moment I thought he wasn't in again. A navy jacket hung on the back of his chair, a brown leather satchel at the foot of the desk, the slight smell of his after shave lingering in the air.

I wandered the floor, glancing at the top of heads bowed behind computer screens, the tip, tap, tap of nails hitting the keyboards as letters and documents were fired off, the office coming alive with the sounds of production. But there was no sign of Harry.

I pushed through a door right at the back of the office which led to the stairs. It was a barren, stark area, contrasting against the prestige, glass and leather of the rest of the building, but it was cool and a great place to think. I stood in the silence, watching out over the windows that over looked the streets feeding workers to Quayside businesses, tiny people below scurrying around on their way to work, trying to beat the threat of the big black clouds that gathered ominously over Newcastle.

The drawl of a man's voice on the stairwell above me caught my attention.

"I'm not working the case."

The voice was Harry's. I moved closer to the foot of the stairs that led to the next floor.

"So, who is?" the man's voice was much fainter and I had to concentrate hard to make it out.

"Avery Edwards, Ava. Antwill specifically asked for her. Martin agreed it," Harry said again.

"For fuck's sake. He's getting too close."

"What are you going to do?"

"What I need to. I'll deal with him. You make sure you can control her," the quiet voice said again.

I concentrated on the other voice, trying to focus on the way the vowels were put together, the roll of the consonants off the tongue. None of it was remotely familiar. The voice was tinny, robotic almost. Harry was on the phone.

"I can. I will. She's just a junior."

I scowled but just then the conversation stopped and I heard his steps on the stairs above me. I should have stayed where I was and confronted him about the other night, cleared the air between us, but something about the conversation I had just overheard made me uneasy. I crept away from the stairwell, slipping back inside the doors and into the office.

*****

The dark clouds had leached the daylight from the sky, the air cooler with the imminence of rain. I pulled my jacket around me, thankful that my hair was restrained in a bun on the top of my head, escaped strands already turning curly with the dampness in the air. My heels clacked furiously on the pavements, the length of my strides restricted by the tight black dress, as I raced against the downpour. The first drops of rain hit my cheek as I reached the doors to Elijah's nightclub and pushed the intercom button urgently.

"Eli's not in yet, but he said to let you up to his office when you got here," Danny beckoned for me to come in, disappointment stabbing me in the stomach lie a blunt knife.

Danny escorted me up the stairs to the office, watching me carefully as I unpacked my laptop and portable scanner, shifting from foot to foot and fiddling with the cuff of his sleeve. I'd glanced up once or twice but he was still there looking uncomfortable, making *me* uncomfortable.

"Will you be here long?" he asked eventually.

"As long as it takes," I answered, beckoning to the stacks of paperwork either side of me.

He loitered in the doorway still, for what seemed like minutes, almost as if he wanted to say something but didn't. I kept my head down, pretending to be lost in the paperwork at the desk but instead trying to escape the awkwardness. Eventually I heard feet shuffling on the floor, growing quieter, moving away, leaving me in peace. I let out a breath and looked up. I was alone.

I worked through lunch, listening to the rain pound the roof, the windowless room offering no other hint of how bad the weather might be outside. A loud grumble from my stomach grabbed my attention and I checked my watch. It was late afternoon and I was heading towards missing another meal if I didn't pack up soon.

There had been no signs of Elijah all day. The heavy weight of disappointment pushed against my chest, dismay unfolding in my stomach, the sense of loss from something I didn't have in the first place. I shook my head at no one. I was hungry, I was tired and I was sick of the sight of papers, invoices and payslips. Defeated, I packed up my equipment, slipping my feet back into the shoes I'd kicked off under his desk and meandered along the hallway and down the stairs.

The belly of the club was almost quiet, hushed voices somewhere only just audible. At first, I couldn't see them, but as I wandered through the doors, past empty booths towards the club's big double doors I saw them.

Two men talking to Danny, hurried and threatening, tension in their bodies and a meanness on their faces. They were imposing, threatening. I wondered whether I could creep round them to the exit, but as I moved I started to overhear bits of the conversation, Danny's voice growing more frustrated.

"I'm telling you he's not here," Danny said, his voice raising.

"Why don't you just send us to his office and we will wait in there," one of the men said.

He wore black jeans and a hooded, black jackct, with short cropped hair and a certain stance that said 'bully' all over it. The other had a snake tattoo on the side of his neck, just behind his ear, and was tall and wiry. I little knot of fear started tightening in my stomach and I backed away.

"Who's this bit of pussy?" tattoo guy piped up.

I closed my eyes and stopped, my heart beat starting to escalate as he walked towards me as I stood deciding on whether to run or stay still. I stood still. Still like a rabbit in headlights rather than something ready for a fight, fear weighing me down. Sucking in a breath, I braced myself as he approached.

"This Antwill's missus?" the other guy quizzed Danny, who looked between us, panic in his face.

I didn't like this. Not. At All. And Danny's reactions were telling me this was bad. I side-stepped tattoo guy, trying to put more space between us and grappling for a tiny nugget of bravery.

"No, I am not," I steeled myself, pushing the nervousness as far from my voice as I could, "you heard him, Mr Antwill is not currently here, so I suggest you make an appointment to see him at a more convenient time."

"Antwill got himself a posh bitch. I like her," tattoo guy said moving back towards me cutting off any escape route, his tall thin frame looming over the top of me.

He was stood so close I could smell the cigarettes and alcohol on his breath and the slight smell of sweat from the body a few centimetres away from mine. I didn't think he could get any closer, but he did, edging, intimidating. My eyes flicked around the room, looking for something anything, but only seeing the upended stool a few paces away and probably totally useless.

His gaze never wavered, his lips pulling into a sadistic smile, menacing and something about the way he looked at me made the hairs stand up on the back of my neck. Sweat broke across my palms, heat touching my cheeks, the same heat that makes the bile pool in your throat just before you vomit. Maybe vomiting on his feet might be considered self-defence.

But as I stood debating on the best weapon to use, an arm snaked around my waist, pulling me into his body, jamming me against his hips and pressing me into his groin. Maybe vomit was viable after all. I pushed my arms into his chest, digging the point of my elbows into his ribs, creating a fraction of space between us. My heart hammered uncontrollably in my chest and I was sure he could feel it too, panic rising like bread in an oven.

"Let go of me!"

I tried to wriggle away from his grasp but he was far stronger.

"I like fight in my women," his tone lowered, and there was a look in his eyes that I didn't want to think about; a look I'd see on men before, men my mother brought home whose eyes roamed across my body when she wasn't looking.

Pulling my leg back I swung it towards him as hard as I could, connecting the pointed toe of my shoe with his shin with a dull thud. That ought to leave a bruise. I would have liked that to have been the bastard's groin but I was too close to reach so I made do with what I could.

"Bitch!" he yelped, releasing me to cradle his leg and I twisted out of his grip, making for the bar stool.

A deep rumble from the doorway made me turn around. The figure filled it; tall, foreboding, dangerous. His whole body seemed to eclipse the light that tried to spill through from behind him, shadows cast against his face matching the darkness of his voice.

Chapter Fourteen

ಕ Eli ಜ

I'd seen the dark shapes as I walked in, my eyes struggling to adjust from the grey of the rain outside to the dull orange glow of the lights inside. My brain couldn't make it out at first, four shapes slowly coming into focus. A shorter man, thick set and rough was nose to nose with Danny, my eyes trailing along the thick outstretched arm to where it grasped the collar of my barman's t-shirt. Danny's face was contorted in fear and his eyes flitted about him and over to a shadowed corner.

I saw the red hair first as it bobbed on the top of her head and then a dull thud. My stomach lurched, my brain turning to an angry mush of violence inducing thoughts.

"Bitch!" the other man yelped, grabbing at his leg as he hopped on the other and Ava side-stepped him.

"What the fuck are you doing in my club?" I bellowed from the doorway.

The thin man next to Ava straightened up rubbing vigorously at his shin, his attention

95

focussing on me and away from her. I let out a quiet relieved breath as I watched her creep further away from him and towards a stack of bar stools. The other guy spoke.

"Ritchie wants to see you," he said gruffly.

"And Ritchie couldn't pick up the phone because…?"

The first guy continued, "he likes to do his business in person."

"Well tell him to get his fucking arse down here in person then rather than send his little bitches."

The thin guy's eyes narrowed on me and I didn't miss the challenge in his glare. Moving down to the stairs from my vantage point and into the belly of the club I advanced on them, my hands tightly clenched to fists at my sides as I tried to restrain the urge to pummel the face of the taller man who'd had his hands on Ava.

"Well? Fuck off then," I said to the pair of them.

The shorter guy looked over at his friend and flicked his head in an unspoken command to get going. The thinner one looked back at Ava, blowing her a kiss before following him towards the door and I had to keep a tight lid on the rage bubbling within me. He stopped as he got to me, looking me up and down deciding whether he could take me. I had an urge to smash my forehead against his nose to answer his question, but I could feel her eyes boring into me. I held his glare, his stale breath hot on my face until he looked away and walked off after his friend.

"You guys OK?" I asked, looking from one frightened face to another.

"Yes, boss. I'm really sorry. When I opened the door to see what they wanted they, they barged in."

"It's fine, Danny. Take off, I'll finish up."

"I'm really sorry about that, Miss Edwards," I said, moving towards the small figure.

"Ava, call me Ava," she said, her voice shaking.

She was even more stunning when she was scared and fragile, her green eyes still wide with fear, the tremble of her delicious lips. My cock swelled against my jeans. Jesus she was killing me. I reached out slowly, careful not to frighten her anymore and tipped her chin up gently, my eyes scouring her face for any damage and I took advantage of the chance to really look at her. I moved my hands on to the top of her shoulders, feeling the shake of her body.

"Are you OK? You're shaking," I asked.

"I, I, I'll be fine," she answered, her voice coming out in shaky bursts, "what was all that about Mr Antwill? Who's Ritchie?"

"Eli, my name's Eli. Ritchie is a business rival," I guided her to a seat next to the bar then walked round behind it lifting a bottle of whisky from a shelf high above my head.

"I'm so sorry that happened, Ava."

Pouring the bronze liquid into two heavy tumblers I passed one to her, the tips of her fingers brushing mine as she took the glass from me, sending more signals to my already engorged dick. I tilted the glass gulping the whisky down my throat hoping the burn would dull all my senses, all the feelings that seemed to be amplified by just being around her.

"What's this?" she asked, sniffing at the liquid.

"Whisky. Good for shock."

"Oh. I, I, I can't. I'm at work."

I moved closer to her, bending over the bar and catching her eye, the whisky firing in my veins, pushing blood around my body and to my cock. The opposite effect to what I hoped.

"I won't tell, if you don't," my voice was a hoarse whisper and I didn't miss the bob of her throat as she gulped.

She took another careful sip from the glass, her face screwing up after she swallowed, her throating tensing and then she coughed.

"It's better to just swallow it," I said with a hint of mischievous that I couldn't keep restrained.

There were a lot of things I couldn't keep restrained around her. She hesitated, glancing up at me through the shelter of her eyelashes, but I noticed and I couldn't help the smirk that tumbled from my lips.

"The whisky. Swallow it in one."

"Thanks. Sipping is just fine," she replied, stubbornly.

She took another sip and I watched as she drank it, my eyes trailing over the creamy skin of her jaw, down her slender neck, down her chest down to dip of her cleavage. A couple of the buttons on the top of her dress had been torn off in the incident and I really should have diverted my eyes, but I couldn't stop, I wanted to see more. I slipped my gaze sideways quickly when she'd eventually finished the last of the liquid, resisting the urge to find out what some of my best whisky tasted like from her lips.

"It was a bit of a risk kicking him," I warned breaking the silence as I willed myself to find a distraction, "what was your plan after that?"

Her face lightened, a sheepish smile transforming from the fear that had been there earlier.

"I, err, well I was going to whack him with that stool over there," she pointed to a two-foot bar stool stacked on its head on one of the tables.

I couldn't help but laugh. Brutal.

"And then I would have run."

"What, in those heels?"

I couldn't imagine her getting anywhere fast in those bad boys.

"You'd be surprised what I can do in these things," she said innocently.

"I think I'd like to find out."

I leaned in closer. Her cheeks coloured. My eyes lingered on hers, searching in the depths of green and we both fell silent again, our gazes tangled. A heavy atmosphere wrapped around us.

I felt like I was staring into the Mediterranean when I looked at her. She smelled like it too, the citrus-fresh scent of her skin mingled with the jasmine of her perfume. I could have been basking on the Italian coast. She looked away from me suddenly, pushing to her feet.

"I'd better get back to work."

*****

I'd waited for Ritchie to leave his house that evening, keeping a decent distance behind his black Bentley. The car was relatively new, not one of the normal ones I spent my nights following. He loved extravagance and rare things, cars, women, paintings, anything that was difficult to get hold of would pique his interest. But this car was relatively plain compared to his normal acquisitions and made me wonder whether this had been a hasty purchase, perhaps one of his other cars had suddenly disappeared, or even been used as a battering ram.

I followed the vehicle as it travelled through the outskirts of Newcastle, weaving through busy streets, round monotonous one-way systems until it reached the centre and disappearing into an underground car park of a boutique hotel. I'd been pretty certain he'd turn up here, after weeks of tailing him, he'd become pretty predictable. And boring.

I parked my car a few streets away in a public car park, jogging back towards the hotel. I broke into a walk a little way off before muttering a 'good evening' to the doormen as they graciously opened one of the huge gilded doors for me. I worked my way to the bar, popping up on one of the high bar stools which allowed a good view of Ritchie and his girlfriend at the far side of the restaurant. I ordered a glass of red wine and watched for a minute or two as his order was taken and a waiter made their way over with a bottle of wine. I took another sip, slid my glass off the bar and made my way over to join the table.

Dragging a chair from the neighbouring table, I pulled it across the floor so it screeched hideously, fellow diners shooting me angry glares, before joining the couple.

"Hello, Eli," Ritchie's voice was calm.

The brunette, after her initial startled look in Ritchie's direction, averted her eyes as she searched in her wine glass for something. The bruises on her face had faded to the tiniest of yellow hues; for now at least.

"A little bird told me you wanted to see me. Thought we could catch-up over dinner. You know, a little more sophisticated," I shrugged and took a gulp of my wine, my eyes locked on his.

"Like old friends?" he asked, smiling at me graciously.

It goaded me and he knew it. I tried to keep my teeth from grinding.

"What do you want, Ritchie?"

"I want my girl back."

That made me smile. So, this wasn't about Billy the Kid. He mustn't know I had been making enquiries about him. This was about the dancer that I stole.

"Go get another one."

I looked in the direction of the brunette and he followed the path of my eyes.

"That one hasn't paid her debt off yet."

I pushed my lips together trying hard not to let my distaste show.

"And how much has she left to pay?"

"Another grand."

I dug into my suit jacket pocket, took out my cheque book and scribbled on the paper, my signature looking like a drugged-up spider had wandered across the strip. I slid it across the table to him.

"All sorted."

He looked down at the cheque but didn't pick it up. The brunette shifted uncomfortably in the seat next to him. I watched as she glanced nervously at him, my gut feeling suddenly heavy as I realised she'd probably be sporting a fresh bruise tomorrow morning because of me.

"She works for me now, Ritchie. Guess you'll just have to send all her punters over to Opulence. Seems I've had a fair influx of new faces already."

He continued to smile at me, sickeningly. Did this guy ever get riled?

"Are we done?" I asked, tapping the cheque that lay untouched on the table.

"For now, old friend."

I knocked back the last of my wine and stood up, making as much noise as possible with the heavy leather chair as I could. As I turned away from him, he called out to me.

"Don't be a stranger, Eli."

Shooting a glance over my shoulder I left him to his steak supper, unable to any longer stomach that untouchable mask.

Chapter Fifteen

❧ Ava ❧

Despite the intrusion, I'd got the filing finished and all the documents I needed scanned into my laptop that afternoon, returning to the messy office with a glass of whisky to refuel me. But that meant for the rest of the week I had no excuse to go back and instead I sat in the office and worked on his business accounts and turnover. But he was never out of my thoughts.

He'd been so close to me, even over the expanse of the bar top, our faces mere centimetres away from each other, so close I could have lunged forward and kissed him. Christ knows I wanted to. I clenched my legs together under my desk as the warm, throbbing sensation returned to haunt me.

I'd taken to refreshing my emails continuously, hoping for something from him, some excuse to return to the nightclub. But nothing had come and instead I stared at my screen blankly, not reading the words in front of me, my mind wandering off to places it shouldn't, delicious places. I jumped, my heart jolting in my chest at the sudden shadow over the top of me. I glanced up, the office eerily quiet, every other desk around me deserted.

"Ava," Harry said, his voice quiet, uncertain, "about the other night."

He trailed off nervously, pushing the takeaway coffee cup towards me.

"I didn't mean to come on so strongly," he continued, "I was drunk and not thinking clearly."

I nodded quietly, tugging the neck of my blouse up uncomfortably, fighting the heat that prickled at my neck.

"But I want you to know, Ava, I really like you…."

"I like you too, Harry. As a boss, you're a good boss."

He smiled weakly. Then his hand covered mine, warm and slightly clammy. I slid my hand from under his, my eyes sweeping the office, but there was no one there to see us.

"I want to be more than a boss, Ava."

My stomach tightened, memories flooding back.

"No, Harry. Been there and done that, remember? It didn't end well."

"I wouldn't treat you like that."

I shook my head. They all said that but ultimately it all ended with pain. He was so like him. The light blond hair, the expensive suits, the love of a good party. I couldn't go back there again, get dragged back into a world of uncertainty and second guessing.

"Give me a chance, Ava, I'll prove I'm nothing like him."

"I'm sorry, Harry. No."

He pinched his lips together, defeat written across his face and nodded curtly, turning away from me. Walking back to his desk he pulled the navy suit jacket off the back of his chair and flung his satchel over his shoulder.

"Don't work too late, Ava," he said quietly as he passed me, making his way to the lifts and out of the building.

My stomach felt heavy, a flutter of guilt nibbling at my insides chased away just as suddenly by the memory of the conversation I'd overheard. *She's just a junior*, he'd said to the unknown voice on the other end of the phone. I'd been a junior too the last time, and I'd got carried away, consumed, controlled and then dropped from a huge height.

I nearly gave the gym a miss. I had to walk past it on the way home, its neon sign almost staring at me as I tried to slink past in the fading light. I'd walked five paces before guilt trickled into my soul and I turned. Contained in a peculiar position at the tip of a triangular shaped building, it almost cowered under the shadow of the Tyne Bridge, a chilly breeze coursing through the wind tunnel it sat within.

The place was reasonably quiet when I got there, having climbed the millions of stairs into the building, a work out in itself. I could hear the low rumble of voices from the weights room and

I caught a glimpse of Cameron training with another man.

I set off on the running machine, my feet beating against the belt, my breath gathering pace as my heart beat hard in my chest. The mirror in front of me offered me glances of the men training in the room behind me. They grunted with each movement followed by the heavy, low thump of dumbbells hitting the gym floor.

The other man stood out, his vest narrowing between his shoulder blades, the dark ink of an intricate tattoo weaving its way over the whole of his huge right arm and creeping across his chest, losing itself under the white material of his top. Knee length shorts did nothing to hide the thickness of long legs, the solid bulge of muscled calves escaping from where the black baggy shorts ended. He turned his head slightly and I caught his face in the mirror, a pair of bright blue eyes staring back at me. Busted. I dropped my gaze hurriedly, keeping my eyes from creeping back to the mirror.

When I'd finished my run I scuttled off to the studio, not even chancing letting my eyes wander into the room where he was. My mind was already swimming with thoughts I couldn't control. I ran through my abs repertoire, focusing on the heavy beat of my music, keeping the ludicrous notions and day dreams from surfacing.

Arms, legs and stomach shaking, I lowered myself to the ground from the plank, tipping myself onto my back with my knees bent. A sheen of sweat coated my skin and I closed my eyes listening as my breaths slowed from ragged gasps, tension drifting from my muscles. My heart pumped out a steady thumping beat, the smell of sandalwood drifting through the air. Pushing the wisps of hair that had escaped my pony tail from where they gathered against the dampness of my face, the sudden touch of hands on my ankles startled me and I sat up quickly with surprise.

"What the…?"

Blue eyes stared at me; his face way too close to mine.

"Hi to you too," he answered, amused.

"What are you doing?" I asked, trying to stop my already laboured breaths from escalating into hyperventilation at his sudden closeness.

"Thought you could do with a hand with your form."

"My form is fine."

"You're lifting your feet off the ground."

"I wasn't."

Eli raised an eyebrow. His hands tightened around my ankles, electricity ripping through my skin from his touch alone and I pushed my lips together to stop me making noises. He leaned towards me glistening with sweat and I could smell the heat of his body. Super-charged anticipation tingled in my chest. My heart, already beating fast from exertion, seemed to have picked up a whole new rhythm. My eyes traced up his tattooed arm, picking out the details of the tattoo, roses and skulls, all against the winged background of a phoenix.

Catching me inspecting him, he slid me closer, a gasp finally escaping my lips and heat flooding to my face in embarrassment. A satisfied smirk formed on his face, transforming the intensity in his eyes.

"Cross your arms over your chest," he instructed, his voice low with the command, sending a warmth radiating from the bottom of my stomach.

"Err, OK."

"Right, now up quick and back slow," he instructed.

I did just that, exhaling as I sat up and lowering myself down over the count of three.

"Keep going."

His voice was rough, sending the weirdest of sensations washing over me. I tried to close my eyes to concentrate, struggling to focus as the big hands clasped tightly round my ankles keeping my feet firmly in place. A throb pulsed between my legs.

"Now, half way back, hold and pulse."

And I did, until the muscles in my stomach were screeching in pain. I tried to concentrate on the ferocity of the ache in my stomach and not the ache in my core. Eli worked me harder, putting in another round of variations until I could barely take any more.

"Stop, I can't," I panted, "I need a rest."

"No. Keep going, you're almost there," he instructed.

I finished the set and lay flat on my back, legs still bent and held by Eli, my breaths coming in jerky rasps.

"Good girl," the rumble of his light Scottish accent vibrated through me, "I like a girl who does as I tell her."

I propped myself up on my elbows and looked at the man on his knees by my feet. His perfectly shaped and hard pecs visible, straining under the tight fabric of his vest, a twinkle in his blue eyes. He took one hand from my ankles and reached forward grabbing me by the wrist and helping me sit upright so that my head was once again inches from his. My eyes wandered over his face, noticing the faint scar across his left eyebrow, the square jaw covered by his immaculately trimmed beard. My heart danced and my pussy throbbed and I couldn't take my eyes from his.

Grabbing the back of my head he pulled my face to him until there was barely a millimetre between us. I could feel the heat from his breath, my lips tingling just for the feel of his. Then he pushed against me, our lips meeting. For a moment I hesitated, his beard scratching at me as his tongue dipped against me and I let mine meet his, in a soft waltz as we both moved against each other tentatively. He slid the tip of his tongue across my bottom lip and I couldn't keep hold of the moan as it tumbled from my lips against his. It seemed to drive him wild and suddenly his tongue was plunging into my mouth, pushing into me, darting inside fast and desperate, the shock and tension pulsing through my body taking my breath from me.

His hand tightened around my hair, pulling me even closer, forcing my face against his, deepening the kiss until the heat burning between my legs turned to a pulsing rawness, matched by the butterflies tapping out an Irish dance in my stomach. My breaths came in raspy bursts. My hands had formed fists, tangled in the sweaty material of his vest, holding onto him as everything inside me swirled in a sweet whirlwind of lust and want and need. A groan slipped from my mouth to his.

"Ahem," a cough was feigned from behind us.

I broke off the kiss, but Eli didn't let go of me. He didn't move but continued to bare down on me with his eyes, sending all sorts of delicious tingles pulsing through my body.

"What do you want, Cam?" Eli, asked in a sultry voice.

"Just wondering why you two were eating each other on the floor of my gym and not working out," Cam said lightly.

Eli let go of me and instead helped me to my feet as his hand fumbled against the front of his pants straightening himself up.

"Hi, Cam," I said, a new blush rushing to my cheeks.

"I was going to introduce you to my buddy, Eli, here but I see you've already met."

Cameron's smile was infectious and I grinned back.

"Hey, thanks for the sit-ups help," I said to Eli, "I'd, err, best get going."

Chapter Sixteen

ເ໑ Eli ର

I watched Ava leave, her hips gently swaying as she walked, the tight bulge of her arse bobbing just slightly. It was such a good sight. How I'd like to sink my teeth into that pert little backside and then some.

I'd got a good look at her, her gym gear leaving a lot less to the imagination than the suits and dresses I was used to seeing her in. Her cropped top showed off the hint of a six pack. Her shoulders had just the right amount of definition, the caps slightly rounded, her biceps and triceps just peeking through. Her thighs seemed well sculpted, shapely and strong and I'd be imagining those wrapped round me now for days to come; a great addition to the bank. And that tight round arse? I was going hard again just imagining what I'd like to do to that.

"Do you think you can put that away before you scare off my members?" Cam commented dropping his eyes to my groin.

I grinned at him, tucking my erection back under some sort of control under the waistband of my shorts.

"I reckon it would up your membership."

"Yeah, well something needs to."

"Business not so good, huh?"

"Memberships just keep dropping off," he sighed, eyes glancing round at the walls, "look around, it needs investment. People want the fancy machines, the monitors, the classes. I've got none of that."

Cameron was right, the building needed updating. Paint bubbled in the corners of the walls where damp seeped through and deposited salt on the plaster. The machines were dated, seats torn and taped up, patch fixes to the faded leather.

"I tried to fix it a year or so back. I took out a loan but the interest rates keep rising and the memberships are dwindling. I'm not sure how long I can keep going."

Something about what he said made me nervous.

"Who'd you take the loan from, mate?"

Cameron didn't make eye contact, staring away in the distance, the strained pause drawing out.

"Ritchie."

I clenched my jaw, anger firing in my stomach.

"Why didn't you ask me, Cam?"

"I was embarrassed. I thought I could handle it, get it paid back quickly, but instead things just kept going wrong. The building got broken into and trashed, the windows were put out another night. There was just always something and I just kept taking out more to fix it back up again."

"Shit," I exhaled.

I'd bet a huge wad of inheritance that none of that had been coincidental. I wanted to punch him just for being so stupid. Ritchie would never let the loan be paid off in full. That was how loan sharks worked, to trap you in an endless cycle of debt and servitude. And I'd been too obsessed over the years with my own agenda that I hadn't noticed my friend struggling.

*****

Joey had narrowed down some intel for me on Dazza Gray and I sat reading his email. Gray was another street level dealer but he was expanding, progressing. His rap sheet was impressive: drugs, assault, sexual assault, domestic violence. Nice fella. My eyes skipped over the copy of his driving licence and a picture of his dark blue VW Passat with taxi plates on the side. He had to have some friends in high places to get a taxi licence with that long list of offences.

'What about the goons Ritchie sent me? Any intel on them yet?' I typed into the email hitting 'send'.

'Not yet, I'm still digging. The stills from your club cameras weren't the best', his response was instant.

I closed the email app on my phone and popped Dazza's postcode into my satnav, starting the Landrover up and following the directions on the screen. It didn't take me long to arrive in a modern housing estate. It was a new build; streets of similar beige, brick houses dotted about flowing streets that seemed to merge seamlessly into one another. The gardens at the front of the properties were well maintained, adorned with fancy ornaments, lit up by solar lighting and swirling trees flanking front doors, neighbours competing for the 'best dressed' lawn competition or some such shit.

Dazza had done well for himself. His house was a big double fronted detached thing, three storeys high with bay trees standing either side of the door. They were the real things too, none of this plastic shit. The driveway had a brand-new VW Golf on the drive but no other car. Maybe it was in the garage? His shift at the taxi company was not due to start just yet.

I pressed the doorbell, the recorded chimes ringing like some old-fashioned mansion. Eventually I heard the turn of the lock. The middle-aged woman stood there, smartly dressed, hair pulled up into a ponytail. Her hand clasped round a glass of wine, her fake nails the same red colour.

"Mrs Gray, I'm sorry to disturb you," she looked at me blankly, "I err, I've been let down by my usual taxi company tonight and I know Darren does freelance. You wouldn't mind passing his number on to me, would you?"

I smiled apologetically.

She looked me up and down for a little while, her eyes eventually fixing on my chest before deciding I didn't look like an axe-murderer or a policeman. She tipped her head towards the house and I stepped into the doorway after her. She really should take more care.

The hallway was pretty impressive for a new build. Stairs stood back from the door so there was a big square entrance way and my thick soled boots clumped loudly on the white tiles on the floor. The woman turned away from me to a table on the left wall and scribbled something down on a notepad as I gazed around. There were pictures of family all over the walls, hung in a haphazard way; big picture frames, next to tiny ones, all mashed together in a big jumble. None of the frames matched either; there were smooth ones, shiny ones, big ornate ones and they varied from black, grey, silver and mirrored. It was hard to concentrate on the people inside them.

"My husband's number," she said, handing out a piece of note-paper to me.

I smiled at her, holding her gaze. I held my hand out to her and she took it. My fingers closed around hers, holding onto her a little longer than I should, watching as her eyes met mine again, her pupils dilating just a little.

"Nice to meet you," I smiled, making it obvious I was looking her up and down.

"Nice to meet you too," she said, her voice a little quieter, a little huskier.

Then I turned and left, feeling her eyes on me as I walked back up my driveway to my car.

That should stop her asking her husband too much about me. He had a record for violence against her, and I'd bet she wouldn't want to make him angry, or jealous. I doubt she'd give me much of a description when she mentioned me later.

I pulled over just before leaving the estate and typed the mobile number I had been given into an email. Joey's response was almost instant again.

'That phone is currently on the Denesgate Estate. I'll get you an address just give me a few seconds.'

The estate was on the west side of the city and was the leftovers of odd and sods of Council housing; half forgotten about after the worst of the properties had been pulled down. Entire ghost streets still stood: roads and pavements and lamp posts but no houses. It was almost like the housing estate version of the Marie Celeste. The properties that were left were privately owned. After a failed attempt to bring investment to the area, they'd been sold off for a pound a piece but with a minimum investment clause which had never really been observed by the purchaser. Now many were dilapidated and, although inhabited, were mostly drug dens and brothels. The area was fucking awful.

This property looked no different. Luckily for me it was part of an unusually full street of properties so pulling up in my car wasn't quite so conspicuous. I parked a few doors down on the opposite side of the street. There were some cars dotted about and a cluster in front of the property including a VW Passat. I sat and watched. Groups of youths entered the address periodically, leaving shortly afterwards. I took plenty of photos but judging by the age of them they were merely street dealers or just there to buy product for themselves. I needed something that connected Ritchie to all this. Something to bring him down.

Eventually the huddle of cars near the property cleared off one by one till the last one left was the Passat. Footfall at the property had reduced too. I sat and waited some more until the door opened again. Two women left first, their short skirts barely covering their arse cheeks, teetering down the path on huge heels. A dark haired, slim man followed after them and they climbed in the Passat and drove off.

Time to have a poke around. I waited for the car to be completely out of sight before walking up the path, conspicuous by my very build. I pulled the collar up on my jacket and knocked on the door, vibrations running through the hollow wood as music pulsed against it from the other side. No one answered. I gave the door a little push and it sprang open easily. Carefully, listening for any noise, I stepped inside. A sweet, earthy, almost mouldy smell assaulted my nose. But cannabis was not what I was looking for.

The lounge was deserted. Two sagging, dirty sofas stood at right angles to each other with a coffee table in the middle which was long overdue a clean; sticky circles covering the glass top, whilst dust collected on top of it. As I got closer, I realised the dust was brilliantly white, much more like a fine white powder. The lounge led to a kitchen with empty takeaway boxes scattered everywhere and discarded plastic cider bottles strewn on the floor. A half smoked joint was balanced on an ash tray. I picked it up, turning it in my fingers. The paper was still fairly crisp and the smell still hanging in the air. It hadn't been long lit.

I climbed the stairs, careful to make very little noise. Four doors, all closed, were at the top of the landing. I pressed my ear against the first one before pushing it open a crack. Empty. The room had a single bed, its sheets crumpled with a stained, uncovered, duvet rolled back like someone had just got out of it. A can of 'Redstripe' lager sat on the windowsill in front of curtains that were half hanging off the rail. A condom stuck to the floor.

I edged in and carefully lifted the mattress off the bed. There were a couple of foil packets rolled up but a quick sniff told me it wasn't what I was looking for. Pulling the door closed I moved to the next. Rhythmical squeaking came from inside and I nudged it slightly, peering through a crack between the door and the frame, the glimpse of a bare white arse pumping away, a woman's legs propped up either side of him still in those ridiculous high heels. A rustling sound from my left caught my attention but not quick enough as the black figure moved at me striking the side of my head.

Lights danced before my eyes, a chasm of black trying to swallow me and I lurched forward through the door. A woman screamed, the vibrations of her shrill cry hurting my ears as I pushed back to my feet, my head swimming with

120

the sound of swarming flies. I touched the side, something warm and sticky coating my fingers.

"Don't fucking move," a young man in tracksuit bottoms and matching tracksuit top shouted at me.

It took me a few seconds for my eyes to focus but I wasn't expecting to be staring into the mouth of a pistol when they did.

The woman on the bed screamed again, a jabber of words coming from her that I didn't recognise as the naked man yanked on some boxers.

"Shut the fuck up you stupid bitch!" the gun toting man shouted pointing the gun in her direction.

Amateur.

I launched myself at him pushing his gun hand to the ceiling as I drove my elbow up into his nose, feeling the crack as it smashed across his face. He howled, loosening the grip on the weapon as I yanked it from him, throwing him into the room to join the other two.

"If you're gonna pull a gun on someone, sunshine, you'd better be prepared to use it."

I resisted the urge to shoot him in the leg to see if it was actually loaded.

"Get your clothes on and make yourself scarce," I instructed the naked girl on the bed.

"Not before he pays me," she said in a thickly accented voice pulling a top over her big tits.

"You're getting fuck all. I never finished," naked man complained.

"Just pay the woman."

I flicked the gun towards him and he quickly grabbed his jeans, pulling out a few crumpled notes from a pocket and tossing them on the floor. The girl bent forwards, her big tits hanging out the bottom of the ludicrously short cropped top she'd covered her chest with, pulling a short red and black checked skirt over the tangled thong then snatched the money from the ground. She paused beside me, running her hand down the side of the gun, all the way along my arm and down my side as I watched her from the corner of my eye.

"I do first fucks free, handsome," she cooed in an attempt at a seductive voice, the words far harsher with her accent.

"Thanks, but you're not my type."

She looked at me pouting her lips.

"Now get gone," my voice came out as a growl as I cocked the weapon in my hand with an ominous click.

She dropped her hand, hurried down the stairs, leaving the rest of us looking at each other.

"So," I waved the gun between the two men, "who's going to tell me who you work for?"

Both stared at me. I moved a little closer the gun now pointing at tracksuit's forehead.

"I wonder whether this is actually loaded?"

I shifted to the right slightly, pulling the trigger. Tracksuit yelped and dived to the floor holding his head as an ear-splitting bang went off in the small room. The naked guy on the bed pulled the dirty duvet up towards his chin protectively.

"I guess it is," I mused, "now, shall we try that again?"

"You're fucking crazy," the man on the floor spluttered.

"Can't argue with that."

I moved forward pushing the barrel of the gun into the soft flesh of the man's cheek, the skin around the nozzle turning white from the pressure. He put his hands in the air in surrender, blood dribbling down between the left side of his face from the chunk of ear he was now missing.

"Ok, OK. It's Dazza. Dazza Gray," he stammered uncontrollably.

"Just him?"

He nodded. Tears pooling in his eyes.

"Who does he work for?"

"I don't know."

I pushed the gun further into his cheek.

"Please. Please!" he gasped, "I really don't know. We don't get told any more than that. There's more people higher up but I don't know their names and I don't ask."

"So, the drugs, the prostitutes? They're all run by Dazza?"

123

He nodded.

"And the gun? Where did you get that?"

"Dazza."

"And where did he get that?"

"I don't know. Same place as the drugs and the women," he shrugged.

Fuck. Ritchie had to be at the top of all this. I knew about the drugs and I suspected the prostitution and all the usual slime that went along with it. But now he was peddling guns too?

I glanced around the room, careful not to take my eyes off the men for too long. There were little packets of white powder stacked on the dresser; just a bit more than for personal use.

I smiled at the two men, "thanks for your help lads."

"Ok, now fuck off," earache replied.

"You don't mind if I keep this?" I asked gesturing to the gun in my hand.

Track suit shook his head.

"Great."

I dropped the gun down, pulled the trigger and shot him in the leg. He fell backwards screaming as blood trickled steadily out the gunshot wound. The eyes of the naked man on the bed widened to the size of dinner plates.

"You'd better call him an ambulance. Think he might need a doctor."

I switched the safety back on the weapon and tucked it into the back of my trousers, turned and left the room, listening to the cries of the injured man behind me.

Chapter Seventeen

ೞ Ava ೞ

All I'd thought about all weekend was the gym and Eli, a mix of contradicting emotions; a combination of need and regret, uncertainty and desire and the rush of adrenaline that pulsed though my veins every time my eyes closed. Then dread would hit me hard in the stomach. I'd moved from my boss to my client and no matter how much I wanted him, a swell of heat hitting me deep between my legs with every raw thought, this could never end well.

The office was a hive of activity and I felt tired just watching the people sat at their desks, the frantic tapping of keys on keyboards, the shrill ring of phones demanding attention. I clutched two huge takeaway coffee cups and deposited one on Harry's desk: a peace offering. His desk was empty, but his computer was on, an email left open on the screen.

'Those figures don't work for me,' the short text from 'R' read, *'I need to see you urgently'*.

"Ava," a voice behind me made me jump and I glanced up, "any chance you could just run the papers up to Martin's office? Julie's not in yet and I can't leave the front desk."

"Sure," I smiled, trying to conceal the heat threatening to take over my face and hoping that the receptionist hadn't realised I was reading Harry's emails.

I grabbed the bundle of newspapers and made my way up to the next floor, the lift pinging loudly as it arrived, the doors sliding back with a gentle hiss. Martin Fairbrother's office was dark, the dull grey morning providing little illumination through the cracks in the blinds, but even in the gloomy light the headline stood out.

'Man shot in West End Drugs Den'.

A headline like that in London had been common, but here in the North gun crimes were far less usual. London. My mind wandered home, a painful jolt of a memory shooting through me, adding another emotion to the surge I was battling with this morning. Chewing on my lip I concentrated on the article instead before replacing the newspaper and tidying the pile up so they didn't look like they had been dumped.

I'd barely stepped out from Martin's office, when someone walked into me, almost knocking me over. Hands grabbed hold of me gently, keeping me from falling over completely.

"Really sorry," he said as I looked up into the handsome face of a grey-haired older man.

"It's OK," I muttered.

"Ah, Harry, who is this lovely lady?" he asked, reaching out with his hand towards me.

127

I took it lightly, politely shaking it.

"This is Ava, one of my staff."

"Nice to meet you, Ava," his gaze held my eyes.

"You have the loveliest looking assistant, Harry."

Cool grey-blue eyes watched me intensely, roaming over my face, his lips pulling into a smile. The smell from aftershave surrounded me, the gentle, sweet scent from the grey-haired man seeping through the heavy expensive assault of Harry's. I felt hot, agitated.

"Ava, is very capable," Harry answered pointedly.

"Well maybe the very capable Ava should show me out," the grey-haired man spoke suddenly and I glanced towards Harry, the muscle in the side of his jaw tensing, "I'm sure you have lots of things to do this morning," he said to Harry leaving no room for any further negotiation.

"Yes, of course. Thanks for coming in this morning, Mr Robertson."

Harry moved towards the stairs at the back of the building, shooting a glance over his shoulder at me, tension across his face. A soft hand touched the small of my back, gently pushing me towards the lifts.

"So have you worked for the firm long, Ava?" Mr Robertson asked.

"No. About six months or so."

"Ah, I thought I'd not had the pleasure of your company yet."

I kept my eyes on the lift display watching as we passed the second floor, the first floor, feeling extremely uncomfortable in this small space with him. He was pleasant and well-spoken but the way he cast his eyes over me left me apprehensive. Eventually the lift stopped at the ground floor, a rush of cool air coming towards us when the doors parted. I walked towards the main entrance to the building, side by side with Mr Robertson.

"You know Harry often drops the paperwork at my house for me to check and sign. Maybe you should do that next time, saves Harry a trip all the way over, I'm sure he has better things to be doing."

"Oh, I can't. I don't drive."

"That's no problem, I'll send a car."

"I, err, I'm not sure Harry would be happy about that. He, err, he likes to tend to his clients personally," I lied; why did I lie?

"I'm sure I could smooth it over with him."

My excuses were running dry and improvising had never been a strength.

"It was nice to meet you Mr Robertson. I should really be getting back to my desk. Harry will probably need me to help him," that wasn't really a lie.

I held my hand out, making it clear I was saying goodbye. He took it and brought it to his lips instead, kissing the back of my hand gently. I pulled my hand away from him slowly, not wanting to make a scene, but wanting to put a bit more space between us. He studied my face.

"Good bye, Ava," he said, his voice soft, before turning away from me.

*****

It had been dismal and grey all day and the evening no better. Clouds gathered in the sky and the air was fuzzy with the threat of rain. My unruly hair was tied up out of the way, but a cascade of red fell down my back from the pony-tail that had started off straight but had now turned to curls in the damp air. The wind had also started to pick up, whipping around me menacingly.

I picked the pace up, walking briskly to escape the cold; drizzle now starting to fall in tiny droplets of water, clinging to my face and eyelashes. I cowered under the nightclub sign pressing the buzzer, a little impatiently, as the first heavy drops of rain started to fall. When the door opened, I bounded inside, not waiting for the invitation.

"Keen much?" Eli asked as I practically threw myself into the foyer.

"Sorry, I was getting wet."

"No need to apologise for that," he cocked his head, a smirk pulling at the one side of his mouth.

I took a breath, trying not to get caught up in him, my stomach jittery.

"I've brought my computer. I'll take you through my findings. Your office?"

"Whatever the lady prefers."

I ignored him, ignored the tingle in my stomach, between my legs, everywhere. Settling at his desk I scanned the room amazed it was as tidy as I'd left it and took out my laptop. I loaded the document as Eli came round behind me, peering over my shoulder, the woody smell of his aftershave threatening to distract me. I breathed out slowly, composing my thoughts.

"I scanned all the documents that I needed from your cabinet. I've managed to get three years of data from all that," I waved flippantly towards his filing cabinet.

"It makes for interesting reading," I continued, "overall you're making a little profit but there's a lot of waste across all the businesses. If you look at this graph here…."

I pointed to a section of the screen and Eli leaned in closer, resting a hand on the desk next to me, his fingers just skimming my arm as he set it down. I held my breath a moment, worried that when I breathed again, he would hear the shake in it. His hands were so big, scars criss-crossing over the top of his knuckles, veins bulged under his skin.

"This graph?" he prompted me.

"Uh? Err, yes, this graph here….it shows the stock you're purchasing against the stock you are actually selling. There's a lot of waste here. Now if you look at how much alcohol you actually throw away. You're offering too much

131

choice. Stick to a few brands per spirit for each of the businesses and that will see your profits improve 10%."

I went on like that for a while. Showing him the data, the graphs, trends and then what I recommended. It was a simple business improvement plan and would massively increase profits by just tightening up some areas. Eventually as I finished, he'd propped himself up against the desk with his arms folded, his eyes dark, thinking.

"Impressive," he said in a low voice, that seemed to vibrate through me.

I chewed on my lip, desperately keeping my thoughts about him in check. A pop made me jump and the room was suddenly plunged into darkness, the only light from the laptop screen.

"What's happened?"

"Power cut. Wait here. I'll go sort it out."

I sat for a few minutes, the glow from my laptop casting eerie green shadows around the room. I stared into the darkness, trying to force my eyes to adjust but the longer I stared the more I imagined things moving in the dark. Idiot. I tried to think of something else. Eli seemed to be taking ages to get the power back on. I heard a scratching at the far side of the room. Rats? The scratch came again and I listened intently. And again. That was definitely a noise and it definitely was something scratching.

What if it was rats? My heart started to pound in my chest. What if they ran up my leg? I pulled my legs up off the floor, wrapping my arms round my knees. The noise came again. That was it. There was no way I could stay in here with rats. Feeling around for my phone I jolted, nearly falling off the chair completely when I heard something move next to me. It was just my laptop bag. I breathed out. I must have knocked it when I was fumbling for the phone. I let out a sigh.

"Shit. Pull yourself together!" I said out loud to nobody.

Using the light from the torch on my phone I tiptoed out of the office, desperately trying to move without startling the rats. I'd heard they'd actually attack you first if they felt threatened enough so I really didn't want to piss them off. When there were about five strides between me and the door I bolted in a half run, leaping the last stride as if a rat was hot on my heels.

As I dashed through the doorway movement caught in the light of my torch. A shadow came at me; a rush of air and a sudden thump and I spun, falling back towards the doorway. My forehead clattered the door frame and I fell, pain exploding inside my head. I crumpled to my hands and knees. Easy takings for the rats.

Chapter Eighteen

ಐ Eli ಣ

I slid along the corridor, my arm brushing the wall, feeling my way in the dark. I'd stupidly put my phone down on the desk and couldn't find it again. Fumbling across every doorway and eventually coming to the stairs, I cautiously moved down each step until they fell away no more. The walls were cold and rough under my fingertips and I glided my hands along until they stopped suddenly. I popped the door of the box open and pushed down a whole load of switches, the hallway coming alive with bright light in an instant.

There was nothing in the fuse box that seemed off, everything appeared to be normal, but something had to have tripped the electrics for the sudden loss of power. I wandered through the bar and stuck my head out of the doorway. The street outside, now bathed in shadows and the golden glow from the street lights looked all in order, the twinkle of lights in windows of other businesses indicated the power cut wasn't a wider issue.

I bounded back up the stairs and pushed through the doors at the top. I figure rose slowly from the floor at the far end, grabbing hold of the door frame crookedly, and I watched her sway precariously as I got closer.

"Ava? What happened?" I asked, gently grabbing her face with my hands, my eyes swarming over her for any obvious injury.

"Urgh. A noise. Rats with clogs. Then a shadow hit me."

She seemed dazed, confused.

"I think you've hit your head. Time to get you home."

"No. No, I, I'm fine."

Ava shook her head from my grasp and tried to step around me, her legs wobbling before lurching sideways. I caught her by the arm, lifting her back to her feet.

"Home. Now."

"Who put you in charge?" she answered back, petulantly.

"Be a good girl, Ava, and do as you're told."

She turned to face me, a flicker in her eye, a stubbornness on her face, a challenge. My cock twitched, and I took a breath, resisting the urge to push her against the wall and devour her there and then. My cock twitched again. Fuck. I needed to get her out of here.

I parked out the front of the communal entrance to her apartment block having somehow found the place after following her shady, dazed instructions. I turned the engine off, jumping out and opening the door on her side, inhaling a lung full of her sweet jasmine scent as I reached across and unplugged her seatbelt.

"I'm concussed not in a coma," Ava complained.

Her eyes dropped to her laptop bag as she raked around then took out her computer and rifled around in it some more.

"Problem?"

"I've lost my keys."

"Is anyone home?"

She shook her head.

"They must be in your office. I'm really sorry, would you mind taking me back?"

Her stomach growled loudly, interrupting the conversation and she hugged the laptop bag to her.

"Hungry?" I asked.

"Yeah, a little. I had to skip lunch today."

"We'll go back to my place. I'll drop you off later once your flatmate is back."

"No. She might not be back to really late."

"You've hit your head. You shouldn't be alone for the next few hours. Hell, I'll even feed you."

She opened her mouth but I pushed my finger under her chin, closing those pretty lips together, her eyes meeting mine, smouldering, or maybe just concussed, but I didn't care. I pressed closer to her, my face only centimetres from hers, my lips brushing her cheek.

"I promise I won't bite. Not yet anyway."

Her pupils dilated and the tip of her pink tongue darted out, licking nervously at her bottom lip and I couldn't tear my eyes away from her.

"Ok," she squeaked.

I loved the nervousness in her voice, the innocence of the sounds her mouth made. It made me wonder what other sounds that little mouth could make.

I moved the big car through the evening traffic stealing glances at the petite red head sitting next to me as she gazed out the windows into the darkness, street lights snaking past as I sped out of the City Centre.

Finally, despite the speed I drove at, the car rumbled to a stop in front of the big walled complex and I punched in the gatehouse numbers onto the keypad.

"You live here?" Ava asked, casting me a look.

"It's apartments, not all mine, but yes, I live here."

"You call them apartments, I call them mansions stacked on top of each other," she mumbled looking past me and to the building beyond.

I pulled the car down into the underground parking lot, parking it in my numbered space and quickly got out, moving to the passenger side and opening the door.

"Thanks, but I can manage," she said, staring at my outstretched hand as if afraid to touch me.

"I'm sure you can but didn't want you bashing my weekend baby here," I patted the side of the black sports car next to me.

Rolling her eyes at me, she placed her slim hand in mine and I pulled her forwards. For a moment I couldn't let her go. She was squeezed up against me so closely in the space between the cars that I could feel her tits against me. Her hair smelled of fruit and flowers all mixed into one as her face tilted upwards towards me, the green glinting in her eyes even in the dimly lit underground garage. I was supposed to be looking after her, making sure she hadn't got a head injury for one.

Instead, I grabbed her pony tail and brought her head to me, burying my tongue in her mouth as she squeaked in surprise. For a moment she was still under my grasp as I plundered her mouth, taking what I wanted from her, and then she pushed back into me her fingers twisting into the thin fabric of my t-shirt as she matched me pressure for pressure. Her lips were soft, her tongue hot and needy, sweeping across mine, moving in rhythm with me like something choreographed, a perfect togetherness of entanglement.

Fuck I was hard, the throb in my groin almost painful. I moved my lips from hers, pulling them across her jaw bone, nibbling at her with my teeth and she moaned lightly, making me harder still. Fuck. I pulled her hips towards me and she moaned again, her mouth so close to my ear that I could feel the exhale of breath. I ran my lips down her throat, kissing and nibbling and she tilted her head back even further allowing me access. I kissed and sucked at her neck gently enough that I didn't leave a mark. But I would mark her. She wouldn't escape me unscathed, not again.

A door banged beside us making Ava jump and turn her head to the side, her brow furrowing and she murmured.

"Eli," she cautioned, and I followed her gaze.

"It's just my neighbours," I spoke into the soft skin of her neck.

"They can see us," she hissed.

"Let them watch."

Ava's stomach grumbled angrily and I looked down at her eyes and the flush in her cheeks and the nervous glances she shot at the older couple who were now walking away from us muttering to each other.

I tilted her chin up so I could see her better. Her stomach growled again.

"Guess we better get you fed, Princess."

Chapter Nineteen

❧ Ava ☙

Eli wielded the knife with a professional precision as he prepared the meal and I watched, perched on a bar stool at the huge kitchen island. His apartment was as big as it looked from the outside. The kitchen was twice the size as mine, maybe even three times, with granite work tops and shiny cupboards contrasted with the satin sheen of metal back splashes.

The living space was open plan and continued into the dining area with a massive marble dining table and white leather chairs and then the lounge with windows that ran the whole side of the room. From the very top of the apartment block the panoramic windows must have provided an amazing view but in the dark I could only see the twinkle of street lights in the distance and the glow of the complex lights as they lit a strip of soft white light down the driveway.

The glass of wine in my hand was going down quickly, far too quickly and I blamed my thirst on the sudden rush I'd felt with Eli in his underground car park and the ache between my legs that I was trying hard to dull. But the alcohol was not dulling those senses at all. It wasn't helped by the sight of him as he worked over the vegetables that he decimated with the flick of the big knife.

His black V-necked t-shirt clung to his body, bulging over his chest and tapering down his stomach to the light-coloured denim jeans. The black short sleeves strained over the huge muscles in his arms, the intricate tattoo on his right arm coming all the way to his hand, sprawling slightly over his wrist, his hands, thick strong fingers moving with finesses as the knife moved in all directions. I took another mouthful of wine.

"Where did you learn to cook?" I asked after I'd finished the last bite of my second helping.

"My mother."

"She must be a good cook. That was beautiful."

"She was," he pursed his lips, and I didn't miss the flicker of sadness crossing those blue eyes.

I stood up, picking up the pasta bowls and moving towards the kitchen, placing them on the sink side and turned on the taps.

"What are you doing?"

"Just cleaning up."

"Just leave them. I'll sort them later."

"It's fine. Won't take a long," I grabbed the pan from the cooker top.

"I told you to leave them," the growl in his voice came from right behind me.

My hand stilled on the pan handle and he leaned in towards me, so close I could feel the scratch of his beard on my neck.

"Are you always so disobedient?" his voice was low and raspy in my ear, my stomach pushed into the benchtop as he pressed himself against me.

I closed my eyes, gripping onto the bench as I struggled with control. His face was so close to my neck, his breath tickling the exposed skin over my shoulders. Fingers sunk into my waist and he spun me round to face him. I didn't dare look up at him but instead fixed my eyes on his chest trying to focus on something else that wasn't the throb developing between my legs, the heat licking low at my stomach. He pulled my head back roughly, the control over the moan in my throat dissipating, coming out in a gasp as he forced me to look into his eyes. They were intense, smouldering with the promise of darkness. I swallowed. He was so tall, so big, so strong and it frightened me and excited me all at once.

Then he closed the last of the space between us, lips crushing mine, his tongue forcing his way through the gap, pushing into my mouth, and I pushed back, tangling and fighting him, my lips on fire from the beard that scratched me. My hands ran through the black hair brushed over his head, pulling him into me with urgency. The granite work top behind me bit into my back as he kept me in place, unable to escape him. But I didn't want to escape him, any of him.

Heat burned in my stomach, in my pussy, in my mouth, over my lips and my neck where his beard scratched and grazed, over the bulb of my shoulders where his teeth bit into the skin and over my chest where he sucked so hard, I cried out.

My hands weren't my own as they tugged at the bottom of his t-shirt, brushing over the ridges of his stomach muscles as I pushed the fabric over his body and he pulled it over his head. The gasp wasn't mine as my fingers slid over the light hair of his chest, feeling the necklace that dangled over the hard bulge of his pecs, tracing down over the ridges of muscle and the hardened 'V' that led to his groin, his skin smooth and his muscle hard.

Thick hands skimmed under the satin camisole top, dancing over the skin of my stomach, a trail of red-hot tingles everywhere he touched until the rough pads of his fingers dived into my bra, pinching my nipple beautifully painfully, heat flooding between my legs. I squeaked again and he pulled back.

"Don't stop," I whispered.

"If you thought you could stop me now, Princess," his voice growled in my ear, low and guttural.

Then, grabbing the neck of the satin top he yanked on it, the material screaming under his grasp, ripped in two in a split second and the top fell to the floor. His eyes devoured me and then his lips as he kissed my chest sliding the straps of my bra over my shoulders, his hands reaching around me and unhooking it effortlessly. It slid off me, a dull swish as it fell to the floor.

His lips were hot on my skin, over my sensitive peaks that stood pert, inviting his mouth to them. His tongue flicked over the top of them sending shivers coursing through me and I wrapped my hands in his hair again as he devoured them, sucking, lapping, nipping at them with his teeth until I squealed. I could feel the dampness in my knickers pooling, my pussy lips swelling at the anticipation of him, tingling for his touch.

His fingers fumbled over the button of my trousers, flicking it free with a skilfulness that shouldn't come from those big hands. The trousers slid over my hips and down my legs, a rush of cool air hitting my skin as I kicked my legs free. The pads of his fingers slid over my arse rough and harsh as they dug into my flesh, my hips pulled towards him, my legs moved apart with the nudge of his knee. He moved in between them, pulling my right leg up and hooking it around his waist, pushing the denim covered hard-on against my entrance, rubbing the rough material against me, making me feel the hardened length of his cock through his jeans.

Dampness was turning to wetness and if it hadn't been for my lace knickers it would have been running down my leg. I'd never felt so turned on, ever. The ache between my legs was burning hot, a fire desperate to be put out, its flames licking across my pussy and up deep into my core. Lust was overpowering me, taking away my free will.

He pulled his lips away and let go of my leg and I gasped; for air, for release, for him. The pressure between my legs was building; all I could feel was a hot, wet, throbbing need. I needed him. I wanted him. Now. This was killing me; he was killing me.

A hand slid up over my thigh, the muscles in my leg contracting just at his light touch as it snaked round creeping slowly up towards my pussy and I tried to maintain some tiny bit of control of my pulsing, heaving, throbbing body, every nerve ending on fire. Fingers snaked closer, brushing my pussy over the top of my knickers and I whimpered, pushing into his hand, my body begging for him.

Eli wrapped a hand around my neck, his thumb against my jaw, pushing my head up so my eyes met his, fingers pulling the small piece of soaking wet material of my thong to the side and sliding through the wet folds. I shuddered and closed my eyes.

"Look at me," his tone was dark.

I forced my eyes open as the tip of his finger pushed at my entrance and then bit by bit into me, pushing my pussy lips apart as he entered me painfully slowly. My teeth raked my bottom lip as I tried to focus on his blue eyes. His finger moved in and out as if he was feeling every part of me as he went. But then I felt the tip of another finger, pushing at me building the pressure, filling me, wet soaking round them as I tensed down on them.

"Open your eyes, Ava. I want to see you," he growled again and I hadn't even realised I'd shut them.

He moved more quickly, twisting and feeling, relentlessly thrusting, pressure building, my body tightening around him, my pussy clenching round the thick fingers that filled me. His thumb moved across my clit and I cried out.

"Look at me, Princess," he commanded, knowing how close I was to the edge.

His thumb circled over me putting pressure against me, his fingers pummelling twisting as my body erupted in response to him, and I pushed myself down onto his hand, taking it all, my body shaking, my eyes fixed on his as he watched me come undone.

Then, before my ragged breaths even began to slow down, he grabbed my waist, pulling my legs around him and carried me from the kitchen. His lips skimmed across mine, planting little kisses all over me, over my jaw, over my lips down my neck and I was barely aware that we were moving down the corridor in his apartment. Eli backed into a door, pushing it open, then turned and let go of me.

"Eli!" I squeaked, gravity taking hold of me as I scrabbled at him.

The softness of the bed cushioned my fall, and I breathed again, lying still for a moment on my back. Eli's eyes raked over me, his fingers on the waistband of his jeans, pulling them open and pushing down his thick legs. It wasn't the sinewy muscle of strong thighs that caught my attention.

He'd had nothing on underneath his jeans. His cock stood out from his body, hard and phallic, its head bulging, my eyes fixed on the shaft that he held in his hand as thick as the rest of him.

He smirked.

"Like what you see, Princess?"

I bit my bottom lip, propping up on my elbows, trying to slow my breathing and the rapid pace of my heart, as I watched him roll the condom over the tip, stretching over his swollen length. Then he dipped down towards me, ripping my soaking thong down my legs, pushing them wide as he knelt in between.

He rubbed the tip of his cock against me, lubricating it in my own juices and the pressure against me made my stomach tense. Then he pushed into me, cramming the thick head into my entrance, forcing my flesh aside, stuffing me full of him, stretching me to my limits. I couldn't help the cry that escaped my lips when I felt the last of him push into me and then he drew back out again, slowly, pulling through the sensitive flesh and then forcing his way back in. Eli rested his arms either side of my head, his mouth dipping towards my ear and thrusted in again.

"Jesus," he muttered into my ear.

I ran my fingers down his back, muscles solid under my touch as he pulled back out and then rammed back into me, then pulled away again, his thrusts quickening, becoming rougher, each movement making me cry out as he plunged into me.

"So, fucking tight," he growled into my ear again, slamming his hips into me, hitting me hard.

My body started to tense and I pulled my legs around him, tipping my hips to meet his.

"Fuck," he cursed as he slammed his cock back inside of me.

Pressure built in the pit of my stomach and an overwhelming heat radiated through my body.

"Eli," I breathed.

His mouth found mine again, taking the name I called from my lips and then he moved quicker, grunting, grabbing handfuls of my hair and pulling my head back almost painfully, sucking on my neck as his hips flew into me, pounding, thrusting, pulsing. My pussy clenched around him, his pubic bone hit my clit, grinding against it with each furious surge from his hips. I couldn't…. I was going to……

"Fuck," his voiced vibrated against my throat.

Oh. My. Fucking. God.

My body tensed, bright lights jumped behind my eyes, screams tore from my throat and my pussy gripped him tighter and tighter with each thrust as my heart raced frantically in my chest and I buried my face further into his gigantic arm, my teeth tearing at his flesh. His growl became grunts as he thrusted ever harder into me, burying himself inside me as far as he could. Then he stilled, panting, his eyes closed, a bead of sweat rolling down the side of his face, as he lay on top of me, his cock still filling me full, the pant of my own breath mingling with his.

Chapter Twenty

ও Eli ৫

I lay next to her listening to her shallow breaths, her petite body dwarfed next to mine and my cock stirred again. She had me obsessed. I'd fucked her again and again, her screams filling my apartment for hours and I only stopped because she looked so exhausted.

But now I lay awake, a fight going on in my brain. It should have just been a good fuck. Nothing more. I should have just used her tight little pussy just for my benefit. But no matter what I told myself there was something else happening in my head, a swarm of thoughts and emotions battling for dominance. I wanted her, not just her body, not just her sweet little cunt, but all of her. I wanted more.

Realisation made my chest swell painfully, fear and dread hitting me in the stomach, feelings I'd long since buried rising within me, threatening on coming to the surface. Feelings I vowed to never have again. I couldn't be thrown off course, it was too much of a risk, I would never get closure if she derailed me; never.

This had to just be a fuck. It couldn't be anything more.

My chin rested on the top of her head inhaling the citrus, jasmine scent of her perfume and the sweet smell of her sweaty well-fucked body. I glanced down at her, slim and perfect as she lay with her head against my chest, her own chest rising and falling, pert little tits moving to the rhythm of her breathing. My cock was already coming to life again.

Sleep never graced me with its presence for long anyway and after I tossed and turned and fought the urge to impale her on my cock once more, I got up. I pulled on my gym shorts and strode off down the hall to hammer some weights to keep my mind and my dick in check.

Later, I wandered back through the apartment to the kitchen, sweat hanging in droplets on my bare torso, my breathing still laboured. I stalled when I got there. Ava was stretching from the tips of her toes up to the cupboard above her head, one of my white work-out vests riding up showing off the bottom curves of her tight little arse as she strained to reach the glasses and her hair, a mess of wild curls, falling down her back. Her muscles pulled tight across her shoulder blades and the slight curve over the top of her arms down to the tension in her toned thighs and the slight bulge of her calves as she pushed up from the floor, the glass just millimetres from her touch.

I stepped in behind her, pressing myself up against her, my erection pushing into her back as I brought the glass down for her. She startled slightly but I didn't move from behind her, keeping her there stuck between the coolness of the granite counter top and the hardness of my cock. I ran a hand between her legs, her skin silky smooth in contrast to the rough pads of my fingers and she drew in a breath.

My head stooped to the top of her shoulder and she tensed under my touch. I nibbled the muscle that led drown from her neck, covering the top of her shoulder, sliding a hand under the vest, the looseness of it making it so easy to feel for those nipples that hardened under the gentlest pressure of my fingers. My other hand moved over her pussy, still swollen from the pounding I'd given it but wet and ready for me. I glided a finger through the satin of her folds, growing wetter and more slippery with each gentle stroke. Ava moaned, pushing her arse back into me, moving her legs apart giving me better access. God she was irresistible.

I grabbed a condom from one of the drawers in the kitchen then turned back to her. My fingers fumbled for the edge of the vest, pulling it off roughly over her head and pushing her down into the coolness of the counter top, an almost inaudible squeal coming from her throat as the cold granite bit into her warm skin.

Gripping her hips, I pushed myself into her slowly savouring the tight grip of her pussy as it stroked my cock, a low growl vibrating in my throat. She was just so tight. I meant to be gentle. I meant to be slow but that hot, wet pussy pulled me to the edge in seconds and the beast in me took over. With a hand between her shoulders, I pushed her hard into the counter tops, her face turned to the side as I pumped into her with a frantic rhythm, my breathing heavy as the most primal of needs took over me.

My hips slapped against her arse cheeks, my cock disappearing from view and the moans from her sweet little mouth became screams. I pushed in as far as I could, ripping a cry from her gorgeous throat each time before I yanked it back and slammed into her again.

The noise she made, the tightness gripping and stroking my cock sent me wild and soon I realised I was grunting loudly with each thrust.

"Oh, god, Eli" she cried out.

Her cries now closer to screams I knew she was ready to come. I loved the sound of my name on her lips. I loved the way she panted underneath me, fragile and delicate, taking all of me, submitting to my dick. The thought sent me wilder still. I quickened into a relentless pulsing, pulling her hips back into me with every thrust, her moans and screams driving me on and on until my cock pulsed and tensed and I let my load go. It went on for far longer than I expected my balls clenching, shot after shot and I almost fell forward on top of her, my legs shaking, my sweat dripping down onto her back.

With my dick rammed tightly inside of her I kept her pushed down onto the counter top listening to her pant as she stayed there dutifully under my grip. God, she felt so good I didn't want to come out of her. I grabbed the flesh on her arse making her suck in a breath then ran my finger over the shape of her arse cheeks and up her back, following with a line of kisses, the slightly salty taste of her skin making my lips tingle.

Once I'd caught my breath and slipped out of her, I turned her round to face me. Her hair fell over her face as she tried to control her breathing, her small tits bobbing up and down just under my eye line, her tight stomach still tense and pumped so her abs were more visible and a sheen of wetness clung to the inside of her legs.

Grabbing a handful of hair, I pulled her head backwards covering her lips with mine, forcing my tongue inside her, claiming her mouth as I had done with her pussy. My cock had recovered and I pushed it into her stomach. Fuck it I wanted her again.

"Eli," she whispered, her voice hoarse, "I need to get to work."

She laid her hands on my chest, gently pushing, her green eyes almost glassy with the best after-fucked looked I'd ever seen.

"I need to find some clothes," she whispered, wrapping her arms across her body self-consciously as she plucked her trousers from where they had fallen last night.

She bent down again, picking the light blue silky top up from the floor and holding it out as she inspected it, biting her bottom lip as she surveyed the damage before lifting her green eyes to me. I couldn't keep the smile off my face at the top that she held, ripped in half.

"Eli, I liked that top," she'd complained lightly with a nervous chuckle.

I'd buy her another.

A short time later we were dressed and making our way out the door. I'd given her a t-shirt to wear under her suit jacket, but it might as well have been a dress on her.

We caught the lift behind the middle-aged couple who shared the same floor on the opposite side to me, who she'd met in the car park last night. The wife kept sneaking glances at us as the lift glided to the ground floor in awkward silence. The older coupled stepped out first and the husband stooped down to say something quietly to his wife and she peeked back over her shoulder at us.

I glanced at Ava, her pale cheeks showing a light flush of pink.

"Were they your neighbours?" she asked, her voice a whisper.

"I bet they wished they weren't my neighbours."

"Do you think they heard us, heard me?" Ava's head shot towards me, worry on her face.

I chuckled, "sweetheart, I think the whole block heard you."

Her face flushed with colour and she snatched her eyes away from mine. I loved the look on her face, fragile and innocent.

I bent down towards her brushing my lips across her ear, "I'm going to fuck you so hard the next time the entire complex is gonna hear you."

She shivered and bit her bottom lip. I was going to bite that lip next time too. For fuck's sake, this was supposed to be casual, just a one-time thing, but one night of Ava and already I desperately wanted more.

*****

I tried to bury my head in my stock orders when I got in my office and twice had to wander out for a hideously strong coffee. Kelly at the café raised her eyebrows inquisitively at me when I upgraded to a double shot on my second visit. The ping of a text message interrupted me.

'You got a serial number?'

'No,' I answered, *'it's filed off.'*

'So how do you expect me to trace it?'

'We both know there's other ways,' I typed back, my fingers moving over the phone's keypad furiously.

He was always such a dickhead.

'What do you know about gun running in Newcastle?' I quizzed him again.

'Nothing. And you know if I did, I wouldn't tell you, Eli.'

Anger erupted in me and I slammed my fists into the desk, pain shooting through the heel of my hands and vibrations running up my arms. I tossed the phone across the room with a roar, swiping a pile of papers with my arm and then instantly regretted it as they flew all over the floor, all mixed up.

"For fuck's sake," I cursed.

The once tidy pile of papers was now in chaos. I might as well have sat at there and beat my chest acting like the bloody fuckwit I was. But I didn't. I stooped down and brushed them all together back into one jumbled, disorganised pile and put them back on my desk.

Frustrated, I moved to the filing cabinet and heaved it forwards, away from the wall behind, creating enough space to reach my arm in, type a code and open the door to the little safe behind. The cold bite of metal met my fingers and I pulled the handgun out. It sunk into my palm, fitting cleanly, the heavy feeling familiar in my hand. I shut the safe, slid the cabinet back into place and sat back at my desk inspecting the pistol. It was a 9mm Smith & Wesson, a type I was familiar with but this was just a little different. Newer. I turned it over in my hands, thinking.

I opened the bottom of my desk drawer, felt around at the back and flipped the catch to release the false back. I fumbled about, my hand brushing a number of stiff envelopes before my fingers caught an object right at the back. I pulled the burner phone out, fired it up and then dialled the only number it contained.

Chapter Twenty One

❦ Ava ❧

I rushed into my apartment, showering in a hurry and throwing on some fresh clothes. Going to the office in a man's t-shirt would definitely send the wrong message, lots of wrong messages. I swiped on some mascara, hoping it would hide my tiredness, wound my hair up onto my head in a bun, and darted out of my room crashing straight into Kerry.

Kerry looked at my flustered face and giggled.

"Good night?"

"Err, yes," I answered sheepishly, heat flooded to my cheeks, and I escaped to the kitchen with Kerry hot on my heels.

I poured coffee into my travel mug, screwed on the top and took a quick sip, recoiling immediately from the sting on my tongue.

"So, does he have a big cock?"

Metal clattered the wooden counter top as my fingers fumbled to catch the mug before it hit the floor too. I turned and shot a glare at Kerry.

"Come on, you dirty stop-out, let's go," she tugged on my arm.

We left the apartment together, travelling down in the lift. Kerry stealing glances at me, a knowing smile pasted all over her face as mine resembled some sort of beaten-up beetroot, reflecting back at me from the stainless steel of the lift doors.

The black Landrover waited outside the entrance, its engine purring steadily. Kerry raised a well sculpted eyebrow at me.

"No strings then?"

"He's just helping me get to work on time, that's all."

Eli was stood leaning against the driver's side of the door his arms folded across his chest, the tight jumper doing nothing at hiding his muscular frame.

"Would your friend like a lift too?" he asked, as we approached.

"No thanks, I'm good with walking. But I can see why Ava needs a lift this morning," she grinned turning and looking me up and down dramatically, "doesn't look like you'll be walking anywhere today. Can you even sit down?"

I felt my whole face light up like a bonfire and glanced at Eli who had his arms folded across his chest, clearly amused, his face animated with a cheeky smile.

"Sorry about breaking your friend," he said to Kerry.

"You two, just stop," I complained, walking around the side of the car and sitting down tentatively in the passenger seat.

I walked in to the office carefully, trying my utmost not to look like a cowboy with saddle sore. I was tender and aching in places I didn't realise could ache. And I was tired. So tired. I'd need to sleep for a week to recover fully. But I wasn't the only one who looked exhausted.

I'd watched him all day staring intensely at the screen, typing furiously then looking defeated. Staff had packed up for the night around us, the office slowly emptying till we were the last ones left. Harry looked exhausted, leaning back in his chair he pulled his hands down his face. Maybe I should have checked in on him earlier? I brought him a mug of coffee.

He closed the screen down hurriedly as I approached, looking at me sheepishly, his mouth eventually pulling into a weak smile as I handed the coffee to him.

"You OK, Harry?"

"Yeah. Just something giving me a kicking."

"Anything I can help with?"

Harry stared at me for a few seconds, licking his lips self-consciously as if considering what answer to give me.

"No. I got it," he said eventually.

I nodded and half turned to leave him alone but he caught my hand, tugging me gently back to face him.

"Do me a favour?" he asked and I nodded, "stay away from the Robertson contract whatever you do."

I looked at him blankly, my mind swirling in confusion.

"Why?" I asked.

"He's just bad news. You don't need be sucked in by that, by him. I saw how he looked at you yesterday."

The hairs on my arms prickled.

"Antwill too,"

I swallowed, dread creeping over me. Did he know about me and Eli?

His hand covered mine, his skin warm against me and I pulled away from him.

"Look. I'm sorry about the other night, Ava," he paused then shook his head at me in warning as I opened my mouth to respond, "I know I came on far too strong. I care about you. I mean I *really* care about you."

"Harry," I protested.

"I would never hurt you like he did."

Pain and memories flooded me, taking the wind out of my sails and bringing me crashing down to realisation.

"Like Tom did. I would never do that to you."

"Tom promised me the same thing," I whispered, tears prickling at the back of my eyes, my throat dry, "I was stupid to believe that."

161

I turned away and packed up my things. I needed to get out of there. I needed a distraction.

By the time I got to the gym it was after 7pm. There was normally not a soul about at this time of night, except Cam. Tonight was no different. The place was empty and would have been peaceful if not for the whir and hiss of the aging machines. I punched a number into the running machine and plugged my earphones into my ears, tunes blasting from them, a heavy driving beat in the background keeping pace as my feet started to keep time with the treadmill.

I don't know how long I ran for, how long I pushed and sucked air into and out of my lungs, my chest burning with the exertion and a heaviness setting into my thighs. My play list came to a stop. Knocking the machine off I grabbed my towel rubbing it across my face and as I dragged the soft fabric over my eyes, I saw a shape appear over my shoulder.

"For God's sake, Cam!" I hissed, my heart jolting in my chest.

He smiled widely at me.

"Training alone?" he asked giving me a knowing wink.

"Yea. I'm sorry about that the other day, Cam. I don't know what got into me."

He chuckled, "I know what wanted to get into you!"

Heat flowed to my face.

"I'm sorry, Ava," he chuckled, not sorry in the slightest, "how do you know Eli?"

"I, err, I'm doing some work for the company at the moment," I stammered caught off guard, "how do you know him?" I deflected, hoping my reaction had gone unnoticed.

"He's a mate. We served together. Eli's a good guy, just a bit intense at times, but I guess you'll already know that if you *work* for him."

There was a wicked twinkle in his eye. I swallowed; sure, my face must be glowing now like an enraged traffic light.

"I, err, yes, I guess. Does he train here often? Just I'd never seen him here before."

"He comes to train with me once a week or so but he's got his own gym at his place so trains at home most of the time. Have you not seen his gym yet?"

Cameron was staring at me, watching my reaction intently and I tried to remain expressionless. Interrogation. That was what they taught these men in the army, and that was what Cam was doing right now.

"No, I haven't," I answered much too stiffly.

"Eli's a really good guy," he said suddenly, "but he's a player. Just know that before you get sucked in by him."

Too late.

Cam's smile was friendly but I still felt like someone had punched me in the stomach.

Reading my face Cam continued, "I mean, you seem a nice type Ava, just know what you are getting yourself in to."

"I'm good thanks, Cam. There's nothing to be getting myself into," I said resolutely, more to myself than to the gym owner.

"Sorry," he said eventually "You're late tonight?"

"Yeah. Work's busy and I got a lot on my mind."

More now. Thanks Cam. The doorbell rang pulling his attention away from me.

"Gotta go," he said, "looks like someone's forgotten their door code."

I finished up, my thoughts back to ricocheting uncontrollably around my head, eventually giving up entirely and packing my kit away into my backpack and taking my laptop from the gym lockers. I wandered down the stairs and along the corridor passing Cameron's office

"Absolutely not. It's never going to happen. You're wasting your time."

A muffled voice replied but I couldn't hear what was said.

"Time to fuck-off now lads," Cameron's voice was threatening, dark.

I strained to hear, my curiosity getting the better of me and I stepped a little closer. The door to the office was open slightly, the back of a man just visible as he stood in front of the desk. In blue denim jeans a quilted jacket with the hood of his grey jumper poking out over the top, he didn't look like he had come to use the gym.

"Right, you can leave now," Cam's voice was louder.

No one moved. Silence.

"Get. Out," he said again.

The atmosphere was thick and heavy, ominous; like a power surge before a thunderstorm. I probably should have walked away. But I didn't. I stood watching, wondering whether I should see if Cam was alright. Maybe if I let my presence be known it might just be enough.

I crept closer.

"The boss will not be happy that you haven't even heard his proposal fully," the voice inside the door said.

The atmosphere in the room was turning, changing. I could feel it without even being in there.

"I don't need to hear anymore. You can tell him thanks but no thanks."

"You'll regret it," the mystery man said, his voice lowering.

I gulped down a big lump of nerves and knocked on the door, moving it open as I did. Cam peered over the two men in his office, his eyes catching mine. The two men standing in his office turned towards me. The talker was familiar looking, his misshapen long nose, the coldness of his eyes, the snake tattoo on his neck.

"Hey, Cam. You OK?" I asked tentatively.

"Fine thanks, Ava. These guys were just leaving. You need a hand out there?"

"Yes, please," he was looking at me pointedly, "I err, need you to show me one of the machines," I lied.

"Fellas, if you don't mind," I could hear the forced calm back into Cameron's voice, "I'm needed in the gym."

It seemed to have worked. The guy I could see in the crack of the door turned and beckoned for his friend to move. Tattoo guy stared at me as he stepped out of the office, his eyes wrinkling at the corners and a sneer came to his lips.

He stopped in front of me, his eyes roaming all over my face then down to my chest lingering on my bare skin where my cropped sports top ended before continuing over my legs. I wrapped my arms across my stomach. When his eyes returned to my face he smiled. His teeth were crooked and tinged yellow, the smell of alcohol and cigarettes stale on his breath. Breath that was too close to my face. I took a step backwards.

"Ava is it, ey?" his hungry grey eyes didn't leave my face.

Sweat prickled on my palms.

"The Boss would really like this place with this sort of pussy."

My face was hot with a mix of embarrassment and anger and I watched as they left.

"What was that all about?" I asked Cam when I was sure they had gone.

"Their boss wants to buy this place," he looked deflated, "and me," he added more quietly.

"They're Ritchie's men, aren't they?"

Cam looked at me in surprise and I shrugged in response.

"They were in Eli's nightclub a little while back," I said.

"Really?" Cam was suddenly very interested.

"Yeah. Not the nicest of people. Tattoo guy got a bit handsy."

"Shit. Ava are you OK?"

"Sure. Not him though. Poor guy left with a bruise on his shin."

Cam let out a chuckle, his shoulders dropping as he relaxed a little.

"Full of your usual feistiness then, Ava? I'll have to see what Eli thinks," he said again more to himself than me.

I raised an eyebrow in curiosity.

"About these guys, not your feistiness," he laughed reading my expression, "and thanks for earlier. But I could handle it."

I smiled at him, "Really? I think I did a better job at chucking them out than you did!"

Chapter Twenty Two

ഔ Eli ൙

My bedsheets still smelled of her, the fresh jasmine scent disturbed every time I turned over. And now each time I closed my eyes I pictured her naked in my bed, her tits bouncing underneath me, the squeeze of her thighs as they wrapped around me, the feel of her hair wrapped in my hands. Fuck. My head was riddled with her.

Even at work on Saturday night, I cruised each bar as I always did, chatting to my doormen, getting a feel for the mood of the night but this time also watching for a red head in the crowd. I'd distracted myself flirting with some of the clientele which wasn't unusual but found myself becoming quickly bored. Even at the strip club I couldn't settle, naked women all over the place but no one piquing my interest.

Ashley had come over to chat to me and as usual I bought her a drink and we'd sat in a booth together, but her advances hadn't interested me. She was usually my first choice to go to when I needed to let my frustrations out, never ceasing to wake my dick with those dirty words she'd purr into my ear. But tonight she didn't even stir a bit of heat, never mind a hard-on.

I left early, not even staying behind to help close up. Weary from my thoughts I climbed into bed only to be assaulted by her smell again.

I called Cam Sunday afternoon and suggested another session in the gym training with him, but he was no fool and had seen right through me, but humoured me anyway.

"I'm going to have to charge you membership at this rate," Cam grumbled at me.

"Hey buddy, just thank me for the P.T. sessions. You were getting skinny," I said punching him in his arm.

But there was something deflated about him, withdrawn.

"What's up?" I asked.

He tipped his head and I followed him into his office closing the door behind me.

"Ritchie's boys paid me a visit last night," he started.

"What? You alright?"

"Yeah fine. He's trying to pressurise me to sell this place. Sent his boys to do the asking. Told him no of course, but I guess that'll be another rise in the interest rate."

"He's a dickhead," I hissed.

"Ava disturbed us," he continued and my attention doubled at the mention of her name.

"Is she OK?"

"Yeah. They left as soon as she disturbed the party. She'd worked late she'd said. She also said Ritchie's boys had been to see you too?"

I nodded. "I reckon he's expanding his operations."

Cam tilted his head.

"I'm following some leads. The usual drug dealing tip offs. But this time I found a gun. There were rumours he was running guns in Iraq but I could never find the evidence, just slithers of information."

My friend shook his head, "the gunshot victim in the West End?"

"It was self-defence," I shrugged.

Well in a roundabout way. I was defending the public from a street dealer. Protecting the community. I smiled to myself, that would work as excuses go.

"Anyway," I continued, "the serial number was ground off."

"What type is it?"

"Smith and Wesson 9mm. But not quite what I've seen before and not the sort of shit we get here normally. Seb can't, or won't identify it and won't give me anything else."

I could feel the grinding of my teeth, frustration radiating out of me. Cam could see it too.

"You tried the Viking?" Cam asked, his voice low like someone might have bugged his office.

I nodded.

Cam still looked subdued and I could see it was playing on his mind. He was quiet for a moment and seemed to be taking his time to find his words.

"I'm really struggling, Eli, some months anyway. Some months, if memberships drop off, I don't even cover the overheads. I thought about it overnight. Selling it I mean. It may end up being my only option."

I saw the defeat in his eyes. Cameron had built his little empire up after being medically discharged. It had given him focus and helped him through a really tough patch. At one time business had been booming and it had been a vibrant space to train and socialise but I had noticed how quiet it had become.

"Come on," I said, "let's do some work."

I had a plan but I needed the time to think, cover all eventualities, and I was always better at that sort of thing while sweating my arse off.

We joked and chatted as we lifted some weights and Cam seemed a little brighter. I was in the middle of a bicep superset, chatting away and dicking about. He'd always been easy company; we'd known each other a long time and helped each other through some really shitty times. He patted my arm and signalled for me to look in the mirror. I glanced up and saw her stood behind me, her arms folded across her chest.

I stared at her in the mirror, not taking my eyes off her as I finished my set.

171

"Enjoying the view?" I asked, placing my dumbbells onto the floor.

"Actually, I was waiting for you two to finish so I can find some weights in all your mess here."

I smiled at her attitude.

"Go ahead, let's see what you've got, Princess."

She shot me a warning look, half mock annoyance, half might have been actual annoyance. And I liked it. She strode over anyway, eyes darting between the dumbbells we had strewn over the floor, eventually fishing out some lighter ones and positioned herself in front of the mirror, bracing her feet she pulled her arms up towards her. Her slim arms pumped, showing the flex of her muscles, but she rocked too much in her frame, and lost half the work she was putting in. As she started her second set, I stepped up behind her, catching her eye in an exchange in the mirror, her tempo faltered and my hands slipped to her hips.

"What are you doing?" she asked breathless, but keeping eye contact with me in the reflection of the glass.

"Just sorting this out," I muttered quietly brushing my lips across her ear, "you're tipping through your body, keep yourself still, and use that core."

I squeezed my hands into her stomach watching her reaction, the little flicker in her eyes at my touch.

She tightened her stomach muscles and straightened through her back better, following my instructions, doing as I told her. I loosened my grip on her waist as she completed the exercises but continued to stand just a little too close behind her. Ava tried to stay focussed but her eyes kept flicking back to me nervously.

"Ok, now bent over row," I instructed and she shot me a look.

Her eyes conflicted, fighting the urge to be stubborn with another urge to comply but in the end, she gripped the dumbbells towards her chest and bent over in front of me.

"Chest lower."

I watched her pert little arse right there inches away from me and this time as she completed the set, she kept her eyes on me in the mirror. Challenging me. God she was hot.

"Good work, Princess," I said when she'd finished and slapped her backside just before she stood back up.

She let out a little cry of surprise before turning round and shooting me that look again. Cameron rolled his eyes.

"Nice to see you Ava," he said and she smiled warmly back at him, "I've got stuff to do in the office Eli, catch you later." He said back to me before looking over at Ava again. "Hey if he's being a pain in the arse, let me know and I'll bar him," he said playfully giving me a wink and stalking off.

"What are you doing here anyway?" she asked me suddenly wiping at the back of her neck with a towel.

"I came to train," I replied, watching the rise and fall of her chest as her breathing started to recover.

"Why? You've got your own personal gym? Why come here?" she asked looking at me stubbornly.

"It's nice to have some company every now and then. Besides, it's a good view here," I said stepping closer to her so that I towered above her.

She held my gaze in some sort of tenacious stand off and if it hadn't been for a small cough and an 'excuse me' from behind me, we may have stayed there for some time, or I'd at least have grabbed her and kissed her.

We moved out of way for the man standing behind us.

"Are you at the office much this next week?" Ava asked me, packing her towel and gym equipment into her back pack.

"Will be."

"Good. I need to collect some more papers. I need the invoices from the last month. You have an accounts return that needs doing. Can you get them ready for me?"

"Ok. Well, we could do it over dinner?" I could really use another round with her.

She walked towards me pointedly and stopped so she had to tilt her head to look up at me with those emerald green eyes, a smile twitching at the corners of her lips.

"We both know what happened last time we had dinner," Ava said placing her hand on top of my stomach, "get your homework done first, Eli, then we can talk about dinner."

With that she stepped around me and slapped me on the arse before walking off to the locker room. I guess I'd deserved that. My cock twitched in my gym shorts.

*****

Sat in the carpark of an old industrial estate on the other side of the River, I checked the digital display of my watch. He was late. The area was supposed to be undergoing regeneration, greedy developers having acquired it for their land banks; instead, it sat there rotting away. The dilapidated factory unit, complete with its trees which had taken up residence and now snaked upwards, sprouting out of windows to grab at daylight, sat behind me menacingly. The wind was picking up, making it hard to hear anyone approaching. I didn't like wind. It dumbed your senses and made you jumpy, always on high alert as to whether the scraping noise behind you was the wind or someone about to gut you.

A single light became visible in the distance, bobbing slightly as it got closer. I got out the car leaning on the bonnet and watched as the black-as-night motorbike eventually emerged from the darkness. The engine cut out, the heavy roar of the exhaust stilling, the rider kicked out the stand and pulled his helmet off.

"This isn't an audition for a L'Oréal advert," I scoffed as he shook out a mane of long blond hair.

"Good to see ya, Eli. Pity you only call me when you need my ass," he gave me a wink.

"Give over, 'V'. You're not gonna get in my pants."

"Not tonight anyway."

He laughed at me. I'd not seen the Viking in a few years but he hadn't changed, wandering around trying to be some sort of bad-ass male model and charming the pants off as many women as possible. God only knew what his count was now? It had been higher than his body count although what I heard on the down-low was that it had also been creeping up.

"What do you need, Eli?" he folded his arms across his jacket and leaned back on his bike.

"Guns."

"What? You need some?"

"I need to know who's selling them."

I pulled the pistol from where I'd tucked it in the back of my trousers and threw it towards him. Catching it with little effort, he turned it over in his hands, pulling the clip out and emptying a few bullets into his hand. Bronze light reflected on the little missiles as he held one up under the street lightning.

"This is military shit, Eli. It's a Smith & Wesson M2. Pretty new stuff. Smith & Wesson only sell it to law enforcement. For this to be here at all it's had to come from the States."

"Do you know who's bringing this shit in?"

The Viking tilted his head to the side and looked at me a long time before answering.

"You still obsessed with him, Eli?"

Heat rose in my chest, like a volcanic eruption ready to go off. I felt the darkness circling in my thoughts, behind my eyes, as pressure built in me.

"You know why, V," I said through clenched teeth.

"You think Ally would want you to be still doing this? All this time later?"

I launched for him, my hands balled in fists, my jaw clenched, but something stopped me a stride out and I exhaled. Normally I would have punched him in his pretty face, he was used to that reaction from me. The Viking relaxed from his defensive stance when I took a step back.

"I will get Ritchie. Even if it I die trying."

The Viking put his hands up in surrender.

"I know of a few gangs that have been getting gun shipments. Not these though. Leave it with me. I'll find something."

He tossed the gun back at me and pulled his helmet on kicking his leg back over the bike. The black motorbike came alive with a roar as the ground under my feet vibrated. And then he took off, leaving me alone with my thoughts, memories long since buried threatening to rise from the depths of darkness.

Chapter Twenty Three

❧ Ava ☙

After I had finished at the office late Wednesday afternoon, I made my way over to Eli's nightclub to scan in the documents I needed for the return and take him through my report. My laptop was weighing heavy on my shoulder, the files I had piled into the bag before I left causing the strap to bite into my flesh. Work was hitting me left, right and centre. The firm had an influx of new contracts each one requiring me to set them up and negotiate terms because Harry was distracted.

The weather had really started to turn these last few days, October now in full swing. I'd spent the last two days getting soaked on the way home from work and I hadn't even bothered with the gym.

Danny let me in after I buzzed through on the intercom and led me through the club.

"Miss Edwards, are you here for long?" he asked swiping me in through the security door up to the offices above.

"No. Just a flying visit. Lots to get home and do," I patted my bag to show it was full of work.

He gave me a weak smile, tension showing in his jaw. I climbed the stairs alone, the heavy bag making me dip from my right shoulder, each step becoming more laboured and not helped by the tight black dress I wore or the stiletto heels that were currently making the balls of my feet burn like I'd just walked over hot coal. I knocked on Eli's office door, entering when I heard the low growl of his voice.

"Hey," I said, a little nervously.

I'd been keeping my distance from him, trying to keep a tight hold of the emotions spinning round my head that mingled with the various warnings from Harry and Cameron that I'd tried to shake off. Yet every recollection of their words filled me with self-doubt and contradiction.

"Hi, Princess, got you a coffee," he responded, smiling at me and waving me into the seat he was sitting at as he slid the takeaway coffee cup towards me.

"Thanks, just what I needed."

"Tough day?"

"Pretty much. Could do with some sort of time machine to get all this work done," I grumbled.

I took a sip of the latte and slid my laptop out from its bag, pressing the power button and watching it as it whirred to life.

"Ok. What have you got for me?" I asked looking around for the documents I had been promised.

"They're all in that pile there," Eli pointed, distracted by something he was reading on his phone.

A prickle of annoyance tugged at my stomach as I eyed the messy pile of paper, a pile I had not long ago tidied up and left in some semblance of order. I let out a loud sigh, hoping he would sense I was a little pissed off, but his eyes didn't move from the device in his hand. So instead, I got to work, thumbing through the bits of paper, pulling all the relevant documents out into a neat pile. Payslips, stock invoices, electric bills, private investigation invoices from Insight Tech Ltd. What?

"Eli, what are you investigating?" I asked, reading the invoice and wondering which bar or club this need to be attributed to.

It was recent, just days old in fact. Eli turned to me, his lips pressed tight, plucking the papers from my hands.

"Sorry, that's not business stuff."

He pulled his desk drawer out, a low rumble in the uncomfortable silence, and stuffed the invoice inside. I sat back at the laptop, using my portable scanner to capture the documents and typing the details I needed right now into my spreadsheet. I worked quietly for ten minutes, popping the last of the data in and then running the macro that produced the return.

"Ok, all done. I just need you to have a quick look over this."

Eli stooped over me, reading the document over the top of my shoulder, his arm brushing up against the side of me. His hand rested on the desk next to mine, not quite touching but close enough so that I could feel the heat from him. I bit my bottom lip trying to ignore the smell of him, the deep cedar wood aroma interlaced with his own musky, male scent. A tingle of electricity seemed to jump between us as I leant in to move the cursor down the page.

"I've refocused the business proposal, with predicted profits. The stats will show the trends across all businesses and then this line here…"

"Great stuff, Ava," he said, his hand slipping over mine, the brush of his beard against my neck.

I swallowed, feeling something igniting within me, the windowless office suddenly feeling like a sauna.

"This demonstrates, based on my modelling, where the business will be performing over the next five, then ten years," I continued trying to control the waver of my voice.

Eli dropped his hand below the desk, the tips of his fingers ran up my thigh snaking under my dress.

"I, I've put the recommendations here," I tried to move the document down on the screen just as his fingertips bit into my flesh, his lips hovering over my ear.

"I don't want to talk shop, Princess. I want to talk about how I'm gonna fuck you right here on my desk and how you're going to take every inch of me like a good girl."

A shiver I couldn't control shot up my spine and I breathed heavily, biting hard on my bottom lip as I tried to stifle the shock at his words, clenching my thighs together to stop the throb of my pussy.

Eli yanked my head back by my hair so that I was staring up at him before he plunged his lips down on mine, his tongue thrusting into my mouth. Then suddenly the chair was spun and he was lifting me out of it and onto my feet, my arse pressing into his desk.

Big hands pushed my dress up my thighs till it bunched around my waist and he tipped me backwards onto the desk stepping between my legs, pushing them open for them, his fingers moving over the thin scrap of material that stood between us, his other hand wrapped around my throat as he held me down. Heat and anticipation coursed through me, my body clenching as he swirled his hand over me. Then, lowering his head so I had nowhere to look but into his eyes, he pulled my knickers aside and pushed a finger into me.

I squirmed around him, desperately trying not to let go so soon as his fingers invaded me, pushing against me, filling me, as he moved in and out, twisting and thrusting, rubbing his thumb over my clit making me gasp and writhe uncontrollably on his desk. He increased the pressure, fucking me hard with his fingers, heat and fire swarming inside me as I cried out.

"Oh, god, Eli. Danny's going to hear me," I gasped, clasping a hand over my mouth.

"Good," he growled bending over the top of me, the thumb on my clit pushing against me harder "I'm going to fuck you so hard you're going to forget who you even are," he grunted at me, his fingers thrusting with each syllable.

"Take your hand away, Ava. I want Danny to hear me fuck you."

A whimper escaped me as I squeezed my eyes shut, so close to the edge just from his slightest touch, the way his fingers moved in me, how they touched every sensitive spot, how they applied pressure in all the right measures, like he could read my pussy like a book from just the one night together.

Eli stopped suddenly and I couldn't help the disappointed cry that tumbled from my lips as his fingers slid back out. But then those fingers tugged at my knickers, pulling them roughly down my legs. Eli pulled away from me, dropping between my legs, his beard scratching at my delicate skin, hot tendrils of breath at my entrance, his mouth poised ready to take me, teasing me with its mere presence. I reached into his hair, trying to pull him closer.

"What do you want Princess?" the vibrations of his voice alone making my insides clench.

"Please," I breathed.

"Tell me what you want."

"You. Your mouth. Your lips. Fuck me with your tongue, Eli"

Jesus. What was he doing to me? I'd never begged a man to eat me out before. Not once. Never. He was turning me into a maniac. Dripping wet and needy.

Wrenching my legs apart suddenly he buried his face in me, his tongue sliding through my folds before, licking and sucking, pulling my clit into his mouth. He probed at my entrance, his tongue surprisingly strong and hard, thrusting it into me, his beard prickling against my clit, sending my eyes rolling back into my head and I pushed myself against his face, clenching my thighs around his head.

"Legs, Ava," he growled against me sending me gasping for air and arching my back so I could push my aching, desperate pussy further into his face.

I obeyed, spreading my thighs wider, baring everything to him, his tongue forcing into me, swirling inside me, in and out and over my clit.

"Eli!"

Then he sucked and nibbled and I bucked my hips, shamelessly riding his face, pushing myself into him, my stomach and core tensing, my entire being quivering as his tongue flicked over my clit, the orgasm ripping through my body, my hand no longer dulling the noise from my strangled cries as he devoured my pussy.

There was a sudden knock on the door and we both jumped, startled.

"Boss?" Danny's voice called as the door started to gently glide open.

Eli stood up quickly wiping a hand over his jaw, pulling me to my feet as I tugged my skirt back into position, forcing my eyes shut, willing my orgasm to stop as it continued to radiate though me.

"Boss. Ritchie's boys are in the bar. They want to see you."

"Fuck's sake", I heard Eli growl. "Ava, stay here," he instructed before following Danny out of the door leaving me glancing around dumbly.

Chapter Twenty Four

✀ Eli ❧

I didn't know what I was more annoyed at as I stormed out of my office; Ritchie sending his boys back here or that it had stopped me fucking Ava all over my desk. Dickhead. She'd looked stunning stepping into my office in that tight dress hugging her hips and showing off the curves of her toned legs. I struggled to think of anything other than burying myself in the moment she got here and she had been a sweet distraction from the demands my father had just emailed me.

Fuck Ritchie for his interruption. I followed Danny out of my office, readjusting my cock on the way down the stairs. The two goons from the other week were stood in my club.

"What do you want?" I growled, watching the tattooed one lean against the bar, a tumbler in hand with my whisky in it. Prick.

"Boss wants to see you," the shorter, sturdier guy started, his hands clasped behind his back, a fake reassurance he wasn't going to pummel my face in. What was he? Ex-military too?

"I thought I told you guys to tell him to get his arse here to see me?"

"Boss says it don't work like that," the tattooed guy joined in, "he says when he calls you come running."

"Is that so?"

"Look, Mr Antwill," the shorter one started again, "we're just here to tell you boss wants to see you. Right now. He sent a car."

I was losing my patience with these fuckwits. Folding my arms across my chest, I looked slowly from one to the other, assessing the situation.

"Just get out. Whatever Ritchie wants he's not getting. No amount of you two wandering in to my premises is going to change anything at all. Whatever deal Ritchie is after, it's not going to happen."

The ugly tattooed minion of Ritchie's threw back the last of my whisky, gulping it down his skinny throat, his Adam's apple bobbing. Then he launched the glass into the mirrored optic holder behind the bar. Glass erupted, shards dropping to the floor as the tumbler and the eight-foot mirror exploded into pieces. He swaggered over towards me, hands balled to fists at his side, stopping when there was little more than an inch between us. He had balls, big ones. I out sized him in height and muscle, yet here he was in easy reach of a good bashing. I took a deep breath, trying to keep my temper from unravelling.

"If the boss wants to see you, you go see the boss. Got it?" his words came out slowly, making

188

sure that I heard every one, little flecks of spit covering me.

I didn't flinch, but watched him carefully, studying the flickers of his face, watching for anything that would betray his next move.

"Tell your boss he can go fuck himself."

Looking back over his shoulder he nodded at the other man, some sort of silent communication passing between them and I probably should have put my fist in his face right then. The other one moved towards my bar, stepping around the pair of us holding something against his leg.

"Well Boss said if you don't come when asked we have to make sure you get the message this time."

The club erupted in a cacophony of crazy; bottles of spirit crashed on the floor as they were ripped from optics on the wall, the baseball bat swinging over his shoulder before swiping a load of stacked glasses on the floor, shattering into pieces everywhere.

I ran at the bar, leaping over the top and landing in front of him. He swung at me with the bat and I dodged backwards out of the way. I grabbed a whisky tumbler that had survived the initial onslaught and launched it at him hitting him hard in the forehead, dazing him, buying me an extra second between the swings of the bat. I hauled him off his feet and over the bar where he slid onto the floor, following him over the top before he'd even hit the ground. My fingers curled in the rough material of his jacket, yanking him back to his feet and then slamming my fist into his nose, the bone cracking loudly under my knuckles. Releasing the grip on his jacket I let him crumple to the floor at my feet.

Blood and adrenaline were coursing through my veins, my heart hammering in my chest from exertion and the rage that simmered. Then I heard the sudden gasp.

"Eli!" I heard her voice

Fuck, had she just seen me beat that guy? But turning towards her I realised that wasn't the reason for her shriek. The thin wiry one pulled her across the floor, his fist tight in her hair, her head pulled painfully towards him as she scrabbled to keep upright in her heels.

"Get, the fuck off me," she shouted at him, her arms flailing wildly, striking out but missing him repeatedly. She was like a wild cat, her fingers outstretched, trying to land a talon of sharp nails against him, but the pummelling she was giving him was no use. He yanked her roughly and her ankle bent, and she squeaked landing on her knees.

"It's the only place you should be, bitch."

Then he was pulling her again, lifting her back to her feet by her hair, her hands scrabbling over the top of his as her green eyes winced in pain.

"Get the hell off my woman," I growled and started striding over to him only to stop suddenly as he waved a shard of a broken bottle towards her face.

Ava didn't miss it, her eyes opening wide as saucers, turning them on me, the look of fear and pleading across her beautiful face. The anger that had been simmering away now burnt white hot, my fingernails biting into my palms from the tension of my clenched fists.

"Ah, so you are Antwill's bit of pussy after all?" he crooned in her ear, his mouth mere millimetres from her skin.

The sight of another man touching her, hurting her; anger and rage was all I could feel, dumbing my other senses, the darkness lurking in my head unleashed. I would kill him for touching her. I would torture him in return for the fear that raged in her beautiful eyes. But right now, I needed control.

I calmed my voice, and forced my brain to slow down. "The girl has nothing to do with this. Let her go."

"No," he mocked, his eyes holding mine, "I like the feel of her arse against my cock. I'm gonna find out how tight she is, Antwill."

Moving his hand from her hair to her neck he pulled her further in towards him and pushed his hips up against her backside. Ava closed her eyes, but I could see her breath hitch in her chest as she bit down on her bottom lip, the muscles in her neck tight with tension. But she stayed still, the piece of glass resting on her neck. Good. Stay still, Princess.

"Hmmm, I bet Antwill has already been here," he spoke into her ear, his eyes holding mine.

He pushed his pelvis forward, grinding into her. Her eyes shot open, and she searched my face for something, fear and uncertainty from her green eyes burning a hole into me. I held her gaze, feigning a calmness, hoping it looked like I had it all under control. Inside I was raging. I would tear him apart. The cock that he had pushed against her, I would slice it to ragged pieces before ripping his throat out with my fingers.

His hand moved down her neck and I watched Ava stiffen, but when she looked up, she tipped her head up and down. A slight nod. A signal. There was a change in her green eyes. Anger, resolve. Her eyes dropped to the right-hand side, watching the hand clutching the jagged glass that had started to drop away from her. Then she looked at me again, winking, before quickly stamping her foot down, stiletto heel first into the middle of his trainer clad foot.

He yelled and Ava turned pulling her dress up and forcing her knee so hard into his groin that tears even came to my eyes.

"Bitch!" he shrieked, unsure whether to cradle his dick first or his foot.

Ava ducked away as I ran at him, driving my fist into the side of his face, his head snapping sideways and blood bursting from his mouth like a knock-out blow in a boxing match. The broken bottle clanged loudly on the floor and I kicked it hard, sending it flying under one of the booths, unreachable.

"Eli! Watch out!" I heard Ava's cry, footsteps advancing.

I side stepped and struck a blow into the other one's side, the dull thump against his ribs and an exhalation of air. He straightened quickly, throwing a wild punch. I ducked, the whoosh of his fist close as it skimmed over my head, my fists flying into his stomach with as much force as I could muster.

I glanced over the top of him as he doubled over in pain, rolling to the ground. 'Ugly' had staggered back to his feet, rubbing at his jaw and eyeing me first then Ava. I stepped left cutting off his path to her.

"Do you need to take a seat, Princess?" I shouted glancing to my right, hoping she got it.

She blinked once, then narrowed her eyes, darting sideways towards a booth she kicked the bar stool over towards me. Grabbing it I swung it hard into the side of the tattooed guy, knocking him sideways and breaking the stool into pieces. I picked up the legs that had fallen off, one in each hand stalking towards them. 'Ugly' was scrabbling to his feet, his friend already leaving him behind as he bolted for the doors.

"You'll fucking regret this, Antwill!" 'Ugly' shouted before limping away like an injured Quasimodo towards the doors.

"The fuck I will," I shouted at his back, "tell Ritchie I'm coming for him."

And with that they staggered out to the street. I looked behind me searching for Ava. She'd sunk to the floor, her breathing short and raspy.

Chapter Twenty Five

❦ Ava ❧

I couldn't breathe. My heart was racing, thumping against my chest. I could hear it in my ears, feel it thundering against my spine, resonating through me fast and frantic. My ribs were squeezing my lungs, strangling me in a vice like, bony grip as my vision flashed from light to dark, dizziness consuming me.

Eli touched my arm gently, his low voice somewhere in front of me but I couldn't see him, only darkness; black and enveloping darkness.

"I can't see," a strangled voice said.

"You're having a panic attack," his voice came again, he was right next to me, "breath with me, Ava. You'll be OK."

I felt his hair brush my forehead, his warm skin touching mine, the tickle of his breath on my face and for a moment I focussed on the sound of his deep breaths not the burn in my chest.

"That's it. You got this, Princess," he rumbled, his voice calm and low.

Heavy hands were placed on my shoulders, rubbing over my skin. My heart steadied and shadows sharpened to shapes; grey and black morphing to blues, greens, reds, oranges, pinks and eventually the off-white colour of artificial light swamping the nightclub in a light yellow glow. My lungs peeled off my ribs, filling with air, cool and refreshing, my heart dropping from my throat allowing more oxygen to flood into me. Something wet rolled down my cheek.

Eli pulled his face from mine, his blue eyes calm, the earlier storm in them having stilled and he swiped a thumb gently across the top of my cheek, catching the tear that had escaped. I took another deep breath, my brain no longer spinning in a chaotic waltz.

I studied his face, his jaw still tight with tension, his dark eyebrows pushed together. His t-shirt was ripped at the front, exposing the hard muscles of his chest and the brown beaded necklace he wore and for the first time I really noticed the collection of metal circles that hung off it; dog tags. There was a scratch on his left bicep, a small trickle of blood running gently down his arm, already partly congealed.

The bar was smashed to pieces, shards of glass littering the floor and bar top, glinting in the lights. Liquid from the bottles that had been wrenched off the walls spilt all over, glistening off every surface, dripping down the parts of the mirror that was still somehow clinging to the back wall, splattered all over the wooden counter and running down the other side.

"They've made such a mess."

"I know. Nothing I can't put right tomorrow," Eli's voice was steady.

He glanced sideways, "take off Danny," he growled at the traumatised barman that crept out of his hiding place.

"Come, on. Let's get you home," he said, gently pulling me gently to my feet.

I gazed around the club again, suddenly cold and wrapped my hands around myself, tears of shock and fear burning the back of my eyes. Eli stopped and looked at me again, tipping my chin gently with his fingers. I swallowed

"Eli?" I whispered, my voice uncertain, "can I stay with you? I don't want to be alone."

"'Course you can, Princess."

*****

A couple of glasses of wine later my hands and my insides had stopped shaking and I was snuggled into Eli's big arms on his couch, resting my head on his chest.

"It's so quiet out here in the countryside," I breathed, my eyes watching out into the darkness, tiny specs of light from cars and civilisation moving in the distance.

Eli laughed, a deep booming noise vibrating in his chest and over my skin.

"Countryside? Hardly, Ava. We're really just in the middle of fields. It's still Newcastle."

"Well, it looks like countryside to me."

"Have you actually ever seen the country before?" he mocked.

196

But his words cut deep and I fell silent.

"Ava?" he said again after a few moments.

I sighed, "I've never been in the country, Eli. The most green I saw when I was growing up was a park, sometimes occasionally on TV, but that was it. The first time I left London was only a few months ago. I saw it on the train."

He looked at me, something in his eyes I couldn't really read; surprise, sadness, pity? The silence was thick, oppressive. The alcohol in me didn't like that.

"But I mean, I can't be missing much really? Isn't it just damp, cold, and you fall over sheep poo everywhere you go? I can't see the attraction."

"You've never been anywhere else but London?"

She shook her head.

"Shit! You've led a sheltered life."

"Not by choice. I didn't have the life choices you had growing up."

"Money doesn't always make those life choices any better, Ava," Eli said, his voice cool.

I looked at him, waiting for more but it didn't come, the room descending into silence, heavy and uncomfortable between us.

"Well London's pretty awesome," I continued, "you've got everything you need there, and there are some parks and trees, and I'm sure if you look hard enough, you'd find the odd cow!"

"If it was so awesome, why are you here?"

His voice held a sharpness to it and I stared into my wine glass, looking for the answer. I let out a sigh.

"Because I found my boyfriend in bed with someone else."

"Shit. I'm sorry."

"Don't be. Wasn't you!"

"I didn't mean to upset you."

"You haven't," I sighed, "he was my boss. He'd recruited me fresh out of college, just as an office junior and somehow, somewhere, we fell in love. Well, I fell in love; or something like that. I was naïve and completely taken in by his kindness, the gifts, the clothes and shoes and everything I'd never had before. I thought I was leaving my old life behind. I should have known. I ignored the smell of perfume all over him when he came home, bought all his excuses for why he worked late, even though I worked in the same office; for him.

We'd had a huge contract on for weeks and I was in late finishing things off for him. He'd said he had a headache and needed to finish early. I worked and he went home. Guess I finished the stuff quicker than he thought I would, so I packed up early too. I walked in on him shagging one of the new office juniors. In our bed."

Eli's eyes were dark, his brow furrowed.

"What a dick."

"Yeah. Well things happen for a reason, supposedly. He paid me through University, I escaped the shitty Council estate I was living in, and escaped my mum and that lifestyle."

"What lifestyle was that?"

The wine was loosening my tongue and bringing back memories I'd buried, long hidden. My chest hurt and tears prickled at the back of my eyes, thoughts descending into a darkness I thought I'd climbed out of.

"You mind if I take a shower?" I asked, ignoring his last question.

"Sure."

I stood under the hot water, letting it pour down my back and over my skin, flooding over my face and mixing with the tears that I finally let fall. I'd never told anyone all the details about Tom. Recounting it all tonight, to someone I barely knew, had been a bad idea. I should have left it buried, left it all where it was, carefully contained in the back of my head. I wasn't that girl anymore; I'd had my eyes opened and my heart ripped out. I scrubbed my hands over my face angrily, washing the rest of the soap off and switching off the shower.

I rifled in Eli's massive wardrobe, pushing jumpers and t-shirts out of the way, pulling a white shirt off the hanger and slipping it on. The arms hung off me, material thick at the ends where I'd rolled the sleeves up countless times.

As I padded down the hallway on bare feet, I heard the low rumble of his voice.

"I'll kill him, Cam. I should have done it long ago."

199

The ice in his voice made me stop.

"Bud, you can't just walk in there and get near him. He's surrounded by people."

I recognised Cameron's voice.

"The Viking can."

"So, you're going to pay the Viking to take the hit?"

"He owes me a favour or two."

"Eli," Cameron's voice was quieter, "don't you think you need to let this drop now?"

"Fuck you, Cam. I'm so close, so close to bringing him and his whole operation down."

"So why go charging in then? Do it properly. Bring it crashing down around him."

"Because all I can think of right now is ripping his throat out," Eli growled, low and thick.

"Why? Because he smashed your club up?"

"Because his boys touched her. They put their stinking hands on her. If he thinks for a minute I'll let that drop…."

My nose tickled suddenly and my eyes watered. The sneeze escaped my throat, loudly.

Chapter Twenty Six

๑ Eli ๛

The sudden sneeze from the corridor stopped the conversation and both of us glanced in the direction, Cameron fixing me with a stare that I refused to read into.

"Hey, Ava," he said, as she moved round the corner, his eyes passing over her and then back to me with a knowing smile.

I glared at him.

"Err, hi, Cam," she answered nervously, pulling the shirt further down her legs self-consciously.

"I'm gonna get going," Cameron grinned, "nice to see you again, Ava, with Eli…again, and in his clothes."

Ava smiled back weakly, a tinge of red forming across her cheeks and creeping up her neck.

"Get the fuck out of here," I growled.

Cameron turned towards the door, grinning ridiculously as he grasped the handle and pulled it open, but the smile quickly faded.

"Don't do anything stupid, mate."

The door closed, leaving us alone.

My dress shirt hung off her shoulders, damp red curls contrasted against the crisp white material, the arms folded up so many times the cuff was thick as it lay against her forearm. She hugged her arms around her nervously, watching me carefully as my eyes raked across her body.

"What was Cameron doing here?" Ava asked.

I ignored the question, instead listening to the pressure starting in my pants.

"Take it off."

"What?" she asked, startled.

"The shirt. Take it off."

"But I've not got anything underneath."

"I know."

Ava hesitated looking around with uncertainty for a split second.

"Now, Ava," I warned, my voice taking on a tone even I'd never heard before.

Her fingers skipped over the little buttons clumsily, undoing the first two before pulling on the hem and lifting it over her head. Her tits were perfect; round and pert, her nipples hardening the minute the air touched her. Her stomach was taught, skin pulled tight over the slight muscle underneath and my eyes drifted down from her belly button to the bulb of the mound between her legs; a wispy patch of dark red hair, carefully trimmed, pulling my eye down further, revealing the lips of her pussy.

I remembered the taste of her; sweet and earthy, the smell of her wet mound still clinging to my beard, making me hard in an instant.

I moved my gaze back to her face, her green eyes uncertain, unsure of what to do with herself, vulnerable and fragile, yet not realising the power she wielded over my body, over my cock and my brain. Her hands moved to cover herself, cutting off my view between her legs.

I moved forward, closing the space between us and resting my arm next to her head on the corridor wall. My face was inches from hers, her scent teasing me, the heat rising from her body and I could almost taste her. I dropped my other hand between her legs, nudging hers away, my fingers gliding through the slick juices that were already pooling, waiting for me to fuck her.

I slid a finger inside her, the soft flesh of her pussy gripping me hard and she exhaled into my chest.

"You're so incredibly tight," I said, my voice low in her ear and she turned her head to brush her lips against mine.

I pulled out of her.

"I want to see you fuck yourself, Princess."

Her eyes opened wide.

"Wh, what?"

"Your fingers. Show me how you like it."

She looked at me again.

Grabbing her slim hand I pushed it against her entrance, rubbing her fingers back and forth over her folds.

"Show me how you finger yourself."

Her hand stilled for a moment, uncertainty showing in her eyes, but then I felt her fingers move under my hand, rubbing over her pussy lips. I took a step back, watching two of them disappear inside of her, gliding slowly in and out, building up the rhythm and she slipped in another, her palm covering her clit. She closed her eyes and tilted her head back.

"Open your eyes and look at me," my voice sounded almost like a growl.

Ava's hips started to rock as her fingers moved, pushing her pussy intro her hand, riding her own fingers, a moan escaping from her mouth.

I dropped to my knees and kissed her stomach, my lips trailing over the delicate skin just above her hand, nipping and pulling and she bucked harder, her breath coming in rasps.

"Eli," she whispered, the orgasm just riding on her breath.

I swirled my tongue over her skin, biting and sucking harder.

"Eli," she said again louder, my name becoming a strangled gasp on her tongue.

"Harder, Princess. Come all over your fingers for me."

I bit down on her skin, my fingers digging into the flesh of her arse cheeks as I pulled her towards my mouth, her hips moving against me and her hand.

"Ahh fuck," I heard the words fall from her mouth, her body quivering.

Fuck she was incredible. I pulled my tattered t-shirt over my head, pulled the condom from my pocket and wriggled my jeans off with one hand as I started to roll the rubber over my dick with the other. Then pushing her hands away, I nudged her legs apart, pulling one up to my hip as I glided the head of my cock over her entrance. Heat radiated out of her, her own juices running over my shaft, lubricating the tip as it glided inside in one tight go.

"Fuck," I cursed into her neck as her pussy stretched around me, pressure building in my balls instantly.

I moved against her, pushing her into the wall as I punished her pussy with my cock. I couldn't go slow, I couldn't wait, instead I thrusted in and out of her like a wild animal, any sense of restraint and control going the minute I entered her. Her arms clasped around my neck, pulling me into her, her breathing ragged.

"Fuck."

I slammed harder against her, ramming her body against the wall, her cries growing louder to the point I couldn't tell whether I was hurting her or pleasuring her, but I couldn't stop, I needed this, her, us. Fuck.

"Eli!" she screamed suddenly, nails biting into my back, her body convulsing and shaking around me.

The pain in my skin mixed with the heat in my groin, my balls tensing, my cock straining.

"Ah fuck!" I growled, biting down onto her neck, shoving hard into her, pushing my pubic bone against her as light and darkness exploded around me.

"Fuck," I whispered again as I tasted the slight saltiness of her skin on my lips.

*****

Ava's hair fell over my chest where she lay, an arm stretched across me, her chest gently rising and falling, the heat of her naked skin against mine. She fit so well in my arms, in my bed, in my heart. Or maybe I was just infatuated with the way I fit in her, how incredible she felt, like nothing I could remember, hot and wet and tight. Had she really crept into my head or was I just thinking with my cock?

The drawer beside the bed buzzed and I wriggled free from the drape of her slim arm, slipping out from under her. I grabbed the burner phone and hit the green button, silencing the angry vibrations as I let my bedroom door close gently behind me.

"Hey, bud," came the voice on the other end.

"What have you got for me V?"

"There's a shipment coming into Leith Docks next Friday. Think you might find it interesting."

"Time?"

"7pm."

"Thanks, mate."

The phone disconnected and I glanced back towards the door of my bedroom, thoughts flying round my head, contradicting and confusing.

Chapter Twenty Seven

❧ Ava ☙

A dull light filtered in through Eli's thick curtains, the room bathed in a soft, pale glow. I shivered against the cold air, despite the warmth of Eli's arms wrapped around me. His skin looked deeply tanned against my pale pallor. I turned into him and traced the definition of his muscle as it mingled with the detail of the tattoo. Red roses stood out against the dark ink, snakes entwined around the flowers, skulls and various shapes embedded in the artwork, only identifiable on close inspection. It spilled across the top of his shoulder, small tendrils stroking his chest, the dusting of dark hair softening the edges as they faded away into his skin.

Eli was a sculpture of a beast, manly, strong, rugged, ruthless; dangerous. I'd seen the look in his eyes yesterday. Cold and hard, his glare like the concentration of a killer not a protector, his beautiful blue eyes dark with rage. It had frightened me and excited me all at the same time. A pull of heat prickled inside of me.

I moved my mouth over his skin, feeling the tightness of the muscle underneath with my lips and my tongue, tasting the gentle saltiness of his body, still smelling woody and musky as my hand slipped down over the hard ripple of his stomach, brushing the courser hair with my fingers, the tight muscles of his groin like warmed marble and, my fingers brushing the smooth bulging head of his erection.

The tip was smooth, almost satiny, bulbous and I slid my hand over the top and down his length, not able to fully close my fingers around it. The veins pushed against me as I moved my hand gently up and down, feeling for every ridge, every vein.

"Morning, Princess," Eli's voice rumbled, a low purr vibrating from his chest.

Then he pulled me on top of him, his cock pushing hard against me, nudging at the folds, pushing to get access. Eli pulled my face to his, his lips grabbing at mine, his tongue joining mine in a dual for dominance as wetness pooled between my legs, warm and damp.

I dragged myself over his shaft till I was poised over the head and lowered myself down, feeling his hardness at my entrance, forcing its way in, pushing my tissues apart as I slid bit by deliciously full bit down on top of him. I couldn't keep the moan from my lips as I settled onto his cock and his hands moved to my hips, guiding me up and down the entire length of him. I rocked, my clit sliding over the muscle covering his pubic bone, the rough hair between his legs rubbing my swollen nub, heat bubbling within me.

I moved faster, grinding myself against him shamelessly, selfishly, my finger nails cutting into the flesh of his chest. Shit.

God, I loved this, his cock, the way it filled me, the way it moved in me prizing me open and impaling my insides, sending flames licking through me, burning heat and electric ripples pulsing through my stomach. My hips moved faster, pushing myself down onto him, taking all of him, his length, his girth.

I closed my eyes for a moment. Behind the darkness of my lids the sensations moving through my body threatened to consume me. My thighs tensed around him, my stomach clenching with each dip of my hips as I slid down his thickness and the tip of his cock hitting my cervix as I ground my clit against him.

When I opened my eyes again Eli's were staring at me, the blue deeper than I'd ever seen them before, his dark hair contrasted against the crisp white pillows, his lips pushed together in concentration, on me, on control.

"Tell me how it feels, Princess."

I hesitated feeling awkward all of a sudden, dropping forwards towards him. Eli grabbed my head in his hands.

"I want to know how my cock feels in you, every time you slide down it what do you feel? Every time I impale you on it how do you feel?"

He moved his hips up into me.

"I want to know what it feels like to fill you, to stretch you. Tell me and I promise I'll make you feel so much more, do much more that you won't be able to find the words to describe it, that I'll snatch those words right out of your very being and replace them with my dick. I'll fuck you like you've never been fucked before. I'll fuck those words right out of you."

My pussy tightened, reacting to the delicious words that tumbled from his sinful mouth, my cheeks flushing hot and a formidable pulsing deep in my stomach.

"So full," I panted, moving up and down his shaft, "so full that I feel like it's going to split me in two. Like it pulls me apart and puts me back together again and when your cock bottoms out I can't think of anything else. It's like it takes away my thoughts and my reason, and it takes away my free will and all I want is more of you. No one has made me feel that, no one has made me orgasm like a wild animal in heat, and I'm addicted to you. You've ruined me."

Eli growled and bucked his hips into mine roughly, the tip of his cock smashing into my cervix and I shouted, lights erupting behind my eyes. His hand sank between us, rubbing me as I moved my hips against him, heat swarming, building. Shit.

His thumb worked harder, his fingers alternating between rubbing and nipping and pulling, his face watching me riding his cock and his hips moving to meet mine, thrusting upwards at the same time as I slid down him. My stomach tensed, the sensation building to a crescendo.

"Shit, Eli,"

He smiled, moving his fingers faster, pushing up into me with more force until I threw my head back, light and dark busting behind my eyes, pulses coursing through my body, exploding in my stomach and radiating outwards, reaching every part of me, my toes, my fingertips, everywhere. Eli grunted from underneath me, sending a shot of sticky, wet warmth inside of me before stilling and pulling me onto his chest.

"I'm sorry," he breathed into my ear as I lay on top of him, "I should have stopped for a condom. I didn't mean to let you do that."

"If it worries you, I'm on contraception."

"Well, that helps with some things," he said, smoothing the hair from my face.

We lay there for a little while longer, tangled together, the soaking wet sensation still between my legs where he'd emptied himself inside of me, his fingertips brushing over my back.

"I've got to get to work," I said eventually.

"Come on, I'll drive you in."

*****

Eli pulled the car up to the door of the big glass atrium entrance of Fairbrother Williams' offices. The day was bright but cooled by a stiff wind, making October seem a harsher month than it otherwise was. The breeze was rolling off the River Tyne, bringing with it a further nip in the air and I glanced around, watching people scurry up and down the river front street, clutching tightly to anything that might be swiftly whipped away from them.

"Thanks," I muttered to Eli, suddenly self-consciously and turned to open the door.

But just as I moved away from him, he grabbed hold of me and yanked me back towards him, crushing his lips into mine, but this time the kiss was something else. Less urgent, but sensual, gentle, his lips grazing over mine, his tongue slowly stroking my mouth. I melted against him, a longing ache starting between my legs, the light pads of his fingers brushing the sensitive skin between my legs. A growl vibrated against my lips, and my thong was pulled aside and I parted my legs letting him get closer. He dipped into me, sending me gasping into his mouth, his fingers suddenly assaulting, thrusting and swirling, his thumb pushed against my clit. Then as quick as he'd entered me, he pulled them away.

"Remember me today, Princess. Remember who's cock you rode this morning, who's fingers were in you in front of the office."

My head was whirling, my body clenching, begging for more of him. Then he patted my leg and sat back in his seat.

"Off you go then."

I opened my mouth, not knowing what to say, not able to think about anything else but him. My pussy throbbed and stomach tightened. Shit.

I swung my legs out of the car, stepping onto the pavement and pulled my coat around me against the wind, the gusts whipping my hair around my face as I clutched my laptop bag tightly. The black SUV roared way, turning the head of those it past as Eli revved it down the road and out of sight.

"Morning, Ava."

I turned, staring into the face of Harry, his eyes roaming over me, searching for something.

"Was that Antwill's car you just got out of?"

"I, err, he just offered me a lift, saw me walking and, er the weather, and, erm, yeah."

The most unconvincing sentence ever had just slipped from my lips. Harry studied me for a moment, a solemn look on his face and then he gave me a weak smile.

"Shall we get in then?" he asked as I stood there looking at him, waiting for something although not sure what.

I nodded and followed him through the revolving glass doors and into the lift behind another couple of office workers who were chattering animatedly and masking the difficult silence that was growing between us.

I watched Harry intermittently all day; partly because I was distracted by my own rampant thoughts and partly because he seemed so off. He'd spent more time resting his head in his hands than striking the keys on the keyboard angrily. His eyes had darted back and forth, his attention neither on the computer screen nor whatever messages had pinged through on his phone all day. And as the afternoon had ebbed away, he'd looked more and more stressed.

I wandered over to his desk, a sudden sense of needing to see if I could help washing over me, although I wasn't certain there wasn't a little pang of my own guilt wrapped up in my gesture.

"You OK, Harry?"

He dropped the screen down to the task bar at the bottom of the computer screen as I got closer.

"Fine," he answered abruptly.

"Do you need me to help with anything?"

"You can't help me, Ava," Harry's voice held a sigh and his eyes cradled the look of defeat.

I swallowed carefully.

"You sure? You don't seem yourself?"

"I'm fine," his voice hardened, "I'm sure you've got plenty things to concern yourself with Ava, like Elijah Antwill?"

The last of his words felt loaded, directed right at me as his shoulders stiffened defensively. I nodded and retreated to my desk, watching as his head fell into his hands once more.

Chapter Twenty Eight

ဆ Eli ର

I followed Dazza Gray around all afternoon, keeping well back, but I was sure the arrogant fuck hadn't even noticed the big black car that was continuously three to four cars behind him. He'd picked up a few fares, dropped a few off and done a number of laps around the City Centre eventually moving westwards towards the edge of the city but this time with an empty cab.

He stopped at a house in one of Newcastle's Council estates, pulling onto a make shift drive way. I parked further down the street, trying not to draw too much attention to myself as I focussed the lens of my camera on him, watching as he opened the boot, pulling something back and handing a number of well wrapped packages to the lanky youths who had come to meet him.

The group looked around wistfully and, satisfied, they carried on, more packages being passed out the back of the big VW Passat. Then he pushed the boot closed and drove off and I took up my position behind him.

I tailed him all day, tediously following him with one fare to the next, not pulling up any more information than earlier. By the end of the day, I was fed up and starving and about to give up. He dropped the last fare of the day off and returned to the city centre but instead of parking back up to the taxi rank in front of the station he drove straight past moving out of the city and over the bridge.

I followed, weaving in and out through traffic as we crossed the Tyne Bridge, and cutting across the lanes as he turned off to the right as the bridge ended. The road was quiet, a scattering of small business, mostly car repair garages littering what was otherwise a big back lane. I hung right back, letting the Passat almost go out of view, aware of my sudden conspicuousness.

Most of the businesses had, or were, shutting up for the day, heavy metal roller doors being pulled over shop fronts, protecting against unwanted visitors. The Passat has stopped further up, pulling up onto a small forecourt and in the distance, I could see the shape of Dazza getting out and ducking under the partially closed roller shutter over the front door. I drove slowly past, sneaking quick glances but not really seeing what was on the other side of the metal fortress.

A car passed me coming from the other direction, speeding down the road and I watched in my rear-view mirror as it pulled up across the front of the building. I slowed, pulling the big car into the side of the road, watching the suited man get out of the car and going into the shop.

Turning round at the top of the street I took a chance, driving back the way I'd come, knowing that I'd most likely blow any form of cover out the water. As I got closer two men were talking next to the Passat, the blond suited man striking a feeling of déjà vu in me as I got closer. I rolled the car past, watching the interactions, the animated conversation, the suit turning and glancing at me.

The familiarity hit me, the memory of him all over Ava in my pub, his hands roaming over her, not taking 'no' for an answer. Rage ignited in my stomach. What was her boss doing here? What was in that building?

His eyes held mine but I didn't shrink from his gaze, watching the realisation cross his face, the furrow of his brow. I wanted him to know I'd seen him. And I knew he had seen me.

I drove away, the image of the man imprinted on my brain. I hardly thought Dazza Gray would be a client of Fairbrother Williams. They dealt with big business and entrepreneurs, it was unlikely his street operations would be anywhere near the turnover they would be interested in, which meant there was another reason that Ava's boss was there.

I parked the car behind the night club, tucking it into the back lane. The mess looked even worse tonight than I remembered from yesterday, the entire mirrored wall at the back of the bar smashed to tiny pieces, liquor now sticky on the floor as my thick soled boots crunched on the glass I walked across. A bar stool lay in pieces to one side, where I'd dropped it reluctantly instead of caving that fuckwit's head in. Years ago, I probably wouldn't have hesitated, but last night I'd reined the monster in, just enough not to completely scare Ava off.

It took a few hours to tidy the club up, sweeping away all the debris and taking down the panel of smashed mirror, ready to be replaced in the morning. I poured myself a whisky from a surviving bottle, swallowing the liquid as it burned the back of my throat, my thoughts flicking back to the garage on the other side of the river, an idea forming.

It was after midnight when I parked my car round the corner, pulling the hood of my jumper up over my head and shoving my arms into the black jacket, before swinging my bag of tricks over my shoulder. The building was deserted, no CCTV, no security lighting and no alarm. I dropped to my haunches beside the roller shutter that covered the door, slipping the crowbar underneath it and forcing my weight onto it until I heard the pop. The metal sprung free and I pushed it up over my head, wedging the crowbar between the frame and the door until wood splintered angrily and the door stuttered, opening inwards.

Stepping inside with my bag, I turned the torch on and pulled the shutter back down behind me. White light washed over the interior, picking up a couple of cars that stood in various stages of being dismantled or repaired. I moved carefully through the building, my eyes scanning every inch, eventually catching the door on the far side leading away from the garage itself.

The handle turned easily in my hand and the door sprung open leading me into a storeroom. Vehicle parts were scattered around, canisters of oil and coolant stacked in piles but as I got further in the haphazard cardboard boxes gave way to thick wooden crates, nailed and secured. I forced the crow bar under the lid, pushing against it hard, my arms and shoulders straining against the screws and nails that kept the lid tightly secured. Eventually the wood splintered, a panel ripping clean off under the force.

I shone the torch over the contents, light bouncing off the numerous tightly wrapped blocks of white brick. I pulled one out, weighing it in my hand. Unsheathing my knife from my boot I cut into the package, taking a small amount of the white powder on the blade and dipping my finger in it before rubbing it across my gum. My mouth filled with a bitterness, turning the area I'd just touched numb.

Fuck, this was good, pure stuff that Ritchie had stashed in the garage, nearly a tonne's worth of cocaine. If the stupid bastard had better security on the building, then there was little chance of it going up in smoke. I grinned to myself as I glanced around the space, eyeing the petrol canisters in the corner. Perfect. I doused the crate with the liquid, giving it a good soaking. Then, already retreating I struck the match, flicking it to the pile of cocaine and watching as the fire caught immediately, flames growing to orange and red beasts, dancing in front of my eyes. I backed out of the room and the garage putting as much space between me and the inferno as quickly as possible. I hoisted my bag over my shoulder and walked back to the car, unable to keep the huge grin off my face.

Chapter Twenty Nine

༄ Ava ༄

'Gateshead Inferno' the caption blazoned in red across the bottom of the television screen as I sipped my coffee the next morning. The cameras zoomed in on the building which was almost entirely destroyed, only bits of blackened, twisted metal were left and randomly, a roller shutter security door hanging at the front.

"Jeez," Kerry commented from next to me buttoning up her white blouse as she watched, "that's a mess."

"Must have been a big fire."

"Yeah, it's taken out the building next to it as well," she commented, "anyway, gotta go. Are you actually coming home tonight?"

Kerry flashed me a wide smile.

"Yeah, probably. Not making any promises though."

She laughed, flicked her blonde hair over her shoulders and grabbed her coat.

"See you later, *Princess*," she mocked, leaving the apartment.

I'd been in the office an hour before Harry turned up. He was red faced and flustered, I assumed because he was late. He peeled off his suit jacket, hanging it on the back of the chair and stooped over the keyboard.

"Morning, Harry. You OK?"

"Why do you even care?" he shot, his words harsh in the air between us.

"I, err…."

His shirt was crinkled, un-ironed and his tie was lop-sided as if he hadn't looked in the mirror yet this morning. He turned towards me, his eyes red and blood shot.

"Seriously, Harry. You look terrible. Maybe you should have called in sick?"

"I'm fine, Ava. Haven't you got a report to do for me today?" his voice was sharper still and I could feel the heat flooding to my cheeks, "go do what you're paid to do."

I nodded silently and wandered back to my desk a knot tightening in my chest.

Harry looked flustered all day, his face changing through various shades of red and purple occasionally diluting to a sickly pale pink, but as the day progressed, he looked more and more pale. He never moved from his desk, not for lunch, a coffee and I don't think I saw him get up to go to the toilet.

By mid-afternoon I tried another peace offering and brought him a mug of coffee, setting it down quietly beside him. Turning to walk away his hand grasped mine, warm and clammy.

"Thank you, Ava. I'm sorry about earlier," his voice was faint, defeated.

"Hey, it's OK," I answered quietly, "but my offer still stands, if you need any help with anything?"

"Actually, there is something. I need to write a report for Martin for tomorrow and this job today is just not playing by the rules," he waved his hand over the computer screen and I glanced at the document that was open, row upon row of numbers.

"Harry, I'll sort it. When do you need it for?"

He grimaced, swallowing hard before answering.

"First thing tomorrow morning."

"That's OK. I'll stay late, but will you please take a break or go home or something?"

He shook his head.

"Harry," I continued, "think of it as a condition of me helping you. You look ill. I'll sort it only of you go home."

He looked up at me from where I stood over him, light blue eyes framed with red. He nodded.

"I'll bring it over later, then if you need any tweaks, I can sort that too."

"Thank you, Ava. I really appreciate it."

I nodded as he stood up, shut down the documents that he had been working on and tidied his desk before leaving for the day.

I sat back at my desk pulling the information in front of me. When I looked up again the office was quiet. People had filed out around me, the huge open plan room deserted and dark, the only light from my computer casting an eerie green glow around me. The sudden vibration next to me made me jump, my heart coming alive in my chest. I checked the display, a number with no name across the screen. I swiped the green button across and held the handset to my ear.

The voice on the other end was low, deep familiar tones sending a tickle straight to my stomach.

"Hey, Princess," his rich voice purred down the phone.

"Eli? How did you get my number?"

"I know a guy…."

"I'm sure that's not legal."

"There's a lot of things I do that's not legal," his voice was light but I could detect a seriousness to it.

"What are you ringing for?" I tried to keep the excitement out of my voice.

"I'm hungry. I wondered whether you wanted to grab something to eat?"

My stomach jumped, excitement fluttering in my chest followed by the bitter taste of disappointment.

"I'm sorry. I'm working late. I have some stuff to finish for Harry. Another night?"

225

Eli paused and a tiny niggle of worry crept inside of me.

"Sure," he said after the lifetime of all silences, his voice a little darker.

The call ended and I sat in the silence of the office, distracted. It was dark outside, the windows letting the night crawl in. I shivered, pulling on my suit jacket and turning my attention back to the computer.

A couple of hours later I was finally finished. Rain splattered the windows, a wind had picked up again, driving it against the building. I packed my laptop away, dialled a taxi as I moved through the quietness of the big glass building and out onto the street.

I stood outside Harry's apartment block angrily pressing the buzzer on the intercom, the rain soaking through my clothes as I stood waiting for him to answer me. Nothing. The door to the block opened and a man stepped out, pulling his collar up against the rain. He dipped his head and charged out into the downpour, leaving the door closing behind him. It stopped clumsily against my outstretched foot and after a quick glance around I wrenched the heavy security door open and ducked inside.

Harry's apartment was right at the top floor and I left a pool of water in the lift as it dripped off me. I marched to his door and hammered on it, the sound echoing around the landing. I waited. And waited. Then I knocked again; louder this time, anger stirring within me.

"Harry?" I called against the door, rattling the handle at the same time.

The door bounded open and startled, I nearly fell in. I looked around, as if somehow, I'd find some sort of invitation or permission before entering his apartment. The place was huge, nearly as big as Eli's and sprawled over two floors. The kitchen and lounge area were open plan, glistening white leather chairs around a glass dining table, a white leather corner settee in the far corner. I carefully popped my bags down on the kitchen bench and wandered across to the settee. Scatter cushions looked like they'd been thrown everywhere, a glass of red wine spilt on one of the seats, the dark red liquid soaking into the leather.

I picked the glass up and set it down on the coffee table, the base making an odd, soft crunching noise as it made contact with surface. I looked down. White powder was strewn across it, spilling from a small clear bag. My stomach dropped, a mixture of dread and disappointment flooding through me. Shit, Harry.

I wandered the rest of the apartment, pushing a few doors and not finding Harry anywhere, yet the place was lit up like a Christmas tree. Every room had a light on, but no room contained Harry. I had walked into the Marie Celeste. Back in the kitchen I dug around for my phone.

"Where are you?"

"I'm sorry, Ava. I'm back at the office. I had something urgent I needed to do."

Fuck's sake, the curse felt harsh. My phone vibrated again.

"I'm so sorry, Ava. Really I am."

The hairs on the back of my neck stood up, a feeling of dread creeping over me. I punched in the number for a taxi and left the apartment, closing the door securely behind me.

The office was swamped in darkness when I returned, no hint of life visible from the outside. The rain had dropped to a steady patter but the intimidating feeling of night that crept around me was foreboding, threatening. Approaching the back of the building I typed in the security code hearing the click of the bolt sliding free from the fire doors.

There were no lights inside, nothing illuminating the stairwells other than the sickly green glow of the fire exit signs. I flicked on the lights, the sudden golden flare chasing away the creeping shadows and bounded up the first flight of stairs and out onto the office floor. I pushed the light switch straight away, sending the lights flickering noisily to life. No Harry.

A scratching above me made me turn back to the stairs and I followed the sound. I took the stairs two at a time, the deepening sensation of unease hot on my heels. My hand brushed something hard and cold sending it swinging away from me. I looked up. Horror filled my throat, taking my breath, my heart forgetting how to beat. For a moment I stood there, my mouth hanging open, my scream only heard by me.

"No. No. No!"

There was a voice. A strangled whisper of pain and fear.

"Shit. No. Oh. God!"

It was my voice. My voice straining into the quietness.

I raced further up the stairs to the next landing, my hands fumbling against the thick blue rope, trembling with fear, trembling with urgency. His eyes bulged out his head, his face a funny pale puce.

"No. No. Harry. Please," I whimpered.

I ran back down the stairs reaching out over the hand rail, grabbing his legs, knocking them as they swung away from my grasp before finally grabbing a handful of his trousers. I pulled them towards me, bracing my legs and with every frantic, desperate strength I had, pushed him upwards. My arms burned and my lungs strained, hysterical breaths ripping from my chest. I couldn't hold him. I couldn't lift him up. I didn't have the strength. A sob tore from my throat.

I fished into my pocket, my hand clasping my phone and swiped the green call button. Harry wobbled in my hands, a sudden surge of pain going through my shoulders and I pushed him upwards again with all my might. My thumb didn't hesitate over the last number on the device. I held the phone to my ear and listened to the burrs as it rang. And rang.

Chapter Thirty

❦ Eli ❧

My phone vibrated in my pocket and I pulled it out, glancing at the name on the screen unable to keep the grin from my face.

"Hey…."

"Eli. Help me!"

Her voice was strained, panicked. My heart stuttered, panic echoing in my own chest.

"Ava, what's wrong?"

Her voice came out garbled and hysterical but I caught the gist. I ended the call and grabbed my jacket, bolting out of the nightclub and down through the city centre. It was faster to run than to battle the City's one-way systems in the car. My arms and legs pumped and my chest burned as I sprinted towards the Quayside, ignoring the astonished looks of those I sped past.

I punched in the code Ava had given me and launched myself at the stairs until, nearly at the top, I slowed.

"Eli!" she screamed, her arms wrapped around his legs holding him up, her face red and panting, "please, help me, get him down."

My eyes scanned the situation. The man was hanging by his neck from thick blue rope, his eyes bulging and glassy. Pulling my knife from my boot I grabbed his legs, pushing Ava off him and handing her the blade. For a moment she looked at it with wide-eyed fear.

"Go up and cut the rope," I instructed calmly and she nodded back at me, racing off up the next flight of stairs.

The body swung suddenly and then for a split second became weightless. I braced myself, then pulled him back over the rail and onto the floor, my thick fingers fumbling over the well knotted rope.

"Pass the knife," I shouted for her as she thundered back down the stairs.

I took the blade from her, wiggling it carefully under the rope and giving it a nudge, the blue binding sprung free.

"Oh, God, Harry," Ava cried from beside me.

I felt for a pulse, the warmth already leaving his skin.

"Go downstairs and wait for the ambulance. I called them on my way here."

"No, no, I can't leave him!"

I started to pump his chest.

"Ava. I need you to let them in. I need to stay here and do this," I looked pointedly down at the body I was uselessly thrusting the heel of my hands against.

Ava nodded, tears streaming down her face.

I continued to pump my arms against his chest, keeping a steady rhythm and watching his skin turn a sickly grey. I had known the minute I saw him he was past the point of no return. I'd seen enough dead bodies over the years. There was a familiarity in the skin tone, the slight stiffness of his body, the coolness of his skin. He'd gone long before I'd got there. I glanced down at him as I worked, noticing the tie he'd loosened off, the shirt sleeves rolled up to his elbows, a funny shadow over one of his forearms. His shirt was missing the last few buttons at the bottom where it had come untucked from his trousers.

Heavy booted feet pounded up the stairs, the noise growing louder as they got closer. The green coat of a paramedic caught in my peripheral vision and then suddenly I was surrounded by green and yellow dressed medics, pulling equipment and drugs out of bags; the sound of zips and Velcro harsh in the air around us. The pumping of my arms never stopped, not even when I felt the brush of arms against me.

"I'll take over," a voice beside me said.

I nodded at the man and in one seamless movement I moved to the side as the paramedic took up a rhythm on his chest. Ava stood behind them, her face pale, lights from the stairwell glistening on the path of the tears that ran down her cheeks. I went to her and wrapped my arms around her, her little body crumpling into mine, vibrating with heartbroken sobs.

I wasn't sure how long the paramedics worked. It seemed like hours and then it seemed like it was seconds, all rolled into one. They talked in hushed voices, huddling together over the body and I knew then that the game was up. The pumping stopped and someone mentioned the time. I grasped Ava more tightly, as if I could protect her against the news I knew she was about to hear. A paramedic walked towards us.

"I'm sorry. We can't help him. He's died."

Her head turned to look at him, daring him to take the words back.

"No," she whispered, "no. Don't stop. He'll be OK. You just need to keep going."

Ava looked between us wildly, her eyes pleading with me to do something.

"Please," she said, more loudly.

"I'm sorry, Ms Antwill."

"Edwards," she whispered.

"Miss Edwards. There's no more we can do. He hasn't responded."

Her body trembled and I felt the strength go out of her. Then she dropped. I caught her before she hit the floor, scooping her up tighter, holding her into me, her whole frame shaking from the sobs. My t-shirt was wet from her tears and my own throat burned in reaction to her pain. A pain I had once been familiar with.

It was long into the night before she finally slept. I'd tried to feed her, gave her alcohol to numb the emotions that were torturing her, but she'd spent most the night standing at the floor to ceiling windows in my lounge looking out into the darkness. I couldn't tell what exactly was going through her mind but I could probably guess. Eventually I'd coaxed her to bed and we'd lain there in silence as I stroked her hair and held her tight.

I needed to head to Scotland in a couple of days. The Board meeting at my father's house had loomed closer all week and I'd buried the thought to the back of my mind. But now I had an even stronger desire to stay. I didn't want to leave her here by herself. I turned onto my side pulling her in against me, the movement sending Ava's floral scent spiralling between us. I sighed. I'd been one foot down the rabbit hole for weeks, I might as well jump in in one go.

Chapter Thirty One

ଞ Ava ଔ

His eyes bulged, his face turning a funny colour of purple, pink and red before fading to a sickly grey. A noise slipped from his throat, gurgling, talon-like shrivelled hands clawing for me. His mouth opening and closing, his words sounding like he was drowning, sending terror racing through my system.

"You could have saved me," Harry's voice was hoarse, "you should have been there for me, Ava."

Tears rolled down my cheeks.

"I'm so sorry," I whispered.

"Ava," he sounded like he was gargling salty water.

"Ava!"

The gentle shake of my shoulder roused me from the dream. Sucking in air, I sat bolt upright, momentarily devoid of memory for where or who I was. My eyes scrabbled around, unable to focus on anything, blurred colours mingling together, blues, greens, darker greens, purples.

"Hey, sleepy head," Eli purred, "we're just about there."

His brow was furrowed, concern and worry creating a mask on his face. I looked about, watching the Scottish countryside fly past the windows as we snaked our way along a road at the foot of a small mountain.

"Mountains," I breathed a mixture of awe and the reverberating terror of my dream.

Eli chuckled, deep and low.

"It's actually only a hill. A big one admittedly but not enough to earn its right as a mountain."

"Oh."

"Don't worry, I'll show you some mountains."

We drove through another village and then out the other side so quickly I wasn't really sure it could be called a village. Consisting of around ten houses, a pub and a little shop, it looked like someone had dropped a random street in the middle of nowhere. Fields had given way to a forest of thick, dark green trees as the car climbed higher and higher, the land turning into a purple and grey patchwork quilt, grey boulders pepper-potting the open countryside until the gentle moorland hills became rockier and more angular. Eli slowed the car coming to a complete stop for a flock of sheep leisurely crossing the road in front of us.

"Eli, stop," I complained when he pulled away from them, the last one hopping into heather and fern on the other side, "we'll have to move them. They might get run over!"

"They roam free up here," he chuckled.

"What like chickens?"

He laughed, a deep, booming belly laugh and turned his dazzling blue eyes on me.

"Yeah, I guess. Free range sheep."

The land dipped away before us the car rolling down a steep hill, before pulling off down a stony track flanked either side by huge fir trees. The road seemed to go on forever, the constant accompaniment of the thick trees making an otherwise bright day, dark and foreboding. And then we slowed to a stop in front of a pair of huge, black iron gates jutting out of a thick, aged stone wall.

"We're here," Eli said quietly, a note of anxiety in his voice.

Sighing, he leant out of the window and punched a code into a black box. The gates immediately whirred to life, swinging inwards in a slow, graceful movement. We travelled down the drive in anxious silence. That was if it could be legitimately called a drive; it was at least a mile long, open fields running off each side. Eventually a fence broke up the land changing it from rolling grazing land to well-tended lawns and carefully sculpted bushes before turning to a fine gravel in front of a huge, 18th century manor house.

"Wow," I breathed, "this is huge. And beautiful."

We walked up the huge stone steps, my hand in Eli's, his big palm wrapped tightly round mine, our fingers interlaced. A housekeeper opened the door and after a brief second his polite smile spread into a huge grin. Eli's grip softened.

"Mr Antwill, Sir. So great to see you," he said in a rich Scottish accent approaching with an outstretched hand but Eli pulled him into a bear-hug instead.

"Callum, this is, Ava."

"Lovely to meet you, Miss Ava," then turning back to Eli he continued, "please, follow me. Your brothers are in the drawing room."

Eli blew out a big sigh, tension back in the hand he wrapped around mine, the muscle in his jaw twitching. We stepped into a huge hallway and I looked around in astonishment. An elaborate chandelier hung from a high ceiling covered in gold-gilded coving. A staircase commandeered the centre, splitting in two part way up, the separated stairwells leading off in different directions. We passed a number of sturdy oak doors, following the housekeeper until he stopped in front of a set of double doors.

The doors swung inwards revealing the room the size of a small pub, three huge windows, framed with heavy, velvet drapes, looking out over the pristine lawns and a lot of unfamiliar faces. Heads turned in our direction, eyes trained on the pair of us and it was my turn to squeeze Eli's hand uncomfortably.

"This is Ava," Eli introduced me breaking the uncomfortable silence, "Ava, Thomas and Timothy, my brothers."

I recognised them from my earlier research on Antwill Industries Limited but in the flesh, they were both taller than I expected. Yet Eli dwarfed them. Eli's eyes were dark with emotions I couldn't determine, like when a river collides with the sea, two forces struggling. His jaw was clenched and I could see the tightness in the ligaments of his neck.

"So, you've graced us with your presence at long last, little brother," Thomas' tone was patronising, almost dismissive, "and you've brought your *secretary* with you?"

Eli's jaw tightened and a slight flush of red crept up his neck.

"Ava is a consultant. And she's not here for business."

Thomas looked me up and down slowly, making sure I could see his disapproval. When his eyes met mine, I held his gaze defiantly.

"Ah, from Fairbrother Williams?" he didn't wait for any sort of answer, "what do you think of my brother's strip club?" he asked and I didn't miss the barbs.

"It's very profitable and well-managed. It has a good future. Sex will always sell in one form or another," I shrugged holding his stare, pretending to both of us the strip club didn't bother me.

Thomas shook his head.

"Father told you to sell that place," he turned back to Eli, his voice losing the professional tone it had earlier, "why can't you just do as you're told for once Elijah? Why are you always trying to drag our name and reputation through the shit?"

Eli didn't respond. For once he looked beaten, the stubbornness fading from his face, replaced with a look a lot like hurt. Timothy patted him on the shoulder.

"Come on. Let's get this over and done with," he said to him more softly.

A sudden commotion at the doorway drew my attention as two women blustered in.

"Elijah!" a slim blonde shouted from just inside the doorway and quickly made her way over to us, her arms outstretched and wrapped them around him. Eli hugged her back, almost picking her up off her feet.

"So great to see you Soph," he said to her and then she turned to me. Her eyes, green like mine, scanning over me, an amused smile on her face.

"This is Ava."

"And Ava is?" she asked looking at Eli to me and back to him again and his lips drew into a broad smile.

"Sophie, Ava is my friend."

"Uh huh?" she said looking between me and Eli with a wide smile, "It's so great to meet you *friend* of Eli," she said ignoring my outstretched hand enveloping me in an enthusiastic hug.

A quiet snort from behind me caught my attention. The other woman was cooler, stunning. Tall and slender, her long dark hair fell in thick waves contrasting against a cream dress and seriously high stilettos making her slim toned legs look seriously long. A model I wondered? She certainly had a catwalk-like air to her, her hips swaying from side-to-side, one foot in front of the other as she made her way towards us.

"Long time no see, Elijah," the woman said, her voice sharp, as if scolding a teenager, "I'm pleased you bothered to make a Board meeting at last."

Eli didn't bite, "lovely to see you too, Felicity."

"Well, now that you are here, Elijah, perhaps we ought to make a start?" Thomas suggested gruffly.

Eli nodded, his faced now steeled, ready for confrontation. Sophie turned to me.

"Come, I'll give you the grand tour, while the boys are talking."

The tour indeed was grand both because of this majestic house and how long it took to get around it. There was room after room on the ground floor. I think I counted four living rooms and then a games room which contained a full-size bar with the biggest whisky collection I had ever seen, and working for Eli I had seen a few by now. The kitchen was the size of one found in a restaurant and had actual chefs working in there, the smell of sautéed onions and garlic making my stomach growl and my mouth water.

A baby cried from right beside me and I glanced around not sure where the sound had come from? Sophie grinned and patted the side of her trousers.

"Baby monitor. The milk bar is on speed-dial unfortunately. Hey, grab a seat in the drawing room and I'll be back in a few minutes, I'll get Callum to bring coffee."

I wandered back into the luxurious room looking at the pictures on the walls and the framed photographs displayed on the tops of the tables. There were many faces, some that I recognised and other's that I didn't. One family photo drew my attention. Alan Antwill stood with a much younger looking lady who wrapped an arm adoringly round him. There was Thomas and his wife, Felicity and two small boys standing in front of them and then Timothy and his wife, Sophie. On the end was Eli, his hair shorter, a five-o'clock shadow covering his face, his strong square jaw much more visible without his beard. His eyes radiated their bright blue, wide and alive. He draped an arm around a slim, tall figure of a woman beside him. Her hair was dark and thick, as dark as Eli's. She was stunning and he was happy. The happiest I had ever seen him.

I picked the photograph up holding it closer, scrutinising it. It was an older picture. The boys in the picture I knew were teenagers now, so it had to have been quite some years ago.

"That was Ally, she was Eli's fiancé," a soft voice from behind me made me jump and I

242

instinctively replaced the picture, feeling guilty for intruding on this family's privacy, Eli's privacy. At the same time a stab of jealousy invaded my thoughts. He'd been engaged? He'd chosen that stunning woman for his wife.

"She was one of very few that Eli ever brought home to meet us," she continued, "you being one of them."

"I, I'm just his consultant."

"Uh huh, sure that's all you are."

She winked at me.

"What happened to them?" I asked, a mix of deflection and the burn of curiosity.

"Ally died."

"Oh. I'm so sorry. I just assumed…."

"That they had split up?" Sophie finished for me, "that would have been kinder for Eli. It was horrible for him, changed him, not for the better. He lost his spark the day Ally died and he never got it back. Not until now. Now I can see that spark is back."

I looked at her and she continued.

"I can see the way he looks at you. Like he wants to devour you and protect you all at once. His eyes have that twinkle. One that I thought I would never see again. I want him to be happy, so whatever this is, consultant, friends, lovers, I'm happy for both of you."

"Surely he must have had other relationships since then?"

243

"It was nine years ago. He's had relationships since, if that's what you can call them, but none have lasted long. You're clearly special to him. It doesn't take a genius to see that, even though I am one."

Sophie winked at me, a broad smile on her face and I couldn't help but like her.

Chapter Thirty Two

ೞ Eli ೞ

When the meeting was finished, I was desperate to find Ava and get out of there. I hated the family Board meetings. I hated looking at the man I called my father and seeing the disdain and disappointment on his face. I'd brought up the idea of purchasing Cameron's gym, more to piss him off, than obtain agreement from them all. I would do it anyway regardless of what they thought.

I knew he would hate the gym idea. It was another thing he despised about me, all the muscles reminding him that I'm a trained killer not a gentleman. They all hated the idea that I've squeezed the life out of someone, beaten the last breath from someone with my bare hands. If only they really knew the monster that I once became, that still now hides within me, deep in the shadows.

A child's laughter rang from the lounge and I moved towards the room stopping and leaning quietly against the doorframe. Ava was playing with the little girl, whilst Sophie sat across from them on the couch feeding the baby and watching her three-year-old daughter giggle in delight. The baby was three months old now and I'd travelled up to Scotland to meet him the day after he was born but hadn't been back since.

Sophie had been like a sister, my childhood friend, the only one who truly knew me, back then at least. We'd drifted apart after my mother died. Another set of memories better buried, better forgotten.

I gave my head a shake. My brain was going to mush in this place. Sophie glanced up at me, the babe still attached to her breast.

"Hey, Elijah. Ava's just distracting Lilly while I get this one fed."

Ava smiled at me but made no effort to stand up and continued with her game.

"No worries, I know where I stand in this pecking order."

It was mid-afternoon by the time I was finally able to steal Ava away and make it out of the house. We'd stayed for lunch with my family, an affair I normally did my best to avoid. I'd actually enjoyed it, on the most part. Ava had fit in well and even Thomas shared some conversation with her. Sophie and Ava had clearly hit it off. My father and his wife, Serena, who was nineteen years his junior, had joined in with lunch and for a short while we felt like a normal, almost happy family. It had been nine years ago since I'd sat with my family, the emotional wounds from my childhood feeling like they may finally close. That was until, barely a year later, they had been ripped wide open. I wasn't going to dwell on that past, not now it felt that I could actually look to the future, however much that scared me.

The drive into the city, negotiating the one-way systems, was relatively straight forward, hitting it just before the rush hour traffic started, which was always earlier on a Friday. I pulled up outside of our hotel and we were met by an enthusiastic valet and bellboy. As our bags were wheeled off, I studied Ava for a second as she gazed up at the huge building positioned in the centre of Edinburgh. I couldn't dismiss her fascination with her surroundings, her eyes as wide as saucers every few seconds at every new thing she had come across.

The huge imposing Victorian hotel was impressive. It occupied a valuable vantage point watching over the City, looking out over the railway, the Prince's Street Gardens and the castle in the distance. After we were checked in, we were led up to the suite I had booked for us, the best one in the building. There were two bedrooms, a huge lounge and a separate dining room. The decoration was opulent and lavish, no detail had gone unnoticed; no luxury has been missed.

"Wow, Eli. This is amazing," Ava swooned over the rooms, dashing from one part of the suite to the other, eyes wide in fascination.

Then in the main bedroom I heard her let out a whistle. Following the high-pitched sound, I found her gazing out of a gigantic window. I walked up behind her wrapping my arms around her, pulling her small body to fit perfectly into mine as we stood for a few moments in silence our eyes trailing over the view of the Castle, stood proud on its jagged rock. This, here and now, my arms around the petite but fiery red-head, this was true ecstasy. For a while we stood like this, quiet in each other's presence, Ava's scent of fresh-cut flowers mixed with warm spice and jasmine entangled my senses.

I sighed, reluctantly pulling away from her.

"I'm just going to the gym for a couple of hours," I spoke into the soft curve of where her neck met her shoulder.

*****

I drove through the busy City streets towards the docks. It had come alive with swarms of people, colourful clothes and bare skin everywhere I looked as the night was closing in bringing a dull greyness with it. Swanky wine bars and restaurants lined the streets, offering fancy food, exciting cocktails and top shelf Gin. Behind all the new splendour the old docks stood, half forgotten by the modernisation of the streets, tucked away behind the bright signs and velvet layered interiors.

I left my car in a busy road a few streets away. The brightly lit streets and clean grey stone withered away, the buildings I approached becoming more neglected, darkened from years of dirt and vehicle exhausts. Cutting down a tight alleyway, I angled my shoulders sideways, my clothes still catching against the rough brick of the tenement style buildings on either side, the smell of salt and seaweed, growing stronger. The ground under my feet was wet and slimy where rain had spilled from botched roof and gutter repairs over the years, a squidgy moss in places cushioning the sound of my trainers as I crept to the south side. Taking a sharp left at what had first looked like a dead end, I skirted round the huge wall which kept the modern lives of revellers and restauranteurs from the graft of the import and export traffic.

Eventually the wall, part of which had crumbled away from lack of maintenance, was replaced with a chain link fence about twenty foot high, metal prongs at the top twisting violently in all directions, threatening to sever the limbs of anyone who dared try and scale the outer fence. I stalked closer until the fence met another building, partially dilapidated and now only really serving as a boundary to the docks. Bushes poked through brickwork driving cracks into the structure, and the holes that were once windows had been boarded up leaving little in the way of entry points.

I glanced up at the building looking for any clue as to where I could breach it, my eyes settling on a boarded window pane three storeys up, the corner soft and wet and coming away from the edge. I tugged on the old lead lined drain pipe, assessing whether it would likely hold my weight. It creaked, moving slightly under the force of my arms but stayed reasonably steady. Gripping the drain pipe with my one hand I pushed the fingers of my other into the link fence, keeping my weight spread across the two structures slowly scaling the wall till I was just above the windowsill. The damp wooden board flapped loosely in the breeze. It ripped off easily and I swung myself onto the lintel then through the gap.

Balancing carefully inside the ledge I switched on the torch from my phone, skimming the void with the light until I was happy there was actually some flooring that would take my bulk and not drop me nearly thirty foot and shatter my legs. The nudge I gave the floorboards confirmed there were no soft patches and carefully, step by step, testing each footing before committing my weight to it, I crept forward.

There were windows at the other side as I crossed two deserted rooms. Dust had taken to the air, I could taste the dry, musty particles as I crept the full length of the building, using the torch from my phone to check for any gaping holes I might fall through. The torch light was suddenly swallowed in blackness and I stopped quickly checking my surroundings. I slid my foot closer, floorboards creaking menacingly, until the sturdy wood softened to sponginess. The torchlight lit up the area in front of me now revealing a huge space of nothing. The floor had completely rotted away leaving a twelve-foot hole, only beams were left.

There was no way round it. I pocketed my phone and dropped to my stomach, lowering my weight down on to it carefully as I checked the chances of it staying up. The beam was good and solid. Carefully and precisely, I inched myself across, sliding my stomach across the wooden bar, feeling my way in the in the dark. Reaching forward my hands detected a change, the beam ended and a rough floorboard, strong under my fingertips, began. Cautiously, I drew my phone from my pocket, my movements slow but sure. If

I dropped it, I'd have to manoeuvre out of here almost totally blind.

Sharp, white light lit up the space, thick strong floorboards forming a metre of platform in front of me. I shuffled cautiously, pulling myself onto the floor on my stomach and rolling onto my side then to my feet, listening for any tell-tale signs that part, or all of the platform might give way under me. The window on this side was a completely empty hole, just rotting wood in the frame remaining. I looked down on the yard below, quiet in the late evening.

The atmosphere had a sharp coldness about it this side of the building, the smell of fish, seaweed and salt hanging heavy in the air. The dock-side was deserted and no one was wandering in the yard below me, not even a security guard. There were cameras secured high on the walls but their placement created useful blind-spots. The shipping containers in the yard below had been unloaded from the ships and awaited pick-up by haulage companies. I needed to get closer. There was a small window of opportunity before the containers were moved on, but getting down into the yard wasn't going to be that easy.

Half a drain pipe and a thirty-foot drop was the only way I was getting into that yard. I edged out the window, catching the metal pipe in one hand and moving slowly across till the tube took my weight. I scaled down the outside of the building as far as the short length of piping would allow and then clinging on right to the very bottom, I let myself drop, tucking my knees underneath me as I hit the ground and rolling on to my side.

The ground hit me hard, my shoulder striking the concrete more heavily than I had hoped, a sear of hot pain shooting through my shoulder-blade and up my neck. I bit into my lip, holding my breath, pushing the sensation of pain away. Then I was off, up on light feet, tugging the dark hood over my head and leaping into the shadows.

Keeping my back flush against the wall, I followed the building to the chain link fence, careful to stay in the camera's blind spot until right at the last minute, then I took a punt the person in the control room wouldn't be checking the cameras that closely and wouldn't notice the dark shape running across the yard. Once I reached the container the rest was quite simple.

The doors were facing away from the camera and so I was sheltered behind them. They'd already been opened for inspection of the goods when they had arrived and had not been properly secured. It wasn't unusual. The docks had a cheap tariff for imports people wanted to keep under wraps so security hadn't seen much investment. Metal screeched, ringing out in the silence of the dock-side as I wrenched the heavy doors open just enough to squeeze inside.

The torchlight from my phone lit up the container as I shined it around expecting to see boxes and crates of imports but instead cars stared back at me. There were four of them, two stacked atop each other. They were either rare or just very fucking expensive. The Maserati at the back, hovering over a vintage Aston Martin, was top of the range. They were all worth a fortune in their own right so it made no sense to send them in via a cheap dock that lacked even the basic security of a dog.

Shining the torch round I looked for anything else in the container, peering through the windows of the cars but they looked like expensive cars should look. Moving to the next container I found exactly the same thing, more cars. Frustrated and angry I closed the containers, denying the urge to slam the doors shut in anger. There was nothing here. Nothing that would tie Ritchie to running guns. Not even anything to do with drugs. Just cars, and shipping these in wasn't illegal. Fuck!

Chapter Thirty Three

❧ Ava ☙

I stared out into the night for a long time, watching the lights from the traffic stream through the centre of the city, spots of red and white tapering off into streams of illumination. The streets were alive with colour, orange, green, blue, pink; the soft lighting of the shops giving way to the bright neon lights of bars and restaurants. I moved from room to room, each view different, twinkling lights varying in colour and intensity, but the view from the bedroom was the most stunning. I watched out over the train station below, with its explosion of activity contrasting against the calm of the soft, amber glow, illuminating the walls of the Castle in the distance, sitting proud atop its jagged rock.

Eventually, I pulled the heavy curtains across the windows shutting myself away from the vibrancy of the city. The suite was huge. The walls carefully painted, ornate coving adorning one side and surrounding an equally grand fire place. There were two bedrooms and a separate dining room; a place fit for a movie star or millionaire. Or Eli.

I could have stayed in the suite for days on end, taking in the views over the city, reading books from the floor to ceiling bookcase. It would have taken days before even the hint of boredom crept in. But something else had start to seep in, creeping into my core, my stomach becoming heavier with the infiltration of dread. My life had come crashing down around me once before, ripping me apart and I still hadn't found all the pieces to put myself fully back together. I couldn't allow the cosy, warm thoughts of relationships to come back. I couldn't get complacent that my life wasn't one big, huge struggle. I couldn't stop looking for the next threat, the next thing that would derail me and try to break me. My stomach felt heavy.

Sending a quick text to Eli that he could find me at the hotel pool, I took the spare key card and ventured off to find it. The pool was empty when I got there and a light instrumental music played in the background. Loungers were neatly arranged around the side, potted palm trees standing in each corner, a warm humidity making me wonder whether this was what it was like to be in a foreign country. All it needed was a swim-up bar and it would look like something out of the holiday brochures I used to read, pretending I was basking on the beach instead of covered in multiple layers of clothes and blankets because my mother had spent the electric money on vodka.

I slipped into the soft caress of the water as it lapped gently against my skin and I became weightless, the water washing away my scars, at least momentarily. The music rang gently in my ears, muddling with the swoosh of the tiny waves I created as I lay on my back, gliding through its gentle viscosity.

After much meaningless splashing, paddling and floating I turned onto my front, dipping my face in the water and pushed my way through the slow lap of the waves in the pool. Each time my fingers touched the sides I counted; one, two, three. The lengths were coming quicker and quicker, my arms cutting through the water as my legs propelled me forwards. By the time I'd swam thirty lengths of the pool my heart pounded against my chest and I struggled to breathe. The poolside was beautifully cool as I pressed my face against it, my cheeks hot. A gentle splash broke my thoughts, water rolling against me as the tide-less pool picked up its own current.

A body pressed against mine, hard, strong, trapping me against the rough side of the pool the scratch of the beard against my neck sending a swarm of heat to my stomach.

"Thought you were at the gym?"

"Been, done it, so thought I would join you."

Eli's erection pressed into my back, his hands running over my stomach, leaving a trail of hot tingles that the water couldn't dilute as his fingers moved over my chest. My nipples reacted to his touch, hardening to peaks, burning and tingling as his hands slipped under my bikini.

"Eli, someone might see!" I gasped.

"There's no one here, Princess," he murmured, his lips sucking gently on my skin.

I moaned, closing my eyes to savour the feel. Eli pulled his lips away and spun me round, his eyes growing dark, a fiery intenseness dancing in the sea blue orbs, coaxing me in to dangerous depths. Then he crushed his lips into me, his kiss urgent and demanding, forcing his tongue through the little gap I created for him. I kissed him back with the same hungry ferocity, my stomach on fire, flames licking at my groin, a pulse throbbing between my legs.

"I think we need to go," my words tangled against our lips.

Eli shook his head, his fingers sliding the bottoms of my bikini to one side, dipping into me, pushing my pussy apart, then retreating; exchanging places with the heavy head of his cock. He pushed against me, forcing me open, my body already surrendering to him as he pulled my legs around his waist. The pressure at my entrance burned as he stretched me, stoking the fire already ablaze, heat pulsing to every part of my body as he slid the head in. Then with a rough thrust he impaled me, a cry bursting from my lips, Eli growling, as his hips pistoned against me, my back banging against the side of the pool, each movement sending a cocktail of pain and pleasure rushing through me.

He growled and grunted with each thrust, quick and hard and I bit into his neck trying to keep my screams muffled against his skin. But every bite of his neck, sent him wild. The tranquil pool around us had turned to crashing waves, a stormy current in the water, turbulent, savage. And just as I couldn't take anymore, just as my insides spasmed and my pussy clenched, and I pushed my head into Eli's neck to prevent the screams from echoing around the swimming pool he rammed every last bit of him inside me, forcing me deeper into the poolside and oblivion.

As our breathing slowed down and the thunderous pace of our hearts returned to a more sophisticated beat, my eyes refocused, noticing the quizzical looks of the old couple, laying their belongings on the loungers on the other side of the pool.

"Eli, how long have they been there?" I whispered, my cheeks glowing hot and red.

Glancing over his shoulder and then back at me, Eli grinned cheekily, sliding himself out of me as I dipped my shoulders under the water reinstating my bikini.

"Dunno. But I'm guessing they may have enjoyed the show."

"Oh, god," I squirmed, not daring to look in their direction

*****

"I'm not really a whisky drinker," I complained, holding the thick, glass tumbler under my nose and giving it a suspicious sniff.

I was stuffed full of the meal we had just eaten at the hotel's restaurant and now, tucked away in a quiet corner of the bar, the alcove lit by candlelight, I was feeling all sorts of cosy.

"You swallowed it all down well the other night," Eli winked at me, a grin illuminating his face and I ignored the flush that ran across my skin.

"That was shock and necessity, Eli," I countered, trying to distract myself with a sip of the harsh liquid.

By the time I finished the glass Eli had slugged back three further glasses of the grotesque drink. I was sure there was something slightly sadistic about his choice of the top shelf whisky as he continually sent the slightly over-weight barman clambering up and down, struggling to reach the premium bottles out of most peoples' reach physically and financially.

"It was nice to meet your family, today," I said after taking the sip of the much easier to drink gin cocktail that I'd negotiated out of the barman from the whisky-only bar, "why do you dislike your father so much?"

Eli drew quiet and at first, I wasn't sure he would answer. For a while he sat searching in the bottom of the whisky glass, swirling the heavy bottomed tumbler in his big palm.

"My mother died when I was 15. I was her last baby. Maybe that was why she spent hours with me, reading to me, teaching me. It annoyed my father. He despised me for taking my mother's attention. I'd hear them argue for hours. Him telling my mother that she was making me 'soft'.

"He wanted disciplined sons, those that would follow in his footsteps, warriors in negotiations, crusaders in business.

"My mother became ill when I was twelve-years old. She fought the cancer for years but then suddenly her health deteriorated. In that last year of her life, when she was undergoing the most gruelling of treatments, in and out of hospital, he was fucking another woman.

"When she found out she just gave up. He killed her; she died because of him."

Eli's gaze sank into his whisky again, his jaw tense. He didn't look up.

"Since then, I've done everything I can to punish him, embarrass him, soil the Antwill name. I joined the Army. He was furious and I fucking loved it. I gave him the warrior he'd always wanted, just not in the Board room. Seeing the look on his face when I told him I'd enlisted was the first time I'd smiled in years.

"I didn't stop there. I specialised, carried out missions more dangerous and dark than many would ever encounter. I was not only a warrior but now I was a killer too. And he liked that even less. I quite literally have blood on my hands. When I eventually left, he thought it was the end of the embarrassment I would cause him, but I bought the bars and clubs with the company money and now the Antwill name is associated with a strip club. It was fucking brilliance."

His tone was so bitter, pain and hate like a barb on his tongue and when he turned to look at me, I could see the same storm playing out in his eyes. His thick eyebrows were drawn together, rage contorting his beautiful features and for a moment he seemed lost in the darkness. He sighed, the clouds suddenly dissipating from his eyes and reached up towards me and pulling me to him. The kiss was more gentle, raw, emotional, but it ignited the same reaction in me. Dominant, angry, sad, vulnerable; it didn't matter, my body, and my heart, they all screamed for him regardless.

*****

I wasn't sure what time it was but I knew it wasn't morning. Not even a sliver of light spilled through the curtains and the suite was cold. But it was the sound of Eli's voice that woke me not the chill that had crept in around us during the night.

"No! No, Ally. Come on I've got you. Come on, baby, I'm here now."

His voice was laced in terror, fear radiating from him. My stomach lurched, my own panic rising, my own body tense. I placed my hand on his chest, my palm sliding in the warm wetness of his sweat.

"Stay with me, Ally! Please baby, don't leave me."

His voice cracked, his arms flailed as he thrashed about the bed. Ducking under a flying arm waving like a bough of a tree in a storm, I leaned over shaking him with a careful urgency.

"Eli! Eli, wake up!"

His eyes sprang open staring wildly then he threw me, rolling over on top of me, pinning me to the bed.

"Wh, what are you doing?" I trembled, his fingers gripping my arms painfully, his eyes full of fury, of hate, tortured.

Blinking, he looked at me, this time really seeing me, before rolling over and sitting on the edge of the bed, wiping his hands over his face. I crawled up behind him, not certain whether to touch him or just wait

"Are you OK?" I asked, worried he would erupt again.

But he didn't. Instead, he took my other hand pulling it to his mouth and kissing it gently.

"I'm sorry," he whispered against my hand, "it was just a nightmare."

I slid off the bed and positioned myself in front of him between his legs. Gently, I cupped his face tilting it to look up at me, his bright blue eyes glinting at me like polished crystal. They glistened more than I had seen before and, in that instant, this giant mass of man and muscle was very simply human.

"What happened to Ally?" I asked, my eyes holding his.

"Sophie?"

I nodded. Eli sighed. For a few moments we stayed like that, staring into each other's eyes as if we were both searching for something deep in the other's soul.

"Tell me about Ally, Eli," I whispered.

Chapter Thirty Four

‍‍஋ Eli ‍ை

Nine years ago

When we made it back to the base the mood was odd. The insurgents we had captured were bagged and tagged and placed in cells awaiting interrogation. I was tired and starving. Thirty-six hours lying in a ditch did that to you. I needed a beer and a good dinner followed by sleep. But the air felt electrified with a feeling of dread and gloom that you could almost taste. We had been off site for weeks gathering intelligence and planning the extraction but something had changed by the time we returned.

"We have a hostage situation," Major Williams stated, not bothering with an official debrief, "one of our units were out patrolling five days ago and were ambushed. The majority escaped but one of the vehicles was hit by a missile. Two have been killed and the other four have been taken."

"Do we know whether they're still alive?" Captain Daniels and my best friend asked.

"Yes, we think so. We have a grainy film of them all, but negotiations are failing and we need to get them out. We've already got a team on reconnaissance but we need Alpha and Beta Team to lead on it."

The Major left Seb and I with a folder of intelligence and we settled down for a few hours to pour over it and make a plan.

"Fuck, I really wanted that beer," I grumbled turning over photographs of the area, concentrating on the landscape.

The hostages were being held in one of the towns, surrounded by Taliban fighters and natives who hated us anyway. We'd be peppered with bullets just trying to breach the walls so a daylight extraction was off the table.

Seb studied the map of the town, surveying the access points, finding its weakness. Aerial photographs with heat seeking apparatus suggested they were right in the middle, heavily guarded. It wouldn't be a straight forward extraction. With the logistics worked out I slid an unopened enveloped towards me, popping it open easily, the gum dry and cracking in the heat, and slid out the pictures of our hostages.

I made a mental note of each one, their facial features, any distinguishing marks, memorising everything I could about them so that in the frenzied few seconds of mayhem when we breached their prison, we could identify them easily.

I slid the last picture out, my eyes combing over the long dark hair, the familiar smile, the

264

faint scar on her eyebrow. I couldn't swallow, I couldn't breathe, I couldn't think and I couldn't put the picture down. I stood there clutching it between my fingers, my hand shaking.

Seb slid around behind me.

"Shit!" I heard him say, as if he were on the other side of the room, not looking directly over my shoulder.

Ally stared back at me, her eyes burning into mine, searing onto my brain. My stomach cartwheeled.

"We'll get her back, Eli. I promise."

We were ready the next night for the extraction and I could almost taste my heart it was that far into my throat. I'd checked and re-checked my weapons and we'd gone over and over the plan and all the contingencies. I'd clock watched all day, desperate for the hours to tick by so we could get this mission over and done with. But with every second the danger to Ally increased.

The town was sleeping, wavering orange glowing in houses and black shadows moved in dimly lit streets. Fear gnawed at me, nibbling at my insides, sending my heart racing and adrenaline bounding round my system. I needed to focus on the bubbling excitement, the fear pulsing through my veins, harness it and not ignore it. Without fear you were reckless, and if you were reckless people died.

We crept through the streets, suspense and tension radiating from the full team as we moved through the darkness kicking up a dusty haze with each shuffle of a thick soled boot. A shout broke out above us and we simultaneously dropped to a crouch. Tucked in the shadows we waited, and listened. The shouts multiplied, a cacophony of deep vices booming in the night, announcing our arrival. My heart beat against my chest so hard I thought the whole town could hear it.

The first shot rang out, stark against the gentle quietness of the night, sending us reaching for our triggers and within seconds we were returning fire. A rough, carnal survival instinct kicked in and without any communication the team moved to contingency one breaking up into smaller groups. Cameron, Joey and the Viking and a couple of others peeled off with me as Seb and Cian took off with the remainder to draw the enemy fire.

Fear and adrenaline raced through my veins, each step driving us towards our targets, closer to Ally. Then poised outside the building where they were held, we hunkered down, assessing the threat. The area was clear apart from the shapes we could see moving inside. The gunfire fight at the far end of town had done its job and pulled some of the enemy away leaving us a bit more breathing space.

I signalled behind me, readied my gun and kicked in the door, wood splintering loudly as it sprung from its frame. The flash bang I threw in front of me exploded, bright light searing across the space on the inside, the shouts of men's voices drowned by the sudden commotion. My heart hammered in my ears as we raced through the building clearing each room with a double-tap for each hostile until we came to a corridor of locked doors.

Systematically we filled each door with a small amount of explosive, popping them open and piling in with our guns raised. Bedraggled figures were tied to chairs, tired red eyes gazing at us with hope and relief. We patted them down checking for any bomb or booby trap before freeing them and sandwiching then in between us as we cleared each of the cells.

By the last door we had them all but Ally. My heart raced and I was sure the resonance from its rapid beat would make it explode through my chest at any second.

"Come on," I growled in frustration at Cameron, pressuring him to get the door open.

And then, with a small explosion the heavy door imploded. It seemed to take forever for the smoke to clear and my eyes to adjust, the blurred body coming into focus, slumped in the seat, only the binds holding her in place.

I raced towards her and lifted her head. Her hair was loose around her face and caked in dried blood, a sickly metallic smell lingering in the air. Ally was barely conscious. Cutting the ropes that held her she fell forward into my arms and I cradled her, pushing the bloodied tats of hair out of her face. Her eyes found mine and a smile twitched at her lips. That was my Ally. My gaze wandered over her and my stomach lurched, bile rising in my throat.

She was covered in gashes. Stale blood had created a gooey, sticky mess underneath fresh, wet claret. There was a deep cut to her leg and as I got closer the smell hit me hard, and I tried desperately to hide the gag from her. I stooped, pulling her into my arms, cradling her against my chest feeling her ragged breaths and the rattle of her lungs. Tears, hot and angry pricked at the back of my eyes.

"We need to get out of here," I growled at Cameron.

"Sure, Eli. I've radioed in. We need more cover to get to the RV point."

I glanced around the darkness of the cells, listening to gunfire not too far from us.

"We don't have time. We need to get everyone out of here. Ally needs a medic now."

"We can't cover this many of us," Cameron complained but I was shaking my head.

"There's no time. She won't make it," I said quietly to Cameron.

I started to retreat through the building, giving orders to round up our freed hostages, arming everyone who was conscious.

"I'm sorry," I whispered into Ally's ear before hoisting her over my shoulder, "let's get out of here."

We ran through the night, skirting along walls and keeping to the shadows. It didn't take long to reach our inception point and carefully we hoisted Ally over the city walls and out into the darkness the other side. By now Seb had pulled the rest of the team back and were already over the other side, helping to lower hostages to the ground.

We ran until we were outside of firing range and then we finally slowed, dropping into the cover of a ditch. I set Ally down, staring into her pale face, the rasping breaths from her chest were nothing but gurgles. She grabbed my hand and forced a smile as Cian, the team's medic got to work dressing wounds and treating her as best he could.

"You found me, Eli," she whispered.

"You're going to be OK," I whispered back, brushing her lips with mine in a gentle kiss, half scared that I'd cause her more pain if I touched her any harder. Her smile was faint.

"I love you, Eli," she whispered.

"I love you too."

Then suddenly the rattling slowed and her breaths became shallower.

"Medic!" I shouted, fear lacing my voice, "come on, Ally. Just hold on a little longer."

Cian rushed over and just as he got there Ally arched her back in agony before her body broke out in convulsions and her eyes rolled to the back of her head.

"Shit! Ally! Come on, stay with me!" I shouted as Cian got to work pumping her chest.

I watched helplessly as he worked hard, forcing her heart to beat, forcing her not to give up. But eventually he stared up at me with pitiful eyes.

I didn't cry or shout. I didn't, couldn't, do anything. I just stared in disbelief, in shock, in denial. Her body had gone limp in my arms, her skin cooling against my fingers. She looked like she was sleeping, the pain and anguish had gone from her face. I couldn't bring myself to close her eyes. I stared into them hoping she could still see me, that she would change her mind and come back. I couldn't bring myself to cover the glassy orbs that looked up into a cloudless sky, because if I did, she was gone forever.

*****

Ava cupped my face, tilting it back so she could look into my eyes and for a moment I was scared to look at her.

"Your necklace," Ava said, touching the round tags that were threaded through the thin plaited leather.

I nodded understanding what she was about to ask.

"Ally's dog tags."

"I'm so sorry that you lost her," Ava whispered, her eyes glistening with tears. "And I'm so pleased you trusted me with her story," she continued.

I pulled her into me burying my face into her chest and we stood there; the sound of her breath, calm and gentle, almost as tranquil as the sound of waves lapping the shore, dulling the pain inside me. Tears rolled down my face, dropping onto the warm skin of her chest and she kneeled quietly in front of me as I poured my grief into her heart, sob after sob.

Eventually we settled back down to catch the last waves of sleep and for the first time since Ally died, I felt at peace.

Chapter Thirty Five

❦ Ava ❧

"I think this is the biggest lake I've ever seen," I commented excitedly, admiring the huge expanse of water.

Eli chuckled beside me and I turned towards him scowling.

"What's so funny?"

"We're in Scotland. This is a Loch, City girl."

I pulled a face in response and he squeezed my thigh before turning off the road. We'd driven three hours North West from Edinburgh. The Scottish countryside had sharpened, swallowing us into a mass of wilderness and mountains, of purple heather and lush green fern, of rock and shale, of jagged peaks coated in snow.

The huge castle now loomed up from the valley floor, sprawling out over well-kept grounds, imposing and beautiful. A doorman took our bags as we checked in before being led to our room tucked away in one of the castle's turrets. The walls were bare stone, warmed by the orange glow of ornate wall lights and the huge cast iron chandelier hanging from the ceiling. A fire was burning away in the hearth at the far side, the crackle and smell giving the room a rustic feel. The semi-circle of the turret was lined with huge windows allowing a panoramic view out over the Loch.

I stood in front of the padded window seat which followed all the way round the curve of the turret, looking out over the water to the snow-capped mountains beyond. Eli stood behind me, wrapping his big arms around me and gently rested his chin on the top of my head. Then he turned away, rummaging in his bag and tossing me a bundle of clothes. I opened them out, staring at the grey material and then looking back at Eli.

"Put them on, we're going for a walk."

"What in just these?" I asked staring back at the bland long sleeved top and leggings.

He snorted, his eyes creasing at the sides in amusement.

"They're long johns. They go *under* your clothes."

I stared at him in silence. Eli tilted his head towards the window.

"You wanted a mountain," he shrugged.

"Are these really necessary?" I asked after I had pulled them on, "I look like I'm wearing my Granny's pyjamas!"

"You rock the Granny night time look," he answered, slapping my backside hard enough that I yelped.

He shot me a cheeky smile.

273

"You will need all of that. It's cold out there," he said, handing me a well-packed backpack that he had brought up from the car.

A knock on our room door stopped me rifling through the bag. Eli returned, thrusting me two parcels wrapped in tin foil whilst packing flasks into his bag.

"Sandwiches," he grunted when I gave him the eyebrow, "pack them carefully, they taste better when they aren't flat. You ready?"

I nodded pulling the woolly hat he held out for me over my head, squashing down the super-volumised curls from the damp Scottish air. I'd not bothered to even dig my straighteners out of my bag this morning; I knew how to pick my battles.

It took nearly an hour to walk to the far side of the Loch and then a further half hour before we reached the bottom of the foot hills. I glanced behind us, watching the well walked path wind away back towards the water, the castle hotel standing proud beside it.

Soon we were clambering higher, up and over the top of the foothills, the hills beyond were steep, becoming rockier with each step. The stony path made the ascent easier but my thighs and calves were already burning from the consistent uphill climb.

The trees became sparser and shorter as we got higher and the purple hue of heather had given way to thick green, highland grasses intermingled with reeds as we stepped around bogs and placed our feet carefully over marshland. The path was

274

steeper, broken up by huge slabs of rocks which jutted out, and the air seemed thinner, colder, the bright day taking on a dull undertone.

Then after what seemed like a gruelling thirty-minute climb, my chest burning hot from the cold air rushing in through my lungs, we stopped on top of a large, flat boulder.

"Tired City girl?" Eli jibed.

"No. I don't want to miss this," my voice seemed barely a whisper, carried away on the wind that was starting to whip around us, "it's just so beautiful."

"Come on. It's much better at the top."

Eli turned and I drew another lung full of cold mountain air before summoning my heavy legs to follow. The grasses had surrendered to rocks and large stones as we climbed higher and higher until there was nothing but a path of loose flinty pebbles. I slipped suddenly, the flat stones moving underneath my feet.

"The scree is hard to walk on," he commented, casually grabbing me by the arm before I landed on my arse.

I glanced up, relief and tiredness came flooding over me, the summit just coming into view below the cloud line. With a burst of energy, I sprang onwards pushing up the steep slope of scree and passing Eli.

"How about that coffee at the top?" I flung over my shoulder and he let out a low chuckle.

Just as I arrived at the top, poised ready to prop my hands on my hips in mock conquest of the mountain I had just climbed, my celebration caught in my throat. It wasn't the top. The path flattened, meandering away far across a ridge before rising steeply up another peak. Eli joined me, wrapping an arm over my shoulders.

"What the fuck?"

A deep laugh rumbled from his chest, "false summit, Princess."

He kissed the top of my head before leading the way over the narrow path, the edges dropping away steeply either side. I swallowed, fear rising in my throat but pushed myself onwards, the safest place was within reaching distance of him. Soon the land reared up in front of us sharper than ever.

"Follow me up this rock face, Ava. Put your feet exactly where I put mine," he instructed, his tone serious.

I watched as Eli tested each foothold of the rocky outcrop before putting his weight on it and hoisting himself up. I followed, using my hands in places to pull myself up, digging my toes into the rock, testing each foot and handhold before committing. The air was getting so much colder with each step; it kissed my cheeks and nipped at my finger ends. Eli paused and I peeked around him, a wall of jagged rock, stood proud against a darkening sky.

"Where's the path gone?" I asked, my voice turning into a squeak.

"It's right here," Eli pointed at the wall of rock in front of us, "just have to climb up this bit and then we are at the top," his said with a casual shrug of broad shoulders.

"We're going to climb that bit?" I asked.

"Yep. Just do what I do."

And off he went, grabbing notches of rock and pulling himself up bit by bit. I studied the wall of rock, feeling the cold smoothness against my fingers. The rock was bumpier than it looked, crevices and ruts in the stone catching against my finger ends but as I looked around my knees buckled. It dropped away viciously on either side and all it would take was one stumble, one fluffed up hand-hold and I would drop to my death.

My heart beat hard against my chest and sweat pearled on my brow despite the cold of the mountain air. Eli was still climbing and, bit by bit, I was getting left behind. I gulped back a pang of nausea and reached up for the rocky nodule above my head. I shuffled my foot into a crevice, gave it a little bounce and then hauled myself upward. And then for a few good strides I was off, testing hand-holds and foot-holds before each effort, scaling up the rock like some sort of lizard; a really slow, frightened lizard.

I was about a foot off the top, having trained my eyes on the rock face in front of me, ignoring the pull to look anywhere else when the foothold I had just tested gave way underneath me. My chest jolted and I squealed like an injured cat. My feet floundered, scrabbling underneath me, trying to find something else to perch on and for a while they went everywhere until suddenly, I felt resistance. I stood still clinging to the rock face, my chest heaving, frightened gasps sending me light-headed. I clutched the rocky bulge of the hand-hold in my hand as panic turned my veins to stone.

"Eli, I can't move!" I shouted at him, as his face appeared over the ledge.

I didn't dare move my eyes, staring at the rock face only centimetres in front of me, my body shaking with fear, breath coming faster.

"I, I can't move," I said through gritted teeth.

"Ava, don't panic. You're OK," he purred, his voice soft and reassuring, "you just need to move your hand here," he pointed.

I shook my head.

"Eli, I can't. I can't move."

"You're OK, Princess. You're nearly there. Just take your right hand and move it up."

Fear racked through my body, a poison moving through my veins.

"Eli, I can't do this," I pleaded.

"Ava, listen to me. This is just a scramble. You are absolutely safe. Just move your hand here."

I shook my head. "I can't move, I'm going to fall," panic laced my voice and my legs started to tremble.

"Just listen to me. You're perfectly safe," Eli paused for a minute, "do you trust me, Ava?"

"Yes," I whispered.

"Then I need you to focus on my voice, on what I'm telling you to do. Take your right hand and move it to where I'm pointing."

I looked up at him, to where he gestured to and could see the firm ledge just above my head. I had to move. Panic had me frozen to the spot on the side of the mountain. I couldn't go down. I could only go up, up towards Eli. I moved my hand and felt for the bulge of the rock.

"OK, that's good. Now run your right toe up the rock face in front of you till you feel a notch. Good. Now your left hand to here."

I followed Eli's instructions, focussing on his voice till I felt his hand clasp around my forearms and he hoisted me up and over the top of the rock ledge.

Chapter Thirty Six

৯০ Eli ଓ

Ava's breathing came in short, fast, shallow breaths, her hands trembling against mine as I pulled her up the smooth rock and into my chest.

"You're OK, Princess."

"You arse hole," she erupted, pushing out of my arms, her green eyes angry, "I can't believe you made me climb up the side of a rock. Shouldn't we have had some ropes or something?"

"It was just a little scramble route, you just panicked that's all. Look," I led her to the edge of the ledge.

Ava shuffled her feet forward one at a time, a tight hold on my arm and together we peered over the edge of the drop that was just over three metres high.

"Well, it felt much bigger than that!" Ava spat, indignantly and I chuckled beside her.

"You want to actually make it to the summit now?" I asked, pointing in the direction of the stone cairn, not much more than a hundred metres in front of us.

She nodded, and grasping her hand, I guided her along beside me as we made our way up another stony path. I'd climbed this mountain many times but I never tired of the view from the top. In front of us the peaks of the other mountains in the range reared up into the sky, their tops covered with varying degrees of snow. Below us the land dropped away down into deep valleys, the stark craggy rocks blurring and softening into grassy hillocks all the way to the Lochs below us.

"Can you see those mountains over there?" I asked, pivoting Ava slightly in that direction.

She nodded, wordlessly.

"That's the Trotternish Peninsula on the Isle of Skye. One day I'll take you there."

"I dunno. Not sure mountain climbing is my thing."

"Hey, you did good for your first mountain. I'm pleased I chose the small one though."

"This was the small one?"

"Yep," I said pointing over my shoulder, and I watched her eyes follow me, "that's the Daddy of this range."

A sharp jagged peak rose up higher than the others, dark, grey rock protruding towards the sky. A soft, light cloud covered some of the peak, like a gentle layer of candyfloss woven across it. But above that the sky was pressing down upon us, thick heavy clouds descending quickly.

"I'll definitely need more practice then," Ava answered.

And that's what drew me to her; vulnerable and delicate but with the heart of a Lion and the fight of a wolf. I turned her round to face me, staring at her beautiful face, her cheeks bright red from the cold mountain air and her eyes blazed bright green. I stooped my head and kissed her gently, savouring the feel of her cold lips on mine, as we stood at the top of one of my favourite places in the world.

"Ava," I said the words gently, searching her gaze, "I don't know what you've done to me, Princess, but I'm hooked. I didn't think I could feel this again. Ever. And somehow, from somewhere, you've crept in and chased the shadows away, shining light into my darkness. I can't promise that monster is locked away for good and I don't know whether my heart will ever be truly redeemable, but what's left of it is yours, if you want it."

"I'm in love with you too," she replied, softly.

A delicate smile pulled at her lips and I pushed mine back on hers, savouring the loneliness at the top of the mountain and the chill of the air as it wrapped around us like a mist. What spell had she cast on me? What curse had she broken? My chest swelled, and my heart, for the first time in nearly nine years, felt warm, the shards of ice wedged there melting away.

When we pulled apart, I suddenly realised how cold it was. Ava was shivering delicately and my stomach was growling. The clouds had grown more oppressive, the atmosphere at the summit starting to change and a wind had picked up around us.

"Come on, time to go."

We descended the opposite side that we had climbed, dropping lower and lower until a rocky outcrop slowed us down. The sudden crop of boulders was huge and the path wound through them. I stopped in the middle, peeling the backpack straps from me and pulling out the flask of coffee, passing a little cup to Ava as we propped ourselves against the rock, the big grey slab providing shelter at our backs.

Below us a Loch sprawled across the valley floor, a forest just visible at the far side and we sat in comfortable silence, the sandwiches not lasting long between us. The light was changing as afternoon rolled on and the storm gathering behind us drew closer. I nudged Ava as soon as the last crumb disappeared and we started again, following the stony path which wound around the water before disappearing into the trees.

"Eli, are we climbing another mountain?" Ava asked, as we emerged eventually from thick woodland, the dull light of afternoon brilliantly bright after trekking through the shadows of the thick crowded fir trees.

"I don't think I have another climb in me."

"No," I answered kissing her on the top of her head and leading her up another small incline.

The path ended abruptly, the bumpy tarmac of a single-track road cutting it off, the first sign of civilisation for miles. Ava had started to limp a little, wincing slightly with each step, making the final climb up the steep hill long and laboured, but finally the cottage came in to view. It was nestled against the hill side, the white walls standing out against the green of the ferns and rushes and the grey of the rock.

Gripping Ava's hand, I lead her up to the door and slotted a key into the lock, the wooden door springing open with a creak.

"What's this?" she asked.

"A cottage?" I replied, lifting an eyebrow in a mocking expression.

"Have you hired it?"

"It's mine," I said, pushing the door open wider, "come on in."

The inside was dark, a light musty, damp smell swirling in the air with the sudden disturbance. I pulled back the curtains and opened the window shutters, late afternoon light flooding in. The modestly furnished lounge sported a leather couch and an armchair huddled around a big stone hearth. A thick, rustic oak table with two mismatched chairs was squeezed into the corner of the room, positioned in front of the window and through a low door was the kitchen, with a sink a couple of cupboards and an old Aga.

"It doesn't have any mains electricity," I said as I poked at the fire starting in the hearth, moving the lighted kindling till the flames took hold and the roared to life, crackling and popping loudly.

I lit the oil lamps, sending a warm orange glow around the cottage.

"It doesn't have mains gas either," I called as I walked into the kitchen to light the Aga.

"Eli, it's beautiful," Ava said excitedly, getting to her feet and wandering around, the bare floorboards groaning under her light weight. She stopped in front of the sideboard, her eyes scanning over the photo frames on the top.

"Your mother?" she asked picking the silver frame up gently, "you're so like her. Your eyes," Ava said, looking between her picture and me, putting one down and picking up another.

"You were blonde as a boy?" she asked me incredulously.

I smiled sadly, dropping onto the soft leather of the sofa. "Yes. Blonde hair, blue eyes. Apparently, my father thought she'd had an affair. That was till I got older and my hair started to darken. Ironic really. She was so loyal."

"I have never met my father," Ava said, suddenly, placing the photo down carefully into its original position.

"I know his name is Rob. I don't even know what he looks like never mind whether he is even still alive."

Her tone was flat. She moved from the sideboard and towards me where I'd sat on the leather sofa to get a better look at her.

"Tell me about your family," I instructed, pulling her onto my lap, warmth licking at us from the flames of the fire.

"There's not much to tell. I'm an only child. I grew up all over the London suburbs, anywhere my mum was dossing or renting from time to time. She loves to drink, and take drugs my mum. She's been like that all my life. I would get up on a morning, clear her vomit from the night before and then get myself ready for school. She drank most of our money away. I took a part-time job on as soon as I could just so I could make sure we had food to eat, although she was never sober enough to notice, or care.

"As I got older her drinking and relationships got worse. She'd bring anyone home, mostly just to pay for her gear. I would leave the house and go sit in the library until closing and some days I would wander the streets for hours waiting for them to go or fall asleep before I'd creep back."

She sighed, looking past me before continuing.

"I've never really had many friends. We moved so often that we didn't have anywhere to sit. I'd spent weeks sleeping in a sleeping bag on the floor after one move. I couldn't bring any friends there to see that.

"I left school without much in the way of qualifications. You can't really learn much when you're always tired and hungry. I constantly got detention for falling asleep in class. Somehow, I managed to get a job as an office junior and that's how I met Tom. Pity he ended up being a total dickhead."

Ava stared into the fire and I watched the flames dancing in her eyes.

"I've written to Mum a couple of times since I've been in Newcastle but she's never got in touch. She's probably been kicked out again for not paying the rent."

I pulled her closer, holding her into me, silently promising her that I would take care of her. All her needs I would provide, all her desires I would satisfy. She would be mine to worship, her body mine to claim, her soul mine to protect.

"I'm sorry that happened to you," I whispered into her neck.

"I'm not."

I pulled back looking at her, quizzically.

"What do you mean?"

"Every shit thing that has happened to me, in my childhood, in London, it's all led me here. To you. With you. I wouldn't change any of that. So, no, I'm not sorry. I'm grateful."

I stared at her for what seemed like ages, like I'd never seen her before in my life. And for the first time I felt a fear rise up in me again. I'd used anger to fuel me all these years and rage to dull the pain of losing Ally. My obsession with Ritchie, my quest for revenge had distracted me from anything else. And then Ava happened and for the first time in nine years, in my bar those few nights ago I had felt fear again. I had feared they would hurt her. I thought I'd lost everything nine years ago. Nine years ago I thought I'd lost the ability to ever love again.

*****

287

The waning light broke my concentration as we lay under a thick blanket on the rug in front of the fire. My stomach growled loudly and I scrabbled around for my clothes, that had been scattered around the room in my urgency to bury my cock as deep into Ava as I could get it. I opened the wooden chest in front of the window, rifling through a muddle of tools and weapons until my fingers felt the mix of wood and metal.

"What's the crossbow for?" Ava asked, confused.

"This, Princess, is how we are going to eat tonight."

"You are going to kill something?" she asked, surprise coating her voice.

"No, I'm just going to pop down to the corner shop and demand they hand over a pizza. There's not a shop or another house for mile, Princess."

Confusion made her all the more beautiful.

"Rabbits. They make a good stew. And we need some dinner soon," I continued, turning towards the door. "I won't be too long."

"Be careful what you're doing with that thing, caveman," she said, a wide smile spreading across her face.

I blew her a kiss, prising my eyes from her tits that had escaped from the blanket she held against her body, the pink nipples hardened to peaks. Turning the handle of the door I stepped out into the cold, focussing on the bitter chill rushing against my face rather than the heat pulsing in my groin.

Chapter Thirty Seven

∞ Ava ∞

The only bedroom in the cottage was freezing and I snuggled in closer to Eli, stealing the warmth from him as he lay sleeping peacefully. I tucked my head under his chin, pressing my body against his, running my fingers over his chest, tracing the muscle of his pecs, the sinewy bulb of his shoulders and veins that pushed through the skin over his biceps. He was a mountain of muscle, of hardness, power and strength. The olive tone of his skin, his almost black hair, the way he towered over me, dwarfed me, scared and excited me.

I didn't need to reach between my legs to feel how wet he made me. I didn't need any reminding that just lying beside him, the feel of his hot skin against mine, his masculine scent, the pressure of his erection against my stomach made my pussy tingle and my insides clench. I could spend every minute wrapped in his arms, every second of the day with him buried deep inside of me because every moment I spent with him made me feel whole.

My lips found his chest, placing light kisses over his hot skin, tasting the slight saltiness as my tongue flicked over his pecs, feeling for the little bump of his nipple, grazing my teeth across the top, listening to him groan from the sharp nip against the granite of his muscle.

A hand curled in my hair, yanking my head back suddenly, Eli's eyes sprung open, bright and blue and swirling with an animalistic need. I watched him, pulsing anticipation pumping through me, my pussy clenching and unclenching desperate for pressure, desperate to be stretched and filled. I whimpered biting my lip as I tried to control the burning sensation between my legs, silently begging him to do something, anything. His eyes never left mine, teasing me with promises.

I reached a hand forward towards his cock, my fingers brushing the tip, feeling thc wctness that clung to the end but he knocked my hand away, pushing me over on to my back. Eli grabbed at my hands, pulling them roughly above my head, pinning them together as his fingers stroked down the side of ribs and I squirmed against his touch.

"What do you want, Princess?" he growled into my ear.

"You. I want you."

"Want me where?"

"I need you to fuck me, Eli."

His fingers glided across my stomach leaving a burning trail across my skin and then I felt his thumb against my clit. I pushed myself against him, feeling a rush of pleasure bursting through me and I moaned into the arm that held me still.

"You're soaking, Princess."

Eli grazed his fingertips over my folds, teasing me but never dipping in me. I pushed my hips upwards, trying to feel more of him.

"Are you going to take everything I'm gonna give you?" he breathed huskily against my ear.

"Yes."

"Like a good girl?"

"Yes."

He pulled his hand away, flipping me over onto my front, fingers tangling in my hair, pushing me into the pillows, his weight crushing me into the bed as he rubbed his cock against me. I felt the head moving through the slickness waiting for him, sliding over me, as his fingers prized the cheeks of my arse apart. He pushed the tip against my arsehole, my breath hitching in my throat at the pressure against my tightness, unable to clench my arse cheeks against the threat of his cock against me. The flames licking in my stomach heightened to an all-new level, a rush of heat reaching my cheeks, and I groaned as he pushed it against me, helpless against the feelings he'd incited, helpless against him. My body would give him everything he wanted it. There was no need for him to take anything at all. I was his, all of me every part of me, body mind and soul.

"You're such a good girl," he whispered into my ear pushing his cock into the forbidden tightness of my ass.

Eli bit my neck sharply and I screamed out, pushing my hips back into him, pushing myself further onto his cock as it stretched that hole further.

"Such a good girl," he growled, pulling the head of his cock from where it pressed teasingly my arse, "I love how you would let me take whatever I want from you."

"Eli!" I screamed, as he thrust into my pussy, pushing my legs wide open, his fingertips digging into the flesh of my thighs.

"Take it, Ava," he grunted, his weight against me, pinning me to the bed, "take it all, every inch, every bit."

He sucked hard on my neck and bucked his hips, hitting the bulbous head of his cock hard and deep within me, sending flashes of light whirling around my brain. I cried out at the roughness, at how he pushed me open for him and the way my pussy responded to him, grabbing at him greedily. He fucked me hard, pulling me apart and putting me back together.

"Fuck, Eli," I breathed.

Then with each thrust he spoke to me.

"You're mine, Princess," he pumped his cock hard against me, "your heart, your pussy, your pleasure. It's all mine. I own it all."

His hips moved in long hard, thrusts with every syllable, my stomach jolting against each, my pussy clenching, holding him, throbbing against him. My whole body tensed, my muscles, even my skin, shuddering underneath him. His fingers reached round my neck, grabbing my throat and pulling me back towards him as he thundered into me, crazed and desperate.

"I'm all yours, Eli. Every tiny part of me, every cell, every nerve, every memory. All. Yours."

I panted beneath him, under the intensity of his hips, under the ferocity of the thrusts, under the grip of his hand on my throat. And then I screamed into the mountain air as the next pivot of his hips sent me spiralling over the edge into a fiery oblivion.

*****

I stood outside the glass doors of the office, the rain beating against my umbrella, my breath streaming out before me in a little cloud of white steam as my lungs burned in my chest and my heart pounded. The distractions of the last few days had stopped the racing thoughts, the memories every time I closed my eyes but now, stood on the Quayside in the rain, I struggled to put one foot in front of the other to enter the building. I counted to ten, and then ten again and yet I was still stood staring up at the building, blankly.

A rumble of thunder rolled in the distance, ominous, atmospheric, the heat of tears burned behind my eyes. I swallowed, moving one leg then the other, slowly and carefully as though I might fall through the black floor tiles inside the building with the slightest movement. But I was moving, I was inside the building, the lift was coming closer, the doors were sliding open and then I stepped inside, consumed by the metal box.

The mood was sombre, a feeling like static in the air. Everyone had their eyes down working, exchanging hushed conversations with one another and I didn't need to look up from my computer to see the concerned glances exchanged from desk to desk.

The shrill ring of the phone made me jump, my empty coffee cup crashing to the floor loudly, smashing into a million tiny pieces.

"I'll get it for you," a friendly voice said from beside me as I pressed the receiver against my ear.

"Martin would like to see you in his office straight away," his secretary, instructed.

"Come in," Martin Fairbrother, called in response to the tentative knock on his door.

He waved his hands towards the seat at the other side of the desk from him and I sat carefully, perched on the end as if ready to escape at a moment's notice.

"Avery."

"Ava."

He looked over his dark rimmed glasses, a hint of annoyance on his face.

"I'm sorry about Harry."

A lump formed in my throat.

"I'm sorry you had to witness that. We can arrange counselling if you would like."

"No, I'm fine," I replied hastily, "but thank you. I don't need it."

Liar.

"Very well. Harry will be sorely missed. It's a shame that he sought that as the only way out of his depression."

"He was depressed?"

I knew he had been stressed, that something had changed. But it had been sudden. There had to have been more than that one trigger. He was always so happy-go-lucky; a party animal.

"Yes. He said so in this suicide note."

"He left a note?" I sounded like some sort of parrot.

"Yes. In his apartment."

I scowled.

"Where in his apartment?"

"Does it matter, Avery?"

"Ava," I corrected, "and yes, yes it does."

Martin Fairbrother sighed, his patience waning.

"The Police found it on his coffee table."

"That's strange. I was there not long before ....before the incident. There was no note on the table then."

Mr Fairbrother looked at me, his head tilted to the side, as if considering whether he would continue to entertain me.

"Avery, you've had an awful experience. I'm sure you will have been very shocked. Sometimes, when that happens, we don't always remember things as they were."

I opened my mouth to answer and then thought better of it.

"Yes, probably."

"Avery, with Harry gone I need you to take over the Robertson contract."

My stomach tensed, dread and nausea swirled inside, pushing apprehension around my body like a poison. It seeped into my veins, making my mouth dry. I nodded, unable to form any sort of words.

"Excellent. I'll pass your details on to Mr Robertson. He'll contact you directly."

Chapter Thirty Eight

ഊ Eli ര

"That intel you fed me, it was utter shit, Thor," I growled as he slid onto the bar stool beside me.

"Nice to see you too, mate."

I slid a pint of lager towards him.

"Am I safe to drink this or is it laced with laxatives?"

I rolled my eyes then returned to staring at the whisky I swirled around the tumbler.

"I found nothing, 'V', absolutely fucking nothing."

Even I could hear the disappointment in my voice.

"Mate. I'm sorry. It was decent intel. A decent source. I dunno why it didn't pay off."

The Viking shrugged taking a few good gulps of the pint.

"Cars. Vintage fucking cars. That's all that was there."

The Viking looked across at me scowling.

"And you checked all of them?"

I nodded.

"It was a guns run that, Eli. That was what I was told," he continued, "that source has never let me down."

"Well, he has now."

I took an angry mouthful of whisky, pulling a face as the cheap liquid burned my throat.

"This place really needs to get some better fucking product. This is fucking disgusting," I complained, taking another mouthful.

"It's a biker bar, mate, not some posh shit like you have. We only want to get pissed and get laid."

The bar was a dive. Sticky, partially dried drinks coated the bar top, the beermat my glass had been resting on sticking to the top like it was attached with cement. The carpet hadn't been cleaned in years and my feet had almost squelched in the dirt, grime and damp it had collected in the time that it had been down. And it had that smell: the sweet scent of spilled alcohol, vomit and probably blood.

"What is Ritchie doing with the Russians?" I asked the Viking suddenly.

"Fuck's sake, Eli, keep ya voice down," he looked around, scanning the pub for anyone who might overhear our conversation, "was it definitely the Russians?"

"Yep. That big baldy one, Volkov."

"Lukyan Volkov," the Viking answered, keeping his voice low, "where did you see him?"

"Going into Ritchie's Social club."

"Could be anything mate, drugs, guns, girls."

There was something about that last word in his tone, it had changed, his voice had lowered.

"Tell me about the girls."

"You know strippers and the like."

"No, I don't. There's only me and Ritchie have strippers in the city. Anything else isn't legit. We talking prossies here?"

"Yeah, I guess."

"What am I missing here 'V'?"

He sighed, lifted the pint to his lips and slugged back the rest of his beer, before wiping his mouth on the back of a tattooed hand. The Viking glanced around the bar again, watching the barman stood at the far end, fiddling with the remote for the heavy cube of a TV.

"The Northern Pipeline," he watched my reaction, and I shrugged my shoulders incredulously, "trafficking, Eli, people trafficking."

I looked at him blankly for a moment.

"What? Here in the North East."

The Viking nodded.

"Certain Firms have been getting into it for a while. The Russians have been sniffing around it more recently too. It's big money, Eli, really big."

"And Cian?"

"I dunno mate. I don't get involved in O'Sullivan business. I'm a freelancer, remember."

I looked at him, raising my eyebrow and waiting.

"Nah, mate. I've not heard that the O'Sullivan's are involved. They're too old school for that shit. The Russians though? Yeah, they would do anything for easy money. Still. Might not be that at all."

"I've watched Ritchie for years, mate. He's pushed drugs round this city for ages but things have been hotting up, he's been more careful. We always suspected the guns, 'V', out there, undercover, we knew what he was doing, we just could never prove it. He's never needed the Russians to make his enterprises work, so why now?"

"That's all I know, bro."

The Viking stood, and slapped me on the back as the sudden rumble of motorbike exhausts could be heard in the distance.

"That's my que," the blond biker said pulling his black helmet over his distinctive long hair, and tucking the ponytail down the back of the leather jacket.

"Not a bar you should be in, huh?"

"I don't exist, remember. Besides I'm a nomad to these guys, they don't appreciate a free spirit."

He winked, pulling the opaque black visor down over his face and walking away. I swallowed the last of the hideous, pale gold liquid, feeling another set of skin cells peeling off the roof my mouth and followed him out a few steps behind. A swarm of motorbikes pulled into the pub car park and I pulled the collar of the black jacket up around my neck, unlocking the big black Landrover and climbing in.

Chapter Thirty Nine

৪০ Ava ৪ব

The morning was battling against the darkness, as I stood and watched from Eli's huge, panoramic windows. An orange and pink glow erupted on the horizon, creeping higher, filling the sky with an explosion of colour, daylight seeping across the world. I felt a strange numbness, an oozing sadness.

Images of Harry's bulging eyes as he hung from the rope had dragged me from Eli's bed. The air was cold, but a faint warmth infiltrated the apartment, as the central-heating roared to life. The morning was transforming from a pinky-orange hue to a dull grey; monotonous and ominous.

I felt his presence before he touched me, a shadow stalking through the dusk of the apartment, his earthy, masculine smell reaching me before the arm that snaked around my waist. His beard brushed my neck, gentle tingles erupting across my skin as he planted hot little kisses across my shoulder, pulling me into his chest. And no matter how feral the feelings of sadness and despair that had woken me, the warmth of Eli's heart and the safety of his arms chased it all away. We stood looking out over the fields, watching the dawn roll across the land, light chasing off the darkness.

I was sat at my desk mid-morning checking off tasks on my to-do-list, keeping my brain as engaged as possible to avoid it drifting off into those dark places. A ruffle of paper broke through my concentration and I watched one of the secretary's slide a piece of paper under my nose. I stared at the short lines of text stacked on top of each other for a few seconds before looking up at the woman.

"Mr Robertson called and has requested you take his papers over to him at lunch time," she said stiffly.

"Today?"

"Yes."

"I, I don't drive. "

"Just order a taxi and charge it to the firm. Harry would often do that."

I nodded, turning the little scrap of paper over in my hands, the sound of his name sending a sharp, stabbing sensation to my heart.

The taxi pulled up to a set of black iron gates in the middle of a long street lined with mansions. Each house was obscenely huge, sprawling over bright green well-tended gardens, and hidden behind high walls and big metal gates. The driver spoke into the intercom and the gates peeled back. The drive was long and snaking and entirely block-paved; a huge jigsaw of bricks in various shades of red and terracotta, like the yellow-brick road, but red. The house was modern, designed to mimic a stately home but had missed the mark, gregarious instead of regal.

The taxi left me on the foot of the steps clutching my laptop bag against me awkwardly. I glanced around. The big house seemed busy, multiple cars of varying degrees of worth were pulled around the side of the building and parked so haphazardly one or two actually looked like they'd been dumped.

The steps were so wide that it took two strides just to climb one as I approached front door, pressing a huge brass button to summon someone's attention. The door was pulled open by a tall man who stood there staring at me silently, not a 'hello', not a 'how can I help' just silence. I shifted uncomfortably.

"I'm, err, Ava Edwards."

He filled the space both in height and width. The white shirt he wore was unbuttoned at the neck and the sleeves folded up to his elbows showing muscled forearms and a trail of faded tattoos.

"I'm h, here to see Mr Robertson," I prompted when he continued to say nothing at all.

He looked me up and down silently.

"I, I'm from Fairbrother Williams."

"You the new Harry?" he grunted, eventually.

"Something like that," I muttered, a pang of guilt shooting through me like a bolt of lightning.

He tipped his head and turned away and I took it as a que to follow, my heels clacking nosily off the marble floor as I tried to keep up with his long strides. Doors lined the marble corridor and I peered in each inquisitively as we passed, my head swivelling left and right as if it was held on by a loose pin. Luxury filled every room from the biggest TV I had ever seen to a glass dining table that sprawled across two rooms and looked as if it would seat at least twenty guests. But at very end of the corridor, when we could go no further, a thick oak door barred the way.

The big man grasped the handle, pushing the door inwards and entering without a knock or introduction. My eyes scanned the room wildly. It was cavernous but sparsely decorated, running across the full width of the property.

"Ah Miss Edwards, thank you for coming," Mr Robertson said, lifting his head from the papers he was studying, crowded by another couple of men who stared at me with interest, "please, take a seat," he gestured towards a leather sofa next to the desk.

He muttered something to the men beside him, who promptly shuffled the papers into a pile, and left the room. Mr Robertson shut the door behind him and then walked across to the room to a bar that was almost as big and as well stocked as one of Eli's pubs.

"I, I'm sorry Mr Robertson, I don't drink at work," I apologised as he pushed a wine glass towards me.

"I'm sure it will be fine. It's just one glass. To toast a new working arrangement."

There was a command in his voice, an authoritarian tone, compelling and encouraging and I nodded and took the glass taking the smallest, modest sip. The taste exploded in my mouth, bold and thick, a hint of acidity battling against a sweet tartness; not quite enjoyable. I set the glass down on the side table fumbling around my laptop bag and pulling out a cardboard folder.

"Harry had already prepared the paperwork," I said passing a small pile of papers to Mr Robertson and handing him my pen, "just need you to sign here and here," I said leaning towards him slightly, pointing to the spaces for his signature.

He dropped his eyes to the paperwork and scribbled his signature over the various pieces before handing them back to me, cool grey-blue eyes holding my gaze uncomfortably. His arm moved across me and I stiffened, the uncomfortable prickle of a nervous sweat starting on my palms. He picked the wine off the table and handed it back to me.

"This is Chateau Petrus," he said, bringing his own glass under his nose and swilling it round as he sniffed at it, "this particular vintage is 1978, older than you."

Explained the taste. I nodded.

"Do you know a good wine is determined by how well it has aged?" he said to me, his eyes burning into mine.

I took another sip of the liquid nervously, pulling the hem of my grey suit skirt further down over my knees.

"Sounds expensive," I mumbled.

"£1,300 a bottle in fact."

I nearly spat the wine back into the glass.

"Then maybe it would be a shame to waste it," I answered, trying to keep the shock from my tone.

He reached out towards me and I froze, staring at him like I was caught in headlights.

"It's not wasted on you," he said pushing one of my loose curls behind my ear.

I stiffened at his touch, my brain frantically trying to fathom an escape plan.

"You know," nudging up closer to me, "this looks like the start of a very promising relationship. Harry was very efficient but I think you and I will get on very well."

He rested a hand on my thigh. I gulped back the last of my wine, the strong taste burning my throat, and set the empty glass back on the table and stuffed the signed papers back into the bag with my lap top.

"I need to get back to the office."

"Surely you have time for another. I know Martin won't mind."

"I have a lot of work to do."

I got to my feet smoothing down my skirt, self-consciously, my throat dry despite the wine.

Mr Robertson guided me out, a hand placed on the small of my back, not just lightly positioned but a heavy, deliberate pressure. I felt uneasy and I fought the urge to just bolt down the corridor away from him the first chance I got. He wasn't unattractive. His light grey-blue eyes and neatly trimmed goatee, added to the symmetrical shape of his face. His suit was well tailored and showed off a lean, firm frame, even for an older man, but his presence sent prickles standing to attention on the back of my neck, fight or flight senses tingling.

"Gary" his voice authoritative, "bring the car round for Miss Edwards, please."

"Thank you, but I can call a taxi."

"Absolutely not. I'll have my driver drop you back to the office," he moved his hand from my back, touching my elbow lightly and pivoting me round to face him, "perhaps you'd join me for dinner one night, Ava. I'm sure you would love to see the rest of my house."

"Thank you, but I don't join my clients for dinner," miraculously my voice didn't waiver

"Shame," his voice lowered as he bent down towards me, "it would have been nice to have gone over some more of the business with you."

"We have a very comfortable Boardroom for that, Mr Robertson. I'd be happy to meet with you there."

"Please, call me Richard."

A car engine rumbled the other side of the doors.

Chapter Forty

ഌ Eli ‌ൔ

I miss you, Princess, I typed the text, pressed the button and lay my phone back down on my desk.

My conversation with the Viking had rung in my ears, ricocheting through my head so when I wasn't distracted with Ava's body all I could think about was Ritchie. I needed something; some little nugget of information that would lead me to more evidence. I picked my phone back up and scrolled through my contacts, my thumb hovering over Sebastian's number, and then I set it down again. He wouldn't tell me if he knew anyway.

I wriggled out of the thick, black jacket and eyed the filing cabinet before dipping down and wedging my shoulder into the side. The big pile of metal screeched across the floor as I pushed it over just enough to get my hand down the back. The key pad behind it stuck out from the skirting board ever so slightly and my fingers danced across the buttons, remembering the sequence with distinct accuracy until the door of the safe pinged open. I pulled the gun out carefully, placing it on my desk and heaving the cabinet back into place.

I looked at the metal pistol again. Guns and drugs were one thing, but people trafficking was a whole other ball game and that made Ritchie more dangerous than I'd ever anticipated. Floor boards creaked outside my room. I slid out my bottom drawer and dropped the gun at the back, pulling files across it. The drawer rolled shut, rumbling noisily in the small space of my office.

"Boss?" Danny, tapped on the door as he walked in, "the new stock has arrived."

"Be down in a second," I answered, locking my desk drawers behind me and heading down to the bar to help Danny with the crates of alcohol that had just arrived.

*****

I ran my hands down over Ava's stomach, her smooth skin feeling like warmed satin under my fingertips, diving into the front of the black, lacy thong and dancing over the little tuft of hair at the front of her mound. She sucked in a breath, eyeing me in the floor length mirror, her hand poised holding the little tube of mascara just next to her eye.

I brushed the hair from her neck where it was partly restrained, cascading from the back of her head like a waterfall of loose waves. My lips skimmed over the tight muscle in her shoulder, sucking gently at her skin, moving around her neck till I was at her throat. My teeth nibbled along her neck, the alcohol in her perfume stinging my tongue, and I worshipped every taste of her, salty, soapy, perfumed. Everything about her I loved.

The hand in her knickers roamed lower, cupping her pussy, feeling the heat radiating out of her, the wetness pooling against my fingers even at the hint of what I would do to it and I bit down hard on her neck, feasting on the little yelp that slipped from her throat.

"Don't you have an awards ceremony to get ready for?" Ava asked, her voice husky.

"Yes," I whispered against her throat.

"Haven't you got an award to present?"

"Yes," I nibbled at her collar bone.

"And haven't you got a father that will be really pissed off with you if you don't make it?"

"Yes."

I spun her around pushing her back against the mirror so she faced me. I kicked off my boxers, pulled her thong roughly to the side, and pushed into her, not giving her time or space to adjust. Ava screamed out in surprise, the tube of mascara tumbling to the floor and I flicked the black material of her bra from her tits, biting down on a nipple that greeted me eagerly making her cry out again.

"But I've got time to fuck my woman first," I growled, the little pink nub still clenched between my teeth.

And I did exactly that, fucking her hard and ferociously against the mirror, our own groans mixing with the creek of the glass behind us that threatened to come undone before either of us.

Her pussy gripped me hard, my balls tensing and then in an instant her tight cunt was driving me crazy, and I lost all reason, all recollection of who or where I was as the back of my eyes turned black and my lungs stung with pain or pleasure or whatever fucked up shit this was.

I kissed her lips gently, sucking on her gasps as she came down from her own orgasm, plastering little nibbles across her jaw, savouring every taste, every touch as my brain came back from oblivion. She smiled against my kisses, wrapping her arms around my neck, her breathing growing steadier, more controlled.

Pulling away I glanced at my watch.

"Ten minutes, Princess. Chop chop."

"Eli!" she complained turning back to the mirror, bending over in front of me as she scrabbled around on the floor for the make-up she'd dropped.

Watching her tight arse, fire stoked deep inside me again and I fought the desire to bury myself in her once more, to make her brace herself against the mirror while I fucked her from behind. I wondered how much shit my father would give me if I missed the Business Awards?

There was a flutter of activity at the front of the hotel; a red carpet, lots of limousines and fancy cars and gaudy banners with 'North East Business Awards' blazed all over them as they flapped in the breeze. I instructed the taxi driver to pull up a few metres back to avoid the queue of cars at the entrance and helped Ava out.

She threaded her arm through mine, clutching her skirt with her other hand. She was stunning. Her black and gold floor length gown, fastened round her neck, exposing milky shoulders and clinging around the small pert breasts I'd become obsessed with kissing every chance I got. The dress cinched her middle, showing the curve of her hips and the slight lines of her muscle in her abdomen where the material was cut away and then fell from the waistband, full and flowing.

Every man in there noticed her too; the shock of red hair, her emerald eyes and her petite frame. I clutched tightly to her arm laying my claim, staring darkly at anyone who looked at her for too long, my possessiveness of her emanating around the room as I kept my prize close to my side.

I plucked two glasses of fizzing champagne from a tray that was carried passed us, handing one to Ava, who sniffed at it before bringing it to her red lips and taking a sip. The room was already packed, men in suits with beautifully dressed women on their arms, moved about mingling and chatting and I pulled on the collar of my own shirt wondering how soon I could take this fucking bow tie off.

"Hey, I'm just going to the little girl's room," Ava said, pulling her hand from mine.

"Ok. I'll just stand here then and scowl at anyone who looks at my woman's fuckable arse as she walks by then."

"Your woman, huh?" Ava's voice was light above the low music.

She stepped up onto her tip toes and planted a lingering kiss on my lips before turning and walking away. I grabbed another glass from a passing tray, leaning against a pillar and scanning the room casually. I spotted her before she saw me, but as soon as I caught her eye she moved pointedly through the crowd. Her blonde hair was pinned up high on her head, loose wisps hanging down to frame her face and her blues eyes stood out under the huge amount of eye make-up.

"Hey, Eli," she smiled at me, kissing me on the cheek but letting her lips linger too long.

"Evening, Ashley. What, or who has brought you here?"

"I'm here with Ritchie. I had hoped *you* might have invited me," she pouted her lips playfully and fluttered her eyelashes.

"What are you doing messing around with him?" I hissed at her, taking hold of her elbow and pulling her closer to me.

"Now, now Eli. You've got a new toy remember?" she shot back, reaching up and straightening my bow tie with a little wiggle.

She stroked her fingertips up the back of my neck, standing so close that I could feel her fake tits pushing against my chest. I took hold of her hand and gently moved it off me. The roaming light from the rotating disco ball above us sparkled, bouncing off a black and gold dress over Ashley's shoulder. Ashley turned, leaving a freshly manicured hand resting on my chest as Ava's green glare watched me, flaming with an intensity I'd not seen on her before.

Peeling Ashley off me I moved to Ava, scooping my arm around the small of her back and pulling her into me and placing a hot kiss on her lips.

"And for who's benefit was that?" Ava hissed, as I pulled my head away.

"Ashley, this is my girlfriend Ava" my voice was laced with purpose.

"Nice to meet you again, Eva."

"It's Ava," she muttered from beside me although not loud enough for Ashley to hear.

I shot Ashley a glare.

"Excuse me, I'd better get back to my date," she said, flashing me a smile before turning and walking off through the crowd.

Ava watched her walk away, her expression unusual; dark, angry, jealous, but she said nothing more about it. I noticed it though, noticed that her frame was stiffer, her eyes wandered around the crowd of people, not solely consumed by me, a sudden distance between us, tiny, almost unreadable, but there was a distance.

The bar area thinned out, people flocking to the big round tables in the banqueting room and we followed along, locating our names on the plan and then onto our seats. We reached the table the same time as the familiar grey-headed man. My heart sank. His cold grey-blue eyes met mine and he flashed me a smile, poison hidden behind it. His eyes caught Ava and I watched as he looked her up and down his eyes darkening and his gaze lingering too long on her exposed thigh.

"Ah, Elijah. So nice to see you again," he said.

Then turning to Ava, his voice softening just a little, "and nice to see you too, Ava. I didn't think you had dinner with your clients?"

Her cheeks flushed pink.

"Mr Robertson, nice to see you tonight," she said, her tone wavering slightly.

"I didn't realise you two knew each other?" I said flatly.

"Oh, Ava stopped by my place yesterday lunch time. We enjoyed a glass of my best red together."

Ritchie turned to Ava.

"If I realised you were coming tonight I would have been happy to have brought you myself, after all we had such a nice time getting acquainted yesterday."

Ava visibly recoiled, a look of panic on her face. Ritchie and Ashley took their seats on the opposite side of the table from and I turned to Ava, trying to hold back any over exuberant interrogation techniques.

"How do you know Ritchie?"

Her head snapped towards me, her lips parting, pressing together and parting again as the colour almost drained from her face. I looked at her confused.

"That's who?"

"That's Ritchie."

"Oh, god," I didn't think her face could get much paler but in that moment it had definitely dropped a shade.

"Richard Robertson; Ritchie," she whispered.

I sat back in silence, trying to focus on the stage where I would soon be invited up to present my family's awards, but all I could see was my nemesis, sat at the same table as my girlfriend and my ex-whatever-Ashley-was. Ritchie's eyes flicked backwards and forwards, drawing my attention with the way he'd nibble at Ashley's neck while she giggled like a little girl. But I also noticed the long glances at Ava, his eyes growing darker, more sinister. I recognised the expression on his face, I could see how he wanted her, how her unusual features spoke to him. Anger simmered under the surface, my hands wrapped into tight balls under the table.

Chapter Forty One

❧ Ava ❧

I felt sick; a hot, uncomfortable nausea as my emotions ran rampant round my head, stoking up worries and neuroses I thought I'd buried. I'd felt insane jealousy watching the blonde with Eli earlier, her hands all over him, her body far too close to him. A pang of familiarity creeping back, uncertainty, dread, a thick unsettling feeling weighing me down. And then Mr Robertson; Ritchie. How had I never put the two together?

"What's going on?" Eli hissed from beside me.

"I, err, Richard Robertson is a client of Fairbrother Williams. I've been working on his business accounts for the last few months and then since Harry….. I had no idea he was Ritchie. Oh god."

"Why were you at his house?" his tone was harsher than I'd ever heard it.

"Harry used to take his papers to his house to be signed. I was asked to do the same thing. He offered me wine and….."

"And what?" the growl from his throat wasn't sexual, it was dark and accusing.

I glanced nervously across the table worried they'd hear us but they were too busy consumed with each other to give us any attention.

"I, I just felt uncomfortable, something about him, his advances maybe. Shit, I didn't know he was Ritchie, Eli. I didn't know."

I could hear the pleading in my own voice, the desperation to make him believe me.

My head was in turmoil, thoughts flying around just out of reach, unable to be put together into any sort of discernible pattern. My mind flittered back to yesterday at his house. Did Mr Robertson, Ritchie, know I was with Eli? Was he trying to make a move on me to get under Eli's skin? Fuel this feud that they have?

I picked at the courses that were brought out to us in between awards announcements, not really noticing who won what; I was too deeply lost in my thoughts. Eli kept glancing over at me clearly agitated and our conversation seemed to have come to a resounding halt. Couple that with the beady eyes of Ashley who seemed to be watching our interactions, or rather lack of interaction, and I was starting to feel extremely anxious.

Award after award was announced and twice Eli got up, made his way to the stage and presented a big, thick glass trophy to the winner. I watched him move confidently through the tables each time, women turning to look at him as he passed, eyes following him to the stage.

"He likes this award the best," Ashley said into my ear from behind me, "You know, best woman in business category? I'm not sure whether it's because he gets to check-out beautiful women or it's that the women are rich and successful like him?"

She walked around the table and sat down next to Ritchie again and I sat and dwelled on her words, words that resonated in me far more than I realised. *Rich and successful*. I was neither of those things. Did Eli pity me? Would he soon get bored of me? Like Tom did. Like my mother did? Those feelings of rejection rattled me, a tickling warmth starting in the back of my eyes, a tightness in my throat.

As Eli sat back down, I excused myself for the bathroom. I needed some space; space away from Ashley, and Ritchie, and Eli. Space to breath, to think, to fight back the tears threatening to overthrow me. I stood in front of the sink in the ladies' toilets for a few minutes trying to control my whirring thoughts, quell the onslaught of self-pity and self-deprecation. The door opened to my side, blonde hair and perky big tits stepping through it. I picked up my bag, making a quick exit but as I passed, she caught my arm firmly.

"Eli gets tired of new toys eventually," she said quietly, dipping her head towards my ear, "and when he does, he'll come running back to me. And I'll be waiting with open legs."

She smiled smugly at me as I shrugged my arm from her grip and bounded out through the doorway. The corridor seemed to go on forever, the longest corridor I had ever known. I didn't see the man until I collided straight in to him, nearly knocking myself over. He caught me by my arms, stopping me from falling backwards before straightening me up.

"Ava," he said, his voice dark, "what's the rush?"

"Sorry, Mr Robertson."

"I've told you, call me Richard or Ritchie if you prefer," he said, a knowing smile forming across his face.

I swallowed, the heavy lump of dread in my throat refusing to go away, threatening me with suffocation, my heart beat rising and my chest tight.

"I didn't know you knew my old friend, Elijah?"

I swallowed again. Ritchie dropped his hands moving in closer to me. I was sure he could hear the nervous thumping of my heart. He could probably feel it through the skin of the arm he grasped in his hand.

"Martin tells me you are a very obedient employee. Is that right?"

"I, err, yes?"

"I'm pleased to hear it," I could feel his hot breath on the side of my face and I didn't dare turn to look at him, "I like little girls who do what they are told. Are you one of them?" he squeezed my arm a bit tighter his fingers digging in to the muscle.

I froze. I couldn't find the words to answer. His words held meaning, threatening in some way

I didn't yet understand but that trickled a catalyst of thoughts erupting in my head, thoughts I didn't want to entertain, thoughts too dark for this world, my world.

"Ah, there is my girl," his voice changed suddenly, his fingers releasing my arm.

I watched the two of them walk away, Ashley with her arm linked through his, her hips swaying from side to side and the flick of her head as she laughed at something he said. The heavy nauseous feeling in my stomach doubled and sweat wet the palms of my hands. I took a deep breath and made my way back to Eli.

Chapter Forty Two

୬ Eli ୯

Tonight had descended into a shit show. I'd been truly disarmed by the familiarity of Ritchie with Ava, sending my head in a spin and mind reaching into dark places. I sat and sulked at the table, waiting for her to return. Her face was pale when she sat down beside me, tension radiating from her entire body. My mobile vibrated in the pocket of my jacket, saving me from the uncomfortable silence hanging in the air between us. I pulled it out reading the message from my security team.

'Two security threats at Opulence tonight. Might want to pop your head in,' the message from Micky read.

But there was more in that message than those words alone.

'Be right there,' I typed back.

'Boss.'

I leaned in towards Ava making her jump, a look of panic over her face and fear in her eyes and I felt instantly guilty at how vulnerable she looked.

"I need to get over to the club. There's been an issue."

She searched my eyes, waiting for something else from me, but I was angry and confused.

"I'll get you a taxi from the Club," I said again, standing up and beckoning her to follow me, ignoring the look of rejection in her eyes, knowing my words cut through her, dismissing her.

Ava's heels tapped loudly on the pavement, breaking my thoughts, dissipating the mist behind my eyes. Guilt stabbed me in the chest again. I knew I was intentionally being a dickhead to her, cold and distant, but I was angry. Angry at Ritchie for coming here tonight, angry at Ashley for getting mixed up with him, angry at Ava for...for him being a client of hers, for not realising who he was because I'd never told her, never told her the whole truth. Total dickhead.

I stole a glance over my shoulder, watching her rub her bare arms in the cold, the wince as each foot fell, as she tried to keep up with me as I stormed away into the night. My heart stammered in my chest and I slowed my pace, shrugging out of my coat, rage and anger disappearing as I looked into her green eyes, hurt and confused. I was an arsehole. The jacket hung off her, swamping over her shoulders but held off the cold and she clasped it in her slim hands, pulling it around her.

"Come on, Princess," I said softly to her, "we're nearly there."

Her face was fragile, almost about to break, tears collecting in her eyes that I had caused. Me. I was angry again. Angry at myself, at my selfishness, at the darkness that always hid away threatening to consume me just as it had started to do back there.

The strip club was busy, an electric atmosphere super-charged by groups of men, laughing and shouting and whooping. I sat Ava in a booth, waving over a waitress who approached with a big wide smile, her eyes lingering on the little red-head as I ordered a bottle of champagne.

Ava's eyes were wide, her head flicking from side to side, watching, half shocked, half embarrassed as the nearly naked woman spun round the pole again on the main stage, her tits bouncing in the effort, the black, stringy thong the only scrap between imagination and realisation.

Micky tapped me on the shoulder.

"Best come and see the cameras, Boss," he spoke into my ear, his voice barely audible above the thumping music.

I nodded in reply.

"I need to go look at some cameras, Princess. Stay here. Don't move."

There'd been a number of groups of men turned away from the club tonight. We'd often get one or two but we seemed to have suffered a barrage of wankers. When the last group had been forcibly moved on a knife had dropped on the floor. Nothing too big, a small flick knife, but a knife all the same.

The CCTV we'd been watching hadn't shown much. Micky pointed at the camera that looked out over the door, and we watched a bouncer check the pockets of a young man in jeans, pulling something out and then holding it up. A small pen knife. Nothing massive but enough to cause a nasty nick. The second camera, about forty minutes later, showed a group of young men inside my club in a booth towards the back. They took it in turns to bend over the table, their heads mere centimetres from the surface, a small tube of something rolled up passing between them.

"You chucked them out?" I asked Micky who nodded beside me.

"Then they came back, waving a tiny knife around at the door. Scarpered when the Police drove past."

I stared at the cameras but the images were grainy and difficult to make anyone out. If I recognised any of them I couldn't tell from these shots. It was too much in one night, too much agro for a coincidence. Something felt off.

"Boss. The booths. Now," was all that came over the radio.

My stomach dropped. Ava. By herself. Launching out of the CCTV office I bundled through the doors. Inside the main club a fuck-ton of hell was breaking loose. Women were screaming. Men were roaring like animals. My doormen were advancing from the entrance. My poached dancer, Chloe, was clutching her face, a denim jacket coated arm coming at her. She bent over onto her knees as the arm pulled back. The blade of the knife caught in the purple-pink light reflected off the disco balls in the ceiling above.

"Mickey, take the others. I'll get the hostile."

I jumped over the injured dancer on the floor as the knife man moved forward, his arm pulled back baring the six-inch weapon. I crashed into his chest, grabbing his right arm as we hit the floor, his body broke my fall and my fist broke his nose, as I pummelled his face repeatedly, rage devouring me, sucking me under. Micky pulled me off him, as my arms flailed wildly. The attacker was out cold.

I turned to my dancer. There was cut across her face, blood dripping down her chin, but it was the pool of blood on the floor in front of her, spilling out over her fingers where she clasped her stomach. Taking off my shirt, I eased her into a seated position, propped up against the side of the booth and pressed it hard against the wound.

"Mickey, ring an ambulance. Donnie, I need you," I instructed my security team calmly.

Nearly all of them were ex-forces; obedient, diligent and fucking amazing in a crisis, and this was a crisis. Donnie, an ex-medic, and right now my most valuable asset, squatted in front of the girl, pulling supplies from the first aid kit as he lifted the corner of my shirt off the wound, carefully.

"It's not good, Boss," he said quietly, looking up at me, the long scar on his face looking ever angrier under the club lights.

I knelt at Chloe's head and stroked her hair back.

"You're going to be OK," I said calmly, hiding the concern and keeping a lid on my anger.

Anger would have to wait its turn.

"Ava!" I called out, trying to pick her out amongst the crowd that had grown.

She was deathly pale, her face a mix of shock and terror, staring at me, frozen

"Ava!"

Her eyes flicked back and forth across the people on the floor.

"Ava!" her head turned to me, "I need you go to my office. In my desk drawers is a file with employee details. Bring that to me. Jack, go with her."

She nodded, grabbing the keys I threw at her and Jack directed her away down the back stairwell.

"Get everyone out of here," I instructed the doormen, "get the lights on."

"Eli," Chloe whispered through clenched teeth. "The man, who did this…. he said I was Ritchie's girl," she stopped and took a pained breath before continuing, "he said if I wasn't earning money for him, I wasn't earning it for no one."

She screwed her face up and whimpered.

"Don't worry, babe, you're gonna be OK."

Fucking Ritchie!

Chapter Forty Three

৪০ Ava ৪৪

Fists flew everywhere, I couldn't make anything out. I couldn't tell the punters from the security. Bodies slammed into each other, men roaring like animals and women shrieking like angry banshees. I'd got to my feet and walked towards the chaos, pulled in like a moth to a flame. And as I got a few feet away I could see the huge frame of Eli. His face was distorted, anger like I'd never seen it before, pure rage, terror itself as he launched his fists into the face of the man on the floor. Then as the body beneath him stilled he turned his attention to the girl.

The shirt he was wearing was wrenched open and yanked down his arms as he rushed to her, pressing the white material into her stomach, blood soaking straight through it. He shouted instructions that I couldn't hear, men running about in front of him. I could hear his voice, deep, steady, reassuring, but not the words. The words didn't make sense, floating in front of me, just out of reach, intangible.

"Ava!"

I snapped my head towards him trying to concentrate on what he was saying as he held out a set of keys and a card in my direction.

"Ava, I need you go to my office. In my desk drawers is a file with employee details. Bring that to me. Jack, go with her," he instructed to one of the bar staff.

I nodded and followed Jack out the back of the strip club and down a set of stairs at the rear of the building, the noise of the furore still whirling in my ears. The nightclub and the strip club backed onto each other, a mere courtyard the only thing in between. Jack helped me unlock the heavy back door of the night club, swiping a key card across the internal door that barred our way. The corridor looked different from this direction, but I followed Jack, rushing up the stairs, my heart whooshing in my ears, my lungs struggling to properly inflate.

The door to Eli's office opened with an angry screech. I unlocked Eli's desk drawers, thumbing through bits of paper, file dividers, my head fuzzy and light but no files. The last drawer was deep, harbouring all sorts of things, from some leather gloves, a tie and eventually files. Files that stuck as I tried to pull them out.

Putting my hand underneath to dislodge the documents my hand brushed something cold. Distracted, I reached for the object, closing my fingers around it. It was heavier than I expected, firm. I pulled it towards me. My eyes seemed to take a while to adjust to the object in my hand, the handle fitting snuggling in my palm the muzzle sticking out a right angle. Then as if it bit me, I recoiled, dropping it back into the drawer with a dull thud. Why did Eli have a gun? My throat constricted, suddenly going dry and I felt like I was going to choke.

"Have you found it?" Jack's voice made me jump.

"Y, yes. Got it," I answered, glancing at the black object once more before pushing the drawer back into position and turning the lock.

*****

I sat on the bed staring at the blood-stained shirt lying on the bedroom floor, listening to the splatter of water in the bathroom next door. My mind was fuzzy, as if someone had stuffed a load of cotton wool into my head and I was trying to find my thoughts within it. I was still staring at the same space on the wall when Eli came out, his dark hair brushed back over his head, beads of water still glistening in his beard and his eyes softer; no longer burning with the anger I's seen in the club.

"What happened tonight?" I whispered, "was it Ritchie?"

"Yes."

"Who is Ritchie, Eli? Rival business owners don't usually go round trying to murder other people's staff. And why is there a gun in your office?"

Eli looked at me, silent for a long moment, a battle playing out in those azure, blue eyes. Then he sighed and sat beside me, the bottom of the bed dipping under his weight and we stared at each other in the mirror.

"The gun is Ritchie's, only I can't prove it yet. I've spent years trying to get the evidence to put him away. But every time I get close, or get something, it's all swept away. Guns though, that's a different matter. I've been tracking leads for the last few weeks, I know he's running guns through Newcastle, I just don't know how. When I do, that will finish him once and for all."

"So why not report it to the Police? Why deal with it yourself?"

"Ritchie has friends in high places, people who get rid of his problems. But he's never been able to get rid of me. I've been plaguing him for years."

"Why?" I asked, "if the Police and authorities won't do anything why are you?"

Eli drew quiet, a tension creeping across his square jaw, partially hidden by his beard but the tautness of his skin and the muscles in his neck betrayed him. He stared down at his hands, and I followed, noticing the way they balled to fists, relaxing a little and then tightening again, the sinewy muscles of his forearm pulsing through his skin.

"The insurgents that took Ally, they were backed by some influential people. We had intelligence and suspicions but we couldn't be sure. I was broken after she died, consumed by a rage I'd never ever known in my whole life. I hid it well from the shrinks and was soon back out in the field. Seb, Cameron and I went under cover, me deeper than anyone.

"Intelligence led us to Ritchie. He ran a mercenary operation out there, protecting dignitaries, native as well as foreign. I worked for him for a few years, all the time feeding any intelligence I could back to the SAS.

"He was careful though, meticulous and ruthless and in my grief, in my darkest days, I got lost in it all. But I got close to him, really close."

Eli took a shaky breath, glancing at me in the mirror before continuing.

"Opium out there is big money for them and Ritchie exploited every last one of them. I never got the evidence for Ally, but I knew he was behind the cell that took her, funded it, controlled it. I overheard conversations with some of the natives and Ritchie, the cell we took down was often talked about, but I could never get the evidence to do anything about it.

"Ever since Ally died all I've wanted is revenge. The weapons they used were Russian, supplied by Ritchie. The drugs they were moving were for Ritchie and the cash they were making was from the drugs Ritchie bought from them. If it hadn't been for Ritchie Ally would never have died."

His cheeks glistened in the gentle light from the bedroom and I moved my hand over his, he squeezed my fingers back gently.

"The cottage in the mountains? That was my retreat, while I got my head back together. Away from people and reminders of Ally, away

335

from everyone asking if I was OK and giving me the usual shit about how time was a great healer. Revenge was a good healer. But soon all I could think about was Ritchie.

"So, I found him and followed him here and then the only thing in my life was ruining him; his businesses, his operations, him.

"That was until you came along, Princess. Now for the first time in nearly nine years I think of something else other than revenge, something else other than destruction."

My heart swelled, warmth and fuzziness filling my veins. I pushed his head so he looked at me and then placed my lips on his. This time when we kissed it was different, gentle but passionate, intimate but sensual, tasting each other for the first time. Eli's lips were soft and vulnerable, carefully pulling at mine, his tongue probing but not demanding. It was raw and emotional and in that instant we were truly connected.

*****

I was distracted at work and drowning under deadlines. I couldn't focus on one job long enough to finish it and instead I had a number of open pieces of work, each as important as the other, each screaming at me for their attention. But it was the folder with Ritchie's documents that I kept eyeing up, afraid to pick it up like it might somehow poison me, kill me.

A dark memory flashed through my mind and I glanced over at Harry's empty desk, cleaned and tidied, not a speck of him left. And then I wondered, my mind formulating questions and assuming answers that made my stomach drop. The suicide note, the night he….the night he died. He'd come back to the office. He'd said there was something he had to do. Did he really come back to…to kill himself? Or was there something else?

I opened the folder and thumbed through the pages adding them to a hefty pile of papers I'd pulled out of Harry's filing cabinet. Spreading them out on my desk in order, I matched the accounts with bank statements, invoices and stock takes cross referencing them with the accounts return Harry had pulled together but I could not get the numbers to balance. I started again, for the fourth time, dragging the numbers into a spreadsheet, running a formula over them, again, but what I had on the submission papers differed greatly to the spread sheet. How could Harry have got these so wrong?

I leaned my head in my hands, concentrating on the hand written notes that looked like a drunken spider had danced across them, but despite the poor handwriting the formulation of the numbers were clear. I sat staring at the screen, the clock on the wall ticking away in the silence, taunting me as the afternoon was quickly fading to evening. A misgiving that had been forming in the back of my mind had muscled its way to the forefront. I looked at the stock take again and a heaviness started to descend within my stomach.

I searched the server for the folder for the Robertson accounts. I'd seen this before, not as obvious, but I had seen something where the figures didn't match. I pulled the spreadsheet up and scrutinised it, remembering my conversation with Harry. I'd mentioned this last month, told him I'd found some discrepancies but when he'd checked them, he'd told me I'd missed some of the figures. But looking at it now, no figures had been missed, no figures had been corrected like Harry had said. I clicked into the permissions and looked at the last time the document was modified. Harry. Harry had changed my numbers back; Harry had signed off the falsified accounts. Harry.

The light from the computer was the only illumination in the dark. Everyone had packed up around me and gone home as I stared at the documents. The money laundering evidence sat in front of me. Evidence that Eli had been searching so long for. Could this be the final nail in the coffin? Would this be what he needed to take Ritchie down and finally find his own peace? I slotted the memory stick into the side of the computer, watching as the icon waved around, showing me the transfer of the files, as I glanced around suspiciously, guiltily.

Rain hammered my face as I climbed the steep bank out of the Quayside, littered with its offices, restaurants and bars and headed straight for the centre of the City. The air was cold, colder because of the wind that drove the rain at me sideways, soaking my hair and clinging to my legs, my heels clumping loudly on the sparsely populated street.

I spotted Danny at the door, punching in his key code and hurried to catch up to him.

"Let me up to Eli's office, will you?" I asked.

"Sure," he shrugged nonchalantly and I followed him through the doors, happy to be out of the rain.

The door to Eli's office was ajar, hushed voices inside, talking in hurried tones. I hesitated, an unease growing within me, dread and nervousness balling in my stomach, knotting and tightening and I inched the door open.

She was there inside the office with him. That curvaceous figure, poured into a tight black top and figure-hugging jeans, extenuating her long legs. Ashley. Eli held her face, cupped in his hands, his eyes roaming over her, his face inches away from hers. My stomach lurched. Then his eyes connected with mine; the gentleness of his expression turning to surprise and horror. Horror of being caught.

My mouth hung open, shock making me mute as heat pricked at my eyes, fire burning in my throat. Desperately I willed the tears not to fall. Not until I got out of this place. I wouldn't let him see me cry. I wouldn't let her see those tears fall. I turned away.

"Ava, wait!" Eli called out from his office but I kept walking, "please Ava! Just wait!"

I could hear his footsteps coming out of his office. I didn't look back, hurrying down the corridor to the stairs bursting out of the fire escape. And then I ran. Quick, determined steps out into the rain as the burning sensation exploded in my chest and the tears flowed, disguised against the rain that hit my face. Sobs ripped through me, my lungs on fire, my heart pounding, pieces of it falling away with each beat, shattered. And as I ran away into the night all I could see were those eyes, those beautiful blue eyes, looking at her. Like that.

Chapter Forty Four

ৰ Eli ৱ

The strip club had been swamped in a Police presence all day; viewing CCTV, collecting evidence and statements and I'd finally escaped to my office in the night club, enjoying the peace and quiet. I scrolled through my phone, scanning the news articles, dismay weighing heavy in my chest at the publicity the stabbing was receiving and I wasn't surprised when the next bleep of the handset was an email from my father.

'Elijah, I'm disgusted that one of your clubs is in the press for all the wrong reasons. It's time we talked about the disposal of it. In the meantime, I'm putting the family solicitors in contact with you to discuss how we move this matter forwards and clean up the family name.'

'It's OK, dad, I'm already on it. My dancer will be fine by the way. She's serious but stable. Thanks for asking.'

This was all I fucking needed, Alan Antwill breathing down my neck. It was tough enough with the Police crawling all over the place, shrinking my revenge operations. Sighing I walked round my desk to the big, heavy filing cabinet and pushed it away from the wall tucking the burner phone and gun snugly inside the hole. Just as I pushed everything back in place the door screeched loudly across the floor and I jumped, whirling round. Ashley.

"What are you doing here?" I asked her, much more gruffly than I had really meant to.

She dropped her eyes from my gaze quickly, pulling her loose blonde hair awkwardly across her face.

"How's Chloe?"

"She'll be OK. It's serious, but she's stable."

"Do you know who did it?" she asked, her voice unusually faint.

I looked at her. Her hair had shifted slightly and despite the heavy make-up she wore the marks on her face seemed to be growing darker by the second. I crossed the room and gently pushed her hair back.

"Jesus, Ashley!"

Her left eye was nearly swollen shut, the skin below it puffy and black. There was an angry cut on her lip and a purple-blue shadow over her jaw.

"I, I was wondering whether I could take a few days off. The punters aren't going to want to look at this."

Her eyes welled with tears.

"Shit!" anger was growing like a storm inside me, "this was Ritchie, wasn't it?"

She pushed her lips together and then winced.

"Ashley," I coaxed, putting my hands gently on her face and lifting it to look at me.

She nodded.

"He was so angry last night, after the awards."

Fuck. I studied her face again, the mess he had made, the pain and fear she would have felt at the end of his fists. My rage was boiling like a kettle so loudly inside of me, flooding my ears with the thick heat of hatred that I almost didn't hear the sudden intake of air at the doorway. I glanced upwards, green eyes finding mine, staring at me, shock turning to realisation, the look of rejection flashing across her eyes, the bob of her slim neck as she swallowed and the way her face started to crumple; destroyed. Fuck. I dropped my hands from Ashley's face, watching Ava turn, whipping away and bolting out of my office.

"Ava, wait!" I called after her, stepping around the injured woman and following the red-head into the corridor.

She'd reached the end already.

"Ava! Please, just wait. It's not…."

She slipped through the doors, her footsteps ringing out on the stairs running to get away from me. The fire doors clanged below. I followed, bounding down the steps and reaching the back

343

doors of the club just as her small, dark shape disappeared from view into the pouring rain. I hesitated a second, looking out into the downpour and then ran after her, soaked through in seconds, the deluge of rain dampening the rage aflame inside of me, cooling my skin. But as I reached the corner of the street I'd lost her, unsure which way she had turned, the streets absolutely deserted.

I stood for a while, the rain soaking through me, water running down my head, the thin t-shirt I wore clinging to my body, the cold penetrating my skin, making my heart burn. Or maybe that was something else? Turning back, I walked across the courtyard, slipping back in through the fire doors of the night club and pulling them closed behind me.

The metal of the doors was cold against my forehead as I stood against them, trying to calm the thoughts duelling in my brain. Ava. I needed to get to her, explain what she saw. The picture of her face burned across my eyes, her heart breaking right in front of me, her green eyes filling with shock and pain and I saw it all, watched it unfold before me. I had to fix this. I needed her to know it wasn't what it looked like. That there was her and only her. Fuck.

Chapter Forty Five

ᘒ Ava ᘓ

Tears streamed down my face and my chest heaved in frantic gulps as I ran away into darkness, rain soaking me, the cold clinging to my skin. The balls of my feet burned hot and angry as I reached my apartment entrance, diving in out of the rain and ramming my fingers angrily into the buttons of the lift. The doors hissed loudly, sliding shut, as if channelling the throbbing pain pulsing through me. The soaked red-head stared back at me in the dull metal walls of the moving box, bedraggled and broken.

At the very top of the block of flats the lift stopped and I stepped out, Newcastle illuminated in a glow of bright lights as I stared out across the river from the window on the landing. My fingers fumbled in my bag, working automatically as my mind drifted off, over the water and into the office of Eli's nightclub. I'd been a fool to think that someone like that would have been interested in me. I'd been a game to him and he'd played me like a pro. They all did. Tom, Eli, they were all the same. Tears welled in my eyes again, the formidable burn of my throat as I fought against the emotions hijacking my body.

My hand shook, missing the lock the first time and then hesitating the second time and turning the key tentatively. I pushed the door open slowly, listening for Kerry, desperately hoping I could dart in and to my room before she noticed I looked like a drowned and tortured rat. The flat was quiet. But in the stillness was an uneasy silence, the apartment braced to my home coming and I stood, struggling to control the hiccupping sobs that racked my body.

Kicking off my heels I left them scattered at the door, my feet immediately expanding, an agonising burn smoothing out over the rest of my foot as I limped to my room. The door clicked safely behind me and looked out into the night, a momentary numbness washing over me; the calm before the storm. My legs weakened, the coldness biting into me and I slid down the door and onto the floor, pulling my knees up into my chest, my vision blurred by tears. My body shook, shivering from the chill of wet clothes and trembling from the sobs that now came hard, unleashed and uncontrolled.

I watched the phone display light up, vibrating furiously on the floor in front of me. Eli. It rang off, the luminous green light fading into the dark of night and the obsidian of my heart. The phone rang again, ugly green light flooding the room and I stared at it blankly; just seeing his name on the display punched me in the chest. My fingers hovered over the button, millimetres from touching it, seconds from unleashing the fury of heartbreak, of betrayal of his deceit upon him.

Instead, I turned the phone off, left in the darkness of my thoughts. I wasn't falling for the empty promises and excuses again; the declaration of mistakes, the humiliation that I had been too stupid to see the signs. I didn't want it rubbed in my face as he paraded his new girl in front of me, casting me out of the home we shared, removing me from his sight, out of his life, away from our friends and my job. Not again. I wouldn't let that happen again.

Anger, rage, pain bubbled inside me, erupting like a volcano, molten emotion spilling around me. The mirrored wardrobe door smashed, shards of glass sliding down onto the carpet, covering the phone I had just thrown half a moment ago. Shit!

*****

The next few days blended into each other in a thick fuzz of emotion and denial, of numbness and distraction. It took every last bit of effort to control the tears at work and whilst I tried to throw myself into the projects and the reports, Harry's workload reigning down on me, I struggled to keep my mind on anything else but Eli.

And when I closed my eyes at night, it was his that I saw, dazzling, the brightest blue I'd ever seen, burning with intensity as he looked at her. Not me. Her.

Today I was tired and I'd been sat staring at the computer screen for ages, my mind drifting to all the what-ifs and oh-buts, counting the regrets and I was losing count quickly. I struck a line through the first job on my 'to do' list looking down at the next item, a sense of dread filling me.

I pulled up Ritchie's files and scanned the dates. The accounts I'd prepared at the end of last week, they were different, the numbers changed again, just like before, but this time it couldn't be Harry. Someone else had been in this folder and someone else had forged the figures. I searched the documents history, but no name popped up, only a series of numbers and letters. I glanced around the office, the heads of people ducked behind computer screens. A dark shape appeared in front of me, a sudden presence and my heart jolted in my chest.

"Are you OK, Avery? You seem distracted; jumpy even?" Martin Fairbrother asked, towering over me.

"Y, yes sure. I, I just don't feel all that well today," the lie slipped over my tongue more easily than it probably should.

"Hmmm OK. I need the work on John Marshall's new company by tomorrow close of play. Can you bring it up to my office when it's done?"

I nodded, relieved when he left me alone and headed back up to the top floor.

But instead of doing the work I should I switched back into Ritchie's files and poured through the information. Profit and loss accounts showed over inflated prices for the stock in the bars and clubs he owned, selling at a much higher price than I was sure revellers would pay and then there were the vintage car sales

I spent the next few hours searching the internet, finding various vintage and rare cars and comparing the price tags. Was Ritchie charging extortionate prices for these imported cars? It didn't make sense when other sellers were much more competitive and none of his cars seemed to be advertised anywhere. I was intrigued. Switching to the accounts for the car sales side of the business and the discrepancies were consistent with the numbers I'd seen across the bars. Slowly I was building a picture and a pool of evidence. Harry had signed off each bit, or changed the documents, and from the evidence I was compiling, I could prove it all.

Over the strongest cup of coffee I could make I decided that I'd go to Martin and show him what I'd found. The Company had a duty to report money laundering or face criminal charges themselves. I could finish Ritchie for good just by doing my job.

"Close the door. Take a seat," Martin said flatly as I approached.

I sat in the uncomfortable chair the other side of the desk feeling a lot like a naughty school girl in front of the head master, a nervousness radiating through my body, my stomach churning with somersaults of apprehension.

"So?" Martin asked a little softly.

I took a breath.

"I haven't had time to finish the work on the Marshall contracts just yet."

He lifted an eyebrow, half in surprise and half quizzically.

"I was following up some discrepancies on the Robertson accounts."

"Oh?" surprise laced his voice.

"The accounts all have discrepancies. Too much money through the books, accounts that don't stack up. And all those were signed off by Harry. I think he was doctoring the returns to make these businesses legit."

"And why would he do that?" Martin asked, watching me intently.

"I don't know what his motivation is, but the night he hung...he died, the night he died he was here in the office working on something urgent. I've reason to believe that Richard Robertson is involved in a number of crimes and money laundering is just one of them."

Martin cocked his head slightly, a colour rising up his neck, studying me. His hands shifted on the desk, his fingers fiddling against each other. I opened my computer and typed an email, attaching all the documents I had pulled together.

"I've sent you everything I've found. I'm sorry to be the bearer of bad news. If you disclose the full information through the appropriate channels you will be seen to have been acting in good faith. The business might take a little hit on reputation but there shouldn't be any criminal consequences."

Martin's face was dark as his eyes darted across his screen and beads of sweat seemed to have gathered on his brow.

"Thank you, Avery. I'll sort the rest out. You can go now."

It was still fairly busy on my walk home. The Quayside streets were littered with people; some going home from work and others coming out to start off their weekends. Yet despite the number of people passing by I felt uncomfortable and very alone. I stopped and glanced around, not seeing anything out of the ordinary in the dark. Street lights illuminated walkways and passing headlights bathed pedestrians in a warm glow. Dipping my head against the rain I hurried back to my apartment.

I turned off the main road, zipping through the underpass, cars rumbling loudly overhead. The normally quiet road was deserted and my footsteps seemed to echo through the thick night air. The bright sign of the gym lit the side of the building stood on the corner, staring at me as I walked past, and I glanced guiltily at the doors. But I couldn't chance running into Eli. The thought of him brought a lump to my throat and I hesitated, staring across the road, the lights from inside spilling through the glass and onto the road, soft yellow squares reflected on the wet tarmac. A white van crawled past.

For a moment I stood looking, watching the shadow of someone moving in the glow from the windows above. Was it Cameron or someone training? Was it Eli? My stomach felt heavy as I stood staring up at into the light, rain falling on my face. A white van drove past, its tyres hissing against the wet road, slowing as it passed me. I turned, tugged my laptop bag onto my shoulder and walked on, bracing my head as the rain grew stronger, soaking through my trousers.

A white van drove past, catching my eye, the number plate familiar. I stopped, the hairs on the back of my neck prickling, a voice in the back of my head uttering a shrill caution, a lump of dread and fear forming in my stomach and suddenly all my senses were on fire, alert. The van slowed pulling over and bumping onto the pavement fifty metres ahead. I stopped too, watching. Doors opened on either side and two dark shapes stepped out. I looked around the deserted street, not a soul or car around, just me, the van and two shapes that were getting closer.

I turned, clutching my bag tightly and walked back towards the gym, my heart picking up a pace in my chest, adrenaline surging through my veins. I glanced back over my shoulder, the shapes getting closer, one short and stocky and the other tall and wiry; familiar. Then I ran, my heels ringing loudly on the pavement, my arms pumping clumsily as I kept hold of the bag. Footsteps hammered on the road behind me, heavy and menacing. Shit! Terror wrapped round my throat and I looked around wildly, desperately hoping for someone to help me. The lights from the gym caught my eye. I ducked my head down and pumped my arms frantically. Get to the gym. Get to the gym. Get to the gym. My heart hammered in my chest, pushing against my lungs.

I launched myself for the door and punched in my key code, stumbling over the last digit I hit a 9 not a 6. Shit! They were closing in. I hammered on the door, my frantic sounds ringing out into the night.

"Cameron!" I screamed as hands grabbed me around my waist, pulling me backwards.

I flung my legs towards the door, pushing backwards with all my strength hoping to knock him off balance. It worked. We stumbled backwards and I fell on top of him as he crumpled underneath me, his grip loosening. Rolling free, I scrambled to my feet and bolted, kicking off my heels and dropping my bag. Feet pounded behind me, a rasping breath growing closer with each split second then the smell of stale, smoky breath was upon me, followed by pain as he grabbed at me, yanking me back hard by the arm caught in his grip. I struggled and kicked and screamed.

"Hey, babe," the man held me tight, fingers digging into the flesh of my arms.

"Get off me!" I screamed, thrashing my body from side to side.

"Aw babe. Don't be like that," I could hear the smile in his voice from behind me.

"Stop messing around and get her in the van," another voice said, the sound of his voice louder with each syllable.

Shit. I thrashed harder, terror coursing through me, tears pricking in the back of my eyes, useless tears.

"Come on, be a good girl," his voice purred, hot and stale on my cheek, so close I could feel the brush of rough lips against my ear.

"I don't fucking think so!" I spat kicking backwards with my leg.

He chuckled, sending a stream of hot, putrid breath across me, stepping out of the way of my flailing leg.

"Wasn't falling for that again."

My arms were tugged tight behind me, something cold fastened tight around my wrists, muscles straining in my shoulders. I struggled; pulling and writhing and screaming, hoping to attract someone's attention from inside the gym, from a few streets away. Anywhere. Fingers bit into my skin, fighting against me, dragging me closer to the back of the white van. I cursed and shouted and kicked but the doors of the van were getting closer.

The shorter man ran forwards, wrenching them open as I was pushed closer, my bare feet scraping on rough tarmac. I screamed again, forcing my foot against the back of the van and pushing back with all my might. The man behind me staggered backwards, loosening his grip slightly and I rocked myself side to side.

I didn't see the blow coming. My head snapped to the side, pain shooting across my face and I stumbled back into the arms of the man behind me, dazed and desperate to stay on my feet. The street lights swirled in a big circle, the sky blacker than obsidian, my head hot and thick like it had been filled it with expanding foam and I felt the trickle of something warm run down the side of my face.

"Please, let me go," I squeaked, my head spinning, spiking a pang of nausea.

"Not so fucking brave now are you bitch?"

My eyelids felt heavy and legs felt like jelly, boneless. I couldn't see. Blurred lights flickered behind my eyes, neon and white all mixing into one. I hit the floor of the van heavily, pain searing across the top of my chest and into my shoulder. I yelped. There was a dull thunk of metal and then darkness. My eyelids felt heavy, and even the shadows spun, all shades of black swirling around in front of my eyes getting darker and darker. Complete darkness.

Chapter Forty Six

ಔ Eli ಞ

The phone rang and rang and rang; the gentle burr of the dialling tone instilling me with a fear I'd never felt before. Then I heard Ava's voice, beautiful, calm, scripted. The call had gone to voicemail. Again. Taking a deep breath, I started my message.

"Ava, please. I need to talk to you. What you thought you saw….it wasn't what you think it is. Please let me explain, Princess."

I wasn't sure how many voice messages I'd left on her phone but the memory must be almost full. I'd rung and rung, sent voicemail and text after text but she ignored them all. It was days later and I couldn't get in contact with her and my desperation was rising, pressure filling my chest in every waking moment, a crushing anxiety filling every part of me, torturing every nerve, energising the darkness tucked tightly away in the back of my soul.

The night club office was dull, despite the lack of windows the pull of night had crept in, filling the space with an ominous presence, something heavy hanging in the air, the taste of defeat and a thick sadness. I'd felt this before, in the grip of annihilating darkness, and it filled me with a fear, a trepidation and I didn't know whether I could handle again.

Pushing up from the sagging leather desk chair, I raked my car keys from the mess on the desk. I had to reach her. I wasn't going to lose her; I wouldn't let her just walk away. She'd made her way into my heart, pushing the blackness in there aside. Ava was the light to my dark, the beauty to my beast. She was mine and if she thought she could simply walk away she was seriously mistaken. Not. Happening. I would make her listen even if that meant tying her to a chair, or the bed. My dick twitched at the thought. Unhelpful.

The block of apartments where Ava lived was on the other side of the river. Newly built with all the mod cons including video intercom and I pushed my thumb against the button for the flat she shared with her friend on the top floor. The light flashed red but no one answered. I tried again. And again.

I peered through the darkened glass watching movement inside. The door opened and a couple walked out. I watched the screen on my phone, my thumb moving across the keys as if typing a message, my head bowed and feigning distraction as the door was left to swing slowly closed. I stuck my toe out, catching it just a second before it shut completely and slipping inside.

Outside Ava's door I listened carefully, straining to hear any signs of anyone moving around inside. It was quiet. There was no sound of music, of kitchen, appliances of a TV; only silence. I banged loudly, the sound booming in the silence as the door rattled on its hinges. No one answered. I knocked again. And again. And again.

A click on the other side of me drew my attention.

"Mate. I don't think anyone's in…."

I shot the man a look. He dropped his eyes and retreated back inside his flat, the scratching of bolts and door chains as the door clicked back into place. I knocked again.

"Ava. Open the door," I shouted through the wood.

I waited, listening. The steady beat of my heart drumming steadily in my ears.

"Ava. I'm not going anywhere till you talk to me."

I slid down the door onto my haunches and pulled out my phone, dialling her number and holding it to my ear. There was no sound of it ringing in the flat.

I wasn't sure how long I'd sat there for. Waiting, listening, watching the night through the big windows of the top floor landing. I'd sat so still the hallway lights had turned themselves off, but suddenly the lights sprang to life, illuminating the landing as I blinked, rubbing away the sudden assault on my eyes. I hadn't seen the blonde step out of the lift, I hadn't heard the whoosh of the doors opening, but suddenly there she was standing in front of me, bathed in bright light like some sort of angel.

"Eli? What are you doing?" her voice was disapproving.

"I need to see Ava."

"Ava doesn't need to see you."

"Yes, she does. She needs to know what happened."

"I think she already does."

"She doesn't. I promise you. I wouldn't hurt her. It's not what she thinks. I just need five minutes. Five minutes to get her to listen."

I must have looked desperate, broken. She nudged me with her foot and I got to my feet moving out the way of the door. The key turned loudly in the lock and I held my breath. Kerry tipped her head.

"Come in then," she said, flatly, "but if you say anything that upsets her, I'll personally castrate you."

I smiled, a sudden weight lifting off my chest and followed her into the apartment. She flicked on the lights, her keys clattering loudly on the kitchen bench as she kicked off her high heels just inside the door. I looked around. Kerry wandered down a corridor and I heard her call out Ava's name gently but she returned alone.

"She's not back yet, Eli. She must have gone to the gym."

"Thanks," I shouted behind me, charging out the door, the muttering of Kerry's voice behind me discernible.

I pulled the car up onto the curb outside of Cameron's gym, right in front of the entrance and not caring for the double yellow lines I'd parked on top of. I pushed the button on the remote, the indicators flickering orange as it locked itself. The road was deserted, not even a vehicle sauntered up or down it. My eyes focussed on a woman's shoe lying in the road. Turning I punched my code into the keypad and the door sprang free from its lock. I took the stairs two at a time thundering up them heavily and passing Cameron's office.

"Hey bud, how are you doing?" Cam called as I strode past.

I grunted making my way onto the gym floor, scouring the rooms for her red hair, for her small stature, her incredible arse and shapely legs, for the small swell of her perfect tits but there wasn't a soul in. No one, apart from Cam.

"What's going on Eli?" he asked from behind me.

"You seen Ava?" I asked gruffly.

"No mate. She's not been in all week. What's going on?"

I sighed, feeling defeat waiting in the background, disappointment, heartache, all waiting for me.

"She saw me with Ashley the other night."

"You fucking idiot."

"No Cam. It wasn't like that. She'd come in to my office all beaten up. I had my hands on her face, looking at the damage he'd done…."

"Ritchie?"

"Yeah."

"Fucking prick."

"But Ava thought I had kissed her, or was going to kiss her, or something. I've not been able to speak to her since. I thought she was here. I need to see her."

My phone vibrated in my jeans pocket and I pulled it out, a cocktail of emotions washing over me. Relief, happiness, nervousness. Ava's number was illuminated on the screen, a text message, the first message of any sort from her in a week. I didn't care what was in it, just having some communication from her sent my heart soaring.

But as I opened the message my heart started to beat in a completely different rhythm.

"Looking for this?" it read.

My eyes locked on the screen, my heart beating faster, knowing there was something more to come, something not right. A dull ache of nausea ignited in my stomach. The phone vibrated, a video downloading. Unease tugged inside me. And then my stomach felt like it dropped through a hole, fear hitting me like a sledge hammer. Ava's green eyes were looking at the screen, blood dried onto the side of her face and a bluish shadow had crept over her jaw.

361

"Look what we've got," a voice behind the camera said, "look at the camera."

Ava kept her head down, staring at her hands that were clasped tightly in her lap but I noticed the way she fiddled, wringing them together, relaxing and tensing back up again.

"Look at the camera, bitch."

My hand tightened round the phone as Cameron moved in behind me, taking a look over my shoulder.

The screen blurred momentarily and then a slim, wiry man with a shaved head and the distinctive snake tattoo on his neck came into view. Grabbing a handful of her hair he pulled Ava's head back roughly and she let out a little yelp of pain, as he held her so her eyes fixed on the camera. He whispered something into her ear that I couldn't catch on the video before yanking hard on her hair again. When she did eventually speak, her voice was strained and quiet.

"Eli. Help me," she winced, "they'll send you the address. If you're not there by 4am they say they'll k, k, kill me."

There was a pause and I watched the tattooed goon whisper something else as she bit into her bottom lip.

"You have to come alone. If there's any sign of the Police, they say they'll c, c, cut my throat," she said again, stifling a sob.

The camera man moved backwards and the view of her widened and I noticed the plastic sheeting sitting underneath her; a sure as hell sign

Ritchie wasn't going to let either of us walk away from this. I could almost taste my heart in my mouth.

Ritchie's tattooed idiot came round to the side of her, his hand on her throat, fingers digging into her flesh. Ava turned her head away from him.

"I'll give her a nice warming up, Antwill, fucking her in every hole she's got while she waits for you. Think I'll start with this smart little mouth. We can compare notes when you get here."

I watched his other hand bulging under her shirt as she pressed herself as far back into the chair as she could get. Then suddenly she moved, and the man groaned almost dropping on top of her and she dropped her knee down from where she had wedged it in his groin. I smiled slightly but as he stood up, he launched his fist into the side of her mouth, a hideous smack of his knuckles on her skin and the whimper that followed.

Then he turned her head to the camera, fresh blood dribbling down from a cut in her lip, his mouth pushed against her cheek and his fingers digging in to her face.

"Now I've got to teach your little cunt a lesson, Antwill."

The footage became blurred, the camera wobbling and losing focus but in the background I could hear Ava scream.

"Fuck!" the roar ripped from me. "Fuck! Fuck! Fuck!"

"Eli!"

"I'm going to fucking kill him! I'm going to fucking kill them all!" my voice echoed in the deserted gym.

"Eli," Cam grabbed hold of me, squeezing my arm tightly, turning me to face him, "we'll get her back, Eli. I promise. We'll get her."

"I can't lose her, Cam," my voice was almost a whisper, "I can't lose her again."

"You're not going to, Eli. But we do need a plan. And we need the team."

I nodded silently. I slid shaking fingers over my contacts list, selecting people from long ago and making the call.

Chapter Forty Seven

❦ Ava ❧

The thump, thump, thump in my head was monotonous and painful and there was a whirring noise in my ears as if a fly was buzzing around in there. My eyes struggled to function and I wasn't sure whether that was because of the darkness or the fuzziness in my head. I moved an arm to rub them. Pain shot through my shoulder. I frowned. Pain erupted in my head, and my lip, and in my side fire burned against my ribs as my chest tightened.

I glanced around, careful not to move my head too quickly to keep the pounding inside at a minimum. My hands hung, unbound, dangling at my sides and as I moved my left arm pain shot through my entire side. I stifled the cry, reducing it to a whimper which bounced around the walls of the cavernous room.

I'd been dragged roughly out the back of the van and had snatched glimpses of my surroundings but the warehouse unit I had been pushed into was unremarkable. Outside it was metal and white wash, stale and purposeful. The corridors I had been marched through were sterile and barren. No signage. No markings. And with each turn I felt like I had lost my bearings.

Now I sat staring at a huge space. Light spilled from a series of windows above me, casting shadows over a number of cars parked a little way away; vintage cars. I recognised a few of the badges of the ones closest to me, realising I was staring at one of Ritchie's money laundering operations. The sharp prong of fear returned. Did Ritchie know I'd been looking into his businesses? Or was I just bait for Eli? I moved my feet carefully, the heavy plastic sheeting rusting loudly underneath me. I didn't like this either. I'd seen the movies; the bodies rolled carefully in plastic to leave minimal evidence. I knew how helpless I was, how helpless this was.

I'd played the performing monkey role they wanted me to, and now what? I just sit and wait till they decide to slice my throat open? Ritchie's men had wandered off after the video had ended, after the wiry one had driven his foot into my side again and again and again until I couldn't hold the screams back any longer. I'd screamed again when he pulled me up and dumped me back on the chair. I closed my eyes, willing the memory from my mind, of his face too close to mine, his lips covering mine, the horrific taste of his smoky tongue invading my mouth and the very real promises of my fate at his hands. I rubbed the skin on the side of my face, blood still oozing slowly from the cut to my lip and my side screaming with red hot pain every breath I took.

I rose slowly from the chair, shuffling myself forward on shaky legs carefully manoeuvring round a couple of cars and towards the big metal door I'd been brought through. My chest heaved laboured gulps as I willed lead-like legs to the other side of the room. The metal of the door was cold under my fingers, the mere effort of pushing down the handle sending pain searing through me but the lock clicked obligingly and the door sprang open.

The corridor was deserted and I crept silently along it, stopping regularly to catch my breath and force the spinning in my head to slow down. I slid my good side along the wall, my heart pounding quicker with each step, each step closer to the door, each step closer to escape. I slowly moved towards freedom. I rounded the last corner, my eyes fixing on the door out of the building, and despite the pain I quickened my pace. Then, resting my hand on the handle for a tiny fraction of a second, I pushed it down, the door springing away and I stumbled forwards falling into the arms of the man on the other side.

"Mr Fairbrother?" I gasped, surprised and confused, "quick, we need to get out of here."

"I don't think that's a good idea," the ice in Martin Fairbrother's voice made my stomach drop.

A sickening realisation swept over me and I stood staring at him, my mouth gaping open. *Run*, the thought echoed round my head like it I was surrounded by speakers. I darted forward, colliding into him, pushing against him to get out into the night, my side screaming in agony. His hand clasped round my hair, pulling me backwards and slamming me into the corridor wall, pain shooting through me. I cried, falling to my knees, sobbing.

"Please?" I begged, the voice not sounding like mine, "please, let me go."

"Up."

He pulled me to my feet, every hair follicle screaming, as if my entire head of hair was being ripped from my scalp. Stumbling and sobbing, I was pushed up the stairs, tears rolling traitorously down my face and bundled through a door that opened out into an office.

"Lost something?" Martin Fairbrother asked gruffly as Ritchie looked up from behind the computer he was peering into.

"Fuck's sake! Thought she was locked away downstairs."

"Obviously not."

My legs were trembling, threatening to turn to jelly right there and then, my heart drilling against my chest. And I was cold. So cold.

Ritchie motioned to the chair in front of the desk and I was relieved when I was forced into it and the hand removed from my hair. I rubbed the tears from my face, steeled myself and looked up at the grey-haired man staring down at me from the other side of the desk.

"Ava, so nice to see you again," Ritchie said, his grey-blue eyes fixing on my face.

"Is it?" I answered, my voice sounding stronger than I felt inside.

"So, I hear you've been taking an interest in my businesses?"

"Of course. That's what Martin pays me for," I replied coolly, meeting his eyes.

"And what do you think of my businesses? Viable?" he prodded, moving round the front of the desk and perching in front of me.

"You have some accounting errors that need fixing."

Ritchie smiled.

"What's the plan, here then?" I asked trying to keep my voice steady and mask the terror pumping in my veins.

"Well, you seem to have got Martin here in a little bit of a pickle. Your resignation would be a starting point."

"I, err."

"How did she even uncover this anyway?" Ritchie turned to Martin.

"The silly little bitch was snooping, that's how," Martin answered, resting his arms on his well-fed stomach.

"It's called diligence," I spat belligerently at my boss, "and it was hardly well hidden."

Ritchie shot him a glance.

"What? Harry was an easy target, I didn't say he was my best member of staff," Martin shrugged nonchalantly.

Ritchie rolled his eyes, "well he wasn't fucking easy to get rid of."

He turned his attention back to me. His eyes twinkling with malice, cold and piercing, "do you know how hard it is to hang someone?" he continued.

Memories flooded my brain, of his purpling skin and his bulging eyes and the look on his face as his body hung heavily from the blue rope round his neck. Ritchie smiled coldly.

"I'd tried to convince him to do it himself. He'd made one too many mistakes. Shit figures, using too much product, being a general pussy when it came to putting his mistakes right. We did it for him in the end. I did it myself, with these hands."

He held his hands open in front of me. Bile rose in my throat.

"Look. Just let me go," I squeaked, "I can sort the numbers out. I can make your accounts legitimate. No one needs to know anything about this. And then I'll resign."

Ritchie laughed.

"And an intelligent girl like you hasn't got insurance? I found the laptop with my files on in your bag. What were you planning on doing with that?" Ritchie asked.

"I was going to give it to Eli."

"Ah Eli, Eli. Has Elijah not told you why he hates me so much?"

"Course he has. You're the reason Ally is dead."

Ritchie laughed again, his eyes lighting up, gleeful.

"He hates me because I helped him forget about her, helped him replace memories of her, helped him succumb to the thirst for blood and death. I helped him forget that pain, forget Ally."

"Why? How?" I asked.

"He was undercover and I'd unwittingly employed him. He was ruthless; a brilliant mercenary. As tough and as dangerous as any I'd ever had in my team and he couldn't half beat a guy to a pulp. He was one of the best killers I've known, save for me. You know he must have killed over twenty people for me. Nearly all with his bare hands. I've literally watched him rip a guy apart. How does that make you feel to know you've been fucking a monster?"

Ritchie studied me and I could feel my face filling with heat, growing red under his stare, a sticky sheen of sweat developing on my forehead and the palms of my hands, sickly hot nausea radiating through my body, my eyes prickling again with the threat of more tears.

"Unfortunately, he was half mad by then and his team pulled him out. Pity. I think I could have swayed him to dive right into the underworld.

"Of course, he was right. They were my guns in the Taliban's hands. My weapons they'd used to capture her and my torture techniques they used on her, techniques I'd trained them in. Do you know what they would have done to a woman out there?"

I shut my eyes, blocking out the thoughts driving through my brain, blocking out the

371

hideous picture Ritchie's words were painting in my mind.

"So, it would be of no surprise to many that he finally cracked up and killed his beautiful young girlfriend. Not after he'd just beaten his ex-girlfriend in a jealous rage after seeing her with a new man," Ritchie continued.

"Ashley?" I whispered, "what do you mean?"

"She was a beauty but she served a purpose and she'll give evidence that it was Elijah who broke her face not me. Now that she's been taught what's good for her."

In the office, Eli had been staring at her, had he actually been looking at the damage Ritchie had caused her?

"And the dancer he poached from me," Ritchie continued, "she'll tell the Police that Eli stabbed her in a mad rage."

"But the cameras. They'll show what had happened."

"Ah yes they would but I've had Danny wipe all the evidence for me. Everything will look like he finally snapped, and that will end when he kills you."

He smiled, his face alive with excitement as he dropped his hand into a drawer in his desk pulling out a hand-gun wrapped in a cloth and placing it between us. I eyed it nervously.

"You see he's made it really easy for me. This," he pointed at the gun and I noticed he didn't touch it with his bare hands, "this has Eli's prints all over it. The bullets in this will match the bullet I put between your beautiful eyes and all the evidence will point back to Eli."

The gun from Eli's desk. It had to be. Tears spilled down my cheeks. He was going to kill me and frame Eli for it. And it would destroy Eli.

"So now you're going to be a good little girl and tell me where the copies of my accounts are? I assume there are some. It'll save your nice apartment being totally torn apart. You don't want your lovely friend coming home in the middle of it now do you? I'm sure my boys would love to have fun with her."

That threat wasn't idle. She was the only person I could still protect. The rest of us were helpless. And there was nothing I could do about it. There'd be no evidence against Ritchie and he'd get away with all of this. Harry, me, God knows who else and even Eli couldn't stop him.

"The bottom of my wardrobe in my room. There's a keepsake box. There's a memory stick in there with copies of the documents."

Ritchie pulled his phone out of his pocket reciting my instructions. I studied my hands that were grasped together in my lap. Pain throbbed through me but now something else; a sickening, almost numbing feeling of impending doom.

"Better get you secured back down stairs. Don't fancy the clean-up operation if we do it up here."

Ritchie held his hand out for me; the ironic gentlemanly action and an idea formed. As I stood my knees trembled and I lurched forward into him, almost into his arms, my face hitting his chest, the slightest drop of the blood from my bust-up lip smearing against his shirt.

"Steady now, Miss Edwards," his voice was soft, almost soothing.

I wanted to vomit.

Chapter Forty Eight

ಖ Eli ಆ

The wait was killing me. We were sat in my Landrover waiting for the rest of the team to reach the RV point and I was about to get a repetitive strain injury from the number of times I'd turned my wrist to check my watch. My team weren't late, just time seemed to be on a fucking go slow, adding to the knot tightening in my stomach.

The rendezvous point was a car park of a deserted factory unit, some miles away from where we thought Ava was being held, or at least the address I had been summoned to. I pulled my phone out of my pocket and studied the message again. It was too simplistic. Too easy. Ritchie had a plan and that involved us walking into a trap. I just didn't know what type of trap.

I checked my watch. Again. We were going in blind. We had no intelligence, no idea of the numbers of hostiles or even whether Ava was actually in there. The low rumble of an exhaust caught my attention, growing louder as it got closer until the head lights lit up the car park like a fairground.

"For someone so good at creeping up on people he sure as hell likes to make an entrance," Cameron remarked beside me.

I grunted an acknowledgement, not daring to speak in case the anxiety within me escaped. The dark blue van, decked out in pimp-my-ride lights rolled to a stop beside us.

"Love your covert wheels, bro," Cam quipped as the lean frame jumped out.

"She's pretty hot, huh?" Joey answered, rubbing the bonnet lovingly with his hands.

"You might as well have had 'Insight Tech Ltd, spy for hire' plastered across the side of it," Cam quipped.

"Any sign of 'The Viking' yet?" Joey called over his shoulder as he slid the side door of his van open.

"Not yet," I replied gazing into the van, row upon row of computers and screens and other techy shit staring back at me, "what's all this then?" I asked.

"Got some new toys to try out," Joey replied climbing in and switching on some monitors, "couple of signal jammers and some pretty cool bits of hacking equipment. Thought we could do with a bit of a look-see before charging in."

For the first time that night a sliver of hope crept into the darkness. And then the Viking rolled in. The bike was quiet, black as the night and discreet save for the bright headlight. He stopped in the space between the two other vehicles, kicked out the stand and let the bike settle to the left. He pulled off his helmet, long blonde hair pulled back off his head into a ponytail, the intricate Celtic tattoo travelling up one of the sides where his head was shaved. Tonight, he looked vicious, like the killer I knew he was.

"You got what we need, Thor?" I asked, hoping his underworld contacts were just as good as they always had been.

"Yep. These should do."

He untied the holdall from the back of the bike and dropped it on the floor in front of me. I unzipped it eagerly, metal clashing against metal. Knives and hand guns clunked against each other, a jumble of weapons, each as deadly as the next, but the feel of that cold metal was welcome against my fingers. I pulled out a Beretta M9 hand-gun, sliding the chamber back and inspecting it.

"Don't even let those words come out your mouth, Eli. Just accept the gifts," the Viking cautioned.

"Cian?"

The Viking nodded, "he had a few contacts up here."

"I'll owe the fucker a favour for years now," I grumbled lightly, "the frigging mob will never let this go."

But I smiled, despite the situation. We weren't unarmed and we had intelligence. The sliver of hope in me was growing. I grabbed a knife and a gun and tucked them into the back of my trousers.

Relocating closer to the warehouse unit where I was supposed to turn up in half an hour we piled in the back of Joey's van whilst his fingers flew over a keyboard, typing furiously like a secretary on speed. One of the monitors came alive with a digital blueprint of the building. Cameron whistled.

"You're still hacking then, Brains?"

"It's my job. Gotta make an honest living somehow."

"Honest, pfft," the Viking snorted behind me.

"Least I don't kill people for money," Joey shrugged.

"They're bad people," 'V' defended himself, "I just help them on their journey to Hell a little quicker."

"Alright girls, can we fucking focus?" I snapped, watching the seconds tick by on my watch.

"There's air ducts there and there," Joey pointed at the map-like image on the screen, "we can get access to the building through there. You distract them at the front Eli, and we'll breach at the rear."

Joey turned to another screen and let his fingers scrabble across the keyboard working quickly and a jumble of code appeared on one screen, a language I couldn't read, letters, numbers, and symbols. Suddenly the screen was brought to life with a number of small squares, grainy pictures in each one and it took me a little while to work out what I was looking at.

"You hacked the CCTV system?"

"Of course I did, Eli. Didn't let myself go in retirement, bud. Taught myself a few new tricks."

Joey hovered over a screen and zoomed in on the image. It was blurry, the focus soft round the edges but there was no mistaking the slim shape of Ava on a seat in what looked like a huge open factory room.

"Well at least we know she's definitely in there," Cam patted me on the back.

The main image on the monitor changed and we all peered at it. A small light-coloured van could be seen pulling opposite the main entrance. The tall frame of one of Ritchie's goons stepped out, closely followed by his shorter friend.

"There's at least three in there then," the Viking commented from behind us as he leaned against the back wheel arch, picking at his nails with the tip of a huge serrated knife.

"Four," I said, screwing my eyes to the image in the top corner of the monitor.

I recognised one of them as Ritchie, but the other well-dressed man I couldn't place. No matter. If he was in a factory unit in the small hours of the morning which happened to house a hostage, he was certainly no ally.

"Four's good," mumbled the Viking again, flicking the knife through the air, checking its balance in his hand, "four we can take."

"So, what's the plan, Eli?" Joey asked, not looking up from his screens.

"They're expecting me to be armed with something. They'll meet me at the entrance and disarm me. Ritchie will know that I won't have come alone. He'll be expecting you, Cam, so I'll need you to play decoy. 'V', I need you to go in through the back and get Ava out. Joey wait till the Viking has Ava then cut the electricity."

I half-heartedly concealed some weapons, handing the gun back to the Viking.

"Oh, and let's try not to kill anyone; this is civvy street after all."

"Well, you've turned into a bore," 'V' complained, sheathing the knife, "I've been looking for inspiration for a new tattoo for a while."

Time had gone from unbearably slow to ridiculously quick. I checked my watch one last time as I drove up to the front entrance of the warehouse unit, a security light picking up the movement of the car and lit the forecourt in a flood of white light.

I'd kicked Cam out a mile away. That would give him enough time to jog here, feign a distraction and be caught trying. I had ten minutes, ten long minutes to get in the building and start the diversion. I glanced up at the camera focused on the main entrance, holding my glare until I heard the scratch of a lock turning. The tall wiry, tattooed piece of shit opened the door, scrutinising me and the space behind me, watching carefully for movement beyond the reach of the security light. After what seemed like an exceptionally long few seconds he stood to the side and I pushed my way past him, my frame filling the space he'd left me.

The door shut and locked behind me.

"Arms out, Antwill," he said from behind me and I held them out to the sides, my gaze fixing on the shorter man barring my way down the corridor.

Slim hands worked down my arms, across my shoulders and round to my chest before stopping at my lower back and the knife I'd wedged in the back of my pants slid from where it was secured by my belt.

"Impressive," he swooned over the blade as I heard the cover glide off, "packing this because you need to make up for a tiny dick, Antwill?"

He sniggered and continued, his Geordie drawl harsh in the confines of the space.

"Wonder whether your girl would like a real man, Antwill? Someone to give her the pounding of her life."

I pushed the bubble of anger to the side, biting hard on the inside of my mouth as I battled to keep my emotions in check. Not now. Now I needed to focus. Right now, Ava was merely the subject of this extraction. I wouldn't be pulled off course.

The tattooed goon continued down my legs stopping on the right-hand side and pulling up the leg of my thick cargo pants, sliding the small knife out, disarming me entirely. The thump of a fist between my shoulder blades sent me forward a small step and I dropped my arms to my sides and followed the shorter man, my eyes scanning left and right continuously.

I counted the doors as we walked. I counted the steps from the main door. I counted the seconds ticking by, stealing a glance at my watch. Eventually we went through a set of double doors that led to a concrete stairwell, sterile like the corridor; whitewashed walls and grey laminate flooring. Easy to clean. Easy to hide evidence.

At the top of the stairs, we followed another barren corridor, cut off by a thick wooden door. The digital blue print flicked through my mind and I readied myself. Pushed through the door I was directed into Ritchie's office towards a seat in front of a desk. Ritchie stood in front of me and the guy in the navy suit perched his well-dressed arse against a small cabinet to Ritchie's left.

"You don't mind if I sit?" I asked casually, pulling the chair out from in front of the desk and angling it so I had a clear view of the CCTV monitor over his right shoulder. Ritchie waved his hand at the chair I had already sank into.

"So, what we're doing here, Ritchie? What's the game plan?"

"Well, your girlfriend has got us all in a bit of a predicament," Ritchie said distractedly, glancing at his phone.

"And you need me to somehow to help you out this predicament?"

"Yes, that's right. And the evidence she'd stashed which my boys have now got."

Ritchie waved over the shorter one who handed him a small rectangular memory stick. He slotted it into the port in the side of the laptop in front of him. I watched as his eyes jumped across the screen. He hit the mouse pad in the middle and his eyes darted back and forth, each angry thump on the mouse pad of the laptop getting harder and harder.

"Fuck!" he roared angrily, slamming the lid down on the computer and snatching the memory stick from its dock.

"Your little bitch of a girlfriend double crossed me. Frankie, go get her up here. I want to know where the copies of the accounts she made are."

The tall wiry one turned to go and my heart pumped frantically in my chest. I glanced at the CCTV monitor behind Ritchie and then at my watch. When I glanced at the monitor again, Ritchie tilted his head, eyeing me carefully.

"Wait, Frankie," he said not taking his eyes off me.

I snapped my eyes back to him then watched as he turned to look at the screen behind him. The dark shape of Cameron skulked across the carpark catching very slightly in the view of the cameras. Ritchie snapped his head back to me.

"You came alone, huh?" he asked.

I kept my eyes on the CCTV images remaining as expressionless as possible, watching Cameron now the focus of the camera on the door, wedging a crowbar into the frame.

"Go get him before he ruins my door!" Ritchie shouted and the two goons rushed out of the office.

Turning his attention back to me Ritchie tutted.

"You still struggle to follow instructions then, Eli? Guess it'll cost you another girl's life."

I clenched my fist, my nails biting into my palm, the stinging sensation reminding me to stick to the plan and not get side tracked by rage. I'd pummel Ritchie's face in as soon as I knew that the Viking had Ava safe.

I heard the commotion before they even entered the office, shouts and bangs as they crashed into the room, the door flying open and a struggling Cameron was pushed in, blood running from his nose. He shot me a glare and I knew I'd never hear the end of this.

Ritchie's phone buzzed on the desk.

"Yes?" he answered as Cameron cocked his head at me, pulling my attention to the TV monitor behind, something moving on the screen.

"Yes. Send it round the back. I want it unloaded right away," Ritchie barked down the phone as I watched the articulated lorry pull into the car park then out of view. Fuck!

Chapter Forty Nine

෨ Ava ೞ

My arms were now pinned painfully behind my back, the cable ties binding my wrists and my ankles to the chair, biting into my skin. My earlier wriggling had only tightened them and now they felt like they would gnaw my entire limbs off and with the violent shaking of my body, my thin clothes offering me no protection against the cold night air, they cut deeper into my flesh.

I was exhausted and I was in agony. If I moved too quickly or breathed too sharply the fire burning in my side would upgrade to a red-hot stabbing sensation. So, I sat still, listening to the raspy sounds my chest made as I breathed and the chatter of my teeth as I tried to shiver as little as possible. Occasionally I would hear voices; boots stomped on the stairs, men's voices, grumbling, shouting, talking, tailing off and never growing louder. Thankfully.

It was dark in the warehouse room. Lights from the emergency exit signs cast a soft green glow at either end of the huge space, and the dull orange glow of lights from the windows bathed me in rich golden colours, as if I was sat under an amber spotlight.

The bang of doors and the sound of loud voices startled me, my hands jolting against the sharp ties, a pain shooting through my chest, taking my breath away and panic rose in my throat. The voices, angry and raised grew louder, a scuffle of boots on the hard floor followed by a loud clatter and then the voices were moving away again. My heart drilled against my rib cage. Was Eli here? Panic and dread swelled in my throat.

I wriggled my arms again, pain bursting afresh through my side, my wrists burned with each movement. I needed to warn him. I had to tell him it was a trap. The plastic pulled harder against my skin, locking my arms more snuggly into place. I wanted to scream in frustration. But instead, as my breaths became more and more shallow and my brain felt like it was floating away down a river, I stilled. A tear dripped down my cheek. An angry, hot tear.

A scrape from over my head frightened me and I looked around, careful not to move too violently, or hardly at all, pain throbbing through my entire body, my wrists, my ankles, my face, my side. A black shape tumbled from ceiling, hitting the floor with a soft thud. Screwing my eyes, I peered into the nothingness, my breath escalating to frightened gasps. There was a shape, a bundle of darker shadows amongst the blackness, creeping closer. My veins opened, panic coursing through every part of me and I ignored the pain, survival instinct saturating my body. I rocked the chair, trying to move away from the dark figure advancing from the gloom. I rocked harder, gaining momentum, too much momentum. The chair toppled, lurching sideways. My head connected hard against the concrete floor.

Footsteps on the plastic sheeting got louder until thick leather boots stood in front of me and I glanced up, stuck on my side, defeated. Boots led to dark blue jeans over thick set legs to a black belt with a bold brass buckle. He reached a big tattooed hand towards me. Fear took my voice. Shadow-man grabbed my right arm, pulling the seat upright, pain searing through my body. I cried out into the cold air, a tortured whimper.

"Quiet!" he hissed.

I glanced at him as he set the chair down on the plastic, more carefully this time. The murky light lit him up and I stared at the leather biker jacket, his square jaw covered in a light beard. His head was shaved on both sides, a dark tattoo meandered along one side and the rest of his hair was tied back in a ponytail. But it was the huge serrated knife in one hand that caught my eye and sent me pressing myself as far into the chair as I could get.

"Shhh, Ava, it's OK", he rumbled at me in a low voice. "I'm one of Eli's team."

"Eli has a team?"

"Used to."

I nodded in understanding, relief flooding over me. Maybe we could all get out of this alive after all?

The biker-looking man bent behind me and I felt the cold metal of his knife against my wrists. I stiffened, the thought of that nasty blade anywhere near me sending fear spiralling. I felt the ties pop and my arms sprang free, the throb in my side starting up again as freedom returned. I winced loudly as he helped me to my feet.

"Are you hurt?" he asked his eyes scanning my body.

"My side," I indicated to my ribs.

He pulled up my blouse and I opened my mouth to complain about the sudden intrusion but his hands moved gently over my skin applying gentle pressure over my ribs as I gasped at the pain of his touch.

"OK. We'll move slowly, think you've bust them," he said sliding his arm securely around my waist.

"I didn't do this," I complained, speaking alone making me breathless, "someone else did."

"Lean on me," he instructed.

We started shuffling towards the back of the warehouse, away from the door. The pain in my side had increased ten-fold now we were moving and I winced audibly with every step. And then we suddenly stopped.

"What is it, Joey?" the biker-man said to no one I could see.

I stared around in the darkness, my eyes groping the shadows looking for someone, anyone.

"Shit!"

That didn't sound good.

"What is it?" I asked weakly.

"Looks like we're about to get company."

He tugged me to the side, pushing me down behind one of the vintage cars.

"Stay here. Keep your head down," he said dropping down beside me.

Something clicked around us, the warehouse room suddenly darker. No glow from the office windows above and even the green fire escape lights had gone out. I crouched, listening to the slow breaths of the man beside me, feeling the cold of his leather jacket against the arm of my blouse, the frantic thrum of my heart creating an orchestra between us.

We waited in the dark for something or someone. I didn't know which. Something rumbled around the building, growing louder and deeper. I felt sick, my body swamped with unease. A huge rattling sound erupted behind us and I ducked further down, escaping the noise, burrowing uselessly into the concrete below me just as bright white light flooded the warehouse. The shadow of someone caught in the headlights made ghostly apparitions appear on the wall in front of us. The biker drew a deep breath beside me. I could feel the tension coming from his body. I didn't need to see his face or hear his words to know this wasn't good. Unease turned to panic, snowballing slowly, opening out like a flower at dawn deep in my stomach, trickling into my veins and invading my blood stream, hitting my heart with a jolt. Shit.

A shrill ringtone sounded at the back of the warehouse, echoing off the walls around us.

"Yes?" a deep accented voice, boomed.

The warehouse seemed to drop into a hushed atmosphere, the only noise from a series of guttural clicks from behind us. Sounds I'd heard only in movies, but despite not being able to see I knew what it was.

"They've got guns?" I whispered.

"I need you to stay really quiet," he whispered back.

This time the click came from right beside me. I gasped, stifling it with my hand as terror ripped through my body, every part of me shaking.

"Joey we're compromised," he whispered, somewhere.

A huge crack from in front of us made me jump, the cry ripping from my throat before I could stop it, pain bursting in my side. Light spilt from the doorway, illuminating the huge figure from behind, muscular, demonic. A shot rang out and the figure in the doorway dived to the floor with an athleticism unnatural for his size.

The air screamed with gun shots, bursting and crackling behind me, blinding noise filling the room as I cowered against the cold metal of the car, my hands clamped over my ears. The blast from the gun beside me was deafening. Someone further away groaned loudly.

"Cover, me, 'V,'" I heard Eli's voice from behind us, my heart skipping a beat with relief at just the sound of his voice.

Four shots fired from beside my head, footsteps rushing towards me. My eyes strained in the dark, looking for him. But it was his scent that got to me first, cedar wood and spice, and then his hands; gentle hands turning me carefully till I was looking into those beautiful blue eyes. Even in the dark and confusion I could still see them, bright as ever. My heart stuttered, my eyes welled with tears, in that moment forgetting the pain and anguish, forgetting the betrayal and rejection. I wanted to fold into his arms, push my lips against his, feel his heart beating against my body.

"Fuck, Ava," Eli cursed, and I could feel his eyes scanning every inch of me.

"I'm OK. I'm OK," I repeated.

The biker man shook his head, "ribs," he muttered.

"We haven't much time, we need to get out. Ritchie's down but not dead," Eli spoke low but urgently.

"Why didn't you just kill the fucker?" the other man hissed.

"Let's just go!"

"Wait," the biker man said.

I didn't want to wait. I wanted to get out of here now. I wanted to get to that door and run and run and run. Or hobble. Or crawl. Anything as long as we got out of here.

The biker opened his jacket, pulling out a couple of items and pushing them towards Eli who took them and tucked them into the waistband of his jeans.

Eli grabbed me gently, "I know you're hurt but I need you to do everything I say. And right now, I'm going to need you to ignore that pain and move as fast as you can."

"OK," I whispered.

"On three, stay low and move towards the doorway."

On three we scurried in a crouch like run across the floor aiming diagonally to the shelter of another car. Guns fired from behind us, bullets whizzing past my head so close I could hear the air parting as they tore through it, clanging against the metal of the car we ran at. A gun fired from close by behind us, Eli groaned, toppling forwards. I glanced sideways at him, but he was still beside me push-pulling me on until we rounded the other side of the car, sinking against the back wheel arch, the biker a breath of a second behind us.

"Next run?"

"Ready," Eli muttered but he seemed to struggle to his feet, his grip on my arm faltering.

We bolted again, this time for the door. Two shots fired from behind us then a hollow click. The biker cursed.

"Go!" he urged from behind us and Eli pulled me harder, pushing me through the door as someone in the corridor grabbed at me and pulled me forwards. Eli and the biker bowled in behind me, slamming the door across the space.

"Quick, this way," Cameron shouted, wrapping an arm under me and taking my weight as we moved quickly down the corridor.

My heart beat in my ears, blood swooshing around my head. My legs were as sturdy as warm jelly as I focused on the last few steps to freedom passing the stairwell that led to Ritchie's office.

A dark object flew over my head connecting hard against Cameron's face, snapping his head backwards and I tumbled out of his grip. An arm grabbed my throat, hauling me upwards before I hit the ground.

"Not another step," the gruff voice shouted, pulling me into him, the push of something cold and hard against my temple.

Eli and the biker-man halted.

"Whoa, take it easy," Eli stated calmly, his palms in the air, either side of his head.

Cameron groaned from the floor, before carefully pushing himself to his feet.

"You. Back along the corridor," Ritchie pointed the gun at him, motioning for all three of the men to move back into the direction we'd just run from.

I glanced at them, watching as they stood, breathing heavily with their eyes fixed on Ritchie. Were they deciding on their next move? Were they just calling his bluff? I wasn't sure but the one thing I was sure of was if we ended up back in that room we wouldn't be coming out. We needed a distraction.

Ritchie waved his gun again at the men in front of him, the hold on my neck loosing ever so slightly. I dropped my head, my mouth finding his arm, flesh bursting under my teeth, warm fluid filling my mouth. Ritchie yelled, his attention faltering, the gun thrashing in the air. Eli darted forward. The gun fired. Someone screamed, a shrill, harsh sound. It was my lips the noise had come from.

"No! Eli! No!" I screamed.

My ribs screamed back and my legs melted from under me like candles in a furnace.

Chapter Fifty

৯০ Eli ର

Just before Joey had cut the electrical feed to the warehouse, I'd launched myself at Ritchie, throwing myself over his desk, both of us falling hard on the floor. My fists flew into him, pounding and punching his face, not letting him reach for whatever weapons he'd had tucked away on him. But he was still the agile fighter years later, scurrying out from the punishment of my fists and hitting me hard in the side, buying himself enough of a gap to scrabble back to his feet.

He drove his foot hard into my side, once, twice, three times, pain shooting though me, my breath squeezed from my lungs. Hands grabbed me, yanking me to my feet by the arms, exposing my torso to Ritchie. I slammed my head backwards hearing the crunch of bone and the howl of pain. I leaned against the wiry frame of the man behind me as I smashed Ritchie in the face with my foot. His head snapped sideways, blood spattering the plump man in the suit who was cowering in the corner, before crashing to the floor, out cold.

With unexpected extras now cutting off our intended escape route from the rear of the building, I left Cam dealing with who was left and still conscious. I had to get to the Viking and Ava before they did.

Racing down the stairs and along the corridor I kicked in the door with all my strength, my bones and muscles vibrating painfully as it sprang open, clattering off the wall. The bodies at the back of the warehouse were illuminated by the bright lights of the huge HGV truck that I'd seen passing on the camera. There was no way we could take on this many. Not if we weren't suicidal.

I raced forwards, scurrying from side to side, pulling the fire, as the Viking fired cover shots. I crashed to the ground where they huddled beside a car. Even in the dark of shadows I could see the mottled bruising on her delicate face and the agony and fear in her eyes. Abstract rage forced the adrenaline in my system faster round my body, the monster uncurling from the shadows of my soul.

"Ribs," the Viking warned as I scooped her up off the floor.

We moved fast towards the car closest the door, quick urgent steps to our next cover point. Pain erupted in my leg, a red-hot searing bite as the bullet ripped through flesh and muscle. I staggered forward, desperately trying to keep my balance as I pulled Ava with me. I gritted my teeth, focusing on the anger filling my veins, ignoring the pain and the warm sensation of blood leaking through my jeans.

We ran again, pushing Ava through the doorway into Cameron's waiting arms as I half-ran half-limped behind her, the Viking covering us with gunfire from the rear. Cam led the way, charging through the corridors as Ava leaned heavily on him stumbling on weary legs but keeping up the pace.

I saw the object fly from the stairwell recess just as Cam and Ava got alongside. It flew over Ava's head hitting Cameron clean in the side of the face and dropping him to the floor. I threw myself forward but not quick enough to get to Ava first. Fresh blood ran down Ritchie's face, bright red against his white-grey goatee. He moved fast, grabbing Ava round the throat and pulling her into him. I stopped, my eyes fixed on the hand-gun pushed into the side of her head.

There wasn't time to speculate about how and how many guns Ritchie was smuggling into the country but I was pretty certain his next shipment of all things illegal had just arrived. And that meant there was at least ten men back in that room that were extremely well armed. My mind danced with theories, with scenarios but not one of them played out well in my head. Cameron groaned pushing himself to his feet, eyes dazed, a hole over his eyebrow and blood splattered all over his face like some sort of bad Halloween make-up.

Ritchie waved the gun, pushing us back towards the warehouse room. Think. I needed a plan, fast. The shrill howl filled the corridor, my eyes darting back to Ritchie as I watched Ava chomping on his arm like an angry dog. I leapt forward, stumbling with the pain of my injured leg and then the shock of pain hit my left shoulder and I crumpled to the floor.

"No!" Ava screamed, panic and fear ringing in her voice.

"No, Eli!"

My chest hurt, my heart drilling frantically against it, pushing blood out of the wound. I took a deep, painful breath, focusing on the vibration of the beat, slowing it, coaxing a synthetic calmness, ignoring the burn of pain, the blood soaking my clothes, the screams of Ava.

"Let go of me!" Ava screamed somewhere.

"Bitch" I heard Ritchie swear.

Soft hands against my face tilted my head up, emerald green eyes staring down into mine, full of pain, fear and something else? It was a fierce, resonate anger I saw in her eyes, a hatred brimming behind the green orbs, shining with tears that fell from her face as her arms wrapped around me.

"I'm OK, Princess," I whispered, my voice hoarse and my throat dry.

But I wasn't OK. I knew that. And now someone wrenched my hands roughly behind my back securing them together then pulling me to my feet. I yelled out in pain involuntarily, immediately regretting it when I glanced at Ava. Tears streamed down her face. It didn't take a medical expert to see how bad the wound to my chest was.

"Move," Ritchie grunted, a blow to the back of my head in encouragement.

I staggered forward, my breath haggard and unsteady, following Cameron and the Viking who were also trussed up like chickens to the oven. I glanced over my shoulder to see Ritchie towing Ava along with him.

In the warehouse room we were hopelessly surrounded. I fumbled behind me, feeling for the knife I had tucked at the back of my trousers but it had gone, knocked out somewhere, probably lying useless in the hallway. Nausea, mixed with pain, desperation and regret swirled round my brain as we were pushed execution style to our knees, surrounded by guns. I looked at Ava, her eyes wet with tears but her jaw was set in a stubbornness I hadn't seen before. A fight burning in her eyes when everything else was so hopeless. She was stronger than I had ever given her credit for. My heart ached. How had I got her mixed up in my mess? How had I got everyone mixed up in this? And now four lives would be lost.

If only I could have given up my mission of revenge? I should have accepted it. I should have let it go. Then I would never have dragged Ava and my team into all this. I hung my head, staring at the plastic sheeting beneath us, the sheeting that would wrap around our lifeless bodies, that would discard the evidence and Ritchie would walk away. Again.

"So how are you going to pull this murder-suicide off now, Mr Robertson?" Ava spoke suddenly, her voice cutting through the tension in the room, loud and clear.

There was no shaking in her tone, no hesitation, only fight. I recognised the attitude; the nothing-to-lose defiance. Ritchie looked at her, a smirk across his face.

"I'm sure I can think of something," he raised his gun, pointing it towards my head.

"Really? How are you going to explain all his gunshot wounds?" Ava tipped her chin in my direction, "the entry of the bullet to the leg alone would raise queries."

Ritchie paused. She had him second guessing himself.

"There's DNA all over this place now. Your plastic sheeting is no use and there'll be four bodies to get rid of or explain away; whichever way you want to do it."

Ritchie looked at the three of us kneeling before him then back to Ava.

"It's nothing I can't clean," he answered waving his gun nonchalantly.

"Hmmm. But what about my DNA all over your shirt?" Ava asked.

Ritchie was thrown off guard, uncertain, he inspected himself.

"When I fell into you in your office earlier....I wiped my blood all over you."

He looked again and now even I could see the dark red smudge on his suit and shirt.

"Oh, and that memory stick you retrieved from my apartment? There's no evidence on that. It's just a copy of my dissertation. The real the evidence is all in the 'Cloud'. Which, given the amount of suspicion four bodies is gonna raise, plus my DNA, it's going to lead a trail all the way back to you."

"You little bitch!" Ritchie roared launching himself at Ava.

She didn't move out of his way, even when he grabbed a handful of her hair and pulled her into him so her neck was pulled back at such an angle, I thought it would snap clean off.

"I'll snap your little neck!" he bellowed at her but she didn't take her eyes off him.

"But if you do that, who is gonna wipe the evidence?" she continued boldly, "the way I see it we're both in a predicament here. You let us all go and I wipe all the info from the Cloud."

I stole a glance sideways. 'V' and Cameron were watching her intently. She was good. But I knew Ritchie. There was no way he would let us go. And we were surrounded by a whole load of guys with guns.

"I'm a reasonable guy," Ritchie answered, "I'm willing to compromise."

A flicker of hope shone in Ava's eyes. But at that moment Ritchie turned back towards me.

"I'm sure I can explain these bodies but I'll let you go free," he said raising the gun so it was pointed directly between my eyes.

Horror filled Ava's face as Ritchie let go of her neck, pushing her to look at me.

"Say goodbye, Ava," he cajoled.

I took a deep breath and fixed my eyes on my beautiful red-head. She was the last thing on this earth that I wanted to see.

"I love you, Princess," I said softly and watched as tears fell freely down her face.

"Oh, for fuck's sake," Ritchie cursed.

I expected the shot to come then. It wouldn't hurt for long. I probably wouldn't feel any of it. But someone else moved. Ava grabbed something from behind her, pushing her fist into Ritchie's thigh. He roared in pain and surprise; the yell became agonising as her fist dragged up his leg to his groin. The first drop of blood fell, a steady drip before his vein opened and blood gushed down his leg, pooling to his feet and he sank to the floor in agony.

Chapter Fifty One

෨ Ava ෬

Ritchie's flesh popped as the blade sank in. He screamed from beside me. I tried to pull the blade back out to stab him again but the serrated edge caught on something and stuck. I pulled at it again but I couldn't pull it out, only up. Hideous screams filled the air as the blade, bumped over muscle and bone stopping at the top before I managed to dislodge it from Ritchie's thigh. Blood dripped from the tip of the knife to the floor and it seemed the whole room held their breath, a hushed, shocked silence sitting in the air. I glanced down, the wet patch forming on his leg growing darker till blood spilled all over the floor and he crumpled into it, his face screwed up grotesquely as his hands scrabbled against his leg, pushing the flesh together.

My hand was slippery, dark red and glistening, the metallic smell of blood making my stomach lurch, bile filling my throat.

"Ava!"

I stared at Ritchie, now lying on the floor in a puddle of his own blood.

"Ava!"

He stared back at me, eyes full of hatred.

"Ava! The knife. Bring it here. Hurry."

I blinked, the words passing through my head, willowy tendrils of information just out of reach.

"Ava! Hurry"

Eli. I turned, running to him.

"Free us, Ava," his voice was laboured.

I nodded, moving quickly behind him and inserting the knife under the cable tie binding his hands. The plastic bond snapped and his hands sprang free. He took the knife from me and, moving quickly, he cut the ties of Cameron and the biker.

There were shouts from behind us, men rushing at us, men rushing to Ritchie, grabbing his leg and stripping off clothes.

"Get to cover," Eli yelled, struggling to his feet.

Footsteps seemed to echo round the room and then the formidable click in the distance.

"Shit," Cameron cursed from behind me.

Eli pulled me down, a gunshot ringing out behind my head. Then more. Quick, short, loud bursts of gunfire. Then shouts. Multiple deep voices; more voices flooding in and the sound of heavy booted feet moving methodically from behind us. Bright white lights flooded the room, the shadows retreating. I blinked, unable to get my eyes to focus.

"Nobody move!" a voice shouted from right at the very back.

Cameron and the biker glanced at each other, passing an unspoken note of communication between them. I looked across to Eli, slumped against the wheel arch of the car, his face grey in the bright light. His lips twitched in a faint smile as I moved towards him, but his blue eyes were half closed. His hand was pushed against the top of his chest, thick red blood trickling between his fingers. His chest moved slowly in and out, shallow breaths, ragged and unsteady. Blood had soaked through his jeans on his left leg.

"You're safe now, Princess," he whispered.

Cameron appeared at his side, his eyes darting over his face and down over the wound in his chest.

"Shit," he said, "hang on, mate. We'll get you out of here."

Eli smiled, a faint knowing smile. He looked tired, drained.

"Seb!" Cameron shouted to the men at the back of the building; men I realised for the first time were dressed head to toe in black tactical gear, rifles half raised at the mismatch of Ritchie's men, now standing still, arms up in surrender.

"Sebastian! We need help over here. Now!"

A tall man approached, his face hardened and focussed dressed in the same black combat trousers, top and military style vest as the others.

Kneeling down next to Eli, he studied him intently before talking quietly into a headset attached to the side of his helmet.

"I'm sorry I got you into this mess," Eli whispered, his eyes glistening, grabbing for my hand, "I love you, Ava. I'm so sorry."

"Eli. I'm fine. You got me out of it. It's fine. You're fine."

"Ava. I didn't cheat on you."

"You don't have to explain…."

"No, I really do. Ashley. She came in to my office, her face all beaten up. I was looking at her injuries when you walked in on us. I never kissed her. I would never hurt you like that, Princess."

Eli broke off, his eyes glistening and his chest heaving. There was a scurry of activity and we were suddenly surrounded by people and I was pushed backwards away from him. I peered over Cameron's shoulder, watching the biker rip a hole in Eli's top, torn flesh and blood underneath. Dressings were piled onto his chest, Eli wincing as Cameron pushed pressure onto each one.

The tall guy looked worried and shook his head and I glanced from Cameron to the biker who passed a look between them. My heart pounded in fear, my own pain paling away into insignificance, a hole developing in my heart watching men crowding round Eli, hushed voices and strained looks passed back and forth.

And then they lifted him carefully onto a stretcher, four of them grabbing a corner each as

Cameron kept the dressing pushed tightly against Eli's chest. I stood there and watched him go.

Tears pricked at the back of my eyes and my lip trembled. I was tired. So, so tired. I shivered, noticing for the first time in the last few moments the throb in my side. My head pounded. My face ached. But nothing hurt as much as the pain in my heart.

"How bad is it?" I asked staring in the direction Eli had been taken, the biker standing silently beside me.

He took too long to respond. I had my answer.

"Yeah, it's not good," he said eventually, swiping his hand through his hair which had now spilled loose around his shoulders, "come on, darlin', let's get you looked at."

I went to take a step but my legs trembled. My resolve, or at least the tatters I had left broke, tears rushing from my eyes, sobs escaping from me. My knees buckled, exhaustion hitting me like a train. The biker caught me, scooping me up in his arms, just before I tumbled to the floor.

*****

I groaned, carefully swinging one leg over the side of the bed, followed very slowly by the second one. My ribs were still on fire and the painkillers were wearing off, the after effects of extreme exhaustion, mild hypothermia and numerous injuries rushing back. My head spun like the inside of a washing machine.

407

The door to my room opened and a leather clad man walked in, a holdall slung over his shoulder. Long blonde hair was neatly tied back in a ponytail and day-old stubble cast a shadow over his face where it wasn't covered by his light beard. I squeaked and backed up against the bed, pulling the thin cotton, backless hospital gown around me,

"Christ's sake!" I cursed, "don't you knock?"

"Not if I get this sort of welcome," he smirked, looking me up and down, dropping the bag heavily on the end of the hospital bed.

"What do you girls pack?" he grumbled "there's at least a month's worth of clothes in here."

I pulled the thin sheet off the bed and wrapped it around before digging through the contents of the bag, grabbing a handful of clothes and shuffling to the bathroom in the corner of the room.

"Hey babe, do you want a hand in there?" the Viking asked, a cheeky look on his face.

"No, I think I got it."

The shower was bliss, hot water spilling over my body, soothing the aches and washing away the dried blood that had been gradually peeling off my face for the last two days as I lay in bed too weak to move. I washed my hair with one hand, each movement still feeling like someone was stabbing me with a red-hot poker from the inside.

I stood looking at myself in the mirror in the bathroom but the person staring back at me wasn't recognisable. Stitches protruded from my left eyebrow, blood still congealed around the site that had stubbornly withstood my gentle scrubbing. A multi-coloured bruise covered most of the left side of my jaw and there was small angry cut to my bottom lip, cracking and stinging every time I moved my mouth and down my left-hand side my ribs were almost imprinted on my skin, purple-blue bruising all the way from under my arm to my hip.

Carefully, slowly, I pulled on an over-sized sweater, unable to move my arms enough to even attempt to put a bra on. I nearly broke the other ribs as I wobbled on one leg, gasping between spasms of pain as struggled to ease each leg in to a pair of jeans.

When I emerged from the bathroom the biker was sprawled on my bed, his arms folded behind his head and his eyes closed. He cracked open one eye and peered at me.

"You took your time but damn, it was worth it!" he said playfully, grinning widely at me.

"I see you made yourself comfortable."

"Well, you know, needed to catch up on my sleep. That roommate of yours has some appetite."

He closed his eyes again.

"Figures," I muttered as I shuffled across the room.

The ward Eli was on was frightening. The Viking wheeled me passed room after room of equipment; patients wired up to all sorts, a cacophony of beeping and pulsing from machines that were keeping them alive. I could feel panic swelling steadily in my chest.

"Have you seen him?" I asked the Viking suddenly, anticipation weighing on me like a dead weight.

"Yeah, I've been in to see him."

"What does he look like?"

"Like shit. Definitely think you should come home with me instead. I look much better than that beat up," he flashed me that cheeky wide grin that I'd become accustomed to over the last two days.

He paused a moment then walked round to the front of the wheelchair and squatted in front of me where he could meet me eye to eye.

"Eli's a tough bastard and have to admit I thought he was a gonna this time but he's pulled through just to prove us wrong for nothing more than shits and giggles. He looks pretty bad but he'll be OK," his tone soft and reassuring, "stubborn arsehole!"

I nodded silently.

"You ready?"

I swallowed.

"Sure."

The biker backed into the door pulling me into the room. My heart leapt into my mouth, constricting my throat. Eli was propped up on pillows, half upright. His eyes were closed and his skin was sickly pale making his dark hair and beard more prominent. His bare chest was covered in wires meandering all over the place and there was a mass of dressings hiding his left pec. Monitors beeped, all different sounds, meaning something to someone but making me anxious. The room smelled clean, too clean, like a bleach overdose in a swimming pool.

"Hey," I called out, my voice barely higher than a whisper.

Slowly turning his head, he opened his eyes, fixing them on me, a faint smile crawling to his lips.

"Hey, Princess," his voice was hoarse and croaky.

My heart fluttered at the sound.

"Hey, Thor," he looked at the biker, "I hope you've kept your hammer away from my girl."

I opened my mouth, momentarily lost for any sort of response until I glanced at the Viking who grinned back.

"Guess you feel less like death today, huh, bro?"

The creak of the door behind me made me jump, painfully and I glanced behind me, recognising the tall, dark haired and broad-shouldered man who walked in behind Cameron. He was dressed more casually this time in jeans and a white t-shirt. A much more low-key look than the black tactical gear and small armoury he wore the other night. But I didn't recognise the third. He was thinner than the others.

"Good to see you, Ava. You look great," Cam stated cheerfully, perching on the foot of Eli's bed.

I frowned at him, regretting it instantly, my eyebrow objecting to the sudden movement. The dark-haired guy walked round the other side of the bed and I watched him suspiciously.

"Sebastian Daniels," he spoke, nodding in my direction.

I would have raised an eyebrow at his curt introduction but I remembered that it would hurt.

"Our ex-Captain," the biker explained.

"You nearly blew my whole operation," he said sternly to Eli, "do you know how long I'd been gathering intel?"

"No, but I've got a feelin' your gonna tell me," Eli croaked, wincing from either the pain or the telling off we could all hear coming.

"Six fucking years, Eli. Six fucking years of tracking that bastard, watching his every move. And you nearly blew the whole thing out the fucking water."

Eli groaned.

"And you," Sebastian had now turned slightly, his attention on the slim guy at the back of the room who was leaning casually against the window. He rolled his eyes in response.

"You've been tapping into my info for how long and feeding it to this idiot?"

The slim guy shrugged.

"A few years, give or take. Nowt worth getting your tackle in a twist for. You should have better security systems in place. It's pretty shit a 'private eye' like me can go digging around in your intel as easy as a man in a prossie's knickers," he shrugged.

"Fuck's sake."

"Besides. If you'd just have helped Eli in the first place, he wouldn't have gone all Rambo on us."

I was confused. Really confused. And too tired for any more cloak and dagger shit.

"Does someone want to tell me what the actual fuck is going on?"

My tone bit and everyone turned to look at me. Eli chuckled. Sebastian spoke first.

"This idiot has held a grudge against Ritchie for years. He should have left me to deal with it."

The tall dark-haired man shot Eli a look.

"I'm gonna need a bit more than that," I prodded.

The man sighed.

"Eli has been stalking…."

"It was reconnaissance!" Eli interrupted.

"Stalking. It was stalking," the man called Sebastian continued, "for years. Passing me back bits of intel, using these two idiots to gain more."

He motioned at the biker and the slim guy by the door.

"Admittedly most was pretty helpful and has helped us creep closer to snagging Robertson. But gathering this level of evidence for this level of operation is slow going and Eli is an impatient prick. The guns were a good tip-off though. We'd have never got that sort of intel without him."

I cocked an eyebrow, stifling the hiss of pain when I realised it was the wrong one.

"Tell me about the guns," I pushed, "Eli had one in his desk."

Sebastian spun back to him, looking at him darkly.

"I was out on reconnaissance," Eli explained, "and took a gun off some kid who held it to my head. The kid was one of Ritchie's foot soldiers, selling drugs and women on the street. It was one gun off the streets and I needed to find out how Ritchie was getting guns in the country. That was my ticket to that."

"Those vintage cars you saw in there?" Sebastian continued, "they were a front for smuggling drugs and guns into the country. Hidden floors in the cars, lead lined, they were virtually fool proof. Robertson was using his ex-SAS position to secure sources all over the world and earning a fortune here and abroad selling drugs and guns."

"The accounts?" I whispered almost to myself.

"Yep. Using the bars and clubs to clean his dirty money."

"He was after the gym, too," Cam added, "guess that would have helped to clean his money even more. Offered to write off my loan with him if I signed it over."

"You didn't?" I asked, worriedly.

"No. Eli bought me out of the loan and bought half the business in the process."

"With all this evidence he's going to go away for a long time," Sebastian continued.

"Wait! H, h, he's not dead?"

Sebastian shook his head.

"But his leg?"

"Yea he was nearly a gonna. You worked a treat on him. But the docs have stitched him up pretty good. A transfusion or two later and we've got a live one for the trial."

"Where did you get the knife?" Eli asked me.

"From the back of your pants after you were shot. I felt the handle when I went to you and tucked it up my sleeve."

Eli grinned at me.

Sebastian turned to Eli, "there's a shit load of people involved with Robertson and plenty who will give evidence so there's no chance he'll get off with this. One of them worked for you: Danny".

"Fuck!" Eli groaned and winced, "I knew Ritchie was planting people in my clubs to deal shit but I couldn't figure out who it was."

"That night when the power went out in the night club, I was sure I'd seen a shadow coming at me, I'd tried to get away from it and stumbled and hit my head."

Eli nodded at me.

"I'd guess it was Danny looking for the gun. Ritchie would have known I had it. At that point he would have been really fucking livid that I could have been close to rumbling him."

"What would he want that gun for?" Sebastian asked.

"He was going to frame Eli for my murder. He knew his prints were all over the gun. He had it in his desk drawer wrapped in a cloth," I answered.

"Shit, so there's a weapon in evidence with Eli's prints on it somewhere?"

"Not just Eli's," Cameron shook his head, "one of Ritchie's arseholes, the one with the snake tattoo, picked it up off the desk when we were rumbling and came at me with it."

"What about Harry? My colleague," I prompted when Sebastian didn't seem to recognise the name.

"The one that was cooking the books? We don't have any evidence yet that Robertson killed him. But we have plenty that Harry was up to his neck," Sebastian looked at me sheepishly for a second, "sorry, I didn't mean to joke about that."

"Nah, Seb doesn't do humour," the biker piped up from behind me, "the stick up his ass doesn't allow it."

Seb shot him a glare, "we'll get it him on it. There's time yet."

"And Martin Fairbrother? The firm?"

"Well, I'm afraid to say you probably won't have a job with them anymore. Fairbrother is complicit in all of this. He'll not be setting foot outside a jail cell for a long time either. The firm have to be investigated further but I can't see its clients sticking around."

He paused for a moment, "any more questions?"

"Who are you?" I asked.

That one had been burning at the back of my throat for some time. The man looked at me quizzically.

"I know you're not the police. Police don't dress up like some over-excited action man doll."

Sebastian scowled as laughter erupted from all sides of the room.

"I'm with the Special Investigation Branch; Royal Military Police," he continued when he saw the look on my face.

"Huh. Who knew there was a thing?"

Chapter Fifty Two

ꔷ Eli ꔷ

Nine Months Later

The smell of fresh coffee percolating in the apartment made my stomach growl. I set the weights down after the last set and wiped the sweat from my face, pulling my soaked vest off and dumping it on the floor. I should have gone straight into the shower, but instead I walked straight past the bedroom, stopping when I rounded the corner and stared into the kitchen.

Ava was stood at the island in the middle of the room, a coffee cup in hand, her eyes scanning a newspaper as her silk dressing gown fell open down to her waist, a black lacy bra gently cupping her pert tits. My eyes lingered over her chest, my groin coming alive. I walked through the kitchen, nestling in behind her, pushing my hardened shaft into her back as I stroked my fingertips over the satin skin of her legs.

She batted my hands away but I could hear the hint of breathlessness and arousal in her voice as she spoke.

"Not this morning, Eli. I've got to go over all the figures ready for the meeting with your father at lunchtime."

I huffed, partly in jest, partly in frustration. Ava smiled.

"He's stopping on his way up from London. I said I'd take him through this quarter's performance in advance of the Board. I'll pop by the club straight afterwards."

"I'll be at the gym this afternoon."

"Ok, there then."

Ava turned to face me, her green eyes meeting mine. Her fingers stroked over my chest, lingering slightly on the scar just under my left collar bone. It had faded and smoothed out over the months and, the puckered lesion shrinking to a wrinkled mark, healing steadily day by day.

Fairbrother Williams had folded, clients quickly scarpering when the news hit about the firm's dealings with drugs and gun trafficking. But by the time the news came out my father had already offered Ava a post as business analyst with the family Company and now she met with him more than I did.

"Are you filming today?" she asked, turning back and taking another a sip of her coffee, her eyes back on the newspaper.

I nodded, taking my own coffee around the other side of the island. Cam and I had started filming training sessions and posting them on the gym's YouTube channel, another of Ava's ideas, and the whole thing had taken off. We now had a

419

virtual training business that people all over the world subscribed to and the gym was turning over a massive profit.

"You're not going to see anything about Ritchie in there, Princess."

Her eyebrows drew together and I could see the frustration on her face. With years and years of my intelligence and Ava's evidence there was no way Ritchie was going to walk for this. But until she knew that he was securely locked away she'd never truly relax. She still looked over her shoulder constantly, waking in a cold sweat in the middle of the night as nightmares plagued her sleep and while her physical wounds had healed well, the mental ones were still raw.

With a sigh she folded the newspaper and slid it back on the bench.

"I just want to know it's over."

"It is. It's over."

I got up again, making my way around the island in a few easy steps and spinning her round to face me. Pushing her back into the bench top I pushed my face into her neck enjoying the raw scent of her skin, not yet diluted by her perfume, just the light smell of soap and the gentle aroma of her. She groaned as I took a handful of her hair, pulling her head back and exposing her throat to me. I trailed my lips along her smooth skin, gently teasing with my tongue, listening for the little gasps of excitement as I traced down to her collar bone.

"I promise you, Princess, it is over," I whispered against her neck.

I dropped my hand from her hair, pushing the silk gown off her shoulders and it floated to the floor, falling around her bare feet. The black lace bra and thong set contrasted against the bright red of her hair that cascaded in unruly ringlets. I took a step back to appreciate her; the hell fire burning in her green eyes, her sharp cheekbones, the stubborn set of her chin, challenging me to dominate her. And I would do that, I would dominate and worship her, laying her out like a sacrifice on the kitchen worktop. I would worship her with my hands, my tongue, my cock and dominate her with my heart.

Hooking my fingers into her bra I teased the lace material back, her nipples pebbling at the slightest brush of my fingers, breath hitching in her smooth throat. Taking one of those pink nubs in my mouth I sucked on it gently, flicking my tongue over it as her fingers entwined in my hair.

"I've a meeting to get to," she breathed against me, pushing her tits further into my face.

I pulled at her nipple with my teeth and she moaned loudly pulling my head further into her chest.

"I don't care, Princess," I grumbled against the hard peak, her body shivering underneath me.

"I've got reports to prepare."

"Be quiet. Or I'll ring the boss and tell him you can't come in because I'm fucking you all over the kitchen."

My lips moved over her stomach, sucking and nibbling at her pale skin, sliding lower and lower until the top of her knickers brushed my lips. I slid the lace material down over her legs and she stepped out of them. Then I pushed my face between her legs, breathing in the scent of her pussy, hovering there for a moment, my lips brushing hers, listening to the rapid pull of her breathing.

I moved back up, towering above her naked body, my eyes roaming all over her, my cock straining against my gym pants. Then, grabbing her by the waist, I lifted her up onto the kitchen island and pushing her down onto her back.

"Open your legs for me, Princess."

She pushed her legs wide, baring her pussy to me, glisteningly wet, her slick clinging to the skin on either side of her thighs. I grabbed her knees, pushing her legs further apart, rolling her hips up to the ceiling so that her vulnerability was displayed just for me. And then I buried my head into her, my tongue lashing out and tasting the wetness between her legs, sweet and earthy. And I licked and I sucked and nibbled at her, pushing my tongue into her entrance and then swirling it around her clit until she was writhing all over the granite counter top, her fingers wrapped in my hair as I built pressure after pressure within her.

"Eli!" she screamed, as her body shook, convulsions ricocheting through her, her pussy tensing against my face as I licked and sucked her, letting her ride out her orgasm on my face.

Chapter Fifty Three

❧ Ava ☙

"These figures are excellent," Alan Antwill mused looking over the most recent profit and loss accounts for Eli's entertainment businesses.

They should really be renamed profit accounts they had been doing so well. The bars and nightclub had been busier than ever and it had helped that one of the biggest competitors was now out of the picture. Ritchie's premises had been seized under the Proceeds of Crime Act meaning that all the money he'd made from drugs, gun trafficking and money laundering would likely be clawed back by the Government. On top of that he was facing jail time. If I was him, I'd be really pissed off.

"And how is the ex-service personnel initiative going?" Alan asked with genuine interest.

I'd convinced Eli to roll out his programme of employing ex-military personnel into his security team with the security arm becoming a business in its own right. He'd explained how difficult it was to move away from the regimented and controlled life of the army to doing what you wanted when you wanted. The initiative offered armed-forces veterans stability and the chance to transition more gradually to civilian life with Eli at the helm as their Commanding Officer.

I'd seen that night of the stabbing how they had followed his orders exactly, how they'd come alive in the chaos and how they'd worked as a seamless team. And recently Antwill Securities had won contracts all over Newcastle with a specific focus on female ex-military who now nearly entirely ran the Strip Club security.

"The company is profitable, even with re-investment into the charitable side," I advised, "in fact it's been nominated for the 'Heart of the Community Award' at the North East Business Awards in a couple of months' time."

We'd been meeting to go over the finance and general performance every month over lunch. Sometimes Eli would join us, sometimes he was busy with the gym which was now his main interest, but each time the relationship between the two men seemed to be improving; the air less cool when they were together.

"These are fine for the Board Meeting at the weekend, Ava, thank you," the seal of approval for the papers had been provided.

Alan drained the last of his wine as waiters descended on our table to clear away the empty dishes and I collected up the papers, shuffling them into a neat pile and back into the folder.

"I'll get the papers sent by close of play," I advised tucking everything back into my laptop bag.

The older man nodded but as I got up to leave, he touched my hand gently.

"Ava," he said, his voice serious all of a sudden, "thank you."

I looked at him blankly for a moment.

"For Elijah. You've changed him. Completed him. I was losing him and you've brought him back to me. I cannot thank you enough for that."

He looked sad all of a sudden but he continued.

"You see, he was the one that looked most like her; Eleanor. His eyes, his smile, his gentleness. He *was* gentle. When she was diagnosed with cancer and we were told all they could do was preserve her life not cure her, I lost it. She was the love of my life, my absolute everything. And I distanced myself from her. I just couldn't cope with losing her. I did some stupid things then and I understand why Elijah hated me so much. I hated myself too, for being a coward. And then, after Eleanor had gone, I drove Eli further away. Because every time I looked at him, I could see her. Instead of loving what she had left me, I resented having to look at him and see her in him. I was cruel. I'll not lose him again, nor her through him."

For a moment I didn't know what to say and the silence hung uncomfortably between us.

"I've never met my father and my mother, well, I haven't heard from her for months. She was the only family I had, so I can't begin to pretend I know how any of that feels. What I do know is that Eli is a good man who protects the ones he loves. Talk to him, Alan, tell *him* this, not me."

He nodded.

"You're right, Ava. But you've given him hope again. And me, you've given me hope too. You'd be a very welcome member of our family."

Heat flooded to my cheeks.

"I'll see you at the weekend," he finished, smiling brightly as I said my goodbyes.

I drove the short distance from the restaurant to the gym. Having now learnt to drive I'd taken a liking to Eli's black sports car. I was saving up for my own but in the meantime this little beauty more than did the trick. Parking at the back of the gym, I turned the key, the purring engine stilling as I swept my legs out of the car, sliding over the black leather of the seat. I clicked the button on the key fob and the Audi beeped shrilly.

The gym was constantly busy now. Eli and Cameron had extended into the next building to create the space they needed to house both its ever increasing members and also the studios they used to film various workout programmes. Today they were working on the new programme. It didn't take me long to work out which studio they were using. There was a small crowd gathered, watching through the glass windows as the men, leading a group of members, produced their routine.

I caught a glimpse of Eli through gaps in the audience as he flexed, his muscles straining through his skin, his gym vest tight around him. A group of young women by the door talked in hushed, high pitched, excited voices as the class came to an end, the chatter of the small crowd bubbling louder as the door was yanked open and Eli and Cameron walked out.

Men stepped forward, grasping their arms, mentioning something about weights and protein and pre-workouts and the women swooned, desperate for their attention. Eli glanced up, his blue eyes meeting mine across the corridor, a shiver vibrating through me as if we had just met for the first time.

I stood against the wall arms crossed over my chest watching him approach, closing the space between us in a few strides.

"Ooh Eli, you're so pumped," I mocked squeezing his arms, "so strong."

I flashed him my best innocent smile. He growled, the low vibrations of his voice going straight to my core. He pushed me back into the wall suddenly, and I squeaked in surprise. I glanced over his shoulder noticing the eyes trained on us, as he nibbled at my neck and grabbed my waist roughly.

"I think you still have an audience," I rasped, heat pooling between my legs at his touch.

"Better give them a show then," his lips brushed over my ear then across my jaw bone.

Leaning further into me, he crushed his lips to mine, thrusting his tongue into my mouth hungrily and I kissed him back. Then, without warning, he picked me up, hoisted me over his shoulder and continued down the corridor to the office, leaving a soft thrum of hushed voices behind us.

*****

It was reasonably warm but Eli assured me it would feel significantly cooler at the top of the mountain so I packed an extra jumper into the backpack.

We'd driven North West the day after the Board meeting after staying in the Antwill family residence. We'd attended the family dinner, seated at the huge dining table which had involved numerous bottles of vintage wine from the cellar and this time I enjoyed the thick red liquid in better company. I'd watched Eli smile and laugh with his brothers, his stoic outward appearance stripped down to reveal the relaxed mischievous man I spent all my time with. He'd even spent hours playing with the youngest niece and nephew and the three of them had to be coaxed in from the garden for dinner.

Now at the foot of the Torridon Hills we'd packed for a trek over the mountains and a couple of days tucked away in Eli's cottage. The sun was out, the wind was still and August was in full swing. The sky was as beautiful as Eli's eyes and there wasn't even the wisp of a cloud insight. I inhaled the air, the scent of pine from the neighbouring forest mingling with the smell of freshly trampled grass as we made our way around the Loch.

We meandered up the foothills and I kept pace easily with Eli, picking my way over rock and boulders until the path turned to scree. We slowed, crossing the small flinty, flat stones, feeling the slight movement under our feet and soon, we stood at the bottom of what I'd once considered a cliff face. It was the part of the mountain that required a bit of a scramble to the top. But it didn't fill me with fear and dread this time; we'd done a few scrambles over the hills of the Lake District in the North West of England in the last few months and although a little higher, the flat face of rock and sparse handholds did not daunt me as it had the first time.

Eli squeezed my hand, "do you want me to go up first and show you the holds?"

"No. I got this," I said confidently, shaking my head.

Then, deftly, I scaled up the first part of flat rock, carefully testing each hand and foothold, pulling myself up, climbing higher and higher, my legs burning slightly under the exertion. I still felt the twinge of nervousness in the pit of my stomach but I pushed on anyway, concentrating on the route up the rock face and hearing the breathing of Eli behind me as he followed my lead.

Eventually, at the summit, we stopped, looking out across the landscape. It felt like I could see the whole world from up here. Ridges upon ridges carried on before me, sharp peaks giving way to deep valleys and the Lochs below. The view was breath-taking, awe-inspiring.

"It's incredible up here, Eli, isn't it?"

Eli was quiet. I looked around, panic suddenly igniting in my stomach until my eyes caught him, bowed before me on one knee, a black box thrust up towards me. The sun glinting off the little object nestled in red velvet.

"Ava, will you marry me?"

I gazed down upon him, azure blue eyes staring up at me, bright in contrast to his neatly trimmed black beard over that square jaw, his dark hair pushed to one side and the muscles bulging out under the thin black material of the long-sleeved top he wore. And up here on top of a mountain, this god-like man offered his soul to me.

"Yes," I whispered.

ೞ The End ಞ

Want More?

All the books in The Northern Sins Saga can be purchased here:

https://nikterry.link/thenorthernsinssaga

Keep up to date with new releases, get access to bonus scenes and exclusive giveaways by signing up to my newsletter:

https://nikterry.link/newsletter

Follow my Facebook page to learn more about me and join my reader group.

https://nikterry.link/facebook

About the Author

I can't remember a time I haven't written stories. I wrote my first short story collection at six years old and they went a lot like this:

Once upon a time there was a goat. The goat was good. The goat met a witch. The witch was bad.....

Well you get the idea, but the imagination, creativity and story structure was there, even when I'd barely learnt to read and write.

I then took to writing thrillers and fantasy series, none of which I have ever published but are sitting, patiently waiting to be given some attention at a later date.

My very first fascination with romance came from the absolute best series of my generation – Buffy the Vampire Slayer. How I loved bad-boy Spike and how angry I used to get with Buffy over some of her rubbish romantic choices (I only approved of Angel when he lost his soul). Then there was Cole and Phoebe in Charmed and later Bella, Edward and Jacob in

Twilight (I was strictly team Jacob by the way – he was much more my type – I think you're getting the picture).

One day I stumbled into the steamy romance genre (before EL James made Romance so very sexy) and bought a book that looked like a fantasy story – which it was – but with extras. I remember reading it on the commute to work and hiding it in a newspaper because I was worried about what people would think if they read it over my shoulder, because that's what I always did to others. I also remember coming across that first scene totally not expecting it and turning bright red when I realised just what I was reading. But I quickly became hooked and I've read so many in this genre since, falling in love with the passion, action, and angst and the adrenaline rush of a hot scene.

Then, just before the Great Pandemic of 2020 (this will sound much more dramatic in ten years' time), I decided to see if I was capable or writing such scenes. It seemed I was, and my hubby was happy to 'sense check' them with me. Now, between us, we have released the first book in the Northern Sins Saga, set in the North East of England where we live with our two daughters, two cats and three ponies.

I'm really excited to get you all on board the steamy romance train with me because what a ride this is going to be!

Printed in Great Britain
by Amazon

86755727R00251